we play ourselves

JEN SILVERMAN is a New York-based writer and playwright. Jen is the author of the story collection *The Island Dwellers* (2018), which was longlisted for a PEN/Robert W. Bingham Prize for debut fiction, and the poetry chapbook *Bath* (2022), selected by Traci Brimhall for Driftwood Press. Additional work has appeared in *Vogue*, the *Paris Review*, *Ploughshares*, *LitHub* and elsewhere. Residencies and fellowships include: MacDowell, New Dramatists and the National Endowment for the Arts. Jen's plays have been produced across the United States and internationally, in countries including Australia and the UK; they include *Collective Rage: A Play in 5 Betties*, *The Moors*, *The Roommate* and *Witch*. Jen also writes for TV and film. *We Play Ourselves* is Jen's debut novel.

BY JEN SILVERMAN

The Island Dwellers
We Play Ourselves

we play ourselves
jen silverman

atlantic · *fiction*

First published in hardback in the United States of America in 2021 by Random House, an imprint and division of Penguin Random House LLC, New York.

First published in hardback in Great Britain in 2021 by Atlantic Books, an imprint of Atlantic Books Ltd.

This paperback edition published in 2022.

1 2 3 4 5 6 7 8 9

A CIP catalogue record for this book is available from the British Library.

Paperback ISBN: 978 1 83895 433 8
E-book ISBN: 978 1 83895 432 1

Printed and bound by CPI Group (UK) Ltd, Croydon CR0 4YY

Atlantic Books
An imprint of Atlantic Books Ltd
Ormond House
26–27 Boswell Street
London
WC1N 3JZ

www.atlantic-books.co.uk

MIX
Paper from
responsible sources
FSC® C171272

For Dane Laffrey

Odd, for an apocalypse
to announce itself with such bounty.

—KAVEH AKBAR, from "Exciting the Canvas"

We are citizens
of the countries we imagine. We make our homes in the dark.

—NICO AMADOR, from "Elegy for Two"

1

I exit LAX and the warm air slaps me awake. The first thing I smell is car exhaust. Then, just under it: desert. People are already upset, a traffic cop is shouting at a red sports car and waving her arms. I think: *Turn around.* I think: *This is not your city.*

Dylan's van is farther up. I recognize it because there is only one of its kind in the world—this is what Dylan said on the phone last night: "You'll know it when you see it, it's the only one of its kind in the world." And here it is: spray-painted silver, a big gaping mouth splashed across the front, rows of jaggy shark teeth. Two big cartoon eyes goggling out at the smog. The windows are cranked down all the way, and I catch a glimpse of Dylan before he sees me: head tilted back, shaggy mop of hair, bopping along to some featureless beat. He hasn't changed since we were eighteen. In another fifty years he'll still look like this.

As if feeling my gaze, Dylan's eyes snap open—electric blue—and he's staring straight at me in the rearview mirror. "Cass!"

"Hey."

"Welcome! Get in!"

I pull open the van door and a stink hits me. Not any smell I know. Something like tang and decay and sugar.

"Stingray died in here," Dylan says, easy. He pulls me into a hug, ignoring the car behind us that has started to honk. "It's so good to see you."

"You too," I say, as the honking becomes an urgent staccato pulse. "Should we . . . ?"

Dylan lets me go, runs his hand through my hair—"Even shorter than last time"—and pulls us out into the circular creep of traffic around the terminal. "How was your flight?"

"Good." I crank the window the rest of the way down and brace myself for more questions—I did, after all, show up with only a day's notice. But he's navigating the bottleneck leading out of the airport, a frown line carving his forehead, paying exquisite attention to the road. I remember he drove like this in college too—always the designated driver.

We're quiet even after we get onto the highway. It all seems like a strange dream: the palm trees soaring up, up, up, increasingly unlikely parabolas of trunk that explode into fronds at the top. The light is desert light, and the 105 is packed bumper to bumper; it feels like everybody is breathing in unison, barely separated by the thin skins of our cars.

I didn't sleep last night. I left my roommate Nico a month's rent in cash, and a note in which I told him he could sell whatever furniture was mine and keep the money. He's in Berlin for five weeks, and I was aware, as I slipped out, that my exit was neither honest nor brave. And yet the need to leave felt clearer than anything else had felt in the past several months. Or if what I felt was not clarity, at least it was adrenaline.

I told almost no one that I was leaving. There aren't a lot of people who would care—for the right reasons, I mean. People want to know what I'm doing about all of the messy aftermath so that they can report back to each other in low voices. Whether or not Tara-Jean Slater is suing me; if it's true that I got tased; that cops came; that the NYPD put out a bulletin; that my agency dropped me; that I'd been arrested but my agent paid bail; that my agent had refused to pay bail, and I'm still locked up somewhere in lower Manhattan; that Tara-Jean Slater's dad is an attorney and he got me moved to Rikers. Rikers feels like a reach to me, but then again, I'm supposed to be the one out of touch with reality, so what do I know. Maybe Rikers really *was* around the corner.

That isn't why I left—I didn't think I was going to prison—but whenever I ran into vague acquaintances, they looked surprised to see me in public. Eventually that starts to wear on you, and you stop leaving your apartment, and you become a shut-in, and the only way to jog yourself loose from your life, from every detail of your life, is to abandon it.

Other than Dylan, I called only one person last night: Liz, my ex-girlfriend. I was calling to say goodbye, because I felt like it might be strange if she ever came looking for me and I was simply gone, but before I could say anything, she was whispering furiously into the phone: "Cass, we can have *coffee*, sometimes, in a *professional* setting, but if you want to hire me for anything you should have *your* people call *my* people." And then she paused and asked, "Do you still *have* people?" And that was insulting enough—in part because of its accuracy—that I hung up without saying anything at all.

I'm lost in my thoughts when Dylan says abruptly, "So, look, we're really happy to have you, but I wanna give you a heads-up about something."

I snap back. Stingray smell. Dylan's eyes, blue like some improbable crayon.

"What's that?"

Dylan clears his throat, squints at the road. "About me and Daniel."

"Uh . . . okay?" I've only met Dylan's boyfriend a few times in the decade they've been together. Daniel is Australian, five years older than we are. He has always seemed very serious to me, someone who has an adult job and who takes nothing lightly.

Dylan sighs. I wait for any number of possibilities to enter the space between us. *Daniel and I decided to charge you five thousand bucks a month. We're starting a cult. We perform abortions in the living room.*

"Okay," Dylan says. "Well. Daniel and I are . . . in kind of a place." He glances at me. "It's this whole thing about how he never planned to stay in the U.S., and how I should *know* that, because even when we met he always said—but the thing is, I don't think he felt that way then. Which, maybe I just forgot, but my distinct *impression* was that Sydney

was hell for him, because he wasn't *out* in Sydney, and L.A. is like . . .
you know. L.A." This time Dylan says "L.A." like it's a synonym for paradise. I watch the asphalt ribbon of highway, wending slowly ahead of us,
the yellow haze of polluted air hanging above it, and I say, "Uh-huh," in
what I hope is an encouraging tone.

"And *now* he's all like, 'Sydney is my home, *of course* I'm going
back, my *parents* live there, my *sister* had a *baby*,' and he was looking for
jobs in Sydney—which, to be honest, I thought was a phase, because
he'd go through them occasionally—but then he found a job, and he
accepted it, and he bought a plane ticket, and now he's leaving January
first."

"No way," I say, startled. Dylan and I haven't stayed in close touch
over the years, but whenever we've spoken, he's been firmly ensconced
in their house, in their life. Dylan was twenty-three when they met,
and as a consequence he is more accustomed to using "we" than "I."
Although I don't know Daniel well, I think of his presence as a solid,
unchanging fact. "January first," I say. "Jesus. That's very symbolic."
When Dylan darts his eyes from the road to my face, I know it was the
wrong thing to say.

"Tickets are super cheap on January first," Dylan tells me.

"I'm sure, yeah."

"He also didn't tell me any of this until he'd decided," Dylan blurts.
"I was like, *Well, let's talk about this*, and he was like, *I bought the ticket*.
Which. *I* think . . ." And then Dylan presses his lips together in a firm
line and doesn't say what he thinks.

We sit in silence for a long moment. The traffic has slowed to a
crawl, and Dylan stares intensely at the road, as if he's punishing it. I say:
"I'm sorry."

"It's life," Dylan responds automatically, as if he's had to tell this to
a lot of different people over the past few weeks. Then, as the traffic
starts moving again, he takes a deep breath, blows it out, and says, as if
he's back on track with the message he meant to deliver: "So! We're in a
place where we're figuring out, uh, a lot of things. And we both wanted
you to know that coming in. So that you'd sort of—you know, if you

come into the room and the energy is intense, you wouldn't be . . ." He shrugs. "Bummed."

"Got it," I say. "And thanks for letting me stay right now."

"No, no," Dylan says quickly. "That'll be good for us. Having a guest." He grins with one side of his mouth. "Less screaming all around."

"But if you *do* scream, I'll consider myself well warned."

"Oh good." Dylan's tone is dry.

I debate asking the question, and then can't help it. "Do you think you'd move to Sydney?"

Dylan frowns. "Sydney . . ." he says.

I wait for a follow-up, but there isn't one.

We turn from the 105 onto the 110, and the haze thins. Now there's a line of mountains, like a filmy backdrop, against the densely packed city. The trees still look Jurassic, and everything is fifteen degrees hotter than October anywhere should ever be, and I keep feeling like I'm either high or in a movie about a person who has moved to L.A. Dylan fiddles with the radio knob and the background beat turns into something mournful. In New York, Tara-Jean Slater might be suing me and the NYPD might have swarmed my building and armed guards might be standing outside my former apartment door, waiting to take me away.

*

The house is a slightly ramshackle two-story, set back from the street by a narrow path. It's painted a fading blue, and a set of low steps lead up to a wood-planked porch where Daniel stands, barefoot, watching us pull in. As soon as I get out of the van, he says: "Welcome," and Sydney laces through that single word, flattens it out. Daniel has dark eyes and fine, long-fingered hands, and his handshake is warm and firm. He's taller than Dylan, broader in the shoulders, with that kind of relentless good health that Australians radiate.

Dylan wraps an arm around Daniel's shoulders, presses a kiss on his cheek. Standing together like that, the contrast is all the more striking: Dylan is Southern California sun, the brown of sunburn already turning gold. Daniel's hair is dark, everything about his body language is contained. He accepts the kiss but doesn't return it. I don't remember if they kissed last time I saw them, so I can't tell if this is "intense" or normal.

"Let's show her the house," Dylan says. "It's so crazy you've never been here, Cass."

"Have you ever been to L.A.?" Daniel asks.

"No, actually."

Dylan picks up my duffel bag, and I follow obediently as Daniel points out the shadowy kitchen with its old gas stove, leading into a small mudroom with a large washing machine, and beyond that, the door to my bedroom. The bedroom is nice—wood floors, big windows facing out onto a backyard. The bed is a mattress and box spring, no bed frame, across from a large open closet with empty hangers arranged in a line. Everything in the room is old and dented, like the house itself, but generous and full of light.

"Looks great," I say, because they seem to be waiting for something. Daniel puts my duffel down next to a battered dresser.

"Let's show her the back," Dylan suggests. From the kitchen, sliding glass doors open onto the small rectangle of yard my bedroom windows face. It's hemmed by weathered wooden fencing whose many gaps reveal the neighbor's house just beyond, and, running along the western edge, a stretch of side street. A back gate hangs off its hook, facing the street.

As we step outside, I take in boxes of herbs, potted plants, a mysterious army of things that are spiky, spotted, bulbous, shiny, flat, waxy, and wet. A large lemon tree hangs over us, branches fat with fruit. It is the only plant I recognize by name.

Daniel drops down onto a nearby lawn chair. Dylan finds a joint tucked under the ashtray on the patio table and lights it, taking a deep drag. He offers it to Daniel, who shakes his head, and then to me. I shake my head. As Dylan blows smoke out in a steady blue stream, Daniel says: "Dylan said—you've been working in the theatre? Are you an actor?"

"No, no," I say hastily. I'm wondering what else Dylan might have said recently.

"Baby," Dylan murmurs, the subtext being: *You always forget what my friends do.* If he googled me, does that mean *he* knows what I did? And if he knows, has there been pity on his face at any point in the last few hours? Did I mistake it for kindness?

"So—what? A stagehand?"

"*Baby.*" Once, years ago, when we were drunk, Dylan had said: "Daniel only remembers the jobs that he thinks are 'real.'"

"She's a playwright," Dylan says softly, reproachfully.

I pick up one of the fallen lemons from the patio, turn it over in my fingers. "I've never seen a real lemon tree before," I say. "It's so wild that you just have one . . . growing."

After a watchful moment, Daniel lets the subject be changed. "It was here when we moved in," he says, and then, humbly, as if he doesn't mean to brag but can't help saying this, he gestures at the plants around us: "The rest is me, though."

"You did this? It's beautiful."

Daniel smiles. It's surprisingly luminous; it changes his whole face. "I planted them, but they did the hard part themselves."

"No," Dylan objects, "it's impressive. Own it."

"Things growing from small to large is my speed," Daniel says, self-deprecating. And then, teasing: "Dylan prefers roller coasters and fast cars and all that American excess."

Dylan grins, shrugs. The sun plays over the muscles of his upper arms, the cords of his neck. Dylan and I slept together once—college, of course, one of those nights that reseal themselves as soon as they're over. We joked about it from time to time, never did it again. I remember that, when Dylan started dating Daniel, he mentioned that Daniel was a "gold-star gay"—"No women," Dylan had said, sounding impressed, "not once." Dylan and I each had a series of boyfriends and girlfriends over the years, and displays of singular focus were impressive to us both. As they stayed together, Dylan stopped mentioning past girlfriends, until you would have thought that his, too, was a history of singular focus. I'd never asked if he had told Daniel about us.

"Well," Daniel says, after the quiet has stretched back out. "I'll put the sheets in the dryer." He gives me a nod, then vanishes inside the house. Dylan kills the joint, tucks its remainder into the ashtray. I turn the lemon over and over in my fist. *This is a real object. This is a real backyard. This is a real city.* After waiting a moment to make sure Daniel isn't returning, Dylan fishes in his pocket and comes up with a pack of cigarettes. "I know, *so* not L.A.," he says when I glance at them.

"You still smoke?"

"Yes and no." He taps the pack on the inside of his wrist, extracts one. "Daniel hates when I do this, but . . . We're all gonna fall into the ocean, so . . ."

"We are?"

"The entire plate," he says. "L.A.'s tectonic plate is gonna detach and we'll fall into the ocean. Daniel will miss the blessed event, of course, but *we* . . ." He holds out the pack. "Haven't you heard the world is ending?"

"Yeah," I say. "Yeah, I've heard that." And I drop the lemon to take one of his smokes.

*

I went to a therapist for the first and only time when everything was falling apart. With Liz, and my play, and all of it. The therapist was younger than I wanted her to be, and her clothes were more expensive than I expected. I briefly wondered if I should have been a therapist, because then I might be sane and rich as opposed to broke and crazy.

She asked me to talk about all of the reasons that I wanted to see a therapist, and I mentioned that everything I cared about was falling apart in ways that seemed ruthless and uncontrollable. She asked me what kind of things, and I searched for the easiest answer—as an example, as something she might recognize instantly—and landed on Liz. My relationship, I said, seemed to be over, although neither of us had ended it yet.

The therapist asked me to talk about this relationship, and I immediately felt like I'd made the wrong choice in using Liz as an example. I also felt like I'd made the wrong choice in calling it a relationship. Liz was the thing I was doing instead of a variety of other things. And, as far as Liz was concerned, I may have fulfilled the same function. But it felt too complicated to explain all of that, so I started to talk, and I talked for what I remember as a long time.

I talked about meeting Liz on the first day of rehearsal, and I talked about the feeling of being at the beginning of something, like a relationship—or a play—that wild rush of possibility breaking over you all the time, even when you're brushing your teeth, even when you're trying to sleep. How actually you just stop sleeping those first few weeks of rehearsal, because this crazy energy is being generated by all the bodies in the room that are inhabiting the thing that you dreamed up. How it's like being possessed by ghosts, except you're the ghost and everybody else feels suddenly so real—you've never been this invisible and this alive at the exact same time. It's a baffling, terrifying, addictive feeling. It's the best high in the world. The other thing about it is that it feels a lot like religion. I wasn't raised with any, but the people I know who believe in God derive a lot of comfort from the idea that they are being held by something larger than themselves. When I'm in a theatre I feel held. I feel simultaneously very safe and like something very dangerous is about to happen, and that dangerous thing is the wall of my chest peeling back—slowly, so slowly, in time with the curtain rising. And if the play is my play, then everybody present can gather close and peer at my naked heart. And I won't even try to guard myself, because I am being held by the architecture of the theatre, by every pair of arms in every seat, and I will sit still for a time between 75 and 120 minutes, and I will be naked, and I will be invisible, and I will be entirely seen. And all the parts of me that are ugly and lonely and horrible and sad will be the parts of me that other people hold close to themselves and find a secret resonance with, and about which they say to themselves: *I know that thing too, when I'm all alone that's how I feel too*. And even if nobody says those words out loud, right then, we will be feeling the same feelings so strongly that we will forget that we aren't of one body, one mind, one tenuous heart. And if it isn't my play, then I will still be part of that collective witnessing organism, still be a single cell within a warm and gazing animal. It's the sort of feeling that becomes a constant longing. It's the sort of longing upon which you build an entire life.

After a while, the therapist broke in. She said, "Cass. Cass." I remember she was looking at me oddly.

I said: What is it?

She said: You haven't been talking about your girlfriend at all, Cass. Are you aware of that?

I said: What are you talking about, of course I've been talking about my girlfriend.

And the therapist said: No, you've been talking about the theatre.

She said: I would say you've been talking about your career, except none of this is about anything I would normally term a "career," you don't seem to have any separation between yourself and your "job," your "employment," so to speak, there's no professional distance, you haven't even mentioned the word "money."

She said: Honestly, I would never usually put it like this, but I'll just say it—you're in a dysfunctional relationship with the theatre. Your girlfriend, Liz, is beside the point.

I said: I've been getting around to telling you about Liz, I just haven't gotten there yet.

And the therapist said: Well, this is the first time in sixty minutes that you've mentioned her name, Cass, so I think that should tell you something, because it certainly tells *me* quite a bit.

*

My first night in L.A., I lie in bed and have a conversation with myself about my new life. The sheets smell like Meyer's laundry detergent and lemon and sunlight, and I say: *Self, you are going to look so skinny and hot. You are going to have great arm muscles, and a tan, and new jeans, and maybe some new ink. This life is going to be so good for you.*

I say: *Self, nobody knows who you are or what you did. From now on, you will only be around civilians who think "off-Broadway" sounds like directions to nowhere. Nobody you encounter will ever have heard of you, and you are going to be happy.*

I start to hear voices filtering down through the pipes. Dylan and Daniel, upstairs. Is their bedroom directly above mine? The tour hadn't extended to the upper floor of the house. Dylan's voice, stacking tone on top of tone, the voice of somebody making a detailed but reasonable argument. Then Daniel's voice, low and soft, disagreeing. Then Dylan's again, stronger.

I get out of bed. It's not like I'm eavesdropping. I walk over to the window. I'm taking in the backyard. I'm looking at the moonlight. If my ear is directly to the pipe, it's just because I'm leaning on the wall. And right then, staring out the window, I see a group of shadows moving purposefully off the street and toward the back fence of the house next door. I blink. The shadows separate into hoods and jeans, sleeves, the glint of a white-soled sneaker. Teenagers, it looks like—five or six of them. As I watch, they scale the back fence of our neighbor's house and, one by one, drop down out of sight. I'm briefly paralyzed with possibility. Am I witnessing a break-in? The precursor to homicide? Is this like the movies made by disaffected Germans, in which teenagers arbitrarily torture and murder middle-class heteronormative family units? Should I be calling Dylan? Or the neighbor? Or the police?

The last of the bodies, enswathed in its hoodie, drops over the back fence. The shadows are gone. The night is quiet. I stand very still, no longer trying to hear Dylan and Daniel's argument—instead, I listen for the sound of screams, pleading, duct tape being pulled to cover someone's well-intentioned, fatherly mouth. But the silence is broken only by the hush of cars passing by on Fountain Ave. Even Dylan and Daniel are no longer talking.

After enough time has passed, I go back to bed. The mattress is firm and the pillows are soft. I can usually sleep anywhere, it's my superhuman skill, but somehow in this comfortable bed, in this large, calm room, I'm jumpy. Whenever I close my eyes, all I can see is the highway speeding wildly past, trees careening, hills swinging right and left, even though Dylan drove it so slowly earlier that day. I lie awake for a long time, eyes wide and dry, listening for the sound of something somewhere happening to someone before it happens to me.

2

My first week in L.A. is long and strange—simultaneously a repeat of certain basic activities (wake up, make coffee, drink it on the patio, check email, shower in the light-filled downstairs bathroom) and a barrage of smells and shapes that I have no context for. Fruit trees so overburdened with fruit that the sidewalks are littered with it; big squashy-blossomed shrubs; armor-plated cacti; homeless encampments comprised of dust-encrusted outdoor tents, shopping carts piled high with garbage bags.

In New York it gets too cold to be outside all the time, you can't build yourself a city of tents and shopping carts. In L.A., whole private lives are happening in public spaces: cooking, sleeping, laughing, talking, hanging out laundry, reading battered paperbacks. The homeless people ignore me and I try to ignore them, but part of me feels like they're ignoring me because they've all heard about me, and they're signaling to each other: *Don't look at her, failure like that is contagious*.

Daniel isn't around in the daytime. I learn from Dylan that he works a regular nine-to-five for a company doing something called "risk management." I don't know what risk management is, other than a tidy summation of everything I'm bad at. Dylan was an English major in college, which means that he works at a restaurant in Los Feliz. But the thing that Dylan *really* devotes himself to, with the determination that other people bring to their jobs, is lounging. He's always in the sun on the patio with his shirt off, throwing his surfboard into the back of the van, returning from the beach with his wetsuit peeled down to his hip bones and his shaggy hair damp and salt crusted.

I gather that this—like the cigarettes—is a subject of contention between the two of them. It seems that there are a number of these, but I have entered at a time of tenuous détente, so I try not to ask questions that they will then have to try not to answer. This is a state of affairs with which I'm well acquainted.

On the afternoon of the third day, I call my agent. Before I left New York, Marisa had said, "Don't call me again," in the same conversation in which she'd used the phrase "appalling and unprofessional." I think it was also the conversation in which she said something about me being lucky I wasn't getting sued, and also something about this sort of bad-boy behavior not being cute anymore post–Sam Shepard. I don't remember the conversation entirely, because I was drunk at the time—I hadn't planned to be, I had only happened to be drinking heavily when Marisa decided to call me back. And now that it's already sort of fuzzy, I try to maintain as much fuzziness as possible, because I can't be responsible for knowing what I don't remember. Maybe in the light of day, in the light of L.A., we can have a new conversation. America loves a comeback story. Think of Britney. I know I've only been gone a few days, but who says how long you have to be gone before you're ready to come back?

So I call Marisa. Her assistant picks up immediately: "Creative Content Associates, how may I help you?"

"Hey," I say, trying to sound very casual. "Uh, is Marisa in?"

"Who's calling, please?"

"It's Cass."

And: a beat, wherein the assistant tries to figure out what to do. Here is what you need to know about this assistant: Jocelyn / twenty-two / ironic polka dots / parents on the UWS / scarlet lipstick / first job out of Barnard.

After a moment, Jocelyn says, her tone slightly cooler: "One moment, please, let me see if I have her." This means: *She's here, but which will she kill me for: hanging up on you, or transferring you over?*

Silence, and then Jocelyn returns. "I'm so sorry, I don't have her at the moment. Can we return?"

"Yeah, please . . . uh, return."

"Okay, thank you so much for calling."

Jocelyn is about to hang up when I hear myself blurt: "I moved to L.A., will you let her know that I moved to L.A.?"

Jocelyn draws breath, but before she can answer, I amend my request: "Actually don't say I *moved*, just tell her I'm in L.A."

"Okay," Jocelyn says. "Well, thank you—"

"—and tell her I don't remember what she—on the phone, what she said? What we said? So if she thinks I remember all of it, maybe tell her that actually isn't the case, so I'd love to sort of . . . reconnect and reexamine. . . . Hello?"

Click. Jocelyn and her scarlet lipstick have hung up.

*

The Lansing Award was what put me on the radar. And it went like this.

Pre-Lansing, I was nobody. I grew up in small-town New Hampshire, went to a college that was affordable instead of fancy, and moved to New York, where I was immediately broke as balls. I paid my bills by grant writing, dog walking, and cater-waitering, in various combinations. I made weird downtown plays and got my friends to put them up in black-box theatres, basements, or found spaces. I had an unshakable conviction that someday I would hit the "tipping point" (this was something a psychic on West Fourth once told me), after which my career would take off. Everything up to the tipping point would be the story I could tell once things had worked out. My unshakable conviction could be seen as either ambition or delusion, depending who you were (the psychic referred to it as a calling), but either way, it made it easier to work three jobs and self-produce experimental plays.

And then one day, in my tenth year of this New York life, a man called and told me I'd won fifty thousand dollars and I had to show up to the Harvard Club for a ceremony, after which I could collect it.

At first I thought this was a scam, but the man kept going. He told me that it was an inaugural award for emerging playwrights. Two others had also won, and he named them, so I googled them. Tara-Jean Slater was finishing her last year of undergrad at Yale, and she seemed to have already won most of the awards that Yale itself had to offer. In the pictures, she looked very young and blank, and pretty in a prepubescent way. Carter Maxwell was straight out of grad school at Juilliard (he'd done his undergrad at Yale), and his mother was an accomplished interior designer on the Upper East Side. He had recently attended his sister's wedding in Hyannis Port, and he looked dashing in a suit—both in the wedding pictures and in a recent *New York Times* profile that called him "possibly the next Arthur Miller."

I called my roommate at work and asked if I could borrow his suit.

Nico was taller than me, but we shared a similar build. We'd lived together for the last four years, and neither of us were ever home, which made our situation work well. Nico was a choreographer. His dad was from El Salvador, his mom was a New York Jew, and both were musicians. Although they'd divorced while he was young, they still lived down the street from each other in Berkeley, and regularly reconvened for family Thanksgiving. Nico was well-adjusted in a way that defied belief; he did his laundry weekly, he saved money, he paid his taxes on time, and he was always lending me clothes.

The day of the ceremony, I borrowed Nico's blue suit jacket and I put it over skinny black jeans and black Chucks, and I took the subway from 168th Street down to Forty-fourth, then walked east toward Fifth Avenue. I walked around the block three or four times before I got up the courage to go in. After the final lap, I took a deep breath, held it until I felt a little high, and then marched over to the entrance. A woman with a clipboard got my name: "Oh! You're one of the honorees! There's a table over there, please get your name tag and then, if you wouldn't mind, there's a step-and-repeat by the—"

I didn't make it to either the name tag table or the step-and-repeat.

There were crowds. There were cocktails. Open bar. Small glasses of wine circulating on trays. I'd fallen into a blur of dark wood and elegant fabric and chardonnay. I realized that nobody was wearing what I was wearing. I realized that everyone had a plus-one, and I should have brought Nico as well as his suit. I caught a glimpse of Carter Maxwell, who had a girl in a silk dress on his arm. Carter was shaking hands with a series of older men, also in suits, and saying things like "Such a pleasure" and "You know, that's a good question" and "Well, thank you sir, I appreciate that" and "Very recently, but it's nice to be out of school." He held his drink effortlessly, and when the time came to put the empty glass on a tray and receive another drink, he did that effortlessly as well. I was having trouble just standing in the room. It seemed that either everybody was staring at me or I was completely invisible. I had wanted this forever, to be in a room like this, and now that I was here, I felt light-headed and nauseous.

Eventually I stumbled down a series of hallways and a woman pointed me to the ladies' room, where I hid in a stall and texted Nico.

I said: *This is awful, I'm gonna puke.*

Nico said: *Get that monayyy.* Nico in person is innate elegance, but Nico over text is a whole different story.

I said: *Nobody is talking to me*
I think maybe I'm dead and/ or dreaming this
I dunno how to get the food off the trays
like, with your fingers? or like
also nobody is wearing jeans
Carter's girlfriend looks expensive
Can I go home early do you think?

Nico said: *This is your TIME to SHINE.*

I said: *I'm gonna puke on your suit.*

Nico said: *Get my money get my cash get my math everything's funny til that ass gettin trashed*—which I stared at for a few minutes, trying to decipher, until I realized it was Nicki Minaj lyrics.

I exited the bathroom stall, flagged down a caterer, and drank two glasses of wine in the span of ten minutes, and a relaxed curiosity unspooled itself inside me. I bobbed along, now just a pair of eyes. If people glanced at me, I looked back, friendly but noncommittal. Carter was near the bar, laughing as a middle-aged man slapped him jocularly on the back—I couldn't hear them, but I could tell that he was deflecting a compliment with expertise. His girlfriend had clearly gotten tired of this; her mouth was fixed in a smile, but her eyes had traveled over their heads, across the crowd, out and away. Her heels were hurting and the room was hot, and Carter was no longer introducing her to people, because they were happening to him so fast he didn't even know their names. He didn't seem overwhelmed or nervous, though. Maybe he'd always expected to be in a situation where he was being rewarded for his promise, and so he was prepared. I had imagined a Big Break for so long but hadn't known that it would have the power to undo me when it arrived.

I drifted over to the bar. Carter glanced up, took me in.

"You must be Cass," he said.

I glanced down at the front of Nico's jacket, found it blank, and then remembered I'd never visited the name tag table. "How'd you know?"

"You look like a Cass," Carter deadpanned, and then he grinned. "I googled you."

"You did?"

"Yeah, I'd never heard of you." He said it like it could be either an insult or a compliment.

"I'd never heard of you either," I said.

Carter grinned again. "Congrats are in order for all of us," he said. "We're *emerging*." He lifted his glass, then saw I didn't have one. The bartender was at the other end of the bar, a situation that had baffled me—does one wave a hand in an establishment like this? Do you shout louder than the ambient noise?—but Carter reached out languidly and snagged a glass of white wine off a passing tray that I hadn't even clocked. He sniffed it, shrugged, handed it to me. "Bad pinot, I think? Cheers."

We toasted, we drank. I studied Carter over my wineglass. The room had gotten overfilled, and you had to lean in and yell to be heard. He was scanning the crowd with mild interest, but he included me in it—"Oh, *Playbill* is here." And then a moment later, "Oh, Tony Kushner is here." And then: "Oh, Marsha Norman is here." I risked a glance at the room, but it threatened to become a blurred mass again, so I focused on my glass.

"Have you met Tara-Jean Slater yet?" Carter asked.

"No," I said.

"Me neither, but I'm looking forward to it. I keep hearing about her."

"You do?"

"Yeah, she's like—a big deal in New Haven." Carter laughed. "The Yale network, you know."

I didn't know. Instead, I asked: "How does this kind of thing go?"

Carter glanced at me. "You mean big picture? You should talk to your agent about that."

"No, I mean like—right now, what's gonna happen?"

Carter shrugged. "There'll be a bunch of speeches, then we go up and say some words, and they give us a check." He turned to scout out the far corner for more people of note, then turned back to me: "You've done this before, it's like all of them."

"I haven't," I said. "Actually."

"Done this before?"

"Yeah."

"Oh." Carter seemed surprised. "I just figured . . . you know, people usually win things because they won other things."

"I've never won anything in my life," I said.

"Oh." Carter gave me his attention in a real way now. "Who's your agent?"

"I don't have one."

Now Carter was really staring. "Like, you're between agencies?"

"I never got one." I shrugged. "I've been—you know, doing stuff downtown."

Carter opened his mouth, but then his girlfriend appeared, smelling floral, and I let the crowd swallow me back up. I wasn't sure whether I felt ashamed for not having and knowing the things Carter seemed to have and know, or whether I felt floaty and warm and like I didn't give a fuck. The fourth glass of wine was nudging me much closer to floaty and warm, and I was contemplating a fifth when the crowd started moving en masse toward the hall and into a different room, as if they'd all heard a whistle that I couldn't hear.

The ceremony itself was what Carter had predicted. I don't remember much of it, because floaty and warm turned into definitely drunk. I didn't absorb what was said about us in the speeches either, but later I looked it up. Carter had won because of his raw and authentic dissection of male-female relationships and his insights into how masculinity functions within shifting power dynamics. I was selected as a promising female voice, a young woman telling comedic and timely stories about young women. And Tara-Jean Slater . . .

I'm not ready to talk about Tara-Jean Slater.

We were called to the front one by one. Carter talked for a while. I remember watching his girlfriend unobtrusively check her phone a few times, before he walked offstage to thunderous applause. When he reached his seat beside her, she was beaming at him as if she'd been hanging on every word.

My memory of seeing Tara-Jean Slater for the first time is blurry. She was wearing velvet overalls and yellow shoes, and her hair was in two tight pigtails the color of rust. She had a very tiny, very clear voice, like a thimbleful of water. Sometimes I wish I could remember what she'd said, but I was drunk, and I didn't know she mattered.

Someone told me later that when my name was called, I walked to the front of the room, blinked at them all owlishly, said, "Thank you," and then walked back to my seat, completely forgetting to collect the check. One of the facilitators had to chase me down the aisle and hand it to me. I don't remember this, but I do remember that I passed Carter after the ceremony ended, and he gave me a thumbs-up and said, "Short and sweet."

I went home and fell into bed. Woke up hungover and couldn't remember why for a few minutes, until I found Nico's suit jacket on my floor with a check for fifty thousand dollars in the pocket. I went to the bank, deposited it, paid my rent, and then after brief thought, paid the next month in advance. Brought Nico's jacket to the cleaners, met him for burritos to soak up the remaining toxins. By the time I'd made it back to our apartment, my hangover was fading and the Lansing Award ceremony seemed like it had happened years ago.

The next day there were pictures of me on *Playbill* and on Theater-Mania and in the *Times*. I googled myself and there I was: fragmented into frame after frame, intoxicatingly real. In all the photos, I looked startled, like an animal on the highway at night; Nico's jacket was big on me, and the powder blue stood out oddly against everyone else's sleek grays and elegant blacks. I hadn't even won spelling bees in middle school. I had assumed that someday I might win something and it would be nice, but this sensation was to "nice" as "amphetamine-fueled bender" is to "party." I started to read all the good things being said about me online, and I felt that they must be true, and I was dazzled by how talented I had been this whole time. Despite the many years of uncertainty, despite all the dog walking and downtown-low-budget-play making, I had actually been the insightfully comedic voice of my generation. I read about myself for hours, long into the afternoon, and when I thought to check my phone, I saw that Dylan had texted me *Whoa fancy*, and my mother had texted me *What is a Lansing Award?* and Nico had texted me, from the next room, *Nice suit jacket where'd you get it*, and the next day Marisa called me, asking me to meet with her, and then the day after that I had an agent and a reputation and a career.

*

Because I have no idea what I'm doing in L.A. other than not being in New York, I spend the whole first week rattling around the big Silver Lake house. I try to stay off the Internet for fear of what I will see about myself; when I do go online, I find myself seeking out bad reviews of other people's plays. I write down the worst bits on Post-it notes and stick them to the mirror in my bathroom, so that when I wake up in the morning I am immediately surrounded by starbursts of disaster that are not my own. When I brush my teeth or wash my face, I read "Remarkably unfinished and uneven" and "A surprisingly banal attempt at . . ." and "A very, very little play that manages to last three hours nonetheless . . ." and I think: *Someone else somewhere is suffering.*

I try Marisa again at the end of the week. I'm waiting in the line outside La Colombe on Sunset Boulevard. The girl in front of me has tattoos of pinup girls on her shoulders and back, and when a light breeze blows over us, she says to her boyfriend, "Oh my god, it's *arctic.*" A surprising number of French bulldogs are walking past, and they all seem jaded.

"Creative Content Associates, how may I help you?"

"Oh, hey, uh, Jocelyn? Is Marisa in?"

She knows it's me. I know she knows it's me. But she has to ask: "Who's calling, please?"

"It's Cass."

Did she sigh? Maybe not. It's loud out here.

"Hi, Cass," she says, very professionally. "I don't have Marisa right now, can I have her return?"

"Uh, do you know when she'll be back?"

"No, I'm sorry. But I can take a—"

"Is she like, *out* out, or is she like, in a meeting but in the office?"

"I'm sorry?"

"Because I just need to talk to her for a second. Say three minutes, five max. So if she's actually *at* the office, maybe—"

"She's unavailable," Jocelyn says firmly. The tone of her voice says she is trying to remind herself that this is her first job out of college and she has to be good at it.

"Okay, well. Did you give her my message?"

"Yes," Jocelyn says, in a tone that tells me, *No.*

"Jocelyn," I say desperately. "Be honest with me."

But instead of sounding desperate, I sound stern. By total accident. Maybe this reminds her of the time a college professor called her out on her bullshit, or maybe it's a flashback to being yelled at by an older sister, but whatever it is, she gets defensive and deferential. "I gave it to her but like, I'm not in control of her schedule? And like, there's a lot of people on the phone sheet right now? So, if she's not calling you yet, that doesn't mean I didn't give her your message?"

"Okay," I say soothingly. "Okay, I hear you. You're doing a good job, Jocelyn."

"Thanks," she says, muffled.

"Can you just do me one more favor?"

"What is it?"

"Can you tell me if Marisa is around this afternoon? Like, if somebody called—somebody, for example, who wasn't me—would she be around?"

Jocelyn knows she's being asked to step into dangerous territory. "Marisa has meetings all afternoon," she says carefully.

"Uh-huh . . ."

"For most of the afternoon."

"Right."

"Around three P.M., she has eleven minutes between meetings."

"Okay."

"Whether or not she's *around* during those eleven minutes is complicated, depending on whether or not she goes to the bathroom during those eleven minutes, or goes outside, or gets a coffee, or has me get her a coffee."

"Thank you," I say, trying to be casual and fervent at the same time.

Jocelyn's voice firms up, gets more profesh again. "Would you like to leave a message?" Someone must be walking by.

"No, thank you," I say, and I hang up. Another French bulldog saunters past. It gives me a languid, scornful stare. It knows I can't even get my agent on the phone. It's never been less impressed, except for the last time it was in Silver Lake and some low-rent asshole was making desperate calls outside an overpriced coffeeshop. *Sooo sad*, says the French bulldog, and pops a squat by the taco truck.

*

I have two and a half hours to kill. It's not even noon in New York. Theatre people are nocturnal. L.A. is intensely, aggressively diurnal.

I sit outside La Colombe and I watch people biking vehemently—not to work, necessarily, but to their next yoga class, or their early meditation session, or to the place two blocks up called, simply, JUICE. I itch for a cigarette. Dylan warned me that smoking in L.A. is basically the same thing as skinning a baby seal. He told me that he only smokes in the backyard, and when people ask him if he's a smoker, he says no. I hold my pointer and middle finger below my nose so I can smell the soothing residual tobacco scent, and I practice what I'll say to Marisa.

Hi, Marisa. It's me, Cass.

Yes, it's lovely out here.

Listen, I know it got rocky. And I take full responsibility for that. But, look. It was a wake-up call. I got my head together. Meditating, green juices, spin classes . . .

Then I'll go in for the kill. *Here's the thing, Marisa. At the end of the day, all these new offers I'm getting? They don't compare to the trust we had.*

Maybe that's too strong. Maybe this is a terrible idea.

I call the office at three P.M. Jocelyn doesn't pick up. The phone rings and rings. I call back eleven times between 3:00 and 3:11. That's once every sixty seconds. Each time, nobody picks up. At 3:12, I know that Marisa is now definitively in her next meeting. I consider sending Jocelyn a really nasty email, but instead I take a deep breath and practice visualizing positive things. I visualize Jocelyn leaving the agency in her strappy high heels and getting hit by a cab. I visualize Jocelyn getting hit by a truck. In my visualization, Jocelyn gets hit by a series of vehicles and is finished off by a horse-drawn carriage, the kind tourists ride in. I watch Jocelyn's high heels fly up in the air and her hair blow back. I feel positive.

*

I was with Nico when Marisa called to tell me that my play was getting produced off-Broadway. Nico's college friends were visiting, and we were sitting around the living room while they reminisced over entire adventures that I'd never heard about—road trips to Montauk to scatter the ashes of somebody's dead dog, the time that they went to a gathering of Radical Faeries. A skinny lesbian was launching into a story about how she'd walked the High Line recently with her Iowan cousin, who kept calling it "the Skyline," when my phone rang. *Marisa, Creative Content Associates* came up on the screen. I'd recently become one of those people who said things like "I'm so sorry, I have to take this, my agent is calling." I'd never been able to say this sentence before, and now that I could, I never wanted to stop saying it. But when I delivered my line, nobody noticed and the skinny lesbian kept talking, so I stepped into our kitchen.

On the phone Marisa was cheerful and forceful in equal measure. Talking to her always feels like being run over by a tank, even when the tank is going in the same direction you want to go. "Gotta jump, so, real quick," is how she begins most phone calls. This one was no exception, except she followed it with: "You got your off-Broadway debut. Congrats!"

"Wait, what?"

Marisa told me that she'd recently gotten off the phone with a large and well-known Midtown theatre. "They had a play fall through for their first slot, so they read this year's crop of Lansing playwrights, and they love your play. Rehearsals start August, play opens September. Yes?"

"Oh," I said. "Oh wow."

"What else, what else." Marisa ticked her pen against her teeth—I'd seen her do it in person by then, so I knew what the *click, click* over the phone was. "They want to have Hélène Allard direct—she was set to do the other play." She said the last name "Al-lar": very French.

"Uh, okay."

"I said you'd have to meet with her, of course, so we'll set that up. She's great, she'll be good profile for you." Click, click. "There's been a lot of buzz. The Lansing and now this—everybody's talking, they're like, *Where did she come from?*"

"I've been here," I started to say. "For ten years, actually—"

But Marisa didn't hear me. "This is your moment, kiddo. Congrats! So, gotta jump. Call you later when we have the paperwork."

She hung up, and I sat on the floor. Nico came in and found me there.

"You okay?"

"Yeah, um—I'm having a play produced."

"Congrats! Are you guys using Judson Church again?"

"No," I said, and then couldn't stop myself from dropping the name of the theatre like a bomb. Nico's eyebrows jumped.

"That's crazy," he said. "That's amazing!"

"It's totally crazy," I said. "They're giving me a fancy director and everything." All of a sudden, I wanted to explain the feeling I'd had the day after the Lansings, when I was looking at myself online. But I didn't have the right words, and instead what came out was: "It's so bizarre to finally be real."

Nico cocked his head. "You've always been *real*," he said.

"No, but—you know what I mean. I was like . . . super DIY."

"You were making good things," Nico said. "It's not like you didn't *exist*."

But that was exactly how I'd started to feel in these short few weeks. Like a picture coming into focus, my life had been given density and shape by success—and from this new vantage point, I could see that everything behind me had been only blur. I opened my mouth, but the skinny lesbian was calling from the other room: "Nico, we're gonna seamless, we're staaarving!"

"Well," Nico said, resolving the conversation, "anyway, this is so great!" and he returned to the living room.

I sat in the kitchen for a second longer and then texted Dylan and two playwright friends, who were sometimes a couple, so if you texted news to one it was good policy to text it to the other in case they were back together. Then I texted my parents, and then I remembered that my parents still don't know how to text back, so I emailed them, and then I texted a guy I'd been on-again, off-again with, a lighting designer.

He was the first one to text me back. He said: *I'm tech avail in August, FYI.*

Hélène said to me once: "Nobody is ever gonna be as happy as you are about the good things that happen, but everybody is gonna show up to watch when the shit goes down." She was talking about herself at the time, about what she'd learned in a three-plus-decade career in the theatre, so it didn't feel like a prophecy when she said it. Only later. But that was much later.

*

I'm on the back patio when Dylan gets home. The house has stood empty all day, and I feel him even before I hear him—a bright burst of energy, like the wind picking up, as the front door slams. After a long beat, he appears in the window over the kitchen sink. He doesn't see me at first—he looks exhausted. He stands at the sink for a long time with his head down. He's wearing his restaurant outfit: gray button-down and black jeans. Eventually he vanishes and reappears a few moments later through the sliding doors. When he sees me, he hesitates.

"I was just going in," I say, at the same time as he asks, "Mind if I sit?"

"No, please . . ."

Dylan sprawls into a lawn chair across from me. His shirt hitches up enough for me to see the taut handspan of skin just above his jeans.

"Long day?" I ask.

"The longest," he says. He tightens his lips like he isn't going to say any more, then changes his mind: "Daniel and I had a huge fight, actually."

"You did?"

"On the phone. On my lunch break. I was standing behind the restaurant *screaming* at him and I just . . . I had this moment where I was like, Who the fuck *am* I?" Dylan sighs, scrubs a hand through his hair. We're quiet. And then, as casually as he can muster: "You said you had a breakup. In New York."

"Did I say that?"

"On the phone—when you called me."

"Oh." I remember the fact of having made the phone call, but—as with the one with Marisa—the space that would usually be populated by detail is a ringing blank.

"You were pretty out of it," Dylan says, excusing me.

"I guess I was."

We haven't discussed my situation all week. I know that Dylan has been waiting for me to bring up whatever happened. For my part, I've ricocheted between wanting to tell him everything so that someone can witness the depths of my misery and wanting to say nothing at all so that—in a quiet space not desecrated by my past—I can attempt to rebuild.

"How long were you guys together?"

The first time I made out with Liz was right before our play went into previews. After that, in some form or another, we were together. But Liz and her wife were also together. And that entire time, I couldn't stop thinking about Hélène. And Liz was probably, in some form or other, thinking about her wife. What specific constellation of longing, guilt, desire, remorse, and rage constitutes actual togetherness? Maybe it's not either/or, it's and/and/and. This suddenly feels to me like some impossible physics question.

"Not long," I say. "But also, maybe too long."

"Do you talk to her still?"

"Liz and I . . ." I try to find the right way to put this. "There's not much left to say to each other. It wasn't really . . . a relationship, the way yours is."

Dylan closes his eyes against the sun. "Did you know that ten years is a common-law marriage?"

"I didn't."

"It used to be that if a man and a woman were together for ten years, the woman had, like, legal claims on the man." Dylan opens his eyes, gives me a lopsided grin: "Not to be heteronormative."

"Legal claims?"

"Like if he knocked somebody else up, somebody's maidservant or a fishwife—or, worse than that, if *you* were the maidservant or the fishwife, and you had ten years under your belt, and then all of a sudden he married some lady of a higher station—in that case, you could take him to court."

"Which of you is which in this equation?"

Dylan's smile is more real when he says, "I'm probably the fishwife. If you ask Daniel."

"And if I ask you?"

"Still the fishwife."

We both laugh. The sun is directly in our eyes now, and I close mine briefly, letting the heat soak into me.

"Hey, Cass?"

"Yeah?"

"What did it feel like? Right after it ended?"

I know he's asking about Liz, but when I answer, I can't help thinking of all the rest of it too: Hélène and the play and the scandal. "It was like—a physical thing," I say at last. "My stomach hurt all the time. And sometimes I'd forget why my stomach hurt, and I'd be like, Oh, did I eat something weird? And then I'd figure it out." I take a breath. "But—you know. I'm sure it gets better. Probably it's already getting better." I dart a glance at Dylan to see if I've comforted him.

He makes a face. "Daniel . . . he's always so serious, so with him it ended up being serious. He's my first for . . . all of this." He gestures to the house, the garden. "It feels like . . . a divorce more than a breakup."

"And—you going to Sydney is not a thing?"

Dylan sighs. "His parents don't know about me. They don't know he's gay and they sure as hell don't know about me. So. No, it's not a thing."

I mull this over. "What do they think he's been doing for ten years?"

"Living with a roommate." Dylan chokes a laugh. "And dating California girls, maybe. There's probably a reason they don't ask."

"And he's gonna go back, and . . . ?"

"I guess."

"Oh."

We're quiet, lost in our own thoughts. My parents had delivered the classic "We love you no matter what" speech when they thought I was lesbian, but then my girlfriend and I broke up and I dated a boy. He was followed by two girls, and on my second boyfriend, I watched my parents give up on understanding. But lack of understanding is not a lack of love. Not always. I imagine Daniel in his mother's kitchen. His mother is asking him about Los Angeles, and he is saying . . . What is he saying?

A movement through the neighbor's fence catches my eye— someone walking past, a flash of skin, bikini string, the top of a floppy sun hat. I remember when, a week before, I saw a small mob of teenagers drop over the back fence. Maybe I wasn't witnessing a break-in after all. Maybe the neighbor is a Mormon, with eight children who sneak out to drink and party and then sneak back in. A sunbathing Mormon.

"Hey." I gesture to the fence. "Who lives there?"

"Uhhh . . ." Dylan shrugs. "Some woman?"

"Like . . . a Mormon?"

"My guess is a hard no. How come?"

"I thought I saw a bunch of kids the other night, sort of scaling the fence, and . . ." It sounds strange even to my ears. "Never mind."

"Oh, no," Dylan assures me. "That's a new thing this past month, but it's definitely happening. There's always a crowd of kids around there now. Like, high school kids."

"The woman who lives there—is she . . . running a sex-trafficking ring or something?"

Dylan grins. "I only saw her once," he says, "but she looks harmless."

"Don't they always."

I glance back to the fence, but the adjacent backyard is empty again, no sign of a sun hat in sight.

3

Let me tell you about Hélène.

The facts: French, early fifties, director. A career studded with big shows at big theatres in New York and London, Broadway and the West End.

Quieter facts: Hélène in the sunlight. Those smile lines around her eyes and mouth. Looking at me, shaking her head. That wry smile that lives in the no-man's-land between amused and mocking, always keeping me slightly off balance.

Marisa set a meeting for us at the Ace Hotel toward the end of June, and I spent the week beforehand wondering what I should wear. I asked Nico and he said: "Look nice, but don't try too hard, but don't look like you don't care." So I went to the Ace in what I usually wore: battered Chucks and torn jeans and a flannel shirt.

It turned out that Hélène was wearing almost exactly the same thing, the difference being that she looked breeze-blown and French, as if she'd been drinking rosé *près de la Seine* only moments before. Her eyes were a warm brown, her face sun worn and unapologetic. She had rings on her index, middle, and ring fingers, on both hands. When I came in, she was sitting at the bar, squeezing a crescent of lime through the neck of her Negra Modelo. She didn't see me at first, and the pure concentration that she was devoting to the task moved me in some way. I wanted to become a person who would put lime in my beer like that—like a commitment to the future, like every detail mattered when done correctly.

I slipped onto a barstool next to her, and she looked up from her beer and smiled.

"Hélène," she said, holding out a hand. She said it the proper way, the French way.

"Cass," I said. Her skin was cool to the touch.

"It's a pleasure," she said, and sized me up. "You're the new thing."

"I am?"

She laughed. "Later on," she said, "keep that exact tone. People will make a meal of you, but they'll still expect you to seem surprised." She flagged the bartender down, glanced over at me. "Whatever the lady would like," she said.

I realized she was referring to me. "I'll have what she's having," I said, and then I wondered if I should have used this as an opportunity to demonstrate my individuality. But she didn't react; she seemed uninterested in what I was or wasn't drinking.

"So," she said, leaning in, eyes sharp. "Let's hear about you."

Hélène led the conversation as if it were a dog or a donkey, pulling it this way and that. I tried to keep up, which involved answering her questions without a lot of time to consider what I was saying. She wanted to know about my parents (teachers), what I'd been doing for money (scrambling), where I lived (Washington Heights), the other playwrights I loved (Sarah Kane, Caryl Churchill, Martin McDonagh).

"Oh, the Brits," she said. "And the Americans?"

I said, before I thought: "American plays are mostly family-secrets-emerge-at-the-country-house or like, five-people-in-Brooklyn-have-a-dinner-party-and-their-relationships-end."

"Yes, realism. It's the American obsession, always has been. With delicious interruptions. Adrienne Kennedy, God bless her, interrupted it and was shunted to the side for decades. Mostly, America ignores interruptions and continues unchecked . . . in theatre as in most other things."

"I don't care about realism," I said.

Hélène lifted an eyebrow at me. "Go on."

"Life is strange and arbitrary," I said, with all the grandness of someone who is never asked for her opinion being asked for her opinion. "Absurdist theatre holds a mirror up to the audience, reflects back what it feels like to be alive. Realism is ordered, neat, easy. Information in little packets, rolled out gently, bite-size. Why aren't we telling stories about how things feel overwhelming and dangerous, how this is a world where anything can change in a moment?"

Hélène looked at me for a long moment, and then she smiled, and it went all the way to her eyes. "Young and opinionated," she said. "I remember that. It was great." She sipped her beer and added, as an afterthought, "I directed O'Neill on Broadway."

Fuck! I'd forgotten that! I'd seen that when I'd googled her, and I'd forgotten it.

"I didn't mean . . ." I backtracked. "O'Neill is, you know, as far as realism goes, Eugene O'Neill . . ."

"Relax. Opinions are good. Even if you end up eating them later." Hélène shrugged. "Or keeping them; who knows? You're at the beginning of all this, maybe three years from now you write a Connecticut-country-house play. But that's not what you wrote this time, and I like what you wrote this time. I want to work on it with you, if you want that."

"I want that," I said immediately.

Hélène held out her hand again, mock-formal, and I took it. "My people will talk to your people," she said, making it into a joke, and I glowed with the feeling of being a person who suddenly had people.

On our way out of the bar, Hélène stopped on the sidewalk. It was still sunny out, late-afternoon shadows cutting long and easy down Broadway.

"This won't always be as effortless as it seems right now," she said, apropos of nothing, as if it was a standard goodbye. "Enjoy yourself. Being a debutante is always easier than being a member of the tribe." She smiled, touched my shoulder, and then she was moving away, uptown, navigating stripes of sun and shadow like a dancer.

*

When day slides into evening in L.A., I fall into the habit of ordering Fat Dragon on Seamless and eating it in bed, straight from the containers. I've started to branch out in my obsessive consuming of other people's shame. Although I began with the contemporary, I find myself turning to history: Van Gogh (the ear), Sylvia Plath (the oven), Virginia Woolf (the river). This leads me to conclude that actually, in the end, we are all entirely summed up by our single most public failure, and not by any of the nuanced, beautiful, difficult things we accomplished before or after. And this thought is bolstered by all the mean online comments I read about myself before I stopped going online—and this makes me even more undeniably depressed.

Tonight, when I reach a fever pitch of bleakness, I leave the Fat Dragon containers tangled in my sheets and plunge out of the bedroom, into the dark kitchen. Nobody is home—Dylan and Daniel are not people who leave notes, and the house has a tidal quality: People are there and then they are gone.

I check the clock on the microwave. It's only eight P.M. Somehow it seems much later. I have nowhere to go and no way to get there. Dylan has a bottle of Jameson on top of the fridge. I pour a few fingers into a mason jar and add an ice cube to make the drink feel intentional and not defeatist. I go out onto the back patio, but I can't sit still, so I unlatch the gate and step out onto the street.

The night is cool and clear, a light breeze stirring the leaves. The house next door, the Mormon Sex Cartel, is quiet—but as I glance toward it, I see that the side gate is open. I've never seen it open before. Anyone standing on the sidewalk could look in. I'm drawn toward it with a curiosity born of a lifetime of watching horror movies. Drink in hand, I stroll casually up the sidewalk, as if I'm taking an evening constitutional, but when I reach the open gate, I stop and glance in.

A back patio that resembles our patio, but far less populated with plants. Another lemon tree. Wide, flat paving stones create a path to a porch, where the shape of a hammock slumps between column and column. Upstairs, a few windows are lit up like a jewel box—you can see pink wallpaper, a bookcase barely visible—but otherwise, the lights are off. The house seems ominously silent, nothing but electrical energy coursing through its veins. A few feet beyond it, the wood fence curves and becomes our wood fence, our dark house on the other side of it. I squint for signs of human life.

"Can I help you?"

Startled, I turn my head, trying to figure out where the voice is coming from.

"I said, can I *help* you."

A shadow detaches itself from the bank of shadow that is the porch and stands. Black, scuffed cowboy boots, the flash of two white-blond braids, light glancing off glass. She must have been sitting in the dark having a nightcap. Standing, she's about my height, and her voice sounds young.

"Sorry," I say, turning away. But she calls after me, her tone more friendly:

"What're you drinking?"

I turn back around. Lift my mason jar: *This?* She nods.

"Jameson."

She lifts her glass, in a half toast. "Blanton's."

"Cheers." Then, "I'm Cass."

"Caroline," she says. "You new around here?"

"I'm staying next door." I gesture. And then, searching for something else to say that will forestall my return to my own dark house: "Hey—I saw a bunch of kids jumping over your back fence. I'm glad you're not murdered."

Caroline laughs. Her laugh is surprisingly nice. "Those were just the girls," she says, "but I'll tell them you thought they were killers, they'll like that." She hesitates, then gestures with her glass: "Wanna come in?"

I walk up the flat flagstones toward her. She sits back down on the edge of the porch. When I reach her, she lifts her glass and we clink.

"So—Jameson?" She's judging me.

I shrug. "I like it."

"Did you *buy* it, or you're drinking what there is and saying you like it?"

I have to grin. "I didn't buy it," I admit.

"Are you broke or something? Broke actor?" Caroline eyes me up and down. "Broke alternative model?"

"Alternative?"

"Don't be flattered, everybody in L.A. is an alternative model. The ones who are just models are modeling."

"Do I have to be broke to drink Jameson? It's not *that* much cheaper than Blanton's."

"Uh, yeah it is," Caroline says with blunt confidence. I expect her to keep chasing down the "what do you do" path, but she says: "What number are you?"

"What do you mean?"

"Enneagrams. I'm a Three, I'm charismatic but ambitious. You have to watch out for Threes. My guess is you're a Two, but you tell me."

"Why am I a Two?" I ask, insulted. I don't know what Enneagrams are, but she didn't say it like being a Two was a good thing.

"You were worried that I was lying dead on my kitchen floor," Caroline says. "Twos are helpers." She swigs some of her Blanton's. "My agents are a bunch of Fives. *I* think you have to trust in this world, but Fives have no trust."

"Your agents?"

She squints at me. "No matter where you go, nobody's got any trust for the universe. Except me."

"Because you're a Three?"

"No," Caroline says thoughtfully. "It's because I'm a very trusting individual, and so far those methods are working for me. If you know what I mean."

I nod, like I know what she means, without having any idea what she means. Caroline smiles, like my nod was the right thing to do. She goes on: "I was at this salt meditation and the leader came around and told each of us a thing we need to work on? And to me, she was like: *You need to open the doors.* So, after the salt meditation, I went on all these dating apps, but then I was like: Oh, sex isn't *the* door. My *door* is like . . . my *creativity.*" Caroline is looking me very squarely in the eyes. "So I had a meeting with my managers and my agents about my new film, and I told them about the salt meditation, and I decided I was going to put some energy into the universe about it. Like, I said to them: *The right people will come if I open the doors.* And they were like, whatever, blah blah. Ryan gets so hung up on things." She shrugs. "Ryan," she says, like *Just between us, he's a dick.*

I sort through all the possible questions and land at: "What's a salt meditation?"

"Himalayan," Caroline informs me helpfully. "Pink." She notices that my Jameson is gone and reaches behind her for her own bottle. I open my mouth to tell her it's okay, but she directs a healthy splash into my jar. "Come *on,*" she says. "Sit *down.*"

The night deepens without warning. Time disconnects. It feels good to be sitting on Caroline's porch while she flicks her white braids over her shoulder and leans back and forth in rhythm with the points she's making, which are not always points that I understand. My body is warm and heavy, and my head is light, and it's altogether the best I've felt in a while. Caroline doesn't know my last name and she misheard my first name—she keeps calling me "Cath." Instead of asking about me, she tells me that her last film was about the death of the ego, and it won things, and her new film is about being reborn, and when I ask her about plot she says, "Plot is for people who don't care about character." Then she tells me that since she was a little kid, wherever she goes, people stop her and tell her about their childhoods. "All I care about is character," she says, and throws down another Blanton's, because her glass, miraculously, unscientifically, is full again.

Caroline tells me that she made documentary films, because she was obsessed with other people's journeys, but this new film is a narrative feature with docu-realistic tendencies, because she's learning how to foreground her own journey. She tells me that Andrea Arnold is her hero. I ask if that's an athlete. She says, *"Fish Tank, Fish Tank,"* and makes me look up "fish tank" on my phone: it's a movie, which I should have seen coming. She says, "It's a made-up story with real people—or like, it's a real story with made-up people played by real people—or like, people are playing themselves, but Andrea Arnold tells them what they feel." She says, "If I told you what to feel right now, do you think you could do it?"

I'm drunk, so I say, "Yes."

She takes this seriously: "Could you really?"

"Sure."

"Feel angry," Caroline says.

I shoot her a look, like: *Really?* But she's serious. Her eyes are locked onto me, as if I'm going to dazzle her. I can't remember the last time somebody looked at me like I had that capacity. And of course, the moment I think that, I remember the first day I met Hélène—that late afternoon, the bar of the Ace Hotel, rings on her fingers. If you asked me: "When in your life have you ever felt dazzling?" I would skip straight to that exact moment, there across from Hélène.

"I said angry, not sad." Caroline is still here. But she doesn't seem disappointed.

"That *is* my angry," I tell her, "and it's also my sad." I finish my jar, and before I can stop her, she's pouring more in.

"So: Blanton's," she says. "Whaddaya think?"

We've reached the part of the night where all whiskey just tastes like whiskey, but I say, "It's good." I get the sense that this happens a lot in her life: People come into her world, and by the end of it, she's telling them how to feel and they're drinking her drink.

"So, when you're making a movie—or like, a docu-movie," I say, "what are you looking for? If it's not plot?"

Caroline has her head down, each braid hanging in a surprisingly straight line as she rubs the back of her neck with one hand. She looks up at me through the fringe of her lashes. "I had a boyfriend who used to ask me that," she says, fuzzy: "Every time we fucked he'd ask me: *What are you looking for?* And at the beginning of our relationship I was always like, *You, I'm looking for you.* But then I realized the more I said that, the less he valued me, and by the end of our relationship it was like: *My self-respect, dude. I'm looking for my self-respect.*" She yawns without covering her mouth. "And then I won a lot of awards—Sundance Grand Jury Prize, I forget if I told you that—and Cannes—and now it's like, I'm just looking for the next big thing. And if Thomas was here right now, I'd tell him: *It wasn't you.* I'm looking for the next big thing, but it was me all along."

*

This is what it was like to be in the theatre with Hélène.

Hélène was meticulous, rigorous, keen minded. She didn't care for lazy thinking, and she'd hold my scenes up to the light, one by one, and examine them angle by angle. All the weak spots and wrong turns would glow like neon, and then she'd ask me about them. She phrased these discoveries like questions—not because she was particularly diplomatic, but because she was always interested in the possibility of being wrong. Hélène wanted to know what she hadn't thought of, and if it was more interesting than all the things she *had* thought of.

Hélène made me work to keep up—I had to be smarter and more tireless than I'd ever been. I liked the person I was when Hélène and I were bent over the script, batting ideas back and forth. "Absurdist theatre still has rules," Hélène said once. "The audience has to understand what you set up before you knock it all down. There's rhythm and logic. Absurdism has to be far less chaotic than naturalism in order to work." And, hearing her say that, I realized it was true, and it made me love the form in a new and deeper way.

In the room, Hélène commanded respect. The actors didn't argue with her—even Liz, who was a TV star and had done six seasons of a hit network show. Hélène was as rigorous with the actors as she was with me, but she never made them feel stupid. She teased them, and like me, they responded to it like plants in the sun. We all wanted Hélène's attention. Sometimes I'd listen to the way she teased other people, and I'd reassure myself that she was tougher on me. I felt that if she was, it would mean that I was special to her. But I could never tell.

For the first time in my life, there were articles coming out about me, and Hélène seemed to read them all, even ones I hadn't found yet when I googled myself.

"Fierce new voice of the . . ."

"American female empowerment, as seen in . . ."

"Young women playwrights with a lot to say, like . . ."

"Young, queer, feminist, and ready to spill the tea . . ."

It was like I hadn't been there for over a decade, making work. It was like I wasn't thirty-three, but rather that I'd emerged newborn, overnight, from outer space. Adjectives associated with me were: "new," "young," "ascending," "rising." I was a helium balloon conjured from a void. It felt amazing. There were interviews with blogs, then small papers, then a *New York Times* profile. In all the photos I look confused, blinking into the camera in one of Nico's clean shirts. "Recent Lansing Award winner, upcoming off-Broadway debut." People kept asking me about being queer—*You have sex with women* and *men?*—and so for a few weeks all the interviews became stories about my exes—mostly about the women. Somehow, nobody was interested in publishing stories about the men.

Hélène was the one who called my attention to this, in her usual dry way: "Well, you managed to get in most of the gory details." The rehearsal room, glowing with sunlight, empty. She was smiling, but something deeper in her wasn't. "Every single lesbian in the city has your headshot on her wall now."

I cocked an eyebrow at her. "They might not all be lesbians. Some women don't like labels."

Hélène refused to take the bait. She would never talk about her past relationships with me—infuriatingly, she maintained strict boundaries. I did my own extracurricular digging and found a male poet (Scottish), a male Buddhist (American), and most recently—but still quite some time ago—a male photographer (French). But information about her dried up quickly; she didn't have much of a personal presence on the Internet.

"Try talking about the play," Hélène suggested dryly.

"They don't ask me about the play."

"Yes, and they won't, everybody prefers salacious details. But you're more than a collection of salacious details."

I told her that Marisa told me the article was good.

"Marisa's your agent, her job is to make sure you get attention."

"What's wrong with that?"

Hélène sighed, the way she did when she was contemplating how unspeakably young she found me. "Cass," she said, "the point is, what *kind* of attention?" She took a breath, the sort of breath in which—I'd come to know—she was smoking an entire cigarette in her mind. When she had finished mentally smoking her cigarette, she said: "You don't want to sell gossip. You want to sell your work. People will always ask women about two things: their bodies and their sex lives. If you answer any of those questions, you'll be a 'woman writer.' If you talk about the work, the work alone, they'll see you as a 'writer.'"

"But I *am* a woman writer," I said, stubborn now. "I am a woman, and I'm a writer. My generation isn't scared of that."

"I lasted this long," Hélène said bluntly, "because I directed the shit out of big male plays—big, sprawling, muscular, male plays—and nobody ever knew who I was fucking, so they had to concentrate on what I was making." A moment, and then Hélène smiled. "Kids your age, you want a brave new world, but you don't have it yet. You inherited the one we had, we know how it works better than you do."

I was going to say so many things, I was going to refute all of her points so clearly, so intellectually. I opened my mouth to tell her that a brave new world comes about when you refuse to participate in the old one. I opened my mouth to tell her that I wasn't ashamed to talk about making plays as a woman. I opened my mouth to tell her—

"I'm not a kid," I said. That was it, that was what came out. Me staring at her across the rehearsal room table with longing all over me. I was thirteen again, I was younger, I was a ball of cells.

Hélène avoided my eyes by folding the paper, putting it under her script. "I need a coffee before the actors get here," she said, and left the room, closing the door softly behind her.

*

I try Marisa again the next day when I'm getting groceries at the Whole Foods 365 in Silver Lake. I'm squeezing nectarines for ripeness. I tried her earlier, from the dairy section, and I also tried her before that, from the toilet paper / home goods section, right after a pyramid of toilet paper rolls tumbled down on my head.

Jocelyn picks up with: "Cass. You have to stop calling."

"Oh *hi*, Jocelyn," I say. "So good to hear from you again!" I do this in case anybody around me is listening.

"I'm not kidding," Jocelyn says. I can tell nobody is listening on her end, because her voice is small and furious.

"How's Marisa?" I have started asking this instead of *Where's Marisa?* or *Can I speak to Marisa?*

A moment passes in which I hear Jocelyn think: *Can I hang up?* But I'm still maybe a client, or I *was* a client, and it's unclear whether or not I will be again in the future. So she can't hang up. And she can't transfer me to Marisa. So she answers my question.

"In a meeting. She's not gonna call you back."

"What's she wearing today?"

A moment, and then Jocelyn says, "Blue jacket, blue skirt, brown boots."

"And her hair?"

"Up."

"General mood?"

"Impatient."

"Is she on her third coffee?"

"Fifth. But no croissant because no gluten."

"When did she quit gluten?"

"Tara-Jean Slater is doing Whole30, so Marisa is doing it too. Awards season in the spring, so." Jocelyn sighs. "So—now there are no bagels or bread snacks in the kitchen, which is like. Not fabulous, actually."

"How *is* Tara-Jean Slater?" I ask, too casually. Then, before she answers: "Actually, don't answer that. I don't want to know."

"How's L.A.?" Jocelyn asks tentatively, like right then she feels bad for me in a way that she maybe didn't before.

"It's so great," I say, because I don't want to be someone you feel bad for. "I've been really busy, actually." Then I remember that I've been calling Jocelyn regularly, several times a day, so clearly I'm not *that* busy. "How're you?"

"I'm okay." Jocelyn sounds listless.

"Yeah?"

"I got my period today." Jocelyn lowers her voice: "Which is great, because it was late, so I thought I was maybe knocked up? But now these cramps are like. Killing me."

"Do you have Advil?"

"I'm taking four Advil an hour, and I still want to kill myself." Jocelyn raises her voice, enthusiastic and cheerful. "I can certainly take that message!" she says to me, and I know someone is passing behind her. After a beat, her voice becomes quiet and morose again. "Also, it's like, I think I hate this job."

"You've only been doing it for a minute. It gets better."

"I've been doing it for a month," Jocelyn says coolly, "and it just gets worse and worse. Marisa is a nightmare, and it's not like her colleagues are that great, and then there's the clients, who are monsters—I mean, no offense—but also, you call me *twelve times a day*, so like, you're ruining my life."

"I'm sorry." I hadn't thought about Jocelyn's life in ruins, only my own.

Jocelyn sighs. "It's not just you. If you aren't calling, some other asshole is. Theatre people are the worst sort of people, I don't know if you've noticed that, but it's like, everybody just wants what they want.

And Marisa never says no, like, she won't ever tell them no, even when they're being insane? So then time passes, and they don't *get* the thing they wanted, but they were waiting for it because they never heard no, so then they call here and they scream at me. And I'm like: *Let me transfer you to Marisa*, but then she's shaking her head, she's all: *Tell them I'm at lunch*, so then I have to be like: *Marisa isn't actually here right now*, and then they just keep screaming at me. It's like my entire job is to be screamed at, because Marisa doesn't want to get on the fucking phone. You know? And the whole week I thought I was pregnant, I kept thinking: *I am twenty-two years old and I am about to bring a baby into a world where people just want to scream at me*. What kind of a world is that?"

Jocelyn has never said this much all at one time, and I'm amazed. "That sounds miserable."

"Tara-Jean Slater is a year younger than me," Jocelyn says, "and she comes in here and I'm like: *Can I get you a coffee?* I'm like: *Please tell me how I can serve you*, and she's barely twenty-one. I'm kind of glad you did what you did, to be honest. I wish it had been her whole head." And then she adds, "You know my college GPA was a 4.0?"

"No, I didn't—"

"*And* high school. In high school too. Which is like, an 8.0, if that were a thing. And who's getting *me* coffee?"

"There's still time," I offer. "I mean, you're very young. You could finish your entire twenties and *still* be young enough to be considered very young for people to be getting you coffee."

"I guess so," Jocelyn says. "I might have quit caffeine by then anyway."

"Right, you might not even want it."

"When I'm thirty, maybe people will be getting me seltzer water. Like, little seltzers."

"That feels possible." I'm nearly at the checkout line.

"Hey," Jocelyn says, "I have to go, because all these other calls have been coming in and I've been ignoring them, but will you do me a favor and not call back today?"

"I guess I can do that."

"Or tonight. I really don't wanna come in tomorrow and have the phone system be like *You have missed ninety calls,* and it's not even nine A.M. Because tomorrow will be day two of my period and day two is always the worst and I can't deal with ninety missed calls at nine A.M. on day two."

Day two *is* always the worst, everyone knows this, so I concede: "Okay, I won't."

"*Thank* you," Jocelyn says fervently, and this time we hang up mutually, at the same time. Right before I get in the checkout line, I grab a pack of day-old bread rolls to make up for all the gluten that Tara-Jean Slater isn't having.

4

I haven't really talked about Tara-Jean Slater yet.

This is either because I'm trying to play it cool or because I'm afraid to say her name. An incantation too powerful for a mortal soul.

How do I describe Tara-Jean Slater.

Tara-Jean Slater is the person who has everything that I should have.

Tara-Jean Slater is the one person on this planet who is living the life that I should be living, even though she is twelve years younger and has done much less to achieve that life than I—who am not living it—have done. This makes it not her life, exactly, but it isn't *my* life either. It is simultaneously *our* life and *nobody's* life, and yet still Tara-Jean Slater's life. She would not think of it this way, however.

Hélène, Liz, and Tara-Jean.

The way to invoke them properly, as a trio, as they concern each other, might be that crass old party game: Fuck Marry Kill. I fucked Liz, I would marry Hélène, and I pray for Tara-Jean Slater's death on a daily basis.

Or, not her *death*. Maybe not her *death*.

Her *nonbeing*. For the universe to retract its mistake. For all of us to hurtle backward in time twenty-one years so that Tara-Jean Slater's mother and Tara-Jean Slater's father can do something other than meet each other. Like go bowling, as platonic friends. Or catch individual colds and stay home in their individual apartments, never to intersect with each other.

But maybe also her death. On my more challenging days.

I have such a blurred recollection of the entire Lansing Award night that it's hard to extract Tara-Jean Slater from the blur. So if you were to ask me the moment in which she was first seared indelibly into my consciousness, it would not be that night but many months later—right after things had started to go wrong.

Marisa and I were having coffee at St. Kilda on Forty-fourth, and I was trying to get her to tell me if she thought I would ever work again, and Marisa had finished evading that and all other questions—and then she brightened. "Do you know Tara-Jean Slater?" she asked. I shook my head. The name sounded familiar, but I couldn't place it.

"I just signed her," Marisa said, stirring another cube of sugar into her flat white with a tiny spoon. "She's straight out of Yale, I didn't know if you'd met her at the Lansing Awards."

"She's a playwright?"

"Yeah, she was one of the playwrights who got the Lansing when you did. I thought you might've met."

"Oh, right," I said weakly. "No, we didn't meet."

"She's so young—maybe twenty-one? But her plays are magnificent. They're so ambitious and brave and full of heart." Marisa lowered her voice, leaning forward. "Playwrights Horizons commissioned her, actually—she's doing a workshop with them this week. She called me yesterday morning and read her new pages to me over the phone. I said: *Sounds good, Tara-Jean!*" Marisa laughed, shaking her head. "She's a fierce talent."

I tried to imagine reading my new pages to Marisa over the phone. These days, Marisa had become difficult to get on the phone.

"Playwrights Horizons, huh?"

"They were like, *Where did you find her?*" Marisa laughed, pleased with herself. Her little spoon smacked against the side of her mug as she stirred. Then she added as an afterthought, "They said they're so sorry they can't see your play before it closes, but that they hear good things."

"Oh," I said. Then: "They can't see it?"

"No," Marisa said thoughtfully, "they just can't get there." She shrugged. "They're very busy."

"No, sure, but . . ." I tried to think how to say *It's basically up the street!* but Marisa had already moved back to the matter of Tara-Jean Slater.

The work was brave. It was feminist and in your face. Tara-Jean Slater didn't give a fuck, Tara-Jean Slater was refreshing. Tara-Jean Slater was an outsider, with all of the magnetic, visionary qualities of an outsider. Tara-Jean Slater believed in the power of immigrant stories— she herself had immigrated from Maryland to New Jersey at a young age. But even more than that, she said that all stories were immigrant stories, because we begin by immigrating from the mother country of the womb into a cold land that does not love us. Tara-Jean Slater had been sexually abused by her uncle when she was a child, and Tara-Jean Slater fearlessly unpacked that trauma in her work, in ways that were difficult to bear witness to, but vital and necessary. Tara-Jean Slater's new play, the one that Playwrights had commissioned, had a mono-logue in the middle of it that was fifteen minutes long, about the after-noon in which she first had a sexual encounter with her uncle. In the script, Tara-Jean Slater had written the following set of stage directions:

The play comes to a crashing halt. The onstage characters look at each other. They become irrelevant. Tara-Jean Slater, The Play-wright, stands up in the audience. The audience will be confused, and they might not know what is going on, but that is okay. Tara-Jean Slater walks through the audience to the front of the stage and delivers the following monologue.

Marisa recited these stage directions from memory, shaking her head in wonderment. Who would ever have *thought* of that, except for a lively, fearless, and constantly surprising twenty-one-year-old named Tara-Jean Slater?

"So, then she gives the monologue about being raped?"

"Yeah, for fifteen minutes. But she never calls it rape, it's complicated and provocative."

"So, wherever this play is done, Tara-Jean Slater is committed to being in the audience?"

"You know, it's so interesting, Tara-Jean talks about theatre as a commitment in and of itself. A commitment to a sort of—'self-*vivisection*' is the word she uses—in front of an audience. It wouldn't surprise me if this play gets done everywhere . . . and then she'll have *quite* the travel schedule. But you know what else? We got a call yesterday from Claire Danes. Somehow, she'd heard about Tara-Jean's play, which is so funny, because it hasn't been produced yet, but she was like: *I'd be interested in the role of Tara-Jean Slater*. So I feel like there will be some interesting options to stand in for Tara-Jean when she gets tired of performing."

"Claire *Danes*?"

"I know," Marisa said. "What a thrill, right?"

"You'd really like Tara-Jean Slater," Marisa said.

"I'm so excited for you to meet," Marisa said.

"I'm so sorry," Marisa said. "I've got to jump, I have a meeting downtown in thirty."

*

Days pass, and nothing stirs in the house next door. It's as if I'd dreamed the backyard encounter with Caroline. I don't see any girls and I don't see her. I feel vaguely lonely, which surprises me. I'm not even sure she's someone I want to be friends with. I got the feeling that she thinks of herself as the axis around which all else turns. Even so, I find myself glancing out the windows whenever I'm near them, studying the fence.

I'd promised Jocelyn a day or two without a call, and I try to distract myself so that I can keep that promise. I go to the Broad and see a Takashi Murakami piece called *My Arms and Legs Rot Off and Though My Blood Rushes Forth, the Tranquility of My Heart Shall Be Prized Above All*. The media are listed below the painting as: "Red blood, black blood, blood that is not blood." I go to the Last Bookstore, in the cavernous hell that is downtown L.A., and wander through stacks built like spirals. Dylan and I take a hike up through the open bowl of Griffith Canyon, hawks wheeling in wide and reckless circles above our heads, as if they're attached to a small chain and someone is swinging them. These days of doing nothing aren't good for me, but the only thing I've ever done or wanted to do is make theatre, and that is now off-limits.

And then Caroline comes calling.

Or, more accurately, she throws an overripe lemon over the back of the fence onto the patio, nearly hitting me. I'm sitting in one of the lawn chairs, smoking Dylan's cigarettes and disconsolately wondering why there seems to be so much more time in L.A. than anywhere else, when the lemon arrives like a revelation and explodes like a bomb.

I jump up and there's Caroline, peering over the top of the fence to see where it landed.

"Oh, hey," I say, trying to sound casual.

"Hey," Caroline says. "Thought I hit you." I can't tell if she's disappointed.

"Next time."

She puts her mouth dramatically to the slat in the fence, and I catch the cardinal red flash of her lips when she says: "Whatcha doing?"

"Being pelted with rotten fruit. What are you doing?"

"The girls are coming over. Wanna meet them?"

In the sunlight, Caroline's house looks like the other Spanish-style houses in Silver Lake: clean, vivid colors—clay and yellow. Caroline kicks off her sneakers on the porch, and I see that her toenails are painted a deep, rich coral. She opens the side door to reveal a mudroom, and past it, honey-colored wood floors, handwoven rugs, a stained-glass window in a kitchen nook that throws amber light over white walls.

She leads us into the kitchen—white cabinets, a new range, a deep sink. It looks like the kitchen of a chef, but from all the bags of plastic containers, it appears that Caroline uses it more as the kitchen of a fast-food connoisseur. She boils water in an electric kettle and dumps a scoop of coffee grounds into a large French press without asking if I want any; as with the Blanton's, she assumes I want what she's giving me. She works with the quiet confidence of a person who doesn't feel she has to talk to you. After a few minutes, she pushes down on the top of the French press and pours coffee into two mugs. She adds soy milk, and the dark brown lightens to caramel. I'm about to ask if she has real milk and then I stop myself—if Caroline wanted me to have real milk, she would give me real milk. She hands me one mug; it's exactly the right size for my hand, a chip on the edge, the words TRIBECA FILM FESTIVAL emblazoned over the front in white. She leads us back into the sun-filled, open living room.

I realize that Caroline has started talking while I wasn't listening: "—and then there's Mona, you'll meet her, she's another one of the rich kids, but she's got guts. Uh, and Bijou, she'll give you a hard time but don't take it personally, she has a chip on her shoulder but she's very camera ready. And I think that's everyone." As she talks, she puts out bags of chips and plates of dip, transforming the coffee table into a buffet of snackable items.

Before I can ask questions, a new sound reaches us: the approach of a herd of baby rhinoceroses. Either that or this is one of the L.A. earthquakes that you hear so much about. The porch shakes, the walls shake, and then the noise separates itself into specific sounds: sneakers, yelling, the doorbell being rung in staccato bursts.

"Oh my GOD," Caroline bellows, like this is normal, "just come in!" And the door is flung open to reveal a mob of teenage girls.

It turns out that there are only seven of them, but for the first ten minutes I think there are maybe seventy or eighty. Or else that it's a single-bodied organism covered in sticky hands, beanies, lip gloss—a single multilimbed beast wearing many Chuck Taylors and Doc Martens, colored chitinous green and floral pink, all of its bootlaces Day-Glo colors. This beast is clutching cold-pressed juices and packs of gum and canvas bags and skateboards and bike helmets; it is chaining its bikes to the porch railing or leaving them capsized in the small yard; its hair is extensive: bleach blond, curly black, spiky brown. I stand and stare while the teenage animal pours through the door and swirls around the living room touching things, picking things up, yelling over itself, hugging

Caroline, announcing it has to pee, announcing it just peed, yelling at itself about how it has to pee all the time and that's because it stays hydrated, *so back off, cunt*. Finally it settles down and separates out, and now I can see that there are seven girls lounging around on the furniture, reaching for celery sticks and ranch, smacking each other's hands away, dropping crumbs on the floor, socking each other in the shoulder, hard. (*Owwww You're getting CRUMBS! Stop hitting me! YOU stop getting CRUMBS!*)

Caroline beams at them and gestures to me—"Ladies, this is Cath."

Hiiiiiii, the mob says, offering me—briefly—a penetrating attentiveness. I clock three blond white girls who look nearly identical, a redhead with curly hair, a black girl with glasses, an Asian girl with a cuff of piercings around her ear, and an underfed girl with a shaved head who looks like a young Sinéad O'Connor.

"She just moved here from New York," Caroline continues, "and she's a libra." I don't remember having told Caroline that, but it must have been part of that drunken Blanton's night. "Okay, tell her your names," she orders, and suddenly there is a Gregorian chant of names. The second they fall silent, I have the same total lack of knowledge. One of them catches my eye—she's the one with the shaved head, her narrow ass cheek perched on the couch arm, her skinny, bare knees jutting out of her torn jeans. Total baby-dyke in the making. Bijou, called B.B., although it will take me some time to know it. She keeps a long, steady stare trained on me, even as the others turn away, back to their own squabbles.

They seem comfortable in Caroline's space, playing on their phones, occasionally shoving their screens in front of each other to reveal something that sends them into gales of laughter. B.B. sits apart from the rest of them, darting glances around the room to see what everyone else is doing. Sometimes her eyes skate over me, and if I catch her gaze, she prolongs the stare in a way that's almost a challenge.

I feel cripplingly self-conscious. I don't spend that much time around teenagers in my regular life. I turn to see what Caroline is doing and am surprised to find that she has her iPhone out and is filming the girls, although their behavior hasn't shifted. It's as if they aren't even aware of it—or are so used to it that they don't care. When Caroline realizes I'm watching her, she comes over to me. She seems illuminated with a new sense of purpose; wisps of white-blond hair escape from her braid and halo her head.

"I'm acclimating them," Caroline tells me. "Most people stiffen up in front of a camera if they aren't used to it, but the girls don't seem to have much of a problem. I think it's a generational thing. Aren't they great?"

"Yeah," I say, because what else am I gonna say.

"Feel free to ask them anything," Caroline says. "They're all super forthcoming."

I'm not sure what I'm supposed to be asking them about. "Are they actors?"

"Oh, no!" Caroline is horrified. "I don't really . . . *do* actors."

"Oh, okay. So, like. What are they doing? For your movie?"

Caroline fixes me with a startled look. "We didn't talk about this?"

"Uh, no?"

"The other night, I didn't tell you about my movie?"

"No," I say, increasingly apologetic. "Or . . . only the big picture, I guess?"

"Oh my god. This is so funny." Caroline grins and shakes her head at herself forgivingly. "This is *so* like me." She turns her iPhone so it's facing us. "Okay, well, the movie is about them. Them as they are, but also sort of them as constructs."

"Hey," I say, uneasily. "Are you—am I—are we on camera?"

"Uh, yeah," Caroline says. "Is that a problem?"

"Uh . . . I don't know if it's a *problem*, but . . ." I dart a glance at the camera. I feel a muscle in my eyelid start to twitch. "I don't really . . . I'm not . . . acclimated?"

"We sort of record everything around here," Caroline says. "Like I said. I mean, I won't *use* everything, obviously. Life as B-roll." She laughs. I don't; the fact of being recorded is taking up all the space in the room. "It's like *Tangerine*," Caroline says. When I look blank, she says, "The first *serious* movie shot on an iPhone? About trans people? That like, *revolutionized* moviemaking?" I shake my head weakly. "This is very *Tangerine*," Caroline tells me soothingly. Now some of the girls are watching, interested. They smell my discomfort like dogs smell anxiety. "Same methodology as Andrea Arnold," she adds, as if that will finish sorting me out.

"I remember you mentioned her," I say, trying to sound comfortable and casual and in control. I angle my body so the camera will get more hip bone and less fat ass.

"I remember you thought she was an athlete."

I flush. Something tells me that she remembers every moment in which I was clumsy or clueless.

"Anyway," Caroline says, "I told you what these girls *do*, though, right?"

"Uh . . . no."

"Oh," Caroline says. "Oh, man. You know what, this is so good. This is so great. You wanna guess?"

"That feels like a bad idea."

Caroline swings the camera back toward the girls. I take a deep, steadying breath and follow its hot eye. B.B. is perched on the couch, kicking a plump redhead rhythmically but gently in the ribs with the toe of her green Doc. "Stop it," the redhead is saying, without making any attempt to avoid her boot. "*Stop* it, okay?"

"Ladies," Caroline invites, "do you wanna tell Cath what you do?"

The girls all glance up from their screens and trade laden looks, full of shared jokes.

"Hit me with it," I hear myself say, sounding like someone's dad. That's not something I've ever said. Why did I say it now? I might as well have called someone "dude." All the girls explode into teenage laughter. I really hate teenagers. I didn't even like them when I was one.

Ming speaks up. I'll learn her name next, after B.B.—she's outspoken, charismatic. Her left ear is ringed by a series of piercings that travel its curve, and when she moves, sunlight glints off just the one ear. "We fight," she says carelessly, swatting B.B.'s green boot away from the redhead's ribs, as if to illustrate her point.

"You fight what?" I'm already imagining it: *social injustice*. These girls with their cute little handmade signs, Instagramming their cute little fight for—

"Each other," says a nondescript white girl, and turns back to her phone.

I look at Caroline.

"I met them on Santa Monica," Caroline says. The tone of her voice says "*origin story*." All the girls sit up, swing the full weight of their focus her way. This is a story they all know, and it requires their attention to be told the right way. "I was driving home and I passed a group of girls, like crazy girls, yelling—super loud." The girls giggle with pride. "And I notice that they all look beat up. Rough around the edges, blood on their hoodies, Mona is sporting a black eye." The redhead laughs, proud, and Ming elbows her. "And I'm like, Holy shit, these girls are abused. So I get out of my car in the middle of traffic—door open, everybody starts honking, total cacophony—and I go over to these girls. And I'm like, 'Do you need help? Do you need me to take you anywhere?' And they're all like, *Actually, yeah*. So they get into my car and give me directions, but super calm, nobody seems that worried. And I'm trying to figure out if they're okay, I'm like: 'So, what happened to you guys?' And Ming is like, 'We don't really talk about it,' so now I'm certain they're being abused. I'm like, 'I can help you, there are places for girls like you,' and then fuckin' loudmouth over here, she's like—"

Caroline pauses and looks at Bijou. Bijou's mouth does something that isn't quite a smile, and she says, clearly quoting herself: "There *are* no other girls like us."

They all love this.

"And then," Caroline says, "I was interested."

"Caroline asks a lot of questions," the girl with glasses says. This will turn out to be Evie: high cheekbones, short hair, she could be a model. "We were like, Who's this bitch with the questions?"

Ming sees that I'm still a few paces behind. "*Fight Club*," she says, "but girls."

"*Fight Club*, like the movie?" I ask.

"It was a book first," one of the three blondes informs me critically.

"We get up into it," Mona says, by way of further elucidation.

"Pound on each other," says Bijou, but she stares at her Docs while she says this, she can't look at you and talk to you at the same time. "Just fuckin' . . . ya know."

Ming mimes an approximation of an uppercut.

"But like . . . boxing?" I'm still looking for some kind of containment vessel, some institutional sanction. "Like a boxing club?" I look around the room at the girls. Some of their faces are still trained on me, but most of them are back on their phones. The origin story was told in all its glory, but the audience was ultimately dissatisfying.

"No," Caroline says gently, "it's not *boxing*. They read *Fight Club* in English class and then started it. It's a feminist reinterpretation of masculine values." I blink at her. I can't tell if I have too many questions or no questions. "So, anyway," Caroline says, "I was like, These girls *have* to be my next movie. The universe brought them to me." Then she smiles, and I feel it again—the absolute warmth and intensity of her attention. "Just like you," she says, a hand on my wrist, surprisingly soft. "The universe brought you too."

*

This was something Liz said to me once: *The universe brought us together*. We were naked, curled up in her and her wife's bed. This was early on, maybe the second time I'd been to her apartment, and therefore the second time we'd slept together. She was running her fingers through my hair. I was sleepy, content, muscles loose with expended effort. Liz's wife was away at a conference; in her absence, Liz had made me dinner—a kale salad, shiny with olive oil and lemon, and crispy hake studded with bread crumbs—and we had eaten in the kitchen, as if we belonged there together, with that mixture of shyness and delight that happens when two people are doing something very strange to the

order of their lives. In each of our minds we were asking ourselves, pri-
vately: *Who is the Me who is doing these things, and is this Me happier
than I might otherwise be?*

All during dinner, I had been telling myself in the top currents of my
mind that we wouldn't necessarily sleep together again. We were *working*
together; our play was in tech, of *course* we had things to discuss over dinner; we could be friends; I had previously been less clear on the status of
Liz's marriage than I was now, and therefore there was a whole moral
consideration added to the mix. But underneath, in the deep, an undertow was dragging us toward each other and into their king-sized bed.

And so: "The universe," Liz said.

"Don't you think?" she asked, when I was silent. She rubbed the
short hairs at the side of my head with her palm, feeling their bristle.
"When I first saw you, I felt like: *Oh.* It felt so simple. Not even like: I
want to do this, but like: Here she is. Here we go."

I tried to remember how I had felt when I first saw Liz. I had known
about her before I met her, and the things I'd heard had formed a first
impression before she entered the room. I knew that, having become
rich from TV, Liz now wanted something unpurchaseable by monetary
means, which Hélène referred to as "authenticity." I knew that Liz
hadn't done theatre before, which made Hélène sigh when the casting
director kept suggesting her. I also knew that she was too fancy to audi-
tion, which meant she was "offer only." Nonetheless, the casting director called us each individually, and then the two of us together, and then
sent an email saying *I think we need to move fast before we lose her.* There
was so much fuss about Liz that I asked Hélène if she was particularly
good, and Hélène replied: "She is a certain kind of famous, and that is
how you get people to go to the theatre in America." So we cast her.

The first time I saw Liz in person was the first day of rehearsal. We
all crowded into a big open studio with wood floors, and plastic tables
set up in the center with folding chairs arranged around them. Containers of pencils and highlighters, a jug of water, cups, and in the corner, a
folding table with a coffee pot brewing and chunky ceramic mugs. A
normal rehearsal room, and yet, every time, a strange magic gets let

in—the objects feel blessed. And that electric anxiety in the air, the launch of a voyage of some kind. You feel it in your fingertips all day, the low-grade hum of something beginning. Hélène had been cool and effortless—black jeans, a denim shirt, her hair pulled up into a coil on her head. She'd welcomed us, giving the first-rehearsal speech that is mostly a chance to let everybody settle down and look covertly around the room at everybody else.

Liz was sitting apart from the other actors, a notebook open, pen in hand, very serious, like it was the first day of school. Of course, she was beautiful, and of course I had noticed—you can't see Liz without seeing her beauty—but it didn't register for me as a fact about which something had to be done. It was as simple and inarguable as the table or the folding chairs.

Hélène asked me if there was anything I wanted to say, and I think I talked about tone—"We can't play style, the style is like invisible scaffolding. We should treat the text with sincerity, no matter how strange it gets." And I remember Hélène gave me that slight smirk: "She means it's not a parody. But she's a playwright, so she needs a few more sentences than the rest of us."

The other actors laughed, but Liz's eyes went to me quick—checking to see if I was smiling—before she let herself smile too. Much later, Liz said: "She kept prodding you." After we'd started sleeping together, maybe it was the first night or maybe the night of hake and salad, she said: "I didn't know if you guys hated each other." And I remember I said something about that being Hélène's style, that she was a boy's boy and an elegant Frenchwoman at the same time. I didn't say—at that time, whenever it was, or in Liz's bed, after dinner—I did not say: *If you saw me falling in love, it happened right then. If you saw me falling in love, it was with Hélène.*

*

An acquaintance of mine, another playwright, became a parent last year. When I asked her how it was, she said that the thing nobody tells you is that suddenly you are a person whose unguarded heart now moves through the world, embedded inside a small and breakable body. You want to stuff it back inside you, almost every day you want to swallow it whole. But you can't, and day by day it gets bigger, more unwieldy.

Making a play is like this. It is only different in that your heart, which is now moving in the world outside of you, does not reside in the body of a singular creature. It resides inside the bodies of a strange troupe of individuals who have signed up for this ritual. Who, by agreement, have become something precious and unnamable. You will love these people savagely, beyond language, for the moment in time in which all of you are bound to each other. If they love you similarly, it will be with similar caveats.

There is no intimacy like the intimacy of breathing life into something together, mingling breath. There's nothing like sharing creation. For the months in which we are assembled, the only people we feel connected to are the ones who joined us inside this world. There might be a legal contract that says we have all agreed to play pretend for eight or ten weeks, after which this will stop. But we are human and we forget how time works—our entire lives are possible only because we have taught ourselves this trick of lying about time. If we thought about the truth—that every morning we wake up is a morning bringing us closer to death—we wouldn't get out of bed. So we live in this room together with a headlong intensity that approximates "forever," because these are the moments that make us want to live at all. And so, somewhere between how much we need each other and how singularly we share a world that no one else shares, we forget that we will not *always* share this one impenetrable world. And because we forget, we love.

And so: Hélène.

And so: Liz.

Tell me you don't understand that, and I won't believe you. You don't have to work in the theatre to be an accomplished liar to yourself. In fact, if you have survived this long, it's because you too are a practitioner of that ancient skill.

You forget, and you forget, and you love.

*

I wait until a day after Caroline's house before I try Marisa again. I'm at Griffith Park, Dylan and Daniel are walking ahead of me on the trail. Above us, the sky is high and clear. A hawk circles lazily on a warm current as the phone rings and rings in New York.

"Good morning, Creative Content Associates, this is Jocelyn speaking."

"Hi, Jocelyn," I say.

"Cass!" Jocelyn is annoyed. "You promised you wouldn't keep calling!"

"I haven't called in three days!" I do a little math. "Two and a half days. I said I'd give you two days for your period. How's your period?"

"Almost over," Jocelyn says with relief. "Thank God. I thought this one was gonna kill me."

"I know what you mean."

"I ate Advil like candy. And I bled on the subway."

"You did?"

"Yeah, straight through my jeans. Onto the seat. So then I moved and sat next to the bloody seat? Because I knew nobody was gonna sit there, so then I'd have some space. And I was right, nobody did sit there. So that was nice, I guess."

"That's smart," I say. I once bled through my jeans on the subway, but I had felt shame and terror, and it had never occurred to me to profit from it. I think, with a mixture of approval and fear, that the next generation really is the future.

"Anyway," Jocelyn says, "thank you for not calling."

"You're very welcome."

Ahead of me, the trail slants upward sharply. Dylan is telling Daniel a story about someone they both know, gesturing with his hands. Something about a swimming pool filled with champagne. I catch the phrase "West Hollywood A-gay," and then they both laugh.

"How's Marisa?" I ask.

"Whole30 is making her insane. She called me into her office to bring her the phone sheet? And she had these pictures of croissants up on her monitor. Like, she Google-imaged croissants."

"Jesus."

"And she made me do all this research to find Whole30-approved cupcakes so we could send a dozen to the first table read for—" Jocelyn stops herself, and I recognize the size of that stoppage.

"Tara-Jean Slater," I say, just to utter the name.

"Yeah," Jocelyn says apologetically. "The cupcakes are made out of nuts and dates, if you wanna know? They're more cupcake *shaped* than actual—"

"First read for what?"

"Just her play."

"Well, I *know* it's her play, Jocelyn."

"It doesn't matter."

"Where's the first read?"

Jocelyn sighs. "Lincoln Center was interested in hearing her play, that's all," she says in a small voice. "Like, just *hearing* it. Nothing's programmed yet."

"Lincoln Center like LCT3?" That's the second stage, for emerging playwrights.

"No," Jocelyn says, delivering bad news to a terminally ill patient. "Like the Mitzi."

The Mitzi. Okay. That's the space for famous people. Canonical playwrights. Fully baked, highly decorated playwrights. The space for people a decade-plus older than me, and by that measure twenty-two years older than Tara-Jean Slater. It's just the Mitzi. It's just a reading. Only a reading, and only nuts and dates shaped like cupcakes, not even real cupcakes. If I wanted a real cupcake I could have a real cupcake.

"Are you still there?" Jocelyn asks gently.

Up ahead, Dylan looks over his shoulder to see where I went. I signal that I'm on the phone, my agent, very important. I try to make my face look like I'm getting good news.

"Look," Jocelyn says, keeping her voice low. "Maybe you should give things a break. For the time being."

These are the things I could say: *Fuck you. Who do you think you are? I booked a movie! I love L.A.! I'm dating a model. I bought a car.*

I say: "How long is 'the time being'?"

Jocelyn says: "I don't know, Cass, like, a few weeks?"

"A few *weeks*?" I could be hit by a bus. By a mudslide. This is L.A. There are *fires*. Jocelyn is silent. "What about next week?"

"You're still on her DNC, so I think next week is too soon."

"Democratic National—?"

"Do Not Call," says Jocelyn, and after another pause, in which I feel the weight and warmth of her helpless good will, she hangs up.

I stand for a moment. Dylan and Daniel are far ahead by now, giving me space for whatever call they think I'm having, which is not the call I'm actually having. The gap between those two potential calls is briefly so cavernous, so overwhelming, that I can't move. I don't know how to bridge the distance between where I am and where Dylan and Daniel are, where they are expecting me to join them.

My phone vibrates. I glance down. A text from Caroline has materialized, like the lemon over the fence: unexpected, explosive, wholly welcome.

Girls are fighting tmrw night. Txt me for deets if you're in.

And if the question is *How do I bridge the gap*, then of course the answer, the only answer, the disjunctive and instinctual answer is: *Like this*.

It was the answer that presented itself, so it was the one that I took.

5

B efore I tell you what the first fight was like, let me tell you what I imagined:

Dark parking garage. Or basement. Lots of cement. One low light bulb hanging somewhere, maybe in a half-open metal cage. The girls assemble, their soundless, sneakered feet moving on cement. Their jaws are set, their eyes have the faraway look of trained killers. This is where *Fight Club* bleeds into *Kill Bill* for me. Bijou is swinging a ball on a spiked chain. Adults are not welcome here. Once the fighting starts, there's screaming, primal teenage howling, the sound of all those girls who bullied you in high school pursuing you down the school corridors, eager for your blood. That's where my imagination ended—I couldn't reach what the actual violence would be like.

Here is what it is like.

I text Caroline and tell her I happen to be free. I don't say that freedom feels a lot like circling the drain with increasing velocity. I sound casual. She texts back with a Hollywood Hills address and adds: *Five pm.*

I text back: *Five?* I'd expected midnight. Eleven P.M. at the earliest.

Yeah, if they get started too late, they can't finish their homework.

The Lyft drops me at the bottom of an immense driveway with a stone column on either side. A baby lion is perched on each column— one serious, one playful. I walk past the lions and up the driveway. I am thinking to myself: *Where's the cement basement? Where is the howling?*

Once I get far enough up, the house looms into view. I don't know a lot about architecture, so my brain just goes: *glass, glass, glass.* Everything is windows, everything looks like crystal with the sun hitting it. The driveway resolves into a circular loop with a garden in the middle, and I stand there in front of the house trying to figure out what to do next.

"Cath!" Caroline is getting out of her car, parked next to a giant shrub shaped like a candy cane. "You're early!"

"I thought . . . ? You said to . . . ?"

Back turned to me, she's pulling things out of the trunk of her car, examining them, tossing them back in. I catch a glimpse of a yoga mat and a sea of empty plastic water bottles. She extracts a plastic bag that says "Del Taco" and slams the trunk.

"So," she says, launching directly in, "this guy cut me off in traffic? Like total dick move, he saw me a mile away and he waited until I was *right* there and then he cut me off?"

She looks at me very closely. "Oh no," I say.

"And it made me remember how, when I was a kid, if I got mad, my mom would tell me to 'calm down.' She was always like, *Calm down, Caroline.* So I did. I got really, really calm, and then I got depressed, and then they gave me pills for a while to sort of . . . make me more fun to be around? And I guess now whenever something happens and I feel rage? I just feel grateful."

I stare at Caroline. She adds cheerfully, "I'm gonna tell that story in the promo materials for the movie." Camera over her shoulder, she walks toward the giant crystal house. I kick into gear to keep up.

Caroline rings the doorbell and a well-dressed middle-aged woman answers. I only realize she's a maid because of the way Caroline says hello. The maid tells us that the girls are in the rec room, and then we proceed to walk for what feels like twenty minutes through a house that keeps unfolding, new corners and rooms and breakfast nooks, new granite countertops and endless high ceilings. Every time I think we're getting somewhere, we turn an artfully decorated corner, and there's another set of white bookshelves with blue books (all the spines are blue, no other colors) or a white leather armchair with a pastel-blue woven blanket folded neatly over the top. Caroline walks like she knows where she's going, and at a certain point I realize the maid has long vanished. I try to imagine Edward Norton walking through this house, and my brain shorts out. I must have fundamentally misunderstood what it is these girls are gathered to do.

Caroline arrives at a door, tugs it open, and reveals carpeted stairs leading downward. I follow her, our feet thudding silently on the white shag, and there it is: the eighties rec room of your dreams, anchored by low-slung couches, a fireplace, and large windows that point out onto the gradually darkening vista of Los Angeles below. A network of tiny lights glows up from the growing dark. My eyes are drawn first to that muffling sea of carpet and then to the windows, so it takes me a second to notice all the girls lounging around. No nunchuks; no silent, predatory approach; no gleaming killer eyes. Just lots of girls in hoodies and leggings, lying on their stomachs on the floor or couch, maybe an errant limb flung over somebody else's torso. Everybody is wrapped up in their phones. The silence of the room isn't the silence before a storm, it's the silence of a pack of teens who have been hypnotized by screens.

"Hey, bitches," Caroline says, tossing the bag of tacos onto a coffee table. "Come and get it."

It's like throwing a slab of meat into a lion's cage. Suddenly, each of the inert limbs belongs to a crawling, shoving creature. The room rearranges itself, and all of them are gathered around a table except for the redhead, Mona, who is still listless on the couch.

"You don't want anything?" Caroline asks her.

"Last time I ate beforehand, I borfed," Mona says. A few of the girls lift their heads from their relentless, feral feeding to offer agreement—*Oh yeah she did*—while one or two others voice their doubts: *Didn't see her.*

"No," Caroline says putting a pin in this, "she definitely hurled," and then to me: "It was pizza night."

The girls look at me to see if I'm impressed. They catch my eyes flicking toward the carpet, and one of the girls says, comfortingly, "Don't worry, that was at Ming's place."

"Driveway," Ming informs me succinctly.

The girls eat while Caroline takes a camera out of her bag. It's hand-held, compact, and expensive-looking. I don't know much about cameras, but I would guess it's several levels up from her iPhone. Evie offers me a handful of tortilla chips, and I take them to be polite. Suddenly the girls are wrapping up what remains of their tacos, shoving coffee tables and chairs to the side of the room, busy and full of purpose. I realize that the camera was the final member of this gathering, and it has officially arrived.

"Okay," Mona says, scanning the girls. They sit straighter, brush crumbs off their leggings. Ming is tying her hair up. Evie does a few stretches. B.B. is sitting very still, her eyes narrowed. An air of preparation enters the room.

Caroline comes to perch next to me on the arm of the couch, camera balanced on her shoulder. "Mona's house tonight," she says softly, "so Mona does the intro."

"What intro?" I'm still not sure that we're talking about the same kind of thing. I can't imagine too much happening inside this padded room.

"Just watch," Caroline says with a sly smile. I glance over Caroline's shoulder and see that she's framed Mona's face in a dramatic close-up as Mona addresses the girls.

"Good evening," Mona says, suddenly formal. And, to my surprise, the girls chorus back *Good evening*, like we're at a church service. It's so incongruous that I wonder if they're all fucking with me, but they seem sober and focused. My presence has been rendered irrelevant by the start of . . . whatever this is.

Mona takes a breath. "Welcome," she says, and then recites: "You don't need a dick to start a fight. You don't need a dick to win a fight." She speeds up. "Two girls to a fight, you stop when you're done, your fight is a collaboration. Any questions?" The call for questions seems to be rhetorical, although Mona gives it a ceremonial pause. Then she says, "B.B., you and I will be first."

Bijou slides off the couch, loose and ready. The other girls pull back to the edges of the carpet, creating an open square, their sock-feet soundless on the cream shag. I don't remember the book too well, but my fuzzy 2002-era memory of the movie includes a lot of hot men with washboard abs screaming and pumping their fists in the air in some dystopian basement. This focused animal silence is more unsettling.

I expect additional ceremony, but suddenly Mona has launched herself at Bijou's throat, and they're rolling around on the floor, clawing at each other. It's such a shocking segue that I find myself standing, as if I'm about to dive into the ring and separate them. And yet I don't move. There is something mesmerizing about this level of unvarnished feroc- ity. Mona is heavier, but B.B. is a killer. She gets both fists into Mona's red hair and starts banging Mona's head against the thick carpet repeat- edly. It sounds like someone smacking a pillow with a potato. Mona hooks her chubby ankle behind B.B.'s legs, flips her over, and starts choking her. I turn to Caroline, alarmed, but Caroline is crouched down, camera trained on B.B.'s small, furious face as it turns first pink and then fuchsia. Maybe for this reason—or maybe due to simple miscalculation—Mona lets up. The second she does, B.B. lunges straight up at her and attaches her tiny, square teeth to Mona's earlobe. It's as startling for us as it is for Mona. Mona tumbles backward but B.B. remains affixed. And then, without warning, B.B. lets go and the two girls fall apart. They lie still for a second, not moving. Then Mona sits up, holding her earlobe. Blood slicks her fingers.

After a moment of suspended silence, she and Bijou nod to each other. They're done here.

"Round two," Mona chokes out, and Ming stands the fastest.

"Me," she says, and is in the center of the ring before Mona and B.B. have even made it out. After a breathless pause, one of the blond girls stands up—short, stocky, looking like a hockey player. "Georgia," Ming says with appreciation.

Georgia sizes Ming up and then leaps across the room at her. I hear the dull thud of their compact teenage bodies colliding. The edge of Ming's sneaker hits an aluminum tin of leftover rice and beans, and it explodes everywhere, rice decorating the carpet like confetti. I shoot a glance to Caroline to see if this is enough to faze her. For the first time tonight, she looks truly excited. She's down on her hands and knees, courting a close-up: individual rice grains clinging to white carpet fabric. Out of focus, in the background of the frame, Ming gets Georgia in a headlock and squeezes. Mona is crouched in a corner, eyes fixed on the round-two girls, holding a fistful of tissues to her ear. B.B. makes eye contact with me—a long hooded stare—and then, abruptly, she grins. Her teeth are pink.

*

I'm sitting on Mona's porch having one of Dylan's cigarettes when Caroline comes out with her camera bag over her shoulder. "Oh," she says, "I thought you mighta left."

"No," I say.

She glances around the circle. "Where'd you put your car?"

"I don't have one."

"Oh, right!" Caroline points her clicker at her car and it *beep-beep*s. "Need a lift?"

"That would be great." I slide shotgun into Caroline's car. It smells chemically piney. The floor on the passenger side is covered with empty water bottles, similar to the mini-landfill I glimpsed in the trunk.

"What'd you think?" Caroline pulls the car around without really looking in her rearview mirror, which gives me brief, panicked visions of crashing into a cactus or some statuary. But we descend the driveway safely.

"It's pretty intense."

"I know, right?" Caroline says enthusiastically. "I think it might actually be Gianni Lobell."

She catches my blank look and adds, "He's friends with her dad." She realizes I have no idea what we're talking about and says, "The house, the house. Interior design."

"Oh! The house! The house is great."

"Mona's dad is an architect," Caroline says. "You should see their beach house."

"Where *are* her parents?"

"I think her dad is in Costa Rica right now." Caroline pulls onto the freeway. It's emptier than it was this afternoon, cars sailing along, one after the other, with envelopes of space around them. "Her mom runs this modeling company? She was doing something in Namibia, I forget what."

"And nobody notices that these girls beat the shit out of each other on a regular basis?"

Caroline shoots me a look. "Are you upset?"

"No," I say. "But like—Mona's ear? That was real."

"Yeah, it's all real. That's the point. Female rage is real."

Whatever I'm about to say is drowned out by the image that rises up and swamps me. Tara-Jean Slater standing in front of me. Tara-Jean Slater's mouth carved open, a scream. I close my mouth again. Caroline is glancing at me instead of at the road, which seems to be how she generally drives.

"It's *supposed* to be shocking," she says gently.

"Yeah, no, I know."

"And sure, people notice sometimes. But girls basically go unseen. You know? Teenage girls, unless they're using their bodies as *currency*, as commodities of *desire*, they're unseen. What's so fucking cool is that these particular girls are trading on their invisibility to perpetrate revolution." Caroline is excited, driving faster now. I try to stop myself from pressing a foot on an imaginary brake pedal. "The whole *thing* is, these girls are co-opting this macho, patriarchal book about—you know, this myth of masculinity. They're just rubbing their pussies all over it, basically. I feel like that's so . . . revolutionary. Anyway, my team thinks this will go straight to Sundance."

We're passing the dark shapes of tents staked out against the wall of an underpass. I study them closely, but I can't see any movement inside. There's a shopping cart turned on its side a few feet down from the small encampment.

"How do they know when the fight is over?" I ask. "It didn't seem like anybody said stop or tapped out or . . . like, all of a sudden they were done."

"Oh yeah," Caroline says, "that's the other thing that's so feminist and cool about it. They don't need a leader to tell them to stop. And they don't need to knock each other out in some display of male dominance. That's the whole part about the fight being a collaboration—when the rage drains away, they're done. And if you're really listening to your opponent—if you're really in *sync*, the way women can be—then your rage can drain away simultaneously, like with B.B. and Mona tonight. It's like getting your period at the same time. Women's bodies are good listeners when they aren't being drowned out by the patriarchy."

I wonder if this is true. I wonder if it's in the promo materials. I remember Caroline shooting rice grains as Ming cut off Georgia's air supply with the crook of her arm. If you asked me for the mark of a genius auteur, this would have to be it, right? I think of what Marisa said about Tara-Jean Slater's play: *Difficult to bear witness to, but vital and necessary.*

We turn off the freeway, we're on Sunset now, another few turns and we're on Fountain, and there's the shape of Dylan and Daniel's house. Caroline pulls up to the curb.

"Hey," she says. "I'm really glad you came tonight."

"Me too."

"We're down the street," she says, "if you're bored." And then, casual in a way that lets me know she's been thinking about this—"I could probably use a hand, if you're around."

"A hand?"

"Yeah." Caroline is looking through the windshield and not at me. "I mean, nothing crazy, but . . . Making a movie, there's always complexities you don't expect. Would be good to have a pair of hands. If you're free, I mean. Before your next gig kicks in."

From the way she isn't looking at me, I wonder if she expects me to say no.

The way she says "your next gig" makes me want to cry, because I don't know anyone in my real life who thinks that I will ever have a next gig. Even if Caroline has no idea what kind of a gig it would be, even if she knows nothing about me, because she's never asked.

"Yeah," I say, "that sounds good."

She turns so fast the white braid whips past my cheek. "Really?"

"Yeah." The feeling of being wanted washes over me. "Why not?"

Caroline grins at me. "This is gonna be big," she says. "You know?"

Her certainty is like voltage leaping across the distance between us; the second it hits me, my heart speeds up. Caroline has a Lara Croft braid and coral toenails and a house with a stained-glass window and a movie that is about Female Rage, and she has been to Sundance, and she is going again, and she is going to be the thing that saves me. She is going to bring me up the ladder with her, out of the darkness, back into a world in which I am a person and not a punch line. And it is going to be so glorious. And this—Caroline and her movie—this is something I can believe in, when I can't believe in God or fate or even myself. This will get me through.

"I know," I say to her, the two of us grinning maniacally at each other in the dark of her car. "I know."

*

There was a stretch of time before my play opened in which not a day passed without some public acknowledgment that I was promising and relevant, and that my play was also going to be these things, and also a feminist revelation, and also a political comedy, and also a female playwright giving voice to her generation.

Liz was impressed by all this. She made that clear one morning before rehearsal started, when we were waiting for the coffee to brew. "I just think it's so cool to watch a young playwright *take off*," she said. "It's like—you know—who got to meet *Tennessee Williams* when he was young?" I hesitated, wondering if I should tell her that I was thirty-three, but in the end I didn't. *Age is relative*, I thought—and besides, it wasn't really about what she was saying, anyway. It was about the way she was looking at me from under her long eyelashes, eyes shining. Her mouth was saying how much she loved the play, but her eyes were saying: *If you kissed me right now, I would kiss you back.*

I wasn't positive that Liz knew what her eyes were saying, but I felt like she was probably the sort of actor who knew what every part of her was communicating. And as the days passed, my certainty that she was flirting with me built alongside of a new kind of certainty generated by seeing myself so often in the press. I loved the synonymity of my work and my persona, how both were suddenly deemed desirable. And it built and built, all of this electric confidence accumulating inside me—and then it would drain out through the Hélène-sized hole in my heart.

No matter how many people were praising me, Hélène had started being the only one who counted, and I couldn't tell how she felt about me at all. So, every day the same weather system: pressure building, pressure released into self-loathing. Falling in love always makes me hate myself, because eventually all I can see are the parts of myself that other people wouldn't like if they knew about them. In the case of Hélène, it was even worse. She saw me clearly, I knew she did—my weaknesses, my fears, my hope, all of it was there in the play. And yet Hélène refused to visibly like or dislike me-as-myself. She wouldn't give me a sign that she thought about me at all, apart from our collaboration.

Inside the rehearsal room we had an ease, an intimacy, a shared shorthand. We'd glance at each other during a scene and, with a quirk of the mouth or a lifted eyebrow, we'd communicate. When the actors stopped talking, she would give them the note that I would have given. But once we walked out of the studio, even over dinner, Hélène wouldn't let us entertain that same direct current. If I tried to force intimacy by oversharing, Hélène would listen, sometimes with that wry smile playing about her mouth. But she never reciprocated in kind.

Occasionally, and only in the context of rehearsal, Hélène talked about personal details. She mentioned once that she had been married when she was much younger, and although she didn't say more than that, a deep dive in the Internet (this time in French) produced a few pictures of her husband that I'd missed the first time—a good-looking Moroccan guy a decade older than her, a drummer in a French rock band at the time of their wedding. Another time, she mentioned a failure, and I found the reviews quickly—her production of a Molière play in the early 2000s. It had gone well on the West End and reached

New York only to be blasted by the *Times* for being "aggressive," "unpleasant," and "chaotic." I knew better than to ask Hélène for the information I wanted; I knew instinctively to play it cool, like I wasn't gathering up her details like rare gems. But I did ask Hélène about this one seeming failure, though I waited until we were having dinner.

Hélène smiled. "Yes, they hated it. I was so humiliated. It was my first Broadway show, you know, and the review was so embarrassing. My agent, he called me, he said, 'Have you seen the review?' I said, 'Yes I have.' He said, 'Onward and upward.' Didn't even try to make me feel better, because what could he say?"

"He could have said your production was good," I said, angry on her behalf. "He could have said 'Fuck them, what do they know?'"

Hélène laughed ruefully. "It *was* good," she said, suddenly mischievous. "It took me years to feel good about it again, but it was actually very strong work."

"But it didn't hurt you? Your career, I mean."

"It hurt me, yes. It took a few seasons before anyone would take a risk on me again, let me do anything that wasn't a small play on the second stage. But it didn't destroy me." Hélène raised an eyebrow, then: "You know why not?" I shook my head no. "Because they called it 'aggressive.' If he'd called it 'sensitive' or 'feminine' or any of that whole other basket of adjectives, I'd have been done for good."

"That can't be true."

Hélène smiled. "Now it's a fad to hire women," she said, "but back then they didn't want it shoved in their faces that they'd hired one. They'd only keep letting you work if they didn't have to be reminded that there wasn't a cock in your pants."

And, having answered my question, she started talking about my play again—what we should try in rehearsal tomorrow, what I thought of the rewrites I'd done so far. It wasn't until later that I realize she'd completely avoided mentioning what she had felt, how she'd coped in the days after being publicly humiliated.

An amount of time with Hélène passed. It was technically a short time but felt like a lifetime. Night after night, we'd finish rehearsal and head to the Marshal or West Bank or ViceVersa for dinner. We often ate at the bar, sitting side by side with our shoulders nearly touching, light reflecting off the shelves of colored liquors in front of us. There was something magic about the oceanic rush of voices to our backs and the jewel-like glow of Hennessey, Aperol, absinthe in front of us. Increasingly, we'd discuss Liz, who was having trouble with tone. Liz had thought my play was a sincere treatise on The Problems of Being a Woman, until she heard other actors talking about it as an absurdist comedy. Prior to that, something about the complete earnestness with which she'd been acting her role had been simultaneously weirdly moving and hilarious. Once she realized the play was saying the opposite of what her words were saying, she sucked for days. A complete nosedive. In her dry, composed way, Hélène panicked. And so, over our late-night dinners: *What were we thinking? Liz can't do tone, Liz does TV.* Hélène after an extra glass of rioja: *You'll forever know me as the weathered bitch who ruined your play.*

It made me love her all the more to see that she cared so much. She cared about my play the way you'd care about a living thing, an animal, something you were hand raising. She cared about it the way I did. I started imagining us on a French farm somewhere. Hélène would be holding a newborn sheep, keeping it warm under her jacket, feeding it with a tiny bottle of milk, with this same look on her face: intense focus, hope, slight despair. And I would be leaning in the door of our barn in my heavy denim jacket, a pitchfork in hand (or some French farm implement), looking at her exactly the way I was looking at her now: with awe and gratitude and love.

And so: night after night, bar after bar.

And so: longing.

I developed a plan, over time, by bouncing things off Nico. The plan was that I would wait until opening and then I would tell Hélène how I felt. After we opened, there would no longer be the fact of our collaboration, either to keep her from responding to me or to guarantee that I'd see her every day.

These are the things I pitched to Nico that I might say to her:

"I think I'm in love with you."

(Nico: "Absolutely not.")

"The idea of not seeing you every day makes me want to jump off a cliff."

(Nico: "Nobody thinks crazy is hot, especially someone who has made a career out of dealing with actors, for God's sake.")

"I want to run away with you and live on a farm."

(Nico: "I'm not even going to dignify that with a response.")

Finally, I asked him what the hell he wanted me to say then, and he said, "Can't you be normal about these things? Just ask her to get drinks with you. Why does it have to be so intense?"

"We get drinks all the fucking time," I said. "This is the theatre, what the fuck are we doing other than drinking?"

"Well, can't you ask her if she'd like to, you know, go out?"

I tried to imagine asking Hélène if she'd like to, you know, go out. I wasn't sure if she'd laugh in my face or walk out. Or tell me to grow up. Or say yes. Or kill me. Everything seemed equally possible.

Nico's parting words of wisdom: "Just don't say anything about a goddamn *farm*."

As it was, I didn't end up following a plan, because I didn't even last until opening. We were four days out from tech, and Hélène and I had stayed in the theatre after rehearsal ended. Hélène was striding up and down the aisles, sitting in different seats, examining sight lines. Our set designer was going to drop by the next day to have a chat about a few bad angles, and Hélène was meticulous in her preparations. I sat in the front, trying to focus but instead watching her long legs in worn blue jeans, leather boots.

"Cass, can you come up here a sec?" Hélène had reached the back of the theatre and was studying the place we'd decided Liz should stand for her opening monologue. I walked up the aisle toward her. "We gotta move Liz upstage," Hélène announced. "I think it's going to be a problem if you're sitting anywhere back here, we'll lose half her body with the set. I mean, we should talk to Jack about it, but tell me what you think."

We perched side by side on the tops of the folded seats. I kept my eyes trained on the stage, trying to imagine what she was imagining, but I couldn't summon Liz. Hélène smelled like coffee and vanilla. I was aware only of her next to me, her body firm and real. Today she was wearing a button-down, sleeves rolled up, and I was mesmerized by the slim planes of her wrists, the side of her neck, her hair escaping its pony-tail and curling by her ears. I heard my heartbeat, suddenly thundering, and it was only by hearing my heart that I suddenly knew what was going to happen. *Oh. This is where we are.*

She turned toward me—"Cass, what do you think?"—and I took her face and kissed her.

She was very kind. She put her hands on my shoulders, broke the kiss gently. My heart was racing so hard I felt dizzy. At first I didn't know what she said, except that it was some form of *no.* She was saying things that were kind and practical, and she was saying them in a tone that was also both of those things, and either way it added up to *Not you.* I was saying things that didn't make much sense, that were not practical. I was saying things like *But just let me* and *Why can't we?* and variations on *I've never felt this way about anyone.* At a certain point, Hélène stopped trying to shut me up and save my dignity. She let me run myself into the ground. I kept clutching at her hands, her wrists, trying to make her see through some medium other than language, because I wasn't saying it right, I knew that already, but maybe if I could still find the right words and the right order and the right gestures, maybe if I could do that, she'd understand, and everything would be made right, would seem irrefutable even, the fact of our belonging together. But if there wasn't language, then maybe simply her hands in my hands—maybe that would do it.

Eventually I ran out of words—everything was wrong, there was no saving it—and I lapsed into silence. Hélène was silent too. I was too exposed; I slid off the top of the seatback and landed in the seat itself, sinking down deeply, letting the red velvet swallow me. After a moment, Hélène did the same next to me. Both of us in the very back row, facing forward, an audience of two intent on a performance that had gone badly.

"I'm sorry," I said.

"Don't be sorry."

"I'm an idiot."

"Yes," Hélène said, but the side of her mouth was quirked, and this gave me hope. "It's flattering. It's been a long time since anyone has thrown themselves at me. And especially the newest rising star of the American theatre."

Now she *was* making fun of me. "Hélène," I protested.

"You get to a certain age, you no longer expect this kind of tribute."

"It's not tribute, I really do—"

"Cass."

"I do, though."

We were quiet. Hélène wasn't smiling anymore, but she didn't look angry either. She just looked thoughtful and sad. Finally, she said, "Well. Onwards and upwards."

But I couldn't let it go. "Do you not believe me? Or do you think I don't know what I want?"

"Cass, please."

"It's okay if you don't feel—what I feel. Or if women aren't—your thing, that's okay. But I don't get the feeling that—I mean, the way it is sometimes, with us, it doesn't feel like . . ." I was stumbling off the cliff again, and now she was looking at me with sharp, unreadable eyes.

"Like what?"

"Like it's nothing."

"It's not *nothing*, you idiot, we're making a play together, we're—"

"You know what I mean." Did I even know what I meant? "You don't feel straight—or like that would get in your way if—I mean, I take it back, maybe you *are*—but you would've said it if that was the problem— or maybe it doesn't matter to you, whatever the reason is to say no—but it matters to me. Because it's one thing if you don't want me. But it's another thing if you think I don't know what I want, or if you think I'm playing. If you're doubting me, then—you shouldn't. Doubt me. Because I'm certain about you."

I reeled to a halt. I felt like maybe now I'd broken it for real. More silence, both of us staring at the stage. These fucking sight lines. This was gonna be my least favorite seat in the house from now on, I could tell.

"Thank you," Hélène said at last, very gently.

"That's it?"

"Cass, what you said is beautiful. *You* are beautiful. And this whole straight thing, or gay thing—I don't say it because it's an excuse to hide. The partners I've chosen have been men, yes. Is my past an indication of my future? Who knows?"

"But . . . So—then why *not* me?"

Hélène looked straight at me. "You are at the beginning of your entire career. You are at the beginning of working this way with directors—or anyone, for that matter—of the kind of intimacy that is generated when we are the only people that we see for months at a time. There are many kinds øf intimacy, it's so easy to confuse them all."

"So you do doubt me."

"No, I have no doubt that right now you are in love with me."

"You think, once we open the show, I won't be?"

"No, I think . . ." Hélène sighed. "I think that I made a decision many years ago not to get involved with other theatre artists—for my health. For the health of my work. For the . . . clarity, I suppose—that I need, in order to make my work. And that decision has been fundamental to me, to how I live, and that has been . . . necessary. And you may not be a person who needs to make a decision like that. Like I said, you're still young—theatre is a very exciting place to have a very exciting series of affairs. And some people get less damaged by it than others. But I have a feeling that you're more like me than you think right now. And, years from now, you too might need to separate how you make your theatre and how you live your life. And when you do, it's possible that someone very young and very attractive and very convincing will want you to unmake that decision. And if that happens . . ." Hélène's mouth quirked. "If that happens, you can say: 'I knew this French bitch once, she ruined my play *and* she broke my heart.'" Hélène sobered then: "But I hope that neither of those things will be true."

In the silence, I understood that this "no" was far more definitive than any "no" I had ever received.

In the silence, I understood that I loved Hélène enough to completely humiliate myself and then not hate her for it, which was more than I'd ever loved anyone.

In the silence, I understood that there was a gaping pit inside my chest, and I had to put something in it quickly or be consumed.

"Don't worry about it." I slid off the seat and stood up decisively.

"Cass—"

"I'm sorry. And. It's okay. And . . . don't worry about it." I grabbed my messenger bag off the floor on my way down the aisle. "I'll see you tomorrow," I called, without turning. Hélène didn't answer, but I could feel her worried eyes on me as I walked out of the theatre.

I went straight to the nearest bar, and I had two shots very quickly, and then a beer, more slowly. And then I texted Liz: *Feel like a drink?*

Her wife was in Dallas, I learned later. She traveled often. Liz had been eyeing me for weeks. She texted me back within minutes, she was at the bar inside of an hour, we drank until it was long past midnight, and we slept together, but I don't remember it. Later, Liz liked to ask me if I remembered certain details—the green dress she was wearing when she walked into the bar, the way she'd reached down and taken my hand sometime between her third and fourth drink, the cab ride back to her apartment and how I'd fallen asleep in the cab with my head on her shoulder—*And all your hair every which way,* she said, *like a baby bird.* How we'd kissed in the hallway, and then against the door of her apartment, and she'd dropped the keys as I was kissing her, and a dog had started barking in the next-door apartment, and she'd been afraid we'd wake the whole building up. How she'd let us in, and I'd stood there, curiously formal all of a sudden, as if my hand hadn't been down the top of her dress seconds before, and she'd asked if I wanted water, and she'd gone to the cabinet to get us water glasses, and then suddenly I was behind her, my arms around her, and then my hand dipping under her dress, skimming up her bare leg, into the soft clench under the shadow of her underwear. We'd fucked in the kitchen and then in her bed, and she'd cum both times, which seemed like a miracle to her—*Do you remember how I told you it was a miracle? And you said, "You've been sleeping with the wrong women." And I told you, "I'm married, remember? I have a wife"—and you didn't even remember! I couldn't believe it, it was like you hadn't heard a thing I'd said for weeks.*

Liz remembered every detail, and so eventually, later, I could join her in this shared story, the origin myth of our affair. But the truth was, I didn't remember a goddamn thing. It was a total blackout, a complete morass, and when I try to think back, all I get is an image of Hélène's face in profile, her eyes narrow and keen, studying the stage as she says: *There are many kinds of intimacy. It's so easy to confuse them all.*

*

I'm back at Whole Foods 365, wandering through the cleaning-supplies aisle, when someone calls my name. "Cath!" The wrong name that is a new name, a name that I'm starting to call myself in the mornings as I gaze into the bathroom mirror. *Hello, Cath,* I say. *Cath, this is the first morning of your life.*

I turn, and it's Bijou. B.B., the girls call her. She's standing there with her chin jutting, and her green Docs, and a watermelon in her hands.

"Hey," I say, surprised. She only stares at me, like now that she's yelled my name, she's done her part in the conversation. I nod toward the watermelon: "Whatcha gonna do with that?" The second I say it, I feel stupid. I have no idea how to talk to teens, so the lilting tone that comes out of my mouth is more geared toward a particularly slow eight-year-old.

B.B.'s face doesn't change, though. "Drill holes in it," she says.

"Drill holes?"

"Yeah, and then soak it in vodka."

"Oh." This particular combination of actions had never occurred to me, although it sounds like the sort of thing people might do. But then: "With a real drill?"

"Yeah," B.B. says impatiently. "With a real drill."

"And then what?"

"Then you *eat* it." B.B. sounds like she's now the one talking to a slow eight-year-old. "And you get fucked up."

"Why don't you drink the vodka straight?" I have to ask. "It's faster, and that way you don't need either a watermelon or a drill."

B.B. stares at me for a second and then she shakes her head. "Wow," she says decisively. I expect that our conversation is finished, but instead she swings into step next to me as I push my cart down the aisle. I agreed to do a house shop, but I forgot to take the list Dylan made of things like toilet paper and paper towels and soap, and now I'm trying to remember whether they were things *like* toilet paper and paper towels and soap or whether I actually need to *buy* toilet paper and paper towels and soap.

"What are you getting?" B.B. asks, in a tone that suggests she no longer expects anything from me.

"I can't remember. Stuff for the house, but I didn't take the list."

"That was dumb."

"I mean, yeah, I'm realizing that."

"You shoulda put the list on your phone. Why'd you write it *down*?"

"Because, kiddo, grandma and grandpa still practice writing by hand." I snag a roll of paper towels off the shelf. That feels like a productive choice. Somebody could spill a bottle of wine, or a carton of tomato juice, or somebody could murder somebody, and then the more paper towels the better.

B.B. cracks a smile, which surprises me. "So, are you and Caroline dating?"

"Wait, what?" I'm reaching for a bottle of hand soap and almost drop it. "No!"

"But you're like, hooking up?"

"No! No, no." I stow the soap in the cart and turn to B.B. "We're neighbors."

B.B. says, as if it's a reasonable next sentence: "My girlfriend just broke up with me."

"Oh," I say. "I'm sorry."

"She thought she liked girls, but actually, she just wanted to be fashionable."

"I'm sorry to hear that."

B.B. shrugs. "She was a cunt," she says, and walks ahead of me down the aisle. I think she'll vanish, but when she gets to the end, she stops and waits for me.

When I reach her, I say: "So, gay is fashionable?"

B.B. rolls her eyes. "*Gay*," she says, like it's a word in another language.

"What?"

"*Gaa-aaay*."

"What!"

"Nobody *uses* that word anymore," B.B. informs me, and power walks to the checkout line, where she then stands and waits for me. I guess I'm done shopping. I join her in the line, and she steps aside for me to pass with my giant cart holding exactly two items. B.B. clocks that. "That's all you're getting?" she asks, in exactly the same tone that she said "Wow" and "Why'd you write it *down*?"

"I hate shopping," I say.

A moment, and then she kind of smiles. "Maybe that's cuz you're *gaa-aay*," she says before she cuts ahead of me in line for the available next cash register, watermelon clutched to her flat chest.

Out in the parking lot, B.B. and her watermelon follow me to Dylan's van. She takes it in and says, "Okaaay." But this time she says it the way you might say "cool."

"This is my housemate's van," I say. I don't want her thinking I'm cooler than I am—I've learned that it's worse to disappoint people later than up front.

"Is he also *gaa-aay*?"

"Why are you so obsessed with this?"

"No," B.B. says, "why are *you* people so obsessed with it? Why can't people be what they wanna be? Why do they have to slap a fucking label on it? Everybody I know is over it."

"Okay," I say slowly. "That's great that your generation is over it, but *my* generation has discovered there's less chance of somebody saying they're your girlfriend and then deciding they don't even like pussy if you date people who have *self-labeled* as liking pussy."

A moment, in which I wonder if I went too far. But then B.B. shrugs, switching gears. "You're not *that* much older than me."

"I'm three thousand years older than you," I tell her. "I'm several millennia older than you."

B.B. gets in the shotgun seat and takes a cigarette out of her bag. She offers me the pack. I shake my head to be a good role model, and she lifts an eyebrow. "I know you smoke," she says. "I saw you and that guy in your backyard smoking."

"I don't *smoke* per se . . ." I begin, and then I abandon that line of defense. "When did you see me in the backyard?"

"I looked through the fence." B.B. sounds matter-of-fact. "On several occasions."

"Oh." And then I think, *Fuck it*, and I say, "Okay, fuck it." She lights both of our cigarettes with a battered pink Bic lighter. "You don't vape? I thought all the kids your age vaped."

B.B. doesn't deign to reply at first, probably because I used the phrase "kids your age." After a moment she says, cool, "I'm old-fashioned."

She's not getting out of the van, so I ask: "Do you want a ride home or something?"

"You could drop me at Caroline's. Since you're *neighbors*."

"What are you doing at Caroline's?"

"Nothing." B.B. takes a drag. "It's a place to be."

"Do you fight there?"

"We hang out. We don't need to fight all the time."

"Look, don't get mad, I don't know how your whole thing works."

B.B. rolls her eyes and mutters something about "your whole thing," but she pulls her seat belt across her lap and hand-cranks the window down, implying that she's ready to be chauffeured. This is the closest I've been to B.B., and I find myself studying the dirty skin of her neck, her little bulldog jaw, the soft places of her arms. I'm looking for marks from the fight at Mona's. In the light of day, the whole thing feels like a weird dream. She feels me looking and turns her head.

"What," she says, self-conscious.

I shake my head. Then it occurs to me that she might have assumed I was checking her out, which feels creepy, so I admit, "I was looking for bruises."

B.B. grins. Her tiny teeth have an animal sharpness to them, which I remember from seeing them clamp around Mona's earlobe. "You wanna see my bruises?" she asks, like it's a challenge. I'm already saying, "Not really—" when she yanks her T-shirt up. Her skinny ribs are purpling over.

"Jesus," I say. "Did you get that looked at?"

"Ugh," B.B. says. "Please." She pulls her shirt up higher and I catch the lemon yellow of her sports bra. I look away.

"Okay," I say quickly, "I guess I've seen your bruises now."

B.B. waits a beat longer in case I look back, but when I don't, she drops her shirt again.

On the drive to Caroline's, I ask B.B. what she thinks of the fact that Caroline is turning her and her friends into a movie. How she feels about being a character. She seems confused, as if it's a trick question.

"It's cool," she says warily.

"No, I mean, sure," I say. "But is it, like, weird at all? To think that there's gonna be this movie out there about you and your friends?"

"Weird why?"

"I don't know. I guess I just wondered. Maybe it isn't weird."

"It's awesome," B.B. says, with a surprising lack of cynicism. "It's the only cool thing that's ever happened, basically."

"Oh," I say. "Okay."

"I wanna be famous," B.B. tells me—like she's saying I want to be a fireman or I want to be a math teacher.

"Like, a famous actor?"

"No," she says, "just famous."

"For doing what?"

"Who the fuck cares." B.B. is bored already. "Everyone is gonna see the movie, and then probably we'll be famous."

"And then what?"

B.B. glances at me like she can't tell if I'm being deliberately thick. "Who gives a fuck *and then what*? The point is, *and then whatever you want.*"

"Got it." I expect her to follow up with another remark about how stupid I am, but instead she keeps her eyes on me, and after a moment she says, quieter, almost shy, "That's what I think, anyway."

I don't plan to say this, I just hear my voice over the rattle of the van: "Before here, when I was in New York? There was a moment of time in which I was—well, not famous the way *you* mean it. But in the community I was in . . . there was a lot of attention on me."

"Yeah?" B.B. leans her head back against the seat, cigarette hand out the window, studying me. "What did you do?" She sounds sincerely interested.

"I wrote something that got attention."

"That's cool," B.B. says.

"No, I mean—that's not why I'm telling you. I guess what I'm trying to say is that there were a lot of people who thought I was great, and then I did something . . . bad, I guess . . . and then they all thought I was trash. And maybe the way you mean 'famous' is a whole lot more tangible— but also, it's basically the way people talk about you. How many people are talking about you and what they're saying. And that's—really stressful. It turns out."

B.B. is quiet for a minute, and I think she's going to ask what I did. But then she says, "But when they were saying good things, it was awesome?"

"Uh . . ." I have to be honest. "Yeah, I guess when they were saying good things . . ."

"So you want it again."

"Uh . . ." Suddenly I feel like my little teaching moment has gotten out of control.

"Yeah," B.B. says, with quiet, explanatory conviction, like we're saying the same thing. "The problem isn't that people talking about you isn't good, the problem is when they stop. So you just weren't famous enough. So you came here."

"Why do you say that?" I ask, shaken.

B.B. is surprised to have to clarify. "People only come to L.A. if they want to be famous."

"Oh," I say. "No. I came to L.A. to disappear."

"That's so weird," B.B. says softly, and we drive in silence for the next few blocks. I turn onto Effie and pull up in front of Caroline's gate.

B.B. gathers up her watermelon. "Thanks for the ride."

"You're welcome," I say. "Thanks for the smoke."

B.B. glances at me then, and there's something in her face that is both completely unexpected and entirely familiar. In the moment, I can't think what it is, I just feel it, like hearing a song somewhere that you know with unplaceable clarity.

"Yeah," she says. "Well. I'll see you."

She clambers out of the van and slams the door, marching up the drive toward Caroline's house. I stare after her for a moment longer, then pull the van away from the curb and point myself toward home.

6

I start spending more and more time next door at Caroline's house. It is a place where someone is guaranteed to be at any hour of the day. When Mona's parents go on a cruise, she moves in for ten days. One of the blondes inexplicably stays there for three. Her name is Nickey, I learn; I can't always tell her apart from the other two (Aubrey and Georgia), so I've been thinking of them all as Nickey. When Ming and her boyfriend, Chad, break up for a week, Ming moves in. She tells us that her parents found out about Chad and forbid her to see him, so she ran out of their house and went straight to Chad's. It was two P.M. and he was in his sweats, playing a first-person shooter online with a guy in the UK. She looked at Chad, with his hands on the controls and the hairlike situation on his chin, and she thought: *I walked out of my own home for this guy?* But then she didn't want to go home and admit that she was wrong, so she came to Caroline's, and there she stays for the week.

As for me, whenever my house is too quiet—which is often—whenever my phone is not ringing—which is always—and whenever I can't stop thinking of Cass, stupid Cass, whose humiliation is the talk of the entire Eastern Seaboard—then I walk next door and I am, miraculously, Cath.

The house is an epicenter of activity, and the activity feels familiar to me—it is like the constant buzz and shift of a theatre, except there is no distinction made between on- and offstage. Caroline films the girls all the time: at the breakfast table, in the den, on the porch, and eventually even I start to forget about the camera. It is the tenth member of the household. Caroline strides around her office and living room, unbothered by the rest of us coming and going, sleeping and eating, showering and arguing. She gesticulates and pitches into the phone. She talks about the girls like they're characters—*Definitely ensemble, although the relationships between Ming and Chad, and Ming and her mother, are developing as two narrative threads.* They don't seem to care. They take it in stride, sometimes glancing at each other with recognition—*Hey, she's talking about you!*—and then they go back to whatever they were doing.

B.B. slips in and out. Sometimes you think she's in another room, and actually she's left. Sometimes you think she's not coming, and she's actually lying on one of Caroline's low couches with the high arms—"gone to ground" is how Caroline describes B.B.'s stealth mode. *Is B.B. out, or has she gone to ground?* I start to realize that the other girls don't talk shit about B.B. not because they're all equally friends, which I'd naïvely assumed, but because they know about her tendency to be around every corner, out of sight but very much within earshot.

Out of all of the girls, B.B. baffles me most. She treats me with the same casual disdain as before, but she always seems to be around when I'm around. If I'm on the porch, she's on the porch ignoring me. If I'm in the armchair, she's hanging on the back of the armchair talking to Caroline, as if there's nowhere else she can lean. If I'm on the couch, then she's sitting on the opposite couch arm—never closer than that, but also no farther. If I'm shoving my way through the throng of girls to get a piece of pizza, B.B. follows in my wake and reaches into the box. It isn't quite like she's following me, in part because we barely speak. But I start to be aware that if I look for her, she is there, and that despite the fact that she is never looking at me, she seems to know exactly what I'm doing at any given moment.

It takes us an entire week after our encounter at Whole Foods 365 to have a conversation. Some of the girls are in the house lying around the living room on their phones while Caroline is on one of her interminable calls. I'm on the porch looking up Hélène on my laptop—I want to see how her next show went, and where she is now, and if she's mentioned me at all in any of the press she's been asked to do since. Ever since the scandal, I've erased all social media, and that means that in moments where I want news of the world, I have to resort to Google.

I've only been outside for a few minutes when B.B. comes out and collapses into the hammock strung between two columns of the porch.

"Hey," I say, not expecting a reply. I've just discovered that Hélène got a rave review for her *Peer Gynt* adaptation at the Armory. This fuels my conviction that she must think of me as a failure. *In hindsight, Cass was a mistake* is what she is probably saying, regardless of whether or not they're printing those quotes. *In hindsight, I can see that I never should have taken on that show—or Cass herself.* I scroll through the review and it mentions that Hélène's next stop is Berkeley Rep, followed by the National in the spring. This revelation feels unexpectedly searing. I imagine Hélène in London, so far away (both geographically and in terms of success) that she barely remembers stooping to my level. This turns into remembering Hélène in a summer shirt, sleeves rolled up, her top two buttons undone. My heart stutters a missed beat.

"Who's that?" B.B. asks, breaking into my downward spiral.

"Who's what?"

"That old lady." I hadn't even seen her glance at my screen.

"She's not old," I say immediately. And then: "She's a theatre director—she's really well known."

"What for?"

"Making plays." This sounds much less impressive than I meant it to, so I add, "And she's French."

B.B. is quiet for a moment, and then she says, "Theatre is stupid."

"Okay."

"Who even *goes*," she says. "Nobody even *goes*."

"Okay."

"Do *you* go?"

I hesitate. Cass or Cath? After a moment I say, "No, I guess I don't go."

B.B. continues to stare at me, like she's not satisfied by my answer.

After a moment she says, aggressively, "So like, did you date or something?"

"No!" I say it the way I said it about Caroline, except there's a hollow tone in my voice, and B.B. zooms in on the falsity.

"So why are you creeping on her?"

"Listen," I say, using offense as the best defense. "For future reference, I'm a monk. And for future *future* reference, it is possible to be neighbors with people, or look them up on your computer, without dating them. Even if you don't believe in labels of any kind, like *dating* or *not dating*."

B.B. rolls her eyes. After a minute she says, "My ex is dating some guy now."

"I'm sorry to hear that."

"She's like, giving him road head and telling everybody we were just friends and that I got too intense. She's like, *We weren't even anything.*" After a moment B.B. adds, "He drives a BMW."

I don't know if that's a good thing or a bad thing, so I say "Huh," like it's a piece of information that's given me something to mull over.

"I maybe got intense," B.B. admits. "I *maybe* did, but I didn't *make it up*. Like, I didn't *make up* that we were a thing. That was her too." After a few more moments have gone by, B.B. says, in a quieter tone, "The fucked-up thing is, I don't even—" And then she cuts off, and I look up to see Caroline, watching us from the doorway.

"Cath, can I see you a second?"

I stand up automatically, then glance back at B.B. Her face is expressionless. Caroline is still waiting expectantly, so I follow her inside. Once we're in the door, Caroline says, "I think we need more tape."

"Tape?"

"For their hands, all the girls want tape for their hands."

"Oh . . . ?"

"Mona and Evie were watching UFC, they saw it on UFC." Caroline hands me her car keys. "I've got a call with my agents next," she says. "Could you go pick up some tape, please? And gum—they ate all my fucking gum. And toilet paper."

"Oh . . . okay. I can do that."

Caroline hands me her credit card like she doesn't even care how much it costs, instead of giving me cash—which means you have a limit. "And Tic Tacs," she says thoughtfully over her shoulder, already returning to her office. "Light green or white, no orange."

When I get back to the porch, B.B. is gone and her bike is no longer capsized in the grass.

*

Liz and I were discreet at first. Or we thought we were.

In rehearsal, we shared long glances and practiced "casual" tones of voice when speaking to each other. This was so transparent as to be obscene. Hélène caught on quickly, shooting me a measuring gaze the first time Liz very casually asked if I thought her new approach to the scene 2 monologue was working, and I offered, with remarkable detachment, that I thought it was, thanks. But there was nothing to comment on, even as there was everything to observe, so Hélène had to stay silent.

Outside of rehearsal, we were frantic with desire. The whole thing seemed to exist inside a miasma of lust. The air thickened when we were alone together in the narrow spaces of her dressing room, the elevator to her apartment, her bed. We didn't need to talk—it was easier when we didn't. Late nights and rushed kisses and hands rifling inside each other's clothes—that was our language. At first all of it happened at Liz's place, but then she started taking cabs to my apartment at midnight, breathless, after having called to tell me that we absolutely couldn't continue this way. I knew the rhetoric made her hot, and that she had no intention of stopping, so I'd meet her at the door and kiss her punishingly against the doorframe. Sometimes, if Nico was out, we wouldn't even make it to my tiny bedroom, we'd fuck on the kitchen floor.

We fought too, right from the beginning. This didn't seem like a problem so much as a sign that what we were doing made sense: two fiery personalities, the electric tension of secrecy heightening everything. The fights themselves were never remarkable. Liz would be irritated that I was on my laptop instead of talking to her; I would be irritated because she kept missing the last five lines of the monologue in scene 3.

The fact of Liz's wife almost never came up. She was always away on business trips, and while I took time to ransack her bathroom drawers and medicine cabinets, sizing her up by her lotions and perfumes and oat-milk soaps, I wasn't troubled by her. Hélène was the one I was keeping an eagle eye on, and when—more and more—Hélène said she couldn't meet me for dinners because she had plans, I felt jealousy and misery mix inside me like poison. *What plans? Who is he?* But—"No problem," I'd say, using my newfound casual voice. And after Hélène left, Liz would be hanging out around the corner from the theatre, and there it was: the lust, something I could be obliterated by completely. Obliteration is clean. It leaves no room for humiliation or heartbreak or unrequited love.

Tech week arrived like rain after a long drought. Short for "technical rehearsal," tech is the part of the process that carries the same obliterative quality as a love affair. All the designers join us in the theatre and start implementing their work on top of ours—lights, sound, props, costumes, the functioning of the set itself. Rehearsal hours elongate and become "ten out of twelves"—now you're allowed to have actors in the theatre until midnight, a full twelve-hour day with two hours of assorted breaks. Our designers set up their tech tables in the back of the theatre, computer monitors and laptop screens casting an eerie blue glow on their faces. Tech is the designers' domain, and Hélène was a designers' director. I had guessed this from the photos of her previous productions— each still looked like a painting—but I didn't realize it fully until I saw her talking to the lighting designer. The stage was drenched in purple light, and Hélène looked vibrantly excited, gesturing with her hands. She was in her element, an Old World god corralling chaos into beauty. I was mistaken if I'd thought Liz would get Hélène out of my system; tech entrenched her all the more deeply.

The marketing department scheduled a last interview on dinner break, with a women-focused theatre blog. I was supposed to talk about plays and what it meant to be a woman who had written one, but instead I found myself monologuing to the interviewer about love, pacing around her fifth-floor conference room as I declaimed: "We don't need love stories anymore, we need stories about autonomy and survival." By the time I was done, I was sweating through my plaid, and the interviewer's expression looked like the interview had ended long before I thought it had. The clock said 6:30. I could get back to the theatre before the evening session started again. But when I got out into the lobby, Liz was leaning against the far wall, skin-tight white jeans and a cream-colored cashmere, her long hair swinging down in front of her face like a curtain while she played with her phone.

"Liz, what are you doing here?"

She looked up, gave me a grin: "Thought I'd walk you back."

We were on the East Side, the theatre was west and farther down. "Did you eat around here?"

Liz met my eyes with that slow, confident TV smile, the one that made you feel like you were in a scene that could only be on HBO because it was about to get full-frontal. "No, Cass," she said. "I didn't eat around here."

We ended up fucking in a bathroom stall—Liz's back up against a wall, her jeans pulled halfway down her tan thighs. She was wearing these punky black Fryes with many straps, and we found ourselves in a weird pretzel—Liz with her leg lifted and one Frye planted firmly on the wall behind me, and me between her legs, trying to maneuver in a space the size of a time capsule. When I started fucking her, I kept banging her head into the stall door by accident, and then she'd say "Ow," and I'd apologize into her mouth. I was getting a cramp in my left hand from supporting my entire weight on the wall, and I was also getting a cramp in my right hand from fucking her. After I made her cum, I realized my entire shoulder muscle had seized up, and in trying to disentangle from Liz so that she could put her leg down on the floor again, I stumbled backward without looking and tripped over the toilet bowl. It felt like both of us had had finer moments.

I washed my hands in the sink and dried them for a long time, trying to think, but my brain kept going to that interview, all the bullshit I'd said. What if Hélène read that? What if Hélène read that and thought: *I was right, she's a child, she doesn't even believe in love.* And then part of me thought: *Had I said all those things because I hoped, in some part of me, that Hélène would read it?* Liz was waiting out in the lobby, but eventually she shoved back into the bathroom, impatient: "Cass, tech started thirty minutes ago, we gotta go!"

"Wait, we're late?" It felt like we'd entered into a time warp. I thought we'd done a thing that didn't matter and therefore shouldn't have taken any actual time. But by the look on Liz's face, I knew that neither of those things was true for her—the not mattering or the no time.

"Yeah we're late, let's go."

We entered the theatre like guilty schoolgirls, neither of us looking at the other. Hélène didn't say anything to me, she just turned to Liz—"We've been holding for you. As soon as you're ready." The quality of her silence said enough. I sat penitently in the back row and watched Hélène work. When a designer called "hold" to rewrite a cue, Hélène strode down front to discuss scene-work with the actors. I found myself trying to make eye contact as she moved around the theatre, but she didn't acknowledge me. This lasted until tech ended at midnight. The actors went to take off their costumes; Liz hesitated, her eyes finding mine in a theatre now seared by the blast of work lights. I shook my head and Liz vanished backstage. Hélène finished a conversation with the set designer, and then the costume designer asked her to look at a series of different colored hats, and she vanished backstage as well.

I sat in the house, at first pretending that I was examining those fucking sight lines and then abandoning the pretense that I wasn't waiting for Hélène. After ten minutes, I asked the stage manager where she was. He was bent over his laptop, typing up the rehearsal report, and he didn't glance up as he said, "Do you mean Liz?"

"No, I meant Hélène. You know, the director of the show?"

He gave me a cheeky grin. "Just a joke. If she isn't backstage, she's having a smoke."

Hélène was in the alley behind the theatre, leaning on the loading dock. I saw the cherry of her cigarette first. The alley was New York dark, an assortment of shadows with different-colored neons leaking in, so your eye caught chaos first and then sorted it into shapes. I knew when Hélène saw me because she adjusted her posture, stood straighter.

I opened my mouth to start with something easy, but Hélène spoke first. Her voice was calm and cold. "What are you doing?"

"What do you mean?"

"You know what I mean. This is your first professional New York production. This will put you on the radar—for better or worse. I know that means something to you."

"Hélène—"

"Never sabotage yourself to punish someone else," Hélène said, still with that deadly cool. "Never when it comes to your work."

"I'm not—"

"Walking in half an hour late because you're fucking your lead actor? She's already distractible, Cass, she can't remember half the words in the right order at the best of times, and you want her showing up late and thinking about something other than your play? You're smarter than that, even if you don't think you are." Now Hélène was angry, and for some reason the spark of anger was a relief to me. I hadn't known what to do with the cold.

"This isn't about you," I muttered. "Maybe I like her."

"Like your play more," Hélène said, unimpressed. "Choose your play. You want to know how to get another play after this one, and another after that? How to survive an industry that is full of people who want your slot, people who have more access and more money and more powerful friends and a Yale degree and a good PR agent and what-ever the fuck it is that they will have that you won't have?" She turned to look at me fully. "Choose your art, practice your art, *always, always* choose your art over and above anything else. If you can't do that, then you have—what, a few more years? And then it will get too hard, it will be too rough, you won't be the hot young thing anymore, theatres will reject you mercilessly for long stretches of time. You will watch younger people rise up and work, and many of them will make shoddy, lazy plays that will be praised because they're in line with the fashion. People with power will make you feel bad, and then other people will make you feel good, and the ones who made you feel good? You'll let them use you, you'll give them whatever they want—and your work, if you're still making it, will get lost underneath all of that. And eventually you'll quit."

I started to speak, but Hélène cut through me: "I've been doing this for your entire lifetime, Cass. Of the women I knew who started out with me, none are still doing what I'm doing. And it's okay to choose something else if you want something else. But I think you don't want anything else—I think you have something in you that makes you need this—and right now you think I'm a solution—or Liz, maybe you think Liz will be a solution—and we won't be."

In the silence that followed, Hélène dropped her cigarette, grinding it under her boot. She was so fiercely certain. And she would give me only so much of herself, only the smallest part. And I knew her well enough to know that I had to take what was offered, because I wouldn't get more, no matter what I did or said. But I couldn't stop feeling the absence of all those things too.

"Okay," I said, rough.

"Okay?"

"Okay, I hear you."

"And what will you do, having heard me?"

"Not make Liz late for rehearsal."

"And?"

I was half-pissed, half trying not to laugh, and tears under all of that. "Not fuck her?"

"I don't care if you fuck her," Hélène said, "but for god sake don't detonate a bomb in the middle of all this."

"You don't care at all?"

A moment. And then Hélène smiled, like she wanted to be mad but she couldn't help it. "Cass, you have to stop this."

"I'm just asking."

"What do you need to hear? You want me beside myself with

jealousy? Will that help you let this go, if I'm writing poems every night at my kitchen table, very French, a baguette and a jug of red wine, consumed by jealousy? Will you feel better?"

"Maybe." I couldn't help it: "The baguette and red wine sounds good, anyway. I like it when you get very French."

Hélène reined in her smile sternly. "You will behave?"

"I will behave."

"You will choose this play, the thing we're making? And you can drink, you can fuck, but you do it *around* this play, not over it?"

"I choose this play."

"Okay," Hélène said. She vaulted back up onto the loading dock so that she was standing beside me. The thick heat of New York in late August, the frenetic flicker and hum of the city around us. Only a few blocks from here, the main artery of Eighth Ave cut down the island, alive with crowds even at this hour.

I looked at Hélène. She smiled at me swiftly, and it went all the way to her eyes, although she did not touch me. "See you tomorrow," she said, and walked past me into the cool depths of backstage.

*

I've been in L.A. nearly a month when Caroline tells the girls that we'll take a couple weeks off from fighting. She tells them that she wants some footage that chronicles the time before their characters find an outlet in violence—the story of daily lives wracked by monotony. She tells me later that she has two interns coming as soon as their paperwork goes through—"Course credit, so I don't have to pay them"—and that we're days away from landing a serious chunk of financing, which will permit her to have a DP around and add a variety of high-tech cameras. ("To augment. You know, like *Tangerine* but if they had a budget. *Tangerine plus*.") In light of our hiatus for pragmatic concerns, she likes the idea of letting the girls' resentments build up.

To the girls she says only: "Communicate the banality."

She says: "With your eyes, I mean, total dead-in-the-eyes stuff."

She says, "This is the part of the movie where teens in the suburbs will empathize with you."

We spend a week following the girls to CVS, filming them as they buy chewing gum and tampons, filming them as they horse around outside of 365, ramming shopping carts into each other, filming them as they tie their shoelaces and check their texts and call each other "cunt" and sniff under their armpits to see if they forgot deodorant that morning. Caroline commandeers Dylan's van one day, and we drive the girls to a series of particularly desolate parking lots and malls and then trail after them while they meander. Our job is only to follow, and there is a great and comforting simplicity in the singleness of that mandate.

Caroline intervenes only once, when we're standing in line by a Shake Shack. Stationed behind Mona, Ming starts propelling mouthfuls of coffee through the gap in her front teeth, sizzling it into a fine mist all over the back of Mona's neck. It takes Mona a second to realize what's happening, but once she does, she turns around and socks Ming hard in the stomach. The punch lands with a *thwock* and the rest of Ming's mouthful erupts all over the front of Mona's tank top as Ming staggers backward and hits the ground ass first. Before the two of them can start whaling on each other, Caroline steps in: "We're not *at* that part yet," she says forcefully and coldly. "We are *pre-violence*, we are *banal*." A moment, in which the two girls glare at each other, bristling, but then Mona turns back around, and Ming hauls herself off the sidewalk.

At the beginning of week two of Banality, three of the girls get their periods at the same time, and Caroline follows Evie into the bathroom of a McDonald's so that she can film Evie changing her tampon. It's only later that afternoon, when we're back at Caroline's house eating the seemingly bottomless store of snack food and reviewing the day's footage, that she has a realization. We're all rewatching the clip of Evie changing her tampon, the girls clustered around the computer monitor. Evie has the air of a bashful star, her eyes foggy with amazement at herself. And then Caroline drops the bomb.

"We gotta redo this sequence," she tells us.

"How come?" Evie asks.

"This feels too politically loaded," Caroline says, "given the history of the fetishization of the Black female body. I should have thought of that before. We need to reshoot with a white girl."

The room explodes. Three of the white girls are trying to yell "I volunteer" over each other. Evie is yelling: "Wait a minute, that's not fair!" Ming is yelling: "What about an Asian?" B.B. isn't yelling; she has her arms folded, and at one point she says, "Don't look at me," even though nobody is looking at her, which I take to mean that she doesn't volunteer.

"One at a time!" Caroline shouts over the din. "Evie, you first."

"It's not fair," Evie says promptly. "I can be fetishized if I want to, first of all, and second of all, it's not fetishization if I say it's not, because it's my body and the tampon scene is mine. And how come white girls always get to come in and be universal? Fuck that! I'm just as universal. I'm gonna universally change my universal fucking tampon."

I've never heard her say this many words before, and I've never heard her swear.

"Yeah, but if people think we're like, fetishizing Black women, nobody's gonna like our movie," Mona says. "So, if that's a thing, we shouldn't do it." Her cheeks are even more flushed than usual, and her curly red hair seems to be attempting escape from the rest of her.

"Oh my *god*," Evie begins, but Ming is already talking: "Why's this shit always about Black girls and white girls? It's like there's nobody else in the country, goddamn! Asians bleed too, you know."

"Asian women are already *totally* fetishized," one of the Nickeys says. "You're like, even worse than Evie."

That's the last straw. Evie is yelling: "The fuck does that mean, worse than?" and Ming is yelling: "Fuck you," and Mona is yelling at the Nickey: "Oh my god, you're not even really bleeding, I'm the only white girl here who's even really bleeding," and it's pure chaos until Caroline intervenes again.

"Cath!" she bellows. Everyone goes quiet. "Cath is gonna decide," she says.

Everyone looks at me.

"Me?" I have to ask.

"Yeah," says Ming, "why *her*?"

"Because that's her fucking job," Caroline says.

I hesitate. The mantle of power is heavy. But I find, as it settles around my shoulders, that it is not uncomfortable.

"We should keep the footage with Evie," I say after a moment. The room detonates all over again, Evie yelling, "See?" and Ming yelling, "What the fuck!" and two of the Nickeys, outraged: "This is bullshit!" and then Caroline slams her flip-flop on the table a few times, and everybody gets quiet again.

"We already have the footage, and I don't wanna go back to McDonald's, because they didn't like us shooting in the bathrooms there," I say. "And Caroline's bathroom is way less banal, so if we reshoot, we're trading the most banal place in the world for a weaker venue."

I'm quiet.

They're quiet.

Then B.B. says, very quietly, not challenging but inquiring: "But what about race?"

"I think people will have a lot to say about the tampon scene," I say honestly, "but I don't think any of it is gonna be about race."

The girls are interested.

"What do you think people are gonna say?" Evie asks.

"I think they're gonna be upset because you're young and because the subject matter is kind of taboo, and I think we might get accused of making something obscene. Whether it's you or Ming or Nickey or whoever, that's probably what's gonna happen. So I'd rather it happen with the scene set in a bleak, fluorescent McDonald's bathroom than in Caroline's, like, hipster-Martha-Stewart bathroom."

The girls all look at Caroline. She's staring at me in a very focused way, and when she realizes they're all looking to her for a reaction, she shrugs like, *What, you heard her.* The girls look back to me. I shrug too, because I'm not sure what else to say.

"Oh," says Evie.

"Huh," says a Nickey.

"I can puke on camera," Ming offers, switching tactics.

The girls devolve back into a chatter of voices, offering up what they would and wouldn't do on camera. But Caroline keeps looking at me, and then her mouth quirks in a smile. I feel like there was some test and I passed it. This whole time she was trying to decide whether she'd made a mistake on me, and she just received the answer, passed to her through the vibrations of the universe: *Cath is a good idea.* Caroline shoves a baby carrot in her mouth and gives me a thumbs-up and I grin back at her, giddy. It comes to me then that this film is definitely going to Sundance, it's definitely getting attention, Andrea Arnold–meets–*Tangerine* kind of attention. And I want that too. I want to go with it. What I am feeling is proximity to success, and this feeling, after the abyss of its absence, is oxygen. And right then I think that if Caroline asked me to change *my* fucking tampon on camera, I'd do it.

7

Caroline and I are driving to Trader Joe's (snack run) when she learns that I'm queer. I hadn't thought I was dropping a bomb, but Caroline gets so excited that she almost drives into the back of the Prius in front of us.

"Wait," she says. "Like, *girls*?"

"I mean . . . and boys?"

"Bi Sexual," Caroline says with enthusiasm, pointing at me. She makes it two separate words, like it's a title she's heard but never gotten a chance to use.

"And people who don't really—you know, who haven't picked a side."

"How does *that* work?"

Caroline is looking at me instead of the road, as usual. My sneaker has started to do the thing where it jams itself against the floor whenever we get too close to the Prius.

"I mean . . . sometimes people don't feel like they're either gender, or a single gender?"

"But like . . ." Caroline's brow gathers in a furrow. "How does that *work*?"

"Well . . . for some people gender is a continuum. Or a buffet. I mean, I just say I'm queer, because when people ask what you are, they only have space for a one-word answer, but—"

"'Gender is a buffet,'" Caroline says, delighted, pull-quoting me. Her open hand drifts through the air above us, like she's turning my pull quote into a marquee sign. "That's so good!"

"Thank you?"

"Maybe that's a conversation you and B.B. should have."

"We should?"

"On camera," Caroline hastens. "Like, a scene. We want to really build certain character arcs. Identity is so important. And you and B.B. could really . . . go there. Together."

"Oh, uh . . . I'm not an actor."

"Nobody is an actor," Caroline says promptly. "And everybody is."

The Prius peels off into a parking lot, and I briefly feel relief, until Caroline almost hits the Honda Fit that's pulling out into traffic ahead of us. She smacks the horn with the heel of her palm, then turns back to me expectantly.

"I, uh . . . I don't feel like I'm the best . . . like, in front of the camera, I wouldn't . . ."

"Everyone is capable of feeling a thing deeply," Caroline says. "Feeling a thing that resonates with your inner truth, and then, letting that truth spill out—everyone is *capable* of that, people just don't give themselves the permission."

That statement feels true to me, and also oddly beautiful, and it confuses me even more because what I'm trying to say is that I don't want to be in front of a camera. But *why* don't I? Should I? Tara-Jean Slater is ready to play herself in the audience every night, telling the world about her uncle. That is both gutsy and incredibly savvy publicity. Maybe I should be ready to play myself too. Just because I wasn't abused doesn't mean I can't play myself, does it? Or does it?

"I've always wanted to date a woman," Caroline says, swinging the car wildly to the left to cut across the oncoming lane of traffic. My body ricochets off the side of the car as a volley of horns start up. We land, unscathed, in the Trader Joe's parking lot. "Synchrony," she's saying. "Like the part where your periods sync up. I think that's great."

I missed the middle part, because I was expecting to die, so I ask: "Wait, have you?"

"No," Caroline says, sadly. "For me it's men. The wrong men, most of the time. But definitely men."

She looks so dejected that I feel like I'm being called upon to comfort her. "That's okay."

"If I ever brought a woman home? My mom would . . . Oh man." Caroline smiles and frowns at the same time. "She wants to be so open-minded, but actually . . . she'd be so polite, in such a hideous way. She'd smother my girlfriend to death with politeness." She trails off, then adds, as if this is a thought she's had often: "She's gonna hate our movie."

I experience a flicker of delight at hearing her say *our* movie. "Maybe she'll like it," I say encouragingly.

"No, she won't, but that's why I'm making it. In part, anyway." After a moment, Caroline says wistfully: "I think when I'm eighty, and I don't even want to have sex anymore? Then I'll date a woman. And she'll be eighty too, and we'll be like . . . so close."

She pulls into a handicapped space, hitting the curb, but I don't even think she notices; her face is dream-cast and distant. "We'll have plants," she continues, turning the car off, "and cats, and we'll like to bake. I'll like to bake by then. Or cook. Or she'll cook and I'll bake, and we'll like—have these *marathons* where all we do is watch every movie Hitchcock ever made."

Part of me feels like Caroline has completely misunderstood what dating a woman means, and part of me finds myself thinking that she's just described my ideal relationship. Or the sort of relationship that is the opposite of every other relationship I've ever had, and that therefore sounds ideal. I'm not sure which half of this thought to voice, so when the silence extends, I choose the second and say: "That sounds perfect."

Caroline turns to me, and for a moment she looks at me, and I think she's going to say something unguarded and raw—and then her phone starts ringing. She plucks it out of the cup holder and examines it, and then sighs. "My agents," she says. "Would you mind . . . ?" She hands me the shopping list and her pink wallet.

"Oh," I say, surprised.

"I have to take this—Chip! Hello, Chip, would you hang on?" She covers the mouthpiece and says, "Get whatever you want, obviously."

"Oh, uh, sure." I get out of the car and then feel like I have to tell her: "This—this is a handicapped spot, by the way?"

Caroline gives me her best deadpan. "I mean, I'm handicapped by sexism, frankly." And then she turns back to the phone—"Chip! Chip, are you still there?"—and I close the car door gently behind me, her pink wallet clutched in my fist.

We're at the end of the second week of "total dead-in-the-eyes stuff" when Caroline tells me about the potential financiers that she and her team have been locking down. We're sitting on her porch having coffee—Ming is still asleep in the guest room and none of the other girls have showed up yet. Caroline says that they are a wealthy British couple, and that the woman of the couple is an investment banker who seems particularly interested in Evie. Every time she and Caroline talk, she asks about her. "So I make it sound like the movie is about her," Caroline says. "You know: 'It's *Moonlight* but with girls.'"

"*Moonlight*?"

"*Moonlight* is the only coming-of-age movie about Black people she's seen," Caroline explains. "*Moonlight* and *Get Out*, but she didn't like *Get Out*." I start to offer that *Get Out* isn't exactly a coming-of-age story, but Caroline keeps going: "The guy is really into Ming, though, he's like, *So important to change the Hollywood stereotype of Asian women*, and I'm like, *I know*. I think he wants to bone her. It's gross." She sips her coffee. "Anyway, so they're willing to shell out a bunch of money, it sounds like. Chip is gonna lock it down with them this week." She makes a face and adds, "I'm only dealing with Chip right now, Ryan is canned."

"Ryan?"

"My other agent. Or like, I put Ryan on time-out. *Canned*, I don't know, we'll see about canned."

"Oh," I say again. I try to think about Marisa in those exact terms.
Marisa? She's canned.
Marisa? I put her on time-out.

I feel a cool breeze of exhilaration from the driver's seat of my life. I open my mouth—Am I about to say something about once having had an agent? Am I about to say something about Cass? My heart is suddenly a thousand pistons, all going at once—but Caroline is still talking: "—clear fetishist, I mean, all his ex-girlfriends are Korean, by the way, if you needed me to say that, which I bet you didn't."

"How do you even *know* that?"

"I looked him up on Facebook," Caroline tells me, like it should be obvious.

I ask: "Do you worry that they're gonna see the movie and like . . . feel that we lied or something?"

"How did we *lie*?" Caroline is offended.

"Sorry, I don't mean *lie*. That wasn't the right word. But I mean . . . it isn't like *Moonlight* . . . at all?"

Caroline smiles as though I'm being naïve. "Oh, *that*," she says. "No, they're gonna love it. And you want to know why?" I nod. "They will love it," Caroline tells me, "because we're gonna get great press. Nobody is disappointed about financing something that gets great press. Regardless of what they thought they were financing. End of story."

"How do you know that, though?"

Caroline fixes me with a particularly "don't be naïve" gaze. "Come on," she says. "You try giving bad press to a movie about seven girls who look like the goddamn United Colors of Benetton, just trying to make it in a man's world. Who are subverting a *man's book* for their coming-of-age story. You know? You just try." And then she gestures to me, as if she shouldn't even have to add this, and says: "*And* one of the filmmakers is queer."

I consider this. If I'm honest, it's like a three-car pileup in my head: *She called me a filmmaker!* and also *Is this offensive?* and also *Is she right?*

I find myself thinking about Tara-Jean Slater again. I think of Claire

Danes standing in for her; I think of different famous lady actresses all performing the role of Tara-Jean Slater. *You try dismissing a play where a girl gets fingered by her uncle.* Is Tara-Jean Slater exorcising her demons or making smart business decisions? Is it her fault that there is an entire marketing machine that now feeds on these particular demons?

I imagine Caroline seeing the girls from her car window, walking on the highway shoulder, blood on their faces—that whole origin story. Maybe she thought: *There's my next film* long before she thought: *I wonder if they're okay.* But so what if she did? They're all benefiting, aren't they? We, I remind myself, *we* are all benefiting.

"You should come," Caroline is saying.

"Wait, sorry, come where?"

"The meeting," she says, "with Chip. End of next week. That way you'll be there, I won't have to repeat everything later."

"Oh," I say. Then: "*Oh.*"

And then "Yes, of course."

Of course it's a yes.

*

Caroline's two interns show up days later, dewy and aglow with enthusiasm. The girl is named Jaki and the boy is named Whitford, and they're juniors at CalArts. They're both brunettes with square-framed glasses. They have the same coloring in general—Los Angeles tan, big brown eyes—but Caroline tells me in private that Jaki is "Latinx, and I think it's so important to have that perspective," and she doesn't say that about Whitford, so I assume he's just a garden-variety white boy.

Even though the funding hasn't been solidified yet, Caroline decides we're ready to get back to violence. The girls have been increasingly edgy and jumpy, conflict leaking out in a variety of small incidents that never boil over fully. I think Caroline is worried that a fight might break out without waiting for a camera. When she tells us that we're finally ready to shoot a fight, the relief is palpable—so much so that Ming volunteers Chad's house in Laurel Canyon. ("It has a heated pool.") When she mentions him, Mona rolls her eyes and mutters something to Evie.

Caroline's eyes light up in a way that I've started to recognize means she's seeing a shot line up right in front of her. "Great!" she says hastily. "Ming, text Chad's address to the group thread."

The promise of a fight gives me a lift as well. Dylan gets home that evening to find me in the kitchen cooking instead of indulging in my usual descent into the ninth ring of takeout.

"Very civilized, Cass," he says. "What're you making?"

"Spaghetti and meatballs," I say grandly, stirring stewed tomatoes into the hissing pan of onions and garlic. It's thickening into the sauce my mom sometimes makes.

"Very Italian."

"At least I didn't use Newman's Own."

Dylan laughs. "I haven't seen you in like a week. You seem good."

"I do?"

"Yeah." He tilts his head to the side. "Very, in fact."

I hear myself say, "I'm working on a movie."

"A movie! That's cool. What's it about?"

It is as if Caroline speaks through me: "It's a . . . post–Me Too coming-of-age story. About girls channeling their rage."

"Wow." Dylan sounds impressed. "And you're writing it?"

"Uh . . . it's a collaboration. It's—not fully scripted but like, Caroline and I are codirectors. She's my new friend—I think I told you—the one who lives next door?"

"No, you didn't tell me!" Dylan pops the cork on a bottle of red, holds it up for my inspection. To me a bottle of red is a bottle of red, but Dylan's restaurant training is impeccable. "Wait, you're codirecting a film with Mormon Sex Cartel next door? That's the most L.A. thing I've ever heard. I love it."

I wonder if I should walk the whole "codirecting" thing back, but then I think about it and it feels true. I don't know what our actual *titles* are, but we're both making decisions. I think of the upcoming fight and my blood leaps again. Caroline has interns now. And I'm definitely not an intern. So, if the options are intern or decision maker, I'm a decision maker. And what is a decision maker if not a director?

Dylan pours me a splash and waits for me to sniff it.

"Smells like wine," I say.

"The customer has a good nose," Dylan says in his snobby waiter voice, and then pours us each a glass. "Hey—Daniel reminded me that next week is Thanksgiving. We should do something, if you're around."

"Sure," I say, "I'm around." I'd completely lost track of time in L.A.'s endless summer. The concepts of autumn and Thanksgiving seem to be happening on another planet.

"We usually go to my parents'," Dylan says, "but it feels complicated this year. And Daniel has relatives up the coast, buuuut—well. *That's* complicated too."

"He has relatives here?"

"His aunt and uncle," Dylan says. "And I bet you can guess why Daniel's never taken me there." After a moment, he dismisses his note of bitterness: "Anyway, maybe we could grill or something. Daniel was saying that we never see you."

The realization that I've been busy—actually busy, not faux busy— swamps me with a wave of endorphins. I am in demand. I have friends! And work. And even if Caroline hasn't called me a codirector to my face, she definitely thinks of me that way. "I'd love that," I tell Dylan.

"Pencil us in," Dylan teases. Then he nods toward the spaghetti sauce: "Have enough for two?"

As I stir the sauce, he begins to prepare a salad, telling me a story about lunch shift that day—something about a woman with two Pomeranians. I'm only half listening, consumed by the thought that has come to me: *I am happy, I am happy, this is a life in which I am happy*— like a mantra or a triumphal chant. And, right under it: *Take that, Tara-Jean Slater.*

*

When Caroline picks me up the next day, Whitford is in the back seat of her car next to a plethora of objects I've never seen before. A giant cardboard cutout of *Fight Club*–era Brad Pitt is shoved in back with a seat belt across it, and next to him is a box of photos and celebrity mags. I see a few pictures of Robert De Niro on top.

I ask Caroline if they're coming from a garage sale. She laughs.

"Set dressing," she says. "We gotta let the space speak."

"What is it gonna say?"

"The space is gonna tell us how deeply these girls are steeped in the hypermasculinization of violence," Caroline tells me as she pulls onto the highway. "We got Tarantino, we got more *Fight Club* paraphernalia, these are gonna be girls who have learned all their self-expression from men. And as they become more and more empowered, the backgrounds are gonna change. By the last shot we're gonna have images of Ruth Bader Ginsberg in the background."

Whitford, in the back seat, is attentive but silent. I ask where Jaki is. Caroline pulls the steering wheel hard, switching lanes and cutting off a small Buick. "Suck my COCK," Caroline tells the Buick. I'm noticing that the prospect of a fight is filling her with restless, eager energy as well. The weeks of banal footage have taken their toll on everyone.

"Jaki's picking up Thomas," Caroline tells me. "He's a DP—he shot my last movie—he's super eccentric, he doesn't have a car? But he's a genius and he's doing today as sort of . . . good faith. He knows I'll pay him when the funding comes in."

"Oh, that's great."

Caroline lowers her voice, even though Whitford can definitely still hear her from the back seat. "We used to date," she says, sotto voce, "but that doesn't complicate our working relationship."

"Oh," I say uncertainly. "That's great?"

I think Caroline is finished, but then she adds: "For two years, actually. He cheated on me with three other people, and he gave me gonorrhea, which is like—antibiotics are great, but it still *sucks*—and then *he* broke up with *me*. After all that. And, you know . . . the thing about Thomas . . ." Her voice trails away thoughtfully, as if she's remembering something from a great distance away.

"What's the thing about Thomas?" I ask.

Caroline glances into the back seat and lowers her voice even more. Now she's mouthing the words. I can't make them out. I lean in. She mouths bigger. I feel like she's trying to share something really important with me, and I'm missing it through my own deficiencies. I shake my head, and Caroline sighs and sticks out her pinky finger in the universal sign for *tiny dick*. Then we both glance into the back seat. Whitford, aware that his existence is not currently wanted, is holding his phone in front of his face and gazing raptly at it. This is the universal sign for *I'm not even here*.

I am suddenly aware of being the person in the front seat of the car. Chosen.

I am suddenly deliciously aware of existing.

*

Chad is tall, gangly, pale, goofy-looking. As Ming had warned us after their first breakup, something approximating a beard is happening to his chin. His eyes are watery, and as he talks to us, his gaze skates around, missing our faces by a foot or so. He tells us that he's a college senior at UCLA, and then he amends that and says he's a "super senior," which means everyone in his class graduated "a few times" but he's still there. Ming hangs off his arm, glancing up at him with adoration, laughing occasionally as if he's making jokes. At one point, his cupped hand finds the back of Ming's bikini bottoms. I wait for Ming to punch him, but instead she squeals and bats at his wrist.

I look at Caroline, because I am contending with the fact that Ming is seventeen and this guy looks like he's twenty-seven-going-on-Ted-Bundy. But Caroline is electric with thrill, like she has stumbled on an unforeseen treasure trove. She whips her iPhone out and points it at Chad. Without glancing at us: "Cath, can you supervise the setup?"

Whitford turns to me, his round eyes damp with expectation.

"Whitford," I say. I hear the note of authority in my voice. It is intoxicating. He cocks his head to the side like a spaniel; he hears it too. "Whitford, I'd like you to dress the set."

Whitford springs into action, lugging the cardboard *Fight Club*–era

Brad Pitt cutout under one arm to its desired destination, facing the pool. I eye the placement as if with the jaded disinterest of a connoisseur. What I'm really thinking: *Is this not totally on the nose?* I shoot Caroline a glance, but she's filming Chad talking about a videogame tournament he was in. Ming hangs off his skinny arm looking bored. In the absence of Caroline's attention, I realize, it is up to me to say what I'm thinking.

"Whitford," I say. He leaps to attention. "Brad Pitt is too obvious. We're gonna cut Brad Pitt."

"Copy that," says Whitford. He retrieves the cutout, folding it in half as he stores it back under his arm.

"Actually, throw it out. It's terrible."

"Copy that," says Whitford, and he lopes toward the driveway. Under my watchful eye, he carefully places the Brad Pitt cutout into the recycling bin.

When I glance over at Caroline and Chad, I see that Ming is no longer touching him. Chad hasn't clocked this; he's hypnotized by the camera, drugged into performing. "—and all those bitches were up in my grill after that," he's confiding. This current incarnation of Chad seems a lot more Snoop Dogg than white UCLA super senior.

"*Okay*," Ming is saying, as in *Okay, shut up*, but Chad doesn't hear her.

"Bitches talkin' 'bout love," he tells the camera, "put pressure on a man."

"Oh my GOD," Ming says, and jumps into the pool with an explosion of water.

At this moment, Jaki arrives with Thomas in tow. He's an underfed goth with a giant camera bag slung over his shoulder. He has nickel-sized plugs in both ears, and a crown of thorns is tattooed around his half-shaven skull; the other half is covered in lank, damp-colored hair. When Caroline sees him, she puts her phone down, cutting Chad off midsentence, and goes to give Thomas a hug. It lingers for one extra beat. I try to imagine Caroline, with her coral toenails and long braid, tumbling around in bed with Thomas.

Caroline and Thomas talk briefly, their heads close together, as he unzips his camera bag. She peers inside, nodding excitedly, then, glancing up, catches me watching and gestures me over. "Thomas, this is Cath, she's my number two. Cath, this is Thomas." She says a sentence about Thomas, but I don't hear it over the reverberation of "number two."

"Nice to meet you," I say. Thomas gives me a nod.

As he sets up his cameras, Whitford and Jaki stand on the balls of their feet, ready to dash in any direction at any time. Ming's head pops back over the edge of the pool. Her hair is plastered to the side of her skull, but her makeup hasn't even smeared. "The pool is so *warm*," she announces joyfully. I surrender the thought of a big-sisterly talk wherein I tell her that Chad isn't good for her. It's clear that Ming knows this already, and right now that knowledge is not as interesting as fucking him and swimming in his heated pool.

Mona and Evie arrive, and then the three Nickeys, who are embroiled in a loud argument—*I only liked her post because she liked mine, that's not the same thing as being friends!*—that they forget as soon as they see Ming in the pool. "Oh my god, let's go in the pool!" the tallest one whoops. By now I've learned that this one is definitely Aubrey, but I still think of them as the Nickeys.

"Film first, pool later," Caroline announces firmly. "Everybody, put your stuff down and go sit in the living room, we're gonna talk some stuff through before we start." She hands her iPhone to Whitford—"B-roll, Whitford"—and he takes it obediently. We all traipse after her into Chad's living room. As we enter, I see that Thomas has set up a whole situation inside the kitchenette—lights, white screens to bounce the light, fancy-looking camera rigs.

B.B. shows up at the last minute. She's wearing camo cargo pants and a T-shirt that says EAT PUSSY, IT'S ORGANIC. She looks like she's been crying, but she just says, "Hey, bitches," to everyone and goes to slump in a sticky recliner. Chad appears with cases of beer, and the girls help themselves. Ming can't be mad at him now that her friends are here, so she perches on the arm of his chair like the queen of the manor, taking sips from his beer.

I wait for the girls to do what I've begun to think of as the preamble (*you don't need a dick to start a fight*) but instead Caroline introduces Whitford, Jaki, and Thomas. She says that we're going to talk through some blocking before we shoot, and that the girls should of course bring their genuine feelings, but we won't be full force anymore, and also, we have some paperwork for them to sign before we start today. What she is saying, I realize, is that we are gently—all together—crossing the line from being into acting, from life into theatre. I don't know if the girls realize this, but they're listening and nodding, their faces blank.

"Any questions?" Caroline inquires.

"Yeah," Mona says. "Why's *he* here?" And she gestures to Chad, sitting in his armchair.

"It's his *house*, cunt!" Ming yells at Mona from Chad's side.

This unlocks a chorus of ill feeling against Chad; the girls are dried grass, it would take nothing to make this flame leap high. "This isn't about him," Actual Nickey says. "This is a thing we do for us, and frankly it's bullshit that we're gonna do it here? And I kinda think he should leave?"

Evie joins the fray: "I don't care where we fight," she says, "but that guy is an asshole."

"I'm right here," Chad says, mild with surprise.

"Yeah, you," Tall Nickey says, "I see you. You're a dickhole. You're a . . ." She searches for something better, then finds it: "Urethra." A moment, in which some of the girls are impressed and some are confused.

Ming cuts through the moment with a roar: "What did he ever do to you!"

"He treats you like shit!" Mona roars back.

"No he doesn't!"

"You can't even see it, because he's fucking brainwashed you," Short Nickey yells, "but I'm gonna fight Chad! Chad! I'm gonna fight you!"

"You cannot fight Chad!" Ming screams. "Chad is off-limits!"

"You actually *can't* fight Chad," Evie concurs. "Chad isn't invited to participate."

"*Can* she fight Chad?" Mona is intrigued by this development.

"I will fucking kill you!" Ming is beside herself. "I will kill you, Nickey!" This is addressed to Actual Nickey.

I feel a thrill of unease. Everyone looks to Caroline to see if she's going to weigh in on whether or not Chad is fair game. Chad looks terrified. Caroline's face is attentive but expressionless. When she doesn't say anything, Chad says, "I'm not fighting anyone?" It comes out half like a question and half like a plea.

"Yeah that's what I *thought*," says Actual Nickey with exquisite contempt. "Back down, faggot."

B.B. is out of her recliner before anyone knows what's happening, and her punch catches Nickey in the gut. Nickey makes an *unh* noise and doubles over. The girls are shocked. This isn't how these things go. Nobody has been sorted into matches. Even Caroline's jaw is dropped. B.B. stands over Nickey, looking as shocked as any of us. Into the silence Nickey coughs, winded, her breath coming back to her. She looks up at B.B., who seems to have no idea what to do.

A silence extends, and then B.B. storms out of the glass doors toward the pool. I hear the sound of her fighting with the swinging gate. Thomas keeps the camera on the girls and Chad while Whitford swings Caroline's iPhone around to get B.B.'s exit. B.B. gets the latch open and slams the gate as hard as possible, and it's this sound that propels me after her. Whitford takes this as a cue to follow me, and I turn on him. "No," I say, loud and clear, as if I'm talking to a dog. He stops in his tracks, and I keep going without looking back.

B.B. has gotten as far as the road when I catch up with her.

"Hey," I say, "hang on."

B.B. is storming down the street like she knows where she's going. The roads around here are winding and narrow, framed with thick greenery. Giant houses sit back at the ends of pathlike driveways half-obscured by trees, cacti, strange plants. Their glass windows spit sun at the sky. In contrast to the cement and metal of Silver Lake, it feels like wilderness.

"Hey, wait!"

She doesn't slow down. I quicken my pace to keep up, and we walk in silence for a minute. Her face is locked down and her breathing is jagged. After a second I say, "We're gonna get eaten by coyotes."

B.B. flickers a glance at me. "That's stupid."

"And mountain lions. Tell me this isn't a haven for mountain lions."

"This is *Laurel Canyon*."

I gesture around us: "Nature is red in tooth and claw."

B.B. shakes her head like she doesn't know if she wants to punch me or smile. Then she says, "Why aren't you back at *Chad's* house?" She makes "Chad" sound like a disease.

"Because you hit Nickey in the stomach and ran out," I say. B.B.'s mouth twists, and we walk in silence for another minute.

"Was it because Nickey called Chad a faggot?" I try. B.B. shrugs. I have no idea what to say, so I go for a *Good Will Hunting* moment. "Do people call you that?"

B.B. shoots me a glare. "Why don't you ask me about my fucking *childhood*," she says savagely, and speeds up.

I speed up to match. I had been prepared to tell B.B. it wasn't her fault and then hold her while she cried, but I give up on the Robin Williams angle. "Well, you made a good scene, so Caroline's not mad at you. If you come back, probably Nickey wants to fight you, so that's another good scene. If you don't wanna come back . . ."

"Then what?" B.B. asks. She's slowed down now.

"I don't know, where were you headed?"

"I don't know."

"Well, if you wanna go home, I can call you a Lyft."

"I came here by Lyft, I can call myself a fucking Lyft." B.B. keeps looking at me, though, something expectant in her gaze. She's waiting for me to say something amazing, but I have no idea why.

"Well, I need to go back eventually," I say, knowing, even as the words leave my mouth, that this isn't the amazing thing she was waiting for. I'm letting her down in a way I can feel but don't fully understand. I hesitate, not sure if she's going to tell me to fuck off again. Instead, B.B. looks down at the asphalt and nods. "Yeah," she says quietly. "I guess you do."

B.B. comes back with me, which I didn't expect. When we get to the driveway, we can already hear the sounds of a fight in progress: grunting, the crack of something breaking—possibly wicker furniture—then a high-pitched scream like an animal rearing up. I unlatch the side gate and as we let ourselves in, Ming and Mona barrel past us, fists locked in each other's hair, staggering over the edge of the pool and landing in the water. A wave rises up and swamps the side, leaving behind chlorinated puddles. In the pool, Ming and Mona separate. The fight seems to be over. They look to Caroline, who is standing on a crate filming downward. Thomas has brought his tripod to the far end of the pool and is filming the master shot.

He and Caroline exchange a wordless glance, and then Caroline says, "Great! Hang on a sec, girls. Jaki, dress the puddles."

Jaki moves past us and kneels down next to the puddles of water. She has an eyedropper in her hand, and she squeezes out a few drops. The puddles turn dark scarlet, like someone has bled profusely. Caroline gets down off the crate and kneels by the puddles, Jaki and her eyedropper out of frame. She takes a close-up, then lifts her head and sees B.B. and me standing by the gate. "Hey," she says, "welcome back!" The girls turn as one to stare at B.B.

B.B. doesn't show anything with her face, just stands right behind me, jaw set, staring down at the ground. A moment, in which Caroline waits for potential conflict to spark. When it doesn't, she returns to work. "Okay, we're gonna shoot the pool sequence one more time. Ming and Mona, this time I want you to run out of the house and straight for the pool, but Ming, wait until you hit your mark before you grab Mona's hair, and then Mona . . ."

As she gives direction to the girls, Jaki and Whitford glance at me deferentially to see if I have any direction for them. And even though I don't, that new feeling rises like a tidal wave inside me once again. I replay Caroline saying *This is Cath, she's my number two.* I step away from B.B., toward Caroline. I don't do it on purpose. I don't even realize I'm doing it until I've done it, and then I think: *It's just so people understand what I'm doing here.*

*

In the car on the way home, Caroline asks me how I think the day went.

"It was pretty different."

"Huh," Caroline says.

"Didn't you think so?" I hasten to explain myself. "Like, before, we didn't have . . . set dressing, or . . ."

"Right," Caroline says. "Well. I mean, we're making a movie, so . . ."

"No, of course, and the pool scene was amazing."

"I know, right?" Caroline grins at the highway. "Chucking the Brad Pitt was a smart call, by the way. Whitford was the one who picked him out, but I felt like that might be overkill."

Pleasure floods me. "Thank you," I say, trying to sound modest. Caroline basically said that I saved the shoot today with my directorial aesthetic. Then I remember the conversation we were having before the compliment derailed me, and I find my way back toward it, gingerly: "I guess I mean . . . There wasn't fake blood before, for example."

"Right, this isn't, you know, a *documentary*. Andrea *Arnold* makes truthful but nondocu*ment*ary—"

"No, no, I know. It felt different, I think, is all that I'm—"

"And the girls can't get *actually* injured, we could be sued. Our in-house lawyer had a long talk with me about all of that, actually. There have to be certain standards in place." She says this like I've made a mistake that needs to be rectified.

"No, of course," I say apologetically. "That makes sense."

We drive in silence for a few minutes. I dart sideways glances at Caroline. I don't want her to think I was criticizing her. I open my mouth to say something that will let her know I'm on her side, but I hear myself ask, "Why do you think B.B. hit Nickey like that?"

Caroline shrugs. "It was a great scene. After you left, the girls have this moment where they talk about how she's so weird at school—it's great character stuff."

"What do you mean, weird at school?"

"Ming has this whole sequence about how B.B. doesn't have any friends, and then Evie is like: *Aren't we her friends?* and Ming is like: Are *we?* It's brutal."

"I guess I thought B.B. had friends," I say.

Caroline sighs like I'm missing the point. "We shoulda got someone to fight Chad," she says after a moment. "That was a missed opportunity."

When I don't reply, she adds, "It would have to come later in the film, of course. We'd really have to build to get there, and then it would need to be about how female empowerment sort of lends the pack courage that they didn't have before. So probably Ming couldn't be on his side. Actually, Ming should probably fight Chad. Maybe we can get them to do that later."

In the dark car, her voice sounds dreamy and thoughtful. Her eyes are large, she is seeing all the possibilities speeding toward us like the highway signs overhead and the headlights of the cars in the opposite lane. I want to ask her if actually we should tell Ming not to be with Chad, if actually we should ask if B.B. is okay at school or at home, if actually it's confusing to combine real pain with fake blood, if Caroline is sure she knows what she's doing—what *we're* doing—if Caroline is certain enough to make up for my uncertainty. But that's the one answer I have. Caroline is certain. More certain than I have ever been about anything. And I'm a sucker for certainty. So I lean back in the shotgun seat, arms folded, and:

"Yeah," I say, matching her tone. "Maybe we can do it later."

*

On Thanksgiving morning, Dylan and Daniel and I go for a hike in Griffith Park. Dylan and Daniel walk close together, their shoulders bumping, although they don't hold hands. The energy between them feels lighter today. I wonder again if Daniel is actually going to leave all this behind on New Year's Day or if it's a fantasy, a late-thirties crisis in the middle of passing.

We rest once we reach the top. The canyon sprawls out below us, its naked length supple and animal. I remember seeing the mountains from Dylan's van for the first time, the night he met me at LAX. I'd felt as if something living were relaxed in sleep. I've been here for nearly six weeks now, but the landscape still fills me with vague awe and unease.

"That's the observatory, down there," Daniel says lazily, and I follow his finger to the round white curves of the Griffith Observatory, the glint of cars. "Has Dylan taken you there yet?"

"No, *Dad*," Dylan says, and Daniel flicks him off. Dylan tips his head back and laughs. There is something about them together when things are good that they lack separately. They have the grace of two acrobats who long ago perfected a routine, who are relieved to find it again with their bodies.

My phone starts vibrating in my back pocket and when I pull it out, I'm surprised to see a number I don't know. I pick up.

"Hello?"

"Hey." Jocelyn's voice. "Is this—uh—is this an okay time?"

"Jocelyn," I say. "Of course." My heart starts hammering and I put on my professional voice. "Do you have Marisa?"

"Oh, I'm—uh—I'm not at the office. Right now. It's Thanksgiving."

"Oh . . . right. Happy Tha—"

Background noise swells up and drowns me out—something clanging, then a faraway siren. The New Yorkness of New York surges, catches my heart. I swallow it down, stepping away from Dylan and Daniel.

"Where are you?"

"Bushwick, I'm at my apartment—uh, hang on a second." Jocelyn muffles the phone with her hand and I hear her yelling, but I can't make out the words. Then she's back with me, sounding breathless and harried. "So, uh, I think the gas main broke? In my apartment building? Because my apartment smells like gas, and the stove won't go on? And the landlord only speaks Russian and he also doesn't like me? I think he doesn't like girls in general, and he probably thinks I should have a husband? Like if I had a husband, he'd talk to my husband, but he won't talk to me? And I don't even have a boyfriend, and whenever I try to turn the stove on it clicks and clicks, and the gas smell—"

"Jocelyn," I say, "turn the stove off! If you have anything lit—a candle or incense or—"

Jocelyn's voice is small. "There's a candle . . ."

"Blow it out!" I can hear her breath *whoosh* as she blows. "Now grab your keys and get the fuck out."

"But what about later?" Jocelyn asks. She sounds close to tears. "What about tonight?"

"Call ConEd," I say. "They'll notify the fire department."

"Oh my god, the fire department?!" Jocelyn sounds panicked. "Why the fire department?"

"They turn off the gas in the whole building until ConEd finds the leak." I can hear her hesitating. "Jocelyn, I don't hear you moving."

A jangle of keys in the background, the sounds of scuffling, and then a heavy door slams. Jocelyn is on the move. "I feel like, I haven't even *showered*," she says, "and this is *horrible*. It's horrible not to have a boyfriend who can talk to your landlord."

I remember that Jocelyn is twenty-two—older than Caroline's girls, but in this moment, she sounds much younger. I find myself speaking to her with the gentle authority I use with them. "It's gonna be okay. The same thing happened in my old building. But don't go far, because the fire department comes really quick, and you'll need to let them in."

"Great," Jocelyn says. "I'll sit in front of my building in my fucking *pajamas* like a *pigeon lady*, because my life *sucks*." She is crying now, briefly. I don't know what to say, but it doesn't seem like I can get off the phone. After a moment Jocelyn asks, grudgingly, "How's L.A.?" She's no longer crying, although her voice is thicker than usual.

"It's okay," I say. Behind me, on the rocks, Dylan and Daniel are still flopped like seals.

"Is it *sunny*? Is it *warm*?"

A hawk circles overhead, catches an updraft, hangs suspended. I squint to make out the architect's model of tiny houses and streets and apartment buildings scattered far below. "It's not that warm," I lie.

"I bet it's way nicer than here," Jocelyn says.

"You should call ConEd," I tell her. "You can call me back, but call them first."

"Okay." A moment and then, "I'm not gonna call you back."

"You can if you want."

A pause, and then Jocelyn says, "Thanks," softer, and hangs up. I sit in the feeling of being Cath: dependable, reliable, informed. I realize that I like Cath. No wonder other people do too.

"Everything okay?" Dylan calls.

"All good," Cath says, and joins them in the sun.

*

We grill in the backyard when the sun goes down. Dylan arranges halved peppers and onions, while Daniel lines up meat patties. The smell of smoke and starter fluid and meat cooking fills the small backyard, evoking some nostalgic childhood that it takes me a moment to realize I never had. Dylan leans over Daniel's shoulder as he grills, arms draped around him, the side of his face against Daniel's neck. He says something low, teasing, about men who grill—and Daniel laughs and shakes his head, embarrassed but pleased. This is the most affectionate they've been in front of me, and there's a sweetness to it that seems to spin out of the lazy sweetness of our day and evening.

Dylan asks how the movie is going, and Daniel asks what movie, so I find myself telling them about Caroline and her girls. I hear myself describing it as "a feminist engagement with the, sort of, *hypermasculine* aggression of *Fight Club*." It feels more honest than talking about #MeToo, since there aren't even any men in the movie.

"*Fight Club*," Daniel says, searching. "With Edward Norton? I thought he was so hot when I was younger."

"I think he's hot now," Dylan says, and waggles his eyebrows. "He

came to the restaurant like a month ago, but he didn't sit in my section."
He's flipping the peppers with his bare hands and he burns a finger,
hisses, sticks it in his mouth.

"Yeah," I say, "but it was a book first. But—the book *or* the movie—
I mean, both are these celebrations of male rage, right? Like, system-
destroying male rage. And what Caroline and I are doing is we're letting
these girls centralize their rage."

"Sounds terrifying," Dylan says around the finger in his mouth.

Daniel nudges him out of the way to flip a patty that's about to burn.
I hear myself say: "It's about seven girls of different races who are trying
to make it in a man's world. Who are subverting a *man's book* for their
coming-of-age story."

"I stand corrected," Dylan says. "Sounds iconic." He lets Daniel
supplant him at the grill and turns to me. "You know, I was in a movie
once too."

"You were?"

Daniel groans. Dylan's grin widens. "I was," he says. "When I was
very young."

"I knew you when you were very young. When the hell were you an
actor?"

"It was right before I met you," Dylan says. "My last year of high
school."

"*Actor*," Daniel repeats dryly. "That's an interesting choice of words."

"Daniel knows this story," Dylan says, turning his grin toward the
grill. But he says it flirtatiously, like it's a shared joke. "I was dating this
chick—"

"She was forty-five," Daniel corrects.

"I was dating this woman—"

"She was forty-five and he was fifteen, for the record."

"I was *eight*een, and I was dating this woman, and she . . . had this
thing about being watched. Like, knowing she was being watched. But
she didn't want a third person in the room, that would have freaked her
out." Dylan shrugs. "And that was back when home videos were still a
thing, so she'd have us tape ourselves."

"Having sex," I clarify. I'm surprised that Dylan is telling this story at all, but it seems like something Daniel has heard before, has even laughed at before.

"Yeah, having sex. But we sucked at the cinematography thing, so at first we'd be mostly out of frame, or like, it would be five minutes of wall and then somebody's leg would be in frame. So it took a while to perfect."

"And it was just for you two?"

"Yeah, and then we'd watch the tapes back—or she would, mostly, and that would be hot too."

"And then," Daniel says gleefully, "she started organizing viewings. Burgers are done, by the way."

"Her friends," Dylan elaborates. "Her book group." He takes a paper plate off the stack, hands it to me. Hands another to Daniel.

"You're kidding." I accept the plate.

"I mean, I wasn't invited to the viewings," Dylan says. "I didn't know it was happening? But I'd be in the supermarket or at CVS or—you know, doing my thing—and these older women would be *noticing* me. Like in a weird way, noticing me. And I couldn't figure it out. I was smoking a lot of pot in those days too, so I also figured maybe I was kind of imagining it? But I wasn't."

"How did you find out?"

Dylan grins, vigorously squirting ketchup and mustard over his burger. "I cut class and went over to her place once—it was senior year, so we'd all stopped going to class? And I let myself in and I could hear these weird sounds from the living room. Moaning, but also like . . . I don't know, cheering occasionally, like people watching sports? And I walked in, and there were seven or eight middle-aged women sitting around the TV watching grainy footage of me plowing Janine. Except we'd fucked up the camera placement again, so it was like—you could see the end of the bed, and the wall, and Janine's feet in the far edge of the frame, and everything was kind of shaking, and then every five thrusts or so, my ass cheek would come into view. And every time my ass popped up, the ladies would cheer."

"It was a very skinny ass," Daniel tells me as he flops a burger onto my plate, then his own. "Less skinny now."

"So," Dylan says, unfazed. "That was my movie debut."

"Let us all give thanks," Daniel says, "that it ended there."

We laugh, and he eases back into his lawn chair. "That's one way to try it out, though. Carnal relations with the opposite sex." He bites into his burger, shaking his head. "If you're going to try it, that's a hell of a story."

I open my mouth, then close it again. Dylan looks intently at his own plate. I wait for him to say that he tried it a bunch more times after that. Or that he wasn't *trying* anything, necessarily. That he was *doing*. He doesn't say anything, and a silence extends in which each of us realizes that we've landed somewhere none of us, for different reasons, wants to be.

After another moment, Daniel moves the conversation back into safer territory: "Tell us about your misspent youth, Cass."

"Well . . ." I pull a beer from the twelve-pack Daniel brought. "I was a loner. Obviously? There was nothing to do in small-town New Hampshire."

Dylan joins the effort to change the energy. "Grizzly bear trapping? Cow tipping?"

"That's the Midwest, asshole. Or a Coen brothers movie."

Daniel smiles. "So, what *did* you do?"

I tilt my head back. "I mean, a lot of drugs. We all did—the kids I knew."

"Like pot?"

"Yeah, and pills. And whatever we could get our hands on." The truth was that I hadn't thought of them as drugs so much as a means of conveyance: how to get out of my head and go somewhere else. I wonder how to tell this story so that it will be funny instead of fucked up—an anecdote about a mischievous kid, and not a story about a teenager whose desire to self-destruct outstripped her imagination for how to do it. And then I think, Fuck it. If it was Tara-Jean Slater, she would just tell the story.

"There was this guy—he was a student at a nearby community

college? And he sold me most of the shit that I took. And then in my senior year of high school, he got cast as Puck—they were doing *Midsummer Night's Dream*. So whenever I called him for drugs he'd be like, 'You have to meet me here, I have rehearsal.' Like, he was really serious about not skipping rehearsal. So after school ended, I'd drive to the community college and slip into the back of the auditorium and wait for them to have a ten-minute break so I could buy whatever. And then eventually I realized that I wasn't going for the drugs. I was going to watch. And I felt all these strange things when I watched. I didn't want to be *on* the stage, but I wanted to sort of—wrap it all around me, like . . . clothes, or a blanket, or . . . I wanted to be covered in it. And I thought I was in love with him? That feeling was so intense, it had to be love, you know? And eventually I realized that it *was* love, but it wasn't with him."

Dylan and Daniel are both leaning in, their eyes fixed on me. Daniel says, very delicately, as if he's afraid I'll stop: "And then you became a playwright."

"Well . . . when I got to college, I auditioned a bit, but I was a terrible actor, and I stage-managed a couple student shows but I'm not very organized—so then, yeah. I started writing. And it felt . . ." I shrug. "So perfect. I don't know. It was the capital-A answer. So I stopped doing drugs and I started doing theatre. With the same kind of intensity." I make the joke before I mean to: "Drugs are better for you in the end."

Dylan and Daniel exchange a loaded look, and it occurs to me that they both know more than I'd like them to. Daniel gets up, diplomatically, and starts clearing dishes away. I wait for him to take an armload inside, and then I say: "So, you googled me."

"Yeah." Dylan winces. "It seemed like I shouldn't ask you questions, so . . ."

He starts to apologize, but I cut him off: "It's bad, isn't it? What's online."

"You haven't looked?"

"Not for a while."

"Yeah, it's pretty bad."

We're quiet. My hands are clammy with the condensation from my beer. I don't know what I'm going to ask until I hear myself: "So do you think I'm . . . super fucked up?"

Dylan grins, to my surprise. "Cass," he says, "obviously."

"Well . . . Do you think I'll ever not be fucked up?"

Dylan hauls himself out of his chair and crosses over to mine. Without asking, he drops down so that our bodies are pressed against each other, thigh to thigh, rib to rib. He smells like lighter fluid and smoke and under that, the ocean pull of sun and salt.

"You know what I like about you?" he asks.

"No," I say, and realize it's true.

"You always just plunge. Whatever it is: theatre—or love—or a gigantic mistake—or L.A. You are all in. One hundred percent, all the time. And yes, okay, it's fucked up sometimes. But also? I would like everybody to live like that more often, because then I would know exactly who they were, and I would trust them." Dylan runs his fingers through my hair, and although I can't see his face, I think he's looking after Daniel when he says, softly, "I would just like everyone to go for broke all the time, no matter what happens."

"No Matter What isn't as fun as it sounds," I tell him.

"No," Dylan says, "but it sure as hell is honest." And there's nothing to say after that, so we sit together in the lawn chair while the grill cools and the night softens, and Daniel doesn't return.

8

The night that my play opened, my parents came in to New York. I could count on one hand the number of times they'd seen my work; they both hated cities, and theatre left them baffled. My parents had never told me to get a real job, but I knew that they thought of writing as a hobby, and that they were patiently waiting for me to become a teacher.

The last time they had seen one of my plays was when I was twenty-five. I and three other writers had rented out the back room of a bar that came with a small square stage. We put on a night of one-acts, for which we were not only the writers but also the designers, publicists, ticket-takers, ushers, and cleanup crew. My parents had sat on punishingly uncomfortable plastic chairs, hands clasped in their laps, as the ten other audience members around them shifted and snored. I don't remember what my play was about now, only that my father fell asleep too, and my mother kept jabbing his thigh with her knuckle to try to wake him up before I noticed. We never talked about it afterward, and I hadn't asked them to come see my work again. Not until now. And even now, in the days leading up to opening, I found myself having recurring nightmares that the theatre was empty except for my parents and Hélène, and as my play inexorably unfurled, all three were dozing.

On opening night, I got to the theatre forty minutes early, poised to have a nervous breakdown. The lobby was already filling up, and Hélène was sitting to the side, long legs sprawled out. When she saw me, she smiled and stood decisively, motioning to me to follow her. Even before I'd reached her, she was already striding toward the doors to the theatre where two ushers stood on either side like stern guards. The house was not yet open. Hélène gave them a nod and we slipped inside.

"Hélène, what are we . . . ?"

Hélène put a finger over her lips and I smiled back, giving myself over to whatever she was doing. In the last two weeks of previews, we had achieved a careful balance. We'd watched the audiences watch the show, discussed and implemented notes. We never talked about Liz aside from her performance, and when Hélène said she was going to give Liz notes, I never argued with them.

From within the theatre, the murmur of the lobby was muffled and distant. Hélène produced a small stick of wood and a lighter, with only a glance over her shoulder—stage management would *not* approve—and held the flame to the end of the stick. Palo Santo, I realized, as the thin, sweet smoke spiraled up and dissipated. Hélène closed her eyes. I felt something go quieter inside me—not calm, exactly; oxygen reaching deeper places in me as I breathed. Hélène was reminding me, without speaking, that this space was ours—remained ours, no matter who came here tonight, audience or critics. That we were connected to a long and ancient lineage of players, that prayers for success were part of this lineage.

Hélène's lips weren't moving, but she was concentrating hard in a way I knew well. I closed my eyes too. I was silently repeating, "Oh God, let this go well," again and again, but it didn't feel like a prayer, because whenever I said, "Oh God," I imagined *The New York Times*. After a time, I opened my eyes, and Hélène opened hers and smiled at me. She crushed the smoking end of the stick on the side of her boot, waved her hands in the air until there was no sign of smoke, and we both slipped back out into the lobby. The crowd had thickened in the short time we were inside the theatre. People were picking up tickets and finishing overpriced drinks and asking each other to hold their bags while they ran to the bathroom.

I fetched my four tickets from the stage manager, and Nico arrived moments later, wearing the powder-blue suit jacket I'd borrowed for the Lansings. My parents were right behind him. My mom was wearing black slacks and a sweater vest, and my dad had on his teaching uniform of khaki trousers and a worn blazer. I remembered those exact costumes from PTA meetings of my childhood. My parents seemed out of place in the crowd and a little awed by it; as I hugged my father hello, my mother pointed to the poster for my play and said, too loudly, "Cassie! It has your name on it!"

I felt immediately embarrassed, and also thrilled at having managed to impress her. "I know," I said, trying for casual, but my mother knew me too well, and her sharp eyes found mine. "It has your *name*," she said again, as if the first time had been for her but the second one was for me. Something lifted in my chest suddenly, a great balloon of feeling. I was so scared that it would translate itself into tears that I ushered them very abruptly into the theatre, telling them it was time to sit down.

As I joined Nico in the back row, I saw Hélène. She was in the same row but at the far end, sitting with a man her age. For a moment I felt an ugly spark of jealousy, and then I shoved it down.

Listen, I told myself. *There will be this play and the next play and the play after that, and we'll keep doing this—this part, the one we can do, where we make something that is unique to the two of us: two separate strands of DNA swapping around, intertangling, creating life.* This hope settled into me like heat, and the audience settled around us, quieting into watchfulness as the houselights dropped low. Nico gave my knee a swift knock with his, a good-luck knock, and as I strained to make out Hélène's jawline in the dark I thought: *If this is all I get, this can be everything.*

*

It's hard to remember how it felt to watch my play. Not because the memory is blurred—on the contrary, it seems to get sharper with time— but because the memory of unguarded joy is so keenly humiliating in the aftermath.

But if I have to tell you one thing, I can tell you that Hélène and I were good together. That the thing we made was a knitting of all of our best parts, all of our sharpest instincts, all of our daring. That we made each other more daring. That it was, to me, beautiful. That it was somewhere I couldn't have gotten by myself. That it was where I most needed to go. That if I could get back there, even knowing everything that followed, even briefly, I still would.

*

The opening-night party was at West Bank. The roar of voices hit me even before I opened the heavy outer door. Inside, bodies were packed into the corridor by the bar, and a step-and-repeat was set up on the opposite side of the room. In the dining area, people moved in and among the tables, a buffet set up at the end with hot plates, pasta, chicken. Nico made a beeline for the buffet and was swallowed by the crowd. I fought my way to the narrowest corner, between the coat closet and the edge of the bar. Marisa materialized to give me a swift hard hug. She told me that the play was "new and raw and a voice from the *future*" but also at the same time "the voice of the now," and that she thought a lot of theatres were going to be very excited about me.

"How was Hélène?" she asked. "Good match?"

"The best," I said with a fervency that might have given me away, but Marisa was already looking over my shoulder toward a stately gentleman in the buffet line. "Oh, I need to talk to him," she said abruptly. "We've been trading calls." And she released me and slid back into the frenzy.

My parents looked out of place in the seething din, huddled close to each other, wincing whenever someone nearby shouted too loudly. I waved to them and we fought our way toward each other. "More of an audience than that one-act, huh," I said when I reached them. I'd meant it as a joke, but the second I said it, I heard in my own voice how much I wanted them to be impressed.

"It's great, Cassie," my father said. "Your mother and I enjoyed it very much."

I didn't want to turn to my mother, but I immediately turned to my mother. My mother didn't say anything; she put her arms around me and then held on, longer than I'd expected her to. I could sense her pride and her relief, like an electrical current traveling from her body to mine. I knew that she had been worried about me, that she had thought I was wasting years in which I could have been establishing a real profession. I felt that now, for the first time, my life here seemed real to her. That she looked at me and saw success. And this feeling was more of a victory than anything she could have said.

My parents left the party soon after that, and in their absence, I scanned the room for Hélène. Part of me had wanted to introduce them to her, and the rest of me had felt that convergence of worlds to be too dangerous. As I turned, my eyes landed on Liz. She was in a green silk gown, her neck and shoulders bare, her blond hair piled up on her head. Her collarbones shone in the light. She looked like one of her own pictures in the magazines where she often appeared. I so rarely thought of Liz as a celebrity—I mostly thought of her as Liz, and three layers underneath that (although I could only admit it when drunk), as "not-Hélène"—that this image of her gave me pause.

Liz was holding a flute of champagne, laughing at something someone was saying. She lifted her eyes to meet mine across the room and a spark passed between us. She lifted her champagne glass in a toast, and I lifted my wineglass back to her. Just then, a woman came up behind her and put an arm around her waist, and I realized with the shock of surprise that she'd brought her wife to the opening. I'd almost forgotten that she had one.

Her wife was older—in her forties, maybe—and she looked very impressive. She was wearing a stylish but shabby blazer with elbow patches, and serious spectacles perched on her patrician nose. Her hair was cut short and sprinkled with salt and pepper. I didn't know exactly what she did, but she was clearly a Literary Lesbian. Had Liz said that she was on a book tour? Maybe I'd made that up from the fact that she was gone so much. There were stacks of heavyweight books all over their apartment—I'd seen them when I was padding barefoot between their bed and the shower. I tried to imagine what they talked about together. Did Liz talk? I wondered if her wife had Liz read her drafts, if Liz lay on their bed in an off-the-shoulder negligee, surrounded by papers, and said things like *But, darling, did you mean to use a metonym?* Suddenly, in my head, Liz had a light French accent. I shook it away, drained my wine, gestured to the bartender for another.

Liz and her wife were moving toward me through the crowd. I glanced down at the bar in case Liz needed me to not see her, but when they got close enough, I heard her calling my name over the din. "Cass! Hey, Cass!"

She introduced me to her wife, all of us shouting. I didn't catch her wife's name. "This is the playwright," Liz yelled, and the wife leaned in to congratulate me: "Happy opening."

"Thank you!" I yelled back. She was much taller than I was, even in her leather loafers.

"I enjoyed your play," she continued. "It's a real deconstruction of desire."

"It is?"

She lifted an eyebrow at me: "Isn't it?"

I hesitated, not sure if this was friendly banter between intellectuals or if she was saying: *It has come to my attention that you have fucked my wife on multiple occasions.*

I looked to Liz for guidance, but Liz was looking at a reflection of herself in the mirror over the bar. She seemed unconcerned with us both. She adjusted a free curl of hair—tugged it looser, as if a very small and specific wind had swept into the bar.

"Desire both homosexual and homosocial," the wife hastened to clarify. "You've used a facile form, of course—absurdism often feels flippant to me, personally—but it's clearly intentional. Your engagement, I mean, with the form."

Was she calling me lowbrow? I didn't know what she was saying about the play, and I couldn't decipher what she was saying about me and Liz under that. It was giving me a headache—that and all the yelling. Even more people had arrived, and now, every time someone new came in the door, the people around us would push into us. Liz was leaning over the bar flagging down a gin and tonic, and when the crowd backed into her, she would ram the nearest offender with her ass cheek, swiftly and vengefully. Then the offender would ricochet off her and collide with whoever was behind *them*, who then absorbed the impact and shuffled and muttered, "Sorry." The whole bar was full of people shuffling and muttering *Sorry*, and the wife had somehow fixed me with a quizzical and penetrating stare, as if we were in a place where answers were possible.

I gestured to the elbow patches of her jacket. "Those are so great," I said. "Did you do them yourself?"

Liz returned to us at that moment, clutching her G & T, and moved us into safer territory: "Baby, Cass won a big award with this play. It's so exciting to see somebody's career launch like this."

"Yes, very exciting," said the wife. "Congratulations."

"You too," I said automatically, and then it was awkward. "I mean. Liz is amazing in the play. We've been so lucky to have her."

"It's been a great opportunity for her to do something other than TV," said the wife.

"TV has gotten much smarter, honey," Liz said quietly to her wife. "Maybe if you watched it, you'd enjoy it."

"I'm sure that's the case," the wife said in a voice that was sure of the opposite.

A look of pure hurt crossed Liz's face and then smoothed over quickly. It made her look like a kid: Liz in grade school briefly staring out at us from underneath the hair and the collarbones and the career. I felt like I'd just seen Liz more purely and truly than either the Liz in my bed or the Liz in my play.

I was suddenly depressed for her. I imagined all her red carpets, her Emmys, her photoshoots, and her wife's voice in her head the whole time, saying dryly: *I'm sure that's the case.* I gave them both a polite smile and made a muffled excuse about saying hello to somebody somewhere. I pushed off into the crowd, letting it carry me. An assortment of shoulders and hips and elbows bore me along, and I let myself go beautifully limp in the middle of it. I was subject to the room, without desire, without destination. I was a cell in the middle of a frenetic and vibrating body of cells. I had cell mind, which is to say, I was blank. Anything could be.

And it was from that place, receptive and quiescent, that I felt a shift: one tide going out and another coming in. A hush entered the room like a new wind, living underneath the chatter of conversation. People were unobtrusively glancing at their phones while their conversations forged onward absentmindedly without them. At first I couldn't understand it. And then I realized: The review was out.

An engine kicked on inside me. I motored through the tangle of shoulders and arms toward the women's restroom. A waiter passed me with a tray, which I dodged by centimeters. Once inside, I slipped into a stall and locked the door. My breathing filled the sudden silence. The stall was like a small room, the walls and door going all the way to the ground, the floor tiled in clean white. The quiet was astounding after so much noise. I took out my phone, brought up the review, and read the whole thing.

It was dismissive and cool and eviscerating. It questioned the right of the play to exist, and beyond that, my right to have made it. It was bewildered by the disparity between the promise I had exhibited and the failure I'd delivered. Where was my treatise on coming of age, or female sexual awakening? Where was the "fresh and uncompromising" voice that everyone had been promised? This was weird. It was ridiculous. It was European, and not in a good way. How had anyone consented to produce it? It was a travesty that a TV star such as Liz had deigned to do theatre for the first time and been cast in something like this. Why wasn't she playing Ophelia at the Public? Frankly, the whole thing was more than disappointing—it was offensive. There were serious people who had serious things to say. I, clearly, was not among them.

After I finished reading, I sat on the bathroom floor for a long time. It took time to catch up to what I'd read, and then to realize that it applied to me, to my play. That everyone outside was currently reading it and knowing that it applied to me and my play. There was a surprising chasm between the world I had been in before the review came out and the world that I was in now. From the previous side of this chasm, I had projected into the future. I had seen the opening-night party, the celebration, the triumphant hug between myself and Hélène. I had seen the moment in which I paid for a cab, profligate with victory, and went home and slept the sleep of the righteous. I had foreseen the moment in which I awoke to congratulatory emails and texts and offers for more productions, opportunities to go to Hélène and say: *Let's do it again.* To say, underneath that: *I have something to offer you.*

A great flashflood had appeared from nowhere and washed it all away. The bridge between where I was and where I could see myself being was gone. I sat on the bathroom floor, stunned. Nobody had told me what to do if this happened. Nobody had told me that this *could* happen. Nobody had told me what comes next.

*

When Caroline and I arrive in the grand and somewhat forbidding lobby of her agency, my immediate impulse is to take a picture and email it to Marisa. I manage to refrain as Caroline strolls casually over to the giant reception desk. "We're here for Chip," she tells the girl behind the desk. She applies a thin layer of lip balm while the girl clicks away on her computer. She doesn't offer her name but waits until the girl finds it—"Caroline Biel?"—and then she says, "Uh . . . yeah," like she thought it was obvious.

Briefly, I imagine expecting people to know my name without my having to say it. I imagine entering lobbies the way she entered this one, and when the girl tells us to take a seat and asks if she can get us anything, I imagine—for a split second—saying "Sparkling water for me" the way Caroline says it, without feeling the need for a thank-you.

We wait for a few minutes, and then another girl, this one with bangs, comes to take us up in the elevator. Caroline doesn't seem to notice her, and I try to emulate Caroline. The girl asks us how we are and how our days are going, and I am opening my mouth to say "Okay, how about you?" and then I notice Caroline silently but expressively reapplying her lip balm. I'm really starting to wish I'd brought lip balm with me. Instead, I close my mouth, and the elevator is filled with an uncomfortable silence as her question hangs in the air instead of dissipating. I imagine the girl hating us. I imagine her thinking, *These bitches are so full of themselves*. I imagine her at the bar, her equally cute roommate asks how work was, she says: *These two assholes came in, thought they were too good to talk to me. One of them clearly didn't even have an agent.* She says: *Total loser vibe and she couldn't even say hello in the elevator?*

"I'm fine, thank you!" I yelp into the silence as the elevator reaches our floor. "How are you?"

Caroline jumps, and the girl gives me an odd look.

"I'm good, thank you," she says politely, and leads us out onto a busy floor of desks and cubicles, giant glass-walled offices to our left. Everything is hung with exquisite and strange pieces of art.

Chip is in the giant office at the end of the hall. When Caroline barges in, he's finishing up a phone call. "Oh my god," he's saying, rolling his eyes. "It's just Brad Pitt, why are you scared of him?" I'm sure we're not supposed to be hearing this, but Caroline flops down on the couch like it's her living room, and Chip grins at her and does the universal *I'm-wrapping-this-up* gesture. He's in his midforties, and I notice that his teeth and hair are the same reflective bleach color. The assistant asks us if she can get us anything else. Caroline ignores the question. The assistant removes herself with an instantaneous assiduity that speaks of practice.

"Okay, okay," Chip says, and then says *Okay* many more times. His tone goes from "I hear you" to "I agree with you" to "I don't agree with you," to "There is no way you're gonna win this one," and his last *Okay* is a nail in the coffin: *You're dead to me.* Then he hangs up and fixes us with a keen, direct gaze.

"Okay!" he says.

"Hiii, Chip." Caroline stands languorously, phone in hand. He gets up from behind the desk and comes over, and they hug and cheek-kiss. I stand awkwardly, and Caroline says, "Chip, this is Cath."

"Nice to meet you." Chip's handshake is very firm. Caroline doesn't offer any distinguishing details, like what I do or who I am, but he doesn't seem to need them. My being with her is good enough. He asks if he can have anybody get us anything, and then he sits in the armchair across from the couch and says, "Well, Caroline, looks like we've got ourselves some financing."

"Oh good," says Caroline. "So, it's done?"

Chip's eyes flick over to me, including me in the conversation. It feels so good to be included. "I talked to the Wylies again this morning. They said what you're doing is too timely to pass up—really current, really thrilled to participate."

"Oh good," Caroline says again, remarkably cool for what seems like such a large victory.

The rest of the meeting happens around me. I keep my face engaged and think my thoughts across the front of my face as visibly as possible, so that Chip will think: *Wow, Caroline's collaborator is so intelligent. She's quiet, because she has depth, but she's certainly going to have a lot to offer Caroline later, as Caroline relies on her to help process information and make artistic decisions.* It feels good to be in this office, on this couch, in a building that has many, many floors of paintings and leather couches and expensive bottles of bourbon peeking out from shelves, endless possibility and accumulated power. It takes a certain kind of person to sit on this couch and drink this sparkling water, to seem like all of this is familiar enough that I'm not overawed, but new enough that I'm alive with enthusiasm. Being here with Caroline makes me that person.

I come back to the conversation as Chip says, "And that's another thing. The sexual awakening aspect."

"Uh-huh," Caroline is saying. I realize that she's taking notes on her phone.

"The Wylies feel like, you know, it should have more of that kind of thing. The girls experience sexual awakening. Etcetera. Boys or what have you. The gay one—maybe she doesn't know that she's gay. You know? Maybe she's like, trying to figure it out, and the end of the movie is: She figures it out. Through fighting! Like a real—a real triumph, like a GLAAD moment, you know? That stuff is really hot right now. For the markets you're thinking—millennial, whatever. You could really lean into that."

"Cath is gay," Caroline says.

Now they're both looking at me, Chip with interest. "Is that right," he says.

"Oh . . . uh—I mean, I'm queer?" I clear my throat, because my voice sounds funny. "I'm not exclusively—"

"Yeah, this is good," Chip says. "Is Cath in this already? I forget."

"She's gonna be," Caroline says. "We were talking about that last week, actually, so—"

"Maybe there's a scene where she and the gay kid are talking, and the gay kid is like: 'I'm scared to be gay.' Her parents are like Christians or something. And Cath is like: 'It's okay.' And she comes out."

"B.B. already—" I begin, but Caroline cuts me off: "It's a *movie*, Cath, B.B. is a *character*."

Chip is still on his path. "Because I can see this whole thing in the marketing, you know, where you ladies talk about how the movie paralleled B.B.'s life and how the advice she received from Cath really . . . *set her free*. You know? That plays."

"That plays," Caroline repeats. She gives me a bright smile like: *I told you*.

"Ah, what else." Chip contemplates the window briefly. The distant outlines of palm trees are hazy this afternoon, an omnipresent backdrop. I think about being on camera, explaining to B.B. that it's okay to be gay. I think about her laughing in my face. Then I think about winning a GLAAD award, and suddenly I'm less concerned about B.B. laughing at me.

Chip is talking again: "Emotional—grit, you know? Los Angeles. The homeless. What have you. Prostitution. One of your girls, she's a cam girl. Saw something about it on CNN. These girls, they take off their clothes in front of their web cams. But more than that—not *that*, but think about—sex. The industry. Grit. Coming-of-age."

A moment, in which I think he's done listing things. Then he adds: "Men. Threat. What's the danger. Me Too, you know? Me Too."

"Me Too," Caroline echoes, her fingers moving at lightning speed.

"Like, universal themes, but Me Too," Chip says, scratching his jaw. "Like, a balance. But for everybody." A long pause. Into the silence he says, explosively: "Lena Dunham." A moment, we wait. He doesn't follow up.

"Great," Caroline says, unfazed. "Thank you, Chip."

"Great themes, big themes, hard themes," Chip says, seeing us to the door, and I think he's quoting something and it's only when I reach the elevator that I realize that's just the way he says goodbye.

*

After the shoot at Chad's, Caroline and I begin drawing up all the matches. If the girls miss being able to choose their own, they don't say anything. We sit in her office, door closed, and we discuss who has been harboring resentment against whom, who spilled coffee or ice cream on whose borrowed jeans, who isn't over it yet. It soon becomes clear that Caroline is interested less in small grudges that burn themselves out than in finding which girls are diametrically opposed to each other.

"Point of view," Caroline says, when I ask her what she means. "On the world. For example, Mona is forgiving, but B.B. is not. In a match between them, I don't know who will win, but I know that Mona will make mistakes because she doesn't remember what happened last time, and B.B. will make mistakes because she's still angry about last time. For that reason, I'd rather watch Mona fight Evie."

"How come?"

"They're both forgiving—it's like watching two goldfish go at it. They have no access to the past."

"But why is that more interesting?"

"Their emotions are always extra fresh," Caroline says, as if we're talking about produce.

We also start watching the footage with the girls at night, every night, gathered in the living room. They ebb and flow—sometimes it's all of them, sometimes somebody has a date, sometimes somebody's parent laid down the law and someone has to get home—but there's always a pulsing life force in Caroline's space, quieting only when the footage comes on.

Caroline's eye is unerring, and what it catches is hypnotic and delicate. In the midst of fights that are growing increasingly elaborate, supplemented by blocking and choreography and stage blood, Caroline unearths honest detail. The camera finds B.B.'s tight jaw, the little muscle jumping in it as it clenches-unclenches, the only signal that she's about to hurl herself at her opponent. It stays on Ming's balled fists, wrapped in electrical tape (lately, she likes the look) as they one-two, one-two in and out of frame, nothing like the loosely cupped fists that socked Chad on the shoulder with helpless flirtation. It finds Mona on the ground and stays with her, almost comforting, lingering on her purpling shoulder.

The camera finds the girls when they aren't fighting as well, sitting on the sidelines with their faces turned toward the action like flowers toward sunlight. Ming could as easily be waiting in the lobby of a doctor or a dentist. She is casual, easy, she watches the fight and checks her fingernails for chipped polish, and sometimes a dog barks or a car door slams and she turns her head with an unfeigned curiosity that tells you all of this has a similar weight for her: a fist in the face or a dog being walked. B.B. bounces on her toes the whole time—strides back and forth, psyching herself up. The camera finds her one day and stays on her for whole minutes while the fight rages in and out of frame, girls punching and hissing, and B.B. flinching and bouncing.

The camera tells me quietly, intimately, that out of all the girls only B.B. is afraid of the violence. But something in her is called toward it at the same time and to the same degree. I don't know if B.B. sees this when she watches that footage; she gets quiet, she stares at herself with wide eyes, like she's having a vision of some kind. Maybe she is seeing who she *could* be rather than who she *is*, because afterward she starts stealing Ming's trick of wrapping her fists with electrical tape, and whenever the camera comes her way, she raises her fists and shakes them, still bouncing.

These days, watching Caroline work is like watching a very fine laser burning its way through everything in its path. She arranges the world to suit her will, sometimes with an effortlessness that seems magical, other times with a sheer Herculean labor that is equally impressive. When Caroline tells me what she wants to see and I tell the assistants what to do—move that chair to the left, scatter cigarette butts over the piece of the counter within frame—it begins to feel as if I am the conductor of a vast and powerful symphony. Caroline is its composer, but I am its conductor. When people want to know what to do, more and more they look to me. Sometimes, even as Caroline is answering a question, they look to me to see if I am nodding.

Caroline catches me on camera just once, without my being aware of it. When she plays the footage later, all the girls go crazy like they've spotted a celebrity: *Oh my god, that's Cath! You got Cath in there!* And B.B., with quiet awe: "Look at Cath!" None of them are ever this excited to see me in person but seeing me on the screen is mesmerizing for all of us, myself included.

I'm standing against the wall and my eyes are tracking the girls offscreen. You can tell when a punch lands, or when somebody gets her hair pulled, because I flinch as if it's happening to me. I don't look eager, but I also don't look scared. I look like I'm bracing against it, like each punch that lands is a punch I knew was coming. When the fight ends, I look relieved, but at the same time, I look bereft. Like the aftermath of the fight is a more difficult place to be than the fight itself.

"Look at Cath," B.B. says almost involuntarily. And—"Look at Cath," Caroline echoes, but there's something thoughtful in her voice. I can feel her eyes on me, even though I don't lift my own to meet them. I don't look at her for the rest of the night for fear of what else she might unearth in me.

*

This is what a bad review feels like: putting your hand on a burner—the shock of cold that is the precursor to searing.

You keep thinking you should be fine, because there was a moment very recently in which you had been fine, so why aren't you still? It defies your understanding. You have to rethink both what "fine" is and what a "hand" is, and how did your hand even end up on this burner? You find yourself going all the way back to the moment when you even decided you had the right to cook. You should never have thought that anything you could make would be fit for consumption by others. You want to make a promise that you will never again inflict your concoctions on anyone else. At the same time, you want to say: "Who made *you* an authority on any of this?" The critic says: "This is the worst tagine I've ever had," and you are filled with the need to say: "I wasn't trying to make a tagine! I don't even know what a tagine is! This is stir-fry, bitch, I made a stir-fry, you can hate my stir-fry if you are a person who hates my stir-fry, but don't hate my stir-fry because you wanted a tagine." You want to make an appeal, but who do you make it to? Why is this not the sort of thing that the Department of Justice handles? It's so utterly unjust, what is more unjust than this?

When you thought of your play before the review, you were filled with an awe and excitement that didn't feel like pride—it felt like a current of magic wending its way out of that creation and through you. It felt like plugging into something larger than yourself, something old and infinitely powerful. But now when you think about your play, you feel like you transgressed in some way against that larger thing—like you violated a pact not just with your audience, but with an ancient and exacting god.

After the review came out, I learned very quickly that nobody dares to mention your failure to your face, so nobody talks about your play at all. Even asking how you're doing would be too loaded, so your life becomes one in which nobody can ask you anything, for fear that you'll answer. Even Nico moved through the apartment like a timid ghost, but he was in rehearsal for a dance show, so mostly I heard him come home at one or two o'clock in the morning, closing the door quietly in case I was sleeping.

I wasn't sleeping.

In the nights after the review, I was never, it seemed, sleeping.

My relatives, on the other hand, emerged from the woodwork. Beyond the immediate concern from my parents ("Do you want to come home?"), an entire cross section of my family tree, some of whom I hadn't heard from since high school, emailed me links to the review with messages like: *Sorry to read this, cuz.* And, from my aunt: *Oh honey, I'm sure your play is* lovely. There is no humiliation like having your midwestern aunt tell you that she's sure your play is lovely, no matter what *The New York Times* said about it.

Liz was the only person who didn't shy away from talking about the review. In fact, Liz needed to talk about it. Not just because she knew I was depressed, but because now she was secretly afraid that the play might not be good. Sometimes she drifted around my apartment saying, "I don't know how they could write those things, those things aren't *true*," and then she'd glance at me, waiting for me to defend the play, reassert its inherent value.

One night, we were naked in bed when she suggested, with enough off-the-cuff carelessness to make me suspect she'd been practicing on her way over: "I know we're past opening, but I wonder if you could make a few more changes."

"That's what previews are for," I said wearily. "The play is frozen now."

"No, I know," Liz said, "but actually plays get frozen so the actors won't complain, and, you know, I wouldn't complain if there was still work you needed to do. Like on my character, to help her be sort of . . . relevant?"

"*Relevant*," I repeated, stung, and as Liz opened her mouth to walk it back, I heard myself demand, "Like what?"

Liz propped herself up on an elbow. "Well . . . I mean, you're the playwright, but for example, what if my character had this whole trauma in her past? Like, she was at a party—and there was this guy—and he got her drunk, and she woke up—"

I broke in flatly. "You want a monologue about date rape?"

"I mean, it doesn't have to be *rape* exactly, Cass, but the question that haunts her could be like: Was it actually consensual?"

Our bare legs had been entangled; now I pulled mine away and sat up in bed. "It's not that sort of play, Liz, it's not about—and frankly, the fact you think a woman needs a rape monologue to be *relevant* is really fucking upsetting."

Liz moved her arm away from me and sat up on her side of the bed. "Oh my god, women get raped, okay? It's a thing that happens, and maybe it's our job to *talk* about things that are hard to talk about! And I know you like absurdist German plays or whatever, but maybe people aren't connecting to your play because it isn't *topical*. And maybe the audience would *laugh* more—or *cry*, even—if it was *topical*, instead of everybody sitting there silent because nobody knows how to react to things that are fucking weird, frankly!"

In the quiet that followed, Liz understood she'd skated out onto thin ice. She was quiet, her eyes flicking over to my face, then away, then back. After a moment she said, "I'm trying to help you."

"Thank you, Liz, for all the *help*. I really appreciate your *help*."

Liz didn't sleep at my apartment the next few weeks, and I didn't ask her to.

*

I have a dream that B.B. is forty years old. In the dream she comes to me accusingly. She says: "We never had a scene where you told me that it was okay to be gay." She says: "I never had any role models." She says: "How was I supposed to know what it was okay to be, if no one told me?" I am still the age that I am now, and somehow it is even more upsetting to look into B.B.'s haggard adult face and see the disappointment of an older woman. I try to apologize. I try to say that it's hard to know what you should and shouldn't do, and even harder when you want to win a GLAAD award but you don't want to be a hypocrite. B.B. says: "I wanted to win an award too." B.B. says: "We could have gotten an Oscar if you'd just talked about gay things in front of the camera." Even in the dream, I can't help myself: "An Oscar?" I ask, and B.B. leans in, real close, like she's going to tell me a secret from the future—and then, right in my face, she screams.

I wake up in a cold sweat, and by the quality of the air—the delicate ringing, the tenderness of aftermath—I know there has been some loud sound. I lie awake, motionless, and then it happens again: a voice, lifted and sharp. I sit up, rubbing the sleep out of my eyes. My phone says it's three-thirty in the morning.

I get out of bed, moving out into the dark hallway, the cavern of the kitchen. A door flings open upstairs and there's a brief hush. Then Dylan's voice travels clearly down the stairs, waking me completely out of the last shreds of the dream: "Fuck you, I'm not the one going back to Sydney because I'm tired of being a fag." I can tell by Dylan's voice that he's both drunk and furious enough that the adrenaline is balancing the alcohol.

Daniel says, with a real edge in his voice, "Keep your voice down."

"What, are you afraid someone might *hear* us? Are you afraid some-one's gonna hear you have an emotion, Daniel?"

Daniel says, crisply, "We're not doing this right now."

"I sure as fuck am!" Dylan yells. "When do *you* wanna do it? You wanna talk about the *weather* up until you get on a plane!"

"We've been over this." Daniel's voice lifts. "There are more oppor-tunities for me back home careerwise, there's more—"

"Are you gonna tell your parents about me? Yes or no."

Daniel is silent.

"Are you gonna tell them you had a boyfriend for *ten years*? Or are you gonna discuss the motherfucking *weather*? Cuz I hear it's *nice* in Sydney this time of year."

"Dylan, stop." Daniel's voice is rough.

But Dylan continues, implacable now, a Labrador chasing down a bird. "Or are you gonna tell them you were with a girl? Ten years, Cali-fornia girl, couldn't work it out. Is that what you're gonna say?"

"Stop it," Daniel says. He sounds exhausted.

"If you show them pictures, at least make sure she looks like me."

"Dylan!"

Silence, and I think the fight might be over. The hallway is freezing, and the cold radiates up my bare feet. But then Dylan's voice comes again, quieter but sharp—going in for the kill.

"You know what the funny thing is? I might be too gay to meet your family, but at least I can fuck a woman and enjoy it."

Daniel punches him. Even without seeing it, it's a sound that the body recognizes immediately: clean and sudden, fat with weight. Then a shocked silence. I don't know if I should go upstairs or return to my room. I shouldn't have been eavesdropping, but somehow this is the first time that's occurred to me.

Daniel starts to say something, but Dylan is hurtling down the stairs now, fast and hard. He grabs his sneakers and keys, flings the door open, and is gone before I can draw the breath to speak. I don't even know if he saw me.

I ascend the stairs slowly, making enough noise that Daniel can retreat if he wants. The idea of going back to bed and pretending none of this happened feels impossible. Daniel is sitting on the floor, head down. He looks up and sees me but doesn't say anything. The lights in their bedroom are on, spilling fiercely out into the hall, casting strange shadows from molding and doorframe. It's the first time I've been up here.

I sit on the top step, giving Daniel some space.

After a moment he says, flat, "He take the keys?"

"Yeah."

"He shouldn't be driving."

"I didn't hear the van start."

"Oh." He scrubs a hand over his face. "He's drunk."

"Are you?"

Daniel looks up at me. His eyes are bloodshot, but he looks painfully sober. "I hit him." When I don't say anything, he says: "We've never done that before. *I've* never done that." Silence, and then: "If he wanted a fight, he should have hit me back."

"Maybe he didn't want a fight."

"He's been spoiling for a fight for weeks," Daniel says. "But—words, all the *words*, I don't have anything I can say that he wants to hear." After another long moment, Daniel adds, "That's why we were so happy to have you here. The whole thing of it—having a guest so we wouldn't fight all the time, right before it was over." He looks at me then. "I don't mean—it's been lovely to have you. Regardless. But."

"It's okay," I tell him.

Daniel shakes his head, as if to clear it. "I can't believe I hit him."

A moment, in which Tara-Jean Slater's face looms in front of me. Pink, cheeks flushed with shock. Two brilliant spots of pink, and her mouth in a little open bow.

"Sometimes we do things we don't mean to do," I say, before I know I'm going to speak.

"I did mean it," Daniel says. "I just wish I hadn't."

The Tara-Jean Slater specter refuses to dissolve. "I know what that's like too," I tell it.

Daniel takes a breath. "I'm not out. At home."

"Dylan did say that."

"I told him that in the beginning. I never hid that. And at first he was like—you know, *Whatever you need to do*. He was like, *I don't need to meet your parents, we'll make a life here instead* . . . but then . . ." Daniel's voice takes on a real bitterness. "It's the American way, cowboy honesty. Burn it all down, but at least you told the *truth*." He shakes his head. "What good does that do you when it's all burned down?"

"Maybe he feels like you can't be yourself if your family doesn't know that part of you." I keep my voice light, uninflected. Not taking sides, just saying. "Even if you're breaking up, you had ten years together. For your family not to know about that part of you . . ."

"So what?" Daniel turns on me. "We have so many parts of ourselves. Why shouldn't my parents know one and Dylan another? Why should we have only one way to be known?"

I think about Cath. Nobody says Cath's name and laughs. Nobody thinks of her as a punch line. If there was just one self that any of us had, I would still and simply be a failure. Cath is so much more.

I look at Daniel, but his head is in his hands. He has moved from his question into a bottomless despair. But there's merit in the question all the same. I imagine us like tiny isolate diamonds, turning and turning, throwing off light from our innumerable, unknowable facets.

We sit on the landing for a while longer, the house cold around us. When I finally go back downstairs, I leave Daniel hunched there, chin on his knees, waiting for Dylan to come home.

9

In the aftermath of my review, weeks passed. I lived underwater, in a world where information filtered in, piecemeal and gradual, from the outside. Things like laundry and dishes and showering were Herculean tasks. I couldn't concentrate, so I couldn't read. Writing was out of the question.

I didn't see Liz unless I went to the theatre, and I did go. I couldn't help it. Once it got to be about four-thirty or so, I'd leave the apartment and take the A downtown to Fifty-ninth Street, then walk to a bar a few blocks down from the theatre. I tried not to start drinking before five P.M., not because I didn't want to be wasted all the time but because the theatre world—no matter how far you feel from the mothership—is always alive and vibrating with lines of communication. I wanted everybody to go, "Oh, Cass? She's fine!" and not "Cass is falling apart." But once it was five it felt safe to have a few drinks, and each night I'd think that tonight I wouldn't go to the theatre—tonight would be the night I'd stay away. By 6:45 I'd be sweating it. By 6:50 I'd be shaky. By 6:55 I'd be out the door, running the last few blocks, getting to the theatre by 7:05. The ushers knew to let me past them, up the stairs, and into the balcony, where I'd stand at the back and watch the audience and not the show.

At a certain point—crouched in the empty balcony as the curtain rose, drinking vodka from a Poland Spring bottle—I had to admit to myself that Liz had become terrible in this play. The other actors were still executing their parts with the precision of dancers or neurosurgeons; their training left no space for doubt to throw off their craft. But Liz didn't even know what play she was in anymore—her sole point of certainty was that she was in a show that was missing a rape monologue. One night I didn't slip out of the balcony fast enough, and I heard one older woman say to another, "What a strange evening," and her friend replied, "The girl from TV is lovely, but you know what the *Times* said about this play . . ." I made my escape, hood up and head down, in case there was anyone there who knew me.

I did this for two and a half weeks, and then I called Hélène.

She didn't require me to explain anything. I stammered my way through asking if we could get a drink, and when I was done she said, "Come over."

Hélène's apartment was between Avenues A and B, an unobtrusive building of soot-colored brick. The door to the lobby was propped open, so I walked in without buzzing. The building was a walk-up, and as I took the stairs, a cat came streaking down past me and out the open door.

I reached the sixth floor, winded, to find Hélène standing in her open doorway. She was barefoot, smiling at me. "I thought I heard the sound of intense physical labor," she said.

I found myself smiling back at her in a way that felt foreign, as if my face had forgotten how to form that shape. "Hélène."

She gestured to her open door, mocking herself with the formality. "Come in, *s'il vous plaît*."

I followed her inside, toeing off my Chucks in her foyer. Her apartment was small but homey, the rooms narrow and the ceilings high. It felt for all the world like a Parisian treehouse. The walls were lined with bookshelves crammed with books of all shapes and colors; the floor was laid in old honey-colored planks, the windows large and open; small lamps were arranged around the space so that the whole room was bathed in amber light. Everything in the apartment felt soft and gentle and curved, with Hélène cutting through it like a knife. It was not the space I would have imagined her creating for herself, and the contrast of those things reminded me why I loved her, and how I never seemed to know her.

Hélène returned from the open kitchen, two glasses of wine in hand, and gave me one. The wine was a deep, inky red.

"This one is expensive so drink it slowly," Hélène said, and then gave me a wink to let me know she was kidding. I didn't know if the joke was that the wine wasn't expensive, or that it was, but she didn't care how I drank it.

We sat in her living room. I took the threadbare armchair, a blanket thrown over the back as if Hélène had, sometime earlier that day, been napping. Hélène sat on her couch, legs crossed, leaning back. She set her wine precariously on the wooden arm—"No sudden movements"— and lit a hand-rolled cigarette. Pulled the smoke in, held it for a second, then released it, head turned to the side out of politeness. I waited, sipping my wine.

"Well," Hélène said at last. "Welcome to the other side."

I was filled with relief that she'd speak of this so openly. That she knew how to name it. "I hate it," I said, because it was the only thing I could think of to say.

Hélène laughed. "Right," she said. "It's terrible. I suppose no one told you not to read the review? Did I not tell you that? Shame on me."

"It wouldn't have helped not to read it, though," I said. "Then everyone would have been treating me like—this—and I wouldn't have known why."

"Oh yes. I know that state of affairs. The well-intentioned silence . . . that becomes a sort of devouring, implacable silence. That goes on until such time as you're completely cut off from any sort of human community whatsoever." Hélène took another drag.

"When does it stop?"

"Oh, not until the next truly godawful review comes out. The second the axe comes down on another neck, they'll forget all about yours."

We were quiet for a moment. Out in the street the sharp honk of a taxi, then voices raised, a brief burst of laughter. "What do I do?" I asked.

"Do? There's nothing to do."

"Liz wants me to change the script."

Hélène lifted an eyebrow. "Liz has the intellectual acuity of a melted crayon."

"She thinks if I rewrite—"

"To what end? The play is open, the review is the review. And either you stand behind the work or you don't."

"Will I work again?"

Hélène gave me a measuring look, and after a moment she said, "Yes, of course."

"But?"

"But it will take more time for you now than if you'd gotten a good review." Hélène's voice is kind but direct. "You were marked as a risk, and theatres, when they program new plays, don't welcome a risk. But so what? It's a long game, it goes beyond one review."

"*When* will I work, though?"

"Do I look like a fortune teller?" Hélène blew smoke at me. "What does your agent say?"

"I haven't seen her since we opened."

Hélène sighed. "Make the next play," she said.

"But what about this one?"

"Make the next one."

"But can't we *fight* . . . ? Like if I wrote a—piece, an editorial, or—"

Hélène cut me off. "What are you fighting?"

"The *Times* killed my play. Have you been back? The audiences are half the size they were, the house is half-empty. If I could talk about the play, *explain*—"

"What are you explaining? A man has an opinion, he happens to be a powerful man and so his opinion carries economic weight. But it is, after all, his opinion." Hélène shrugged. "This problem is so deeply embedded that, in American theatre, the problem and the institution are the same thing. If you did not know this before, what kind of marriage you're getting into, now you do."

I wanted to offer a coolly removed intellectual opinion about the state of affairs in American theatre, but I had no cool remove. I couldn't say anything that didn't come from a place of lying awake all night, fighting with Liz, avoiding Nico, hating myself. So I said: "I don't know what to do."

"Write the next thing," Hélène repeated, kindly but firmly. "And if you can't do that yet, then see your friends' plays. Try to remember that you chose this form, and that you love it."

"Liz hates our play." I didn't know I was going to say that until it came out of my mouth. Hélène looked neither surprised nor upset, and her tone didn't change when she added a final suggestion to her to-do list: "Stop sleeping with that ridiculous girl."

I didn't stay much longer after that, and when Hélène walked me out to the hallway, she gave me a hug. It was the first time we'd ever hugged.

"This might feel like a death," Hélène said quietly, into the hug. "But remember that it's just theatre. No one died."

As I walked north up Avenue A, I thought that—of all the things that Hélène had said—that one helped the least.

*

The scandal happened a day after my play limped to a close, and the night of Tara-Jean Slater's opening.

It was the play for which she had won her Lansing Award, and the Lansing Foundation reached out to all of us to arrange tickets—*Support your fellow Fellows*, the email read. I thought about Hélène's advice and balanced it against how much I wanted to crawl inside the earth and be swallowed by it, and then I wrote back and said that I would be delighted to attend.

Then I asked Nico if he'd be my plus-one.

Nico gave me a worried look. "Are you sure you wanna do this?" he asked.

"Hélène thinks it's a good idea. Get out, see plays. Etcetera."

Nico shrugged. "Open bar," he said philosophically. "I'm in."

The small crowd milling in the lobby was a mix of donors in their opening-night regalia, theatre staff, artistic leaders, actors who weren't in the play but wanted you to know they were in *a* play, Juilliard playwrights, Yale playwrights, playwrights who held extreme distaste for institutional reputations, and everybody's agents and girlfriends and boyfriends. The agents were standing with drinks in hand, scanning the lobby for the people they should be poaching, and the girlfriends and boyfriends were standing with drinks in hand, scanning the lobby for the people they'd rather be fucking. In these moments, all that comes to mind are David Attenborough documentaries about the animal kingdom.

Nico and I were standing in a corner, watching people introduce themselves to each other, when Marisa blew in through the doors, tall and glamorous, a gold jacket thrown over her black silk jumpsuit. "Oh, that's my agent," I said, to be saying that sentence out loud to someone, even if it was only Nico. I was about to call out to her when I heard a small voice behind me — "Marisa!" — and a vision in leather overalls drifted past me and into Marisa's open embrace.

And that was Tara-Jean Slater.

Porcelain skin. That hair the color of burnt copper, pulled into her two long and coolly unironic pigtails. A delicately crisp white blouse blossomed from beneath her overalls. Tiny scuffed wing tips. Marisa released her from the hug and she handed Marisa a tiny drink ticket, and then I remembered that Marisa was Tara-Jean's agent too.

My face looked funny, and Nico asked, "Are you gonna puke? You look like you might puke," and I said, "No, I'm having a great time, thank you." I stationed us behind a column so that we could observe Tara-Jean Slater and Marisa from a slight distance. I remembered being nauseous with anxiety on my opening, but Tara-Jean didn't look nauseous at all. She wasn't trying to hide in the back either. She seemed perfectly comfortable slouching in the center of the lobby as theatre-goers arrived. Marisa took advantage of this to start flagging down artistic directors and literary managers, introducing them to Tara-Jean Slater as they went to collect their tickets at the box office.

"She doesn't look like a success," I said to Nico grimly. "Does she look like a success to you?"

"I mean . . ." Nico was baffled by the question. Then he rallied. "Not at all," he said gamely.

We kept studying her from behind the pillar. Tara-Jean Slater sipped at her plastic cup of wine, and Marisa looked at her with adoration. Marisa wasn't even scanning the room for people to poach. This was the most insulting thing of all. Marisa definitely scanned the room when she was with me. I'd seen her do it and had simultaneously forgiven her, because it would have been like getting angry at a bird for flying, or a dolphin for emitting bizarre, high-pitched noises. But watching Marisa maintain her attentive focus on Tara-Jean Slater, who was now scratching her scalp with sharp little jerks of her hand, examining beneath her fingernails, then turning a vague, moonlike smile toward the artistic director to whom Marisa was introducing her—*This is my client, Tara-Jean Slater.* I could read Marisa's lips from across the room. *She's about to graduate from Yale.* Watching Marisa reveal herself to be capable of focused attention was a dagger to the heart.

Pleased to meet you, Tara-Jean Slater yawned. She didn't look pleased. She looked bored. She was scratching her scalp again. I glanced at the artistic director to see if he thought that Tara-Jean Slater might have head lice. The artistic director looked mildly enthralled. *She's a visionary,* Marisa was saying, and Tara-Jean Slater remained mysteriously silent. *Working on a brand-new play,* Marisa was saying. *In which she plays herself.*

Tara-Jean Slater had dead eyes which were also the color of pennies.

She plays herself?

Yes, it's about familial trauma, it's a commission for Playwrights Horizons, very exciting.

That sounds fascinating, the artistic director was saying. Older man, straight, his eyes kept going to the open throat of Tara-Jean Slater's white blouse, to the place where the tops of Tara-Jean Slater's pale tits were showing. *I'm very glad to be here tonight.*

We're so thrilled to have you, said Marisa as Tara-Jean Slater's fingernails *scritch-scritched* under the gathering of her left pigtail. And

Tara-Jean Slater smiled with vague benevolence at the room, at the man, at her fingernails, as if she wasn't sure who it all belonged to but she knew she had a place there.

By the time the curtain dropped on Tara-Jean Slater's play, there was a pit in my stomach that I kept falling through. Nico was asleep next to me, and I kicked him gently but hard enough to wake him up, since the applause wasn't doing it. Nico jerked awake: "What did I miss?"

"The play's over."

Nico ran a hand through his hair, cleared his throat. "Did the chick get the abortion?"

"She did it herself, with a coat hanger."

"Oh."

"And she bled out. And her boyfriend came home while she was bleeding out, and she sucked his dick, and he gave a monologue about masculinity."

"Oh, whoa."

"And how his dad abused him, and epigenetics, which is how trauma gets stored in your *cells*, apparently. And then the girl died, and the boyfriend made scrambled eggs. On the stove. Like, he actually scrambled actual eggs."

"I thought the theatre smelled like breakfast," Nico said, pleased with himself. As the applause died down, he added, "Thanks for the replay, now I'm ready to congratulate people." A moment, as he scanned the line of actors filing offstage. "Wait, which one gave the epigenetics monologue?"

"Tyler. With the beard."

"Cool, I'm gonna tell him his monologue made me cry."

"No you're not."

"I one hundred percent am. Is he single?"

"He's straight."

Nico sighed and fished out his iPhone, checking his texts. I turned around in my seat, craning my neck until I caught sight of Tara-Jean Slater a few rows back. She caught me staring at her and gave me that blank, dead-eyed stare, no facial expression whatsoever. Marisa, who was enthusiastically congratulating her, followed her flat gaze to me. Her face shuttered for a second, like she was trying to remember who I was, and then cleared as she remembered. She raised a hand in a little wave and made a facial expression that was 60 percent *Oh my god, what a great surprise to see you here!* and 40 percent *Wasn't this play the most amazing exploration of female trauma–slash–sexual awakening that you've ever seen?* and I made an expression with my face like *I know, right??* on both counts.

We all filed out of the theatre into the lobby and then across the street to the fancy bar where the opening-night party was. It had rained while we were inside, and the air smelled rich and damp. "So meaningful," somebody was saying to my left. "Absolutely incendiary, you know?"

"The female Sam Shepard," someone else replied sagely.

"David Mamet," the first somebody said. "But like . . . a girl!"—and then they were lost behind us.

"Are we really going to this party?" Nico asked. But I'd glimpsed Tara-Jean Slater and Marisa half a block ahead of us, turning to enter the bar. Light from the open door glanced off the luminous cap of Tara-Jean Slater's hair. I couldn't go home now. It would have felt like withdrawing from the battlefield.

"We're really going," I said grimly, speeding up my pace.

"But you're miserable," Nico said. "You're gonna hate it."

"No I won't," I said, jaw muscles locked. "I'm great."

I ended up standing on the outside of a semicircle of theatregoers forming an audience for Tara-Jean Slater. People congratulated her, and she said "Thaaank you" in exactly the same uninflected tone every time. Nobody seemed to know what to say about the blow job / abortion scene. Someone told her that it was "aggressive," and she stared at him unblinkingly until he added, "In a good way." Marisa was doing a lap of the room, shaking hands and agreeing to go out for drinks with various people from various institutions. Every once in a while, as she talked, she gestured toward Tara-Jean Slater. I tried to tell myself that she was gesturing toward Tara-Jean Slater *and* me, that we were standing near each other so of course Marisa was saying, "I represent both of them, that's

Cass right there." I stood closer to Tara-Jean Slater so that it would be easier to see me when looking at her. I knew about sight lines—I'd watched Hélène worry about them for six weeks.

". . . sort of an *arrhythmic* hand job," Tara-Jean Slater was saying in her tiny dead voice. "Just watching my little ten-year-old fist go up and down." She studied all of us, glancing around the half circle, landing on me last. "His dick looked like a naked mole rat," she said, but not directly to me. I realized that she was talking about her uncle and her Playwrights Horizons commission.

"What's a naked mole rat?" someone asked.

Tara-Jean Slater assassinated him with a flat stare. "Google it," she said.

Carter Maxwell came over, flushed with the benefits of an open bar, and Tara-Jean Slater sized him up with interest—his suit, his disheveled hair, his air of bemused success.

"Hi," Tara-Jean Slater said. "I'm Tara-Jean Slater."

"I know," Carter said. "We were at the Lansings together. Congrats and happy opening, your play is really . . . something. It's really something."

Tara-Jean Slater smiled. It was the first time I'd seen her smile all night. "Thanks," she said.

Carter noticed me then and gave me a nod. "Hey, Cass." He was suddenly awkward, and I knew the thoughts racing through his head. Should he say something about my play? Should he say something about my also having received the Lansing? Should he acknowledge the Lansing but not my play? But the Lansing was *for* my play, so if he mentioned the Lansing, he'd either have to pretend he hadn't read the review (he'd read the review), or he'd have to acknowledge the review but then say, "I liked it anyway." But *did* he like it anyway?

Into the weighted silence Tara-Jean Slater said to him, in a voice that shouldn't have carried so clearly for being so small: "I read your Lansing play, and it made my dick hard."

Carter's attention whipped back to her. He looked astonished, and then interested. "Thanks," he said.

"All the stuff about masculinity," said Tara-Jean Slater. "Potent. Very potent."

"Thanks," Carter said again, in a way that was completely different from the way he'd said "thanks" seven seconds earlier.

I looked for Nico. He was by the open bar, chatting to Tyler with the Beard. I looked for Marisa. She was talking to the artistic director of Lincoln Center and gesturing to Tara-Jean Slater. I waved at her so that the artistic director of Lincoln Center would say, "Who's that waving at you?" and Marisa could say, "Oh that's my other client Cass, who is also very talented and should be produced at Lincoln Center." The artistic director of Lincoln Center didn't seem to care that I was waving, and Marisa kept her gaze studiously trained away from me.

I looked back at Tara-Jean Slater. I'd never seen skin so flawless or wrists so tiny. "—right on my taint," she was saying to Carter, who looked enthralled. "And that's how I found out where my taint was. It's in my next play." I felt certain that Tara-Jean Slater's taint was as tiny and well formed and flawless as the rest of her. Like a doll's taint, if dolls had taints.

I realized that I hated Tara-Jean Slater.

I realized that I wanted her dead. That if some hit man walked up to me right now, some total stranger who happened to be a Ukrainian hit man or maybe an Irish assassin—if that person approached me and said, in his accent that was either Ukrainian or Irish, "I'll kill her for you, just say the word," I would say: "Do it." I would say, "Can you do it in the next five to sixty seconds?" I would say: "Money is no object, I'll take out a loan."

What was more, I didn't like myself very much either. I wasn't sure when that transformation had occurred, but I now knew it to be true. And if that Irish Ukrainian hitman had been offered a sum to take me out as well, if he were to say, "By the way, you're next on the list, missy," I wouldn't cry or run away. I would look him in the eyes and say what I said about Tara-Jean Slater: "Do it."

I had another several drinks. Time passed, and Tara-Jean Slater talked to Carter, and Marisa came over to whisk Tara-Jean Slater away to meet the artistic director of Lincoln Center—"I'm so glad you're having fun!" Marisa said to me cheerfully as she passed—and Nico came over to say "Yeah, he's definitely straight" with more disappointment than the situation warranted.

"I told you so," I said, unable to find space for sympathy inside me, because my hatred for Tara-Jean Slater was taking up all the space there was and had ever been.

Nico glanced at me for a few beats too long and then gestured toward the empty glass in my hand. "Time to go home?" he suggested.

"Nope," I said grimly.

"Are you sure?"

"I'm not done yet, Nico."

He shrugged, and we shoved our way through the crowd toward the bar. Marisa had vanished, and Tara-Jean Slater was holding court with a new knot of playwrights. As we approached, she was saying: "—wish they'd stop commissioning me. I mean, I *appreciate* it, but after about the tenth commission it's like, How can I write this many plays? So I told Marisa we should start turning them down. I was like, Where's the Geffen? It sounds far away, let's turn it down." Tara-Jean Slater shrugged. "But we didn't turn it down."

"I've been trying to get a Geffen commission for three years," Carter said easily. He didn't mind admitting defeat to Tara-Jean Slater, because her pigtails were so pullable and because she knew where her taint was. Carter would have admitted anything to Tara-Jean Slater right then.

"You can have mine," Tara-Jean Slater said, and made a half-smile, half-frown face.

Right then, I felt the energy in the room shift. That tidal thing, that lunar pulling. I knew that shift; I'd been feeling it in my nightmares for weeks. All around me I saw people's phone hands starting to twitch as the unobtrusive review checking began. The conversation continued with blithe determination, but people's eyes skated sideways and downward, pretending to each other that they were checking texts, making sure the babysitter hadn't left and their parents were in good health. But really, they were all reading Tara-Jean Slater's review.

So I took out my phone, and I did it too. Right there in the crowd, without pretending to be doing anything other than what I was doing, I pulled up the review.

"Hey," Nico said, alarmed. "What are you doing?"

"Reading," I said, and I read.

The review was a *New York Times* Critic's Pick. It said that Tara-Jean Slater's play was insightful beyond measure, full of an emotional intensity that was devastatingly truthful. It said that her portrayals of fierce and flawed women were groundbreaking, and that it was impressive that someone so young could depict trauma with such wisdom. It said that Tara-Jean Slater was a rising star with a unique ability to speak for women, and that she was pioneering work that challenged the status quo. It said the abortion blow job was a brilliant and challenging moment that recalled scenes in plays by Mamet and Shepard but through a uniquely female lens.

I put my phone down. Maybe on the bar, or on a stool, or in my wineglass, I don't remember. The crowd shifted as more people pushed their way toward the bar to congratulate Tara-Jean Slater. Across the room, Marisa looked flushed and giddy. She was gesturing toward Tara-Jean Slater with increasing excitement, declaiming, signaling. She could see Tara-Jean Slater's future rolling out like a red carpet, and it looked welcoming. She had seen my future roll out the same way, but we had both stood and watched as it rolled itself back up just as neatly. *This* one wasn't going anywhere. *That* one was the right bet.

I turned my head toward Tara-Jean Slater as well. She was surprisingly close now, a foot away, being pushed toward me by the tide of bodies. I examined her like a scientist with a troubling specimen. I wanted to see for myself if fate had left a mark on her, a stamp or a fingerprint, a birthmark of some kind, if you could see it and go: *Well, that's that. Can't be helped.* If that were the case, I thought woozily, I would accept it. I could let go of my hatred, I could say, *Tara-Jean Slater was born underneath a different star.* But without some direct sign from fate, the crushing injustice of it all would kill me. I had been promised success. And now Tara-Jean Slater was our generation's bravest and most authentic voice on the harsh truths of female sexuality, and Carter was our generation's foremost authority on the quiet suffering of masculinity, and who was I? I was nobody. I was thirty-three. Fate hadn't marked me, but it had whispered in my ear. It had said: *Kidding.* It had said: *Psych.* It had said: *Tara-Jean Slater, you're up next!* So where was her goddamn birthmark?

A dusting of freckles, like someone blew a Pixy Stix of copper glitter across her nose and cheeks. Down the white curve of the back of her neck. Fine light hairs, almost invisible hairs, that stirred under my breath. Tara-Jean Slater turned her head. "Hey," she said in that flat little voice. "You're really close." I was trying to count the teeth inside her mouth. Maybe if I understood the sigils and I knew the numbers, the mathematics for the intricate workings of Tara-Jean Slater's relationship to fate—maybe I could replicate those exact calculations and trick the universe into thinking that I was one of its own.

"Hey," said Tara-Jean Slater, louder, "could you give me some room?" She tried to step back but there was a wall of bodies behind her, she couldn't go anywhere. I studied her. I couldn't be Carter. I had nothing to say about masculinity, I didn't look particularly good in a suit, and I didn't go to weddings in Hyannis Port and I didn't have epic plays in me about men who had returned from the war and were searching for tenderness inside themselves. Carter might have the mark of fate somewhere on his body, but it would never be math that I could replicate. Tara-Jean Slater was my only option. Could I be Tara-Jean Slater?

I was a woman. That was a commonality. I wasn't straight, but I sometimes fucked men. What if I wrote about that? *I will write about men,* I said to the Universe. *I will write a rape monologue. I can do this. Give me a sign. Show me the sign you gave to Tara-Jean Slater, and I will write epic, hyperreal American plays about being raped by tender, masculine men who have returned home from the war. I won't even complain about it, just put your hand on me, Fate, reach down from this ceiling right now and anoint me the way you anointed her.*

"Hey," Tara-Jean Slater said. Her breath smelled like wine and crushed spices. "Uh, what's your name? Could you please back up?" Our faces were so close that her eyes looked like one giant copper eye. There were green flecks inside that copper eye. Was that the mark of fate? There inside her eye? Hidden where everyone would see it without recognizing what it was? I took a step closer. "Hey!" I was trying to read the signs and symbols inside her gaze. I reached out. I was touching her skin, the skin of her neck. I had imagined it would be very smooth and cold, hard to the touch, but it just felt like normal skin. Warm, pliant.

"Oh my god," said Tara-Jean Slater, right into my face. "Can somebody please help me?"

I'm told that was when I put my finger in her eye.

I don't remember that part.

They say that she'll lose the eye patch by April. I'm glad for her. It hasn't hurt her career any, if you want the truth. It was all free publicity for her, and I'm not saying I wasn't at fault—clearly, clearly, I was at fault—but she isn't blind. Although, if she *were* blind in just the one eye, she could still write. She could still read. She could still read the *Vogue* profile piece that came out on her in December where she was declared "astonishing" and a "twenty-one-year-old luminary." She could write a monologue about how getting jabbed in the eye is also a violation of sorts, similar to but different from the one her uncle perpetrated on her, and how her life has come full circle, and how we are in a new dawn of feminism because now women can hurt other women just as badly as men do. These are the things Tara-Jean Slater could write with even one eye. But you know what? She still has two. Because she was chosen by Fate. And Fate will not extensively punish its own. Just a little test here or there to make you interesting. "I'm sorry I let my blunt tool jab you in the eye," Fate is saying to her. "Have this *New York Times* Critic's Pick, have this *Vogue* profile, have this Playwrights Horizons commission." And later Fate will say: "Have this Obie, have this Guggenheim, have this MacArthur, have this Pulitzer."

Fate never reached down from the ceiling that day, never gave me a sign beyond the green flecks in Tara-Jean Slater's retinas or the dusting of freckles across her pale skin. Nico reached out—a number of people reached out—there was a lot of shouting and hands shooting out from the crowd to pull me away from Tara-Jean, to hold both of us upright, because Tara-Jean was reeling and screaming, and I was so unsteady on my feet that I had to be carried. This part is half memory and half what Nico told me later. The only thing I remember with any clarity is this: Of the many, many hands that landed on me that night, the only notice-ably absent pair was that of Fate.

*

In the aftermath of putting my finger in Tara-Jean Slater's eye, every-thing changed for me very quickly. There was video on Instagram and Facebook, and there were photos that media outlets picked up, and apparently a few playwrights live-tweeted the whole thing and some gos-sip blogs republished the Twitter thread, but I never saw any of that. Or the memes. I'm told there is a picture of us taken right at the moment I put my finger in her eyeball—Tara-Jean Slater is already screaming, and there's some girl over my shoulder in the crowd whose face is doing jaw-drop shock, which everybody thought was hilarious. Nobody has told me what my face looks like. Nico told me that there were a variety of different captions. One was *You got something in your eye*, and another was *Eye can't with you!* The only one that made me smile for just a sec-ond was *Oedipus Rex the party*, and then I remembered that the caption was about me, and then I couldn't smile, and then I made Nico stop telling me.

Everything happened like a domino effect after that. Liz told me that we couldn't be in contact. She said it had nothing to do with what-ever happened at the party, which she wasn't there for and she sincerely hoped that people were blowing it out of proportion, because it sounded crazy, truly insane, but anyway it wasn't about that, it was about the fact that she was recommitting to her marriage. Then she told me not to call her in the future, and said that if I ever wanted to offer her a role in any-thing, I should have my agent go through her agent.

Marisa was not about to talk to anybody's agent for me. Marisa was not calling me back after the single conversation we had, which was short and brutal and culminated in Marisa hanging up the phone. Radio silence descended. In general, people became very busy. Nico remained a constant, but a less available one—he had been offered a five-week gig choreographing a show in Berlin. Nico is nothing if not loyal, and before he accepted it, he asked if I'd be okay alone. I said "Of course," because I could smell the relief on him at the thought that he'd get a break from all this. From me. He deserved a break. He packed a bag and left, and the apartment lapsed into a deep-space hush, a vacuum so immense it defied all life.

You would think the bad review of my play prepared me for the bad review of my life, but it didn't. It is one thing to think that everyone is talking about what a failure your play is. It is another thing to know, definitively, that you have become a punch line that eclipses even your play. You are never prepared for the things you fear, and that's why you fear them.

*

I knew that Dylan had a large house in Silver Lake. I knew that, even though we'd drifted over the years, he would welcome me without questions. I knew that he didn't work in theatre, and neither did Daniel, and so the chance that they were following my disgrace was less likely than with any other friends I might still have.

But that is not the real reason I went to L.A.

This is how I decided on L.A.: I was alone in my apartment; it was mid-October; it was day nine or twelve or fourteen of Nico's absence; all days had become the same endless day in which I ordered Seamless with my Lansing Award money, and filthy plastic containers and extra pairs of chopsticks formed a slow skin over every surface; the clothes I was wearing when Nico left became the clothes that I was permanently wearing; sometimes, when I started to itch, I would step into the shower and turn on the water and stand underneath it; then I would shut the water off and sit very still in front of a space heater, shivering, until I dried; this could take hours, but time was in endless supply, time was a resource that refused to be spent, and so what were these hours to me? And then, at some point in that expanse of time, Nico's old-school radio was on, and Terry Gross was interviewing an author, some cranky older woman whose voice reminded me of Hélène, and Terry Gross was saying, "And what made you move from Los Angeles to London?" And the author replied: "Because there was absolutely no culture in Los Angeles, you see. The place is a wasteland. There isn't even proper theatre."

And so I went to L.A.

2

10

The morning after Dylan and Daniel's fight, I jolt awake to the thud of the front door closing, signaling Dylan's return. I wait until his footsteps have receded up the stairs before I pull on jeans and Chucks, splash water on my face, and head out to Sunset Junction for coffee. After my own season of destruction, I can't bear to be around another thing in pieces.

The morning air is crisp with early December, the sun glaring. I pass Caroline's house, but all is quiet. I wonder if Thomas has slept over since the shoot at Chad's. But maybe, with all the girls constantly underfoot, Caroline isn't entertaining exes who are bad for her. It occurs to me that, while this may not have been a reason for her to make the movie, it's a positive side effect.

I take a right onto Manzanita, walking quicker now. An image comes to me: Daniel sitting in the dark hallway, head down, light spilling from their open bedroom door. It feels like a thing that happened a long time ago, and simultaneously, like a thing that is still happening. I reach the broad cement stairs leading up to Sunset, thickened on one side by scrub and on the other by scrub that is striving to be a community garden. I take the steps two at a time, unzipping my hoodie, and the breeze lifts my damp T-shirt, makes me shiver.

Intelligentsia is too busy; every unemployed freelancer on the East

Side of Los Angeles is there, camped out over a laptop, scanning the crowd for someone they might know. I pass it in favor of La Colombe, the domain of dog owners who need a coffee mid-walk. On my way in, I pass a fat Saint Bernard and its three yards of tongue, a pit bull mix drinking out of the guest bowl, and a surprisingly butch dalmatian.

I'm waiting in line when a hand comes down hard on my shoulder. I jerk around, startled, and come face-to-face with B.B. She's grinning with the satisfaction of having made me jump.

"Fuck you," I say, recovering my breath. "That's how you give people heart attacks."

"Old people."

"Yeah, like me, so don't do that."

B.B. tilts back on her heels. "Whatcha doin'?"

"What does it look like?"

"Wanna buy me a coffee?"

"I mean, no?"

"Caroline always buys us everything."

"We're not at Caroline's."

"I know," B.B. says, studying me. "And I like you better this way." She turns and saunters out onto the patio without giving me a chance to respond.

When I join her, placing a coffee in front of her, she's got her fingers buried in the Saint Bernard's shag and is scratching its neck.

"You made a new friend, I see."

B.B. gives me a swift smile. "Thanks for the coffee."

"You're so welcome, the idea came to me when I was in line. I thought, Maybe I'll do something nice for the youth of America."

B.B. makes a fake laugh face. She looks like such a kid in that moment that I have to smile. "What're you doing wandering around here, anyway?"

"Caroline didn't answer her phone, so I was killing time."

"You were going to Caroline's this early?"

B.B. rolls her eyes. "It's Saturday?"

"And?"

"Better than being at home all day." She sips her coffee, makes a face. "Be right back." I watch through the glass as she dumps in more half-and-half than I imagined would fit, adds two packets of sugar, stirs aggressively, and returns.

"Hey," she says as soon as she lands. "You wanna see something?"

"Um, okay?"

She starts walking up the street, spilling coffee, not looking to see if I'm following, but walking slowly so that she won't leave me behind.

"Where are we going?"

"I'm gonna show you."

"What do your parents think about your spending all your time at Caroline's?" I've wondered this before, about all the girls.

"I mean, we haven't really sat down and *discussed* it, Cath."

"But aren't they like — 'Who's this older woman you spend so much time with?'"

B.B. snorts. "My sister's in rehab so I'm not really like, the one everyone's worried about. At the moment."

"You have a sister?"

"She's in rehab."

It occurs to me how little I know about any of these girls, although I see them every day. I wonder if Caroline knows the things I don't know, or if details aren't important. I'm mulling this when B.B. asks, "Are you an only?"

"Yeah."

"That explains so much."

"Does it?"

"Yeah, you know, how you are with Caroline."

"How am I with Caroline?"

B.B. glances at me, a sharp, curious glance. "Attached," she says crisply. And then: "It's not much farther. But if you're thinking it's gonna be really cool, you're gonna be disappointed."

"What do you mean 'attached'?"

She ignores the question. "I would say like, whatever level of expectation you're having? Cut it in half right now."

"Wow," I say, giving up on the Caroline part of the conversation. "Don't go into marketing, okay?"

B.B. grins. Sunset flattens out, taking up more space. Now there are car washes and body shops. It's more industrial, dirtier in a way that feels like home. We reach a small tailor shop and B.B. jerks her head toward the narrow alley running alongside.

"In here."

A narrow staircase leads up, each thin cement stair painted like a piano key. The effect is startling, oddly magical in the thin December sunlight. B.B. shoots a glance at my face and then starts up the stairs, and I follow. I wonder how Dylan and Daniel are doing back at the house. If they're talking, if they're making breakfast together, if the fight has resumed. I reach the top of the stairs a few steps behind B.B. She's standing looking out, and when she makes a gesture, I see that this was what she wanted to show me. I turn and look down at the piano keys leading back to Sunset Boulevard, and then out over Silver Lake to the hills beyond. Everything glitters like cold crystal under the sun—the reflections off car bumpers and windshields, off shop windows and dog bowls on the sidewalk, off planes in the sky and mica buried in the pavement.

"It's beautiful," I say.

"You think so?"

"Yeah."

"My stepdad used to live in Silver Lake, before it was cool." B.B. keeps her face turned straight out as she says this, but I can feel the intense focus of her peripheral gaze. "I never used to hang around here much, but then one day we had a day that was just the two of us and he took me here. And then after that we used to come up here sometimes if stuff got too crazy at the house. I was a lot younger, though—eleven, maybe. This was cool when I was eleven."

"It's cool now," I say.

"Everybody around here knows about it," B.B. adds hastily. "It's not a *secret* or anything."

"Your stepdad sounds nice."

"He's the only one who doesn't go in for all the drama. My sister and my mom, it's like . . . But he doesn't do all the crying and yelling, he's like, 'I'll call 911.' My mom has to have all these emotions before she can do anything, like, Ronnie could be overdosing and my mom would have to *express* herself before she did anything."

"Ronnie?"

"Veronica. My sister." B.B. fumbles in the pocket of her oversized hoodie and comes up with a battered pack of cigarettes and her pink Zippo. She offers me one and I shake my head. "I can also tell you're an only because you're so *responsible*," she tells me, dry.

"That's not really how people think of me. People who know me."

"I know you," B.B. says, "and that's how I think of you."

"I guess I meant people in New York."

"Maybe they don't know you that well anymore."

I look at her, startled. She's looking straight out again, at the pale wash of mountains.

"Maybe," I say.

This time she risks a glance at me. "So maybe now I know you better."

I grin into my coffee cup and don't say anything. Sometimes she seems so old and other times she's such a kid, always pushing for a little more than you want to give her. After a moment, I sit on the top step. B.B. sits next to me, all narrow hips and battered sneakers, her leg jostling mine.

"How'd Caroline find you, anyway? Was it the ad?"

"I saw you guys jumping her fence," I say, "and wondered if you'd murdered her." B.B. laughs—and then the second part lands on me. "What ad?" I demand.

"You know," B.B. says. "The—I don't know what you call it, the thing for the movie. Back at the beginning." I shake my head, and B.B. explains, "You know, to be in it. She was like: '*Fight Club* meets *Lord of the Flies*, but girls.'"

"Wait . . . I thought you guys were on the side of the street? She saw you, you were bleeding—?"

B.B.'s eyes dart to my face, startled. "Yeah," she says, "that's the *story*."

"Oh."

"For later, that's for later. For when people ask later."

"Oh." I realize I'm holding the cardboard coffee cup too tightly, and the sides are caving. I put it down on the step. "There was an ad?"

"Caroline didn't tell you?"

"No."

B.B. is surprised. "You thought we made up the fighting ourselves?"

"You didn't . . . ? From *Fight Club*, from English class . . . ?"

B.B. is shaking her head. "No, no," she says. "Caroline thought up how the movie works. It's about us finding an outlet—like, this super masculine outlet, and co-opting it, so that—"

"I *know* what it's *about*," I say, sharper than I meant to. Her eyes widen. "Sorry," I say, quieter. "I'm just—I thought the fighting was . . . I thought it was something you were already doing. Caroline met you and you were doing it."

"No, she had the idea. Like, all this stuff about girls is In now—she said suddenly people care about girls. Or they feel like they should? You know, everything right now is called *Girls, something something Girls*—or *Women*—or *Ladies*—and she was like, 'Now is the time to give people what they want, but also it's a feminist statement.' People want violence. But also they want girls." B.B. shrugs.

I'm reeling. "Caroline came up with this because people like girls," I repeat. "And this isn't . . . you guys didn't . . . because of *Fight Club*, you didn't . . . ?"

"We don't even read *Fight Club* in English class," B.B. says apologetically. "It's not real literature."

"*Have* you read it? On your own?" I don't know why this matters, but it does.

B.B. shakes her head. "Some of the girls watched the movie," she offers. "They said Edward Norton started out dumb but then he got hot. But I don't really care about Edward Norton, so I . . ." She shrugs. "I figured I could whale on someone without having read a book about it."

"And . . . even the thing you used to do at the beginning? *We don't need a dick*—that whole thing?"

"Caroline wrote that for us," B.B. says apologetically. She can tell that she's letting me down. "And Ming sort of edited it? To make it sound cooler? But . . ."

I sit in silence. Below me, the sound of cars on Sunset rises up through the hazy air. The sound of a dog barking wends its way down to us from somewhere higher up, where the rich people's houses are. B.B. sits quietly, darting her eyes at me from time to time. She isn't sure if she fucked up or if someone else did.

"And you answered the ad," I say at last.

"It wasn't exactly an ad," B.B. amends, uneasily. "Caroline knew Ming and Mona already, from this arts mentorship program? So she wrote a few paragraphs about the movie and gave it to them to recruit some friends. She was like, 'We need a Black girl and a gay girl.' And she said we'd be like Joaquin Phoenix in that movie where he was himself but pretending he was crazy. She said our characters will have our real names, but they can still be our characters."

When I don't say anything, she says, "I guess I thought you knew. . . ."

"No," I say. "I'm your first audience member. I bought the backstory."

"She should've told you." B.B. takes my side. "It's fucked up you'd be working on it and she wouldn't tell you." Then she shrugs. "I guess it doesn't really matter, though." And then, studying my face: "Does it?"

"Yeah," I say quietly, "I think it does."

"Because she didn't tell you the truth?"

I shake my head. I feel like we climbed up these stairs to a different planet, where the air is thicker and heavier, where thoughts come slower.

"No," I say, "not just that."

"Then what?"

"It's also about *how* she—like, *who* she—like, nobody's parents are *ever* there. You know? And yours—"

"What about mine," B.B. says, fierce.

"You said it yourself, they're not looking at you right now. I'm not talking shit about your family, B.B., I'm only saying Caroline picked a bunch of kids who—"

"Who wanted to be there." B.B.'s lip is jutting, her whole chin. She looks both pugnacious and scared. "She asked us if we wanted to, and we wanted to. We're basically adults, we know what we want to do."

"I'm thirty-three," I tell her, "and half the time I don't even know what I want to do."

"Then you're weak," B.B. says. "Nobody tells me what to do." But she keeps looking scared as she says it, so it doesn't land like a punch, the way she wants it to.

We sit in silence.

B.B. says, "Are you gonna tell Caroline that I told you?"

"No, why would I do that?"

"She's already mad at me."

"That isn't true," I say.

B.B. takes a breath. "They all want a chance to kick me out."

"B.B., why would you say that?"

B.B. shrugs. "You don't see us at school, but they don't even talk to me there," she says. "Only at Caroline's, when the camera—or if there's a *scene*. It's not like I care, I'm just saying."

"But Caroline invited you directly, B.B., obviously she wanted you here."

"Caroline needed a gay and Ming was like, *This kid at our school is a big dyke*. And that was me."

I'm quiet for so long that B.B. gets nervous again. "You promised," she reminds me.

"B.B., I'm not gonna . . . It's okay."

"Okay," B.B. says, and watches me with large eyes. Her leg jostles up and down anxiously on the step.

After a time she says, "Why do you look so sad?"

After a time she says, "Cath, say something."

Her whole face is as open as a soup dish, dismay and worry and guilt all mixed together.

"B.B. . . . ." I begin, without knowing what I'm going to say. But I don't have to, because without warning she's leaning in, her sticky coffee fingers on either side of my face, and she's kissing me. It takes a second to realize what's happening, because I receive it as a series of revelations: *fingers, coffee, hair, breath*, the angle of her knee against mine, and then when I realize, I put my hands on her shoulders and move her back, very gently.

"Cath," B.B. says again, and in the exact way that she says it, suddenly I know, I get it, exactly who she reminded me of.

"No," I say, keeping my voice as soft as I can.

"Why *not*?"

And the only thing, the only thing I can think, comes to me in Hélène's voice: *There are so many kinds of intimacy, it's easy to confuse them all.*

After a moment B.B. nods, once, like she's putting herself back together. And I see it happen, the shutters fall, even the way she pulls her hoodie closer around her shoulders is an armoring. But her voice isn't angry when she says, "Okay." Just like that: "Okay." She stands, and then she smiles but it isn't a real smile, it's the one she does sometimes for the camera.

"B.B.—"

"Later," she says, and she heads back down all the steps, sneakers pounding the piano keys. I let her go, remembering how Hélène showed me that grace. I wait until B.B. has reached Sunset before I get up and start walking.

*

My feet take me down Hollywood Boulevard toward Vermont, and it becomes clear that I'm walking to Los Feliz, since it's one of the few directions I know to go in. I try not to construct any thoughts that require more than a few components. I wonder what I'll do when the Lansing money runs out. I could dog-walk and grant-write again. I could cater-waiter or bartend again. The thought of having my ass squeezed by guys in blazers makes all of my cells die. I could try to teach, but am I hirable with my name all over the Internet?

Or the movie could come out. The movie could come out with my new name on it, next to Caroline's. Or below, probably below. But still: my new name. "Cath." And there would be money when that happened. There would be a record of Cath's existence. A record of her success. And that would subsume the record of Cass's failure. And if Caroline wasn't 100 percent honest with me, so what? She gave me a chance to join something—doesn't that count for more than pure honesty? And if she was strategic about these girls, then that makes her a good producer, a good entrepreneur. It makes her someone who understands how things work. Maybe you can't just be an artist these days, you also have to be a marketing genius. *We need a gay girl.* Well, it's not like B.B. was complaining.

I'm passing the Goodwill, outside of which a tent encampment stretches the length of the sidewalk for a block. Guys sit on crates or inside the open flaps of their camping tents; someone cooks on a small stove. Nobody glances at me as I pass. I take a right off of Vermont onto Melbourne, cutting through a small jungle of plants for sale outside a flower shop. In the window of the Punchbowl, three male models are waiting for their smoothies as they scroll through their phones. The door to the Punchbowl opens as I approach, and a girl saunters out onto the sidewalk, smoothie in hand. And everything gets very quiet.

I blink a few times. I have entered a new dimension.

Copper hair in two little braids. Overalls with one shoulder unfastened. A belly shirt, tiny leather wingtips. I catch a glimpse of a neck like cream, a dusting of freckles, a lime-green eye patch, and then Tara-Jean Slater is walking away from me up the street.

I stand, pinned to the spot. And then I hurry after her, weaving and ducking behind the parked cars whenever it seems like Tara-Jean Slater might turn around. She doesn't turn. She has her smoothie in one hand, car keys in the other, and she crosses the street to the other side, where a red convertible is parked under a tree. It *beep-beeps* and the door unlocks. She climbs in, starts the engine, and backs out slowly. This takes effort, maybe because of all the other parked cars, maybe because of her eye patch. I dart behind a Honda Fit, but even though she's looking directly my way, she doesn't see me. For a moment Tara-Jean Slater and her red convertible and her smoothie all seem suspended in the air, glowing like emissaries from another world, and then she hits the gas and peels out onto Vermont. A left onto Hollywood, and she's gone.

I sit on the sidewalk. Then I call Jocelyn.

"Hello, this is Creative Content Associates, how may I—"

"You didn't tell me Tara-Jean Slater was coming here."

In the pause, I hear Jocelyn change gears. "Cass," she says, her voice hushed. "Listen." There must be people nearby, because she sounds both stricken and like she can't say anything.

"I told you how to not die in a fire—in a *gas* explosion—on *Thanksgiving!*—and you don't tell me that Tara-Jean Slater is in my neighborhood? Not even the fucking *city*, but my *neighborhood*?"

"It's only for a few weeks," Jocelyn whispers. "Look, can I call you back?"

"Why!"

"I'm gonna call you back on my cell." Jocelyn hangs up.

I sit on the sidewalk for another minute, and then my phone rings. When I pick up, Jocelyn starts talking immediately. Her voice has a strange echo, and I realize that she's in the women's bathroom.

"Look, I meant to tell you, but I wasn't sure you wanted to know, and I don't know anything about L.A., so I figured, if you were on opposite sides of town, then there wasn't any point in *disrupting* your—peace of mind or whatever."

"What is she doing here?"

"I just want you to think about whether or not you want me to answer that." The sound of a thin stream of water falling from a height. Then Jocelyn says, "I'm peeing, tell me if you can hear me peeing."

"I can hear you peeing."

"Oh, sorry. I didn't know this speaker was so good! You always think these things are pieces of shit, because they break so easily."

"Tell me what she's doing. I wanna know, okay?"

Jocelyn sighs. "Okay," she says, like: *You asked for it*. "Netflix optioned her play about her uncle, and they're doing an eight-episode limited series."

"Netflix?"

"Yeah, and she's gonna play herself in it. It's like a whole thing. George Clooney wants to play her uncle, so she's taking a meeting with him to see if there's chemistry."

"*George Clooney?*"

"I mean, there's a list, he's on it."

"Who else is on the list?"

"Oh, it's not like a *crazy* list," Jocelyn says very casually, in a way that doesn't manage to disguise that it is a completely crazy list. "But like, Al Pacino, uh, Samuel L. Jackson, who else . . ."

"Samuel L. *Jackson?*"

"Tara-Jean Slater feels like racially accurate casting isn't necessary," Jocelyn says, "because it's about the *essence* of the character." Into the ensuing pause she adds: "Lea DeLaria!"

"Lea De*Laria?*"

"She felt like Lea DeLaria also might be able to tap into the essence of her uncle. Like, the butch essence. They're gonna hang out." Jocelyn lowers her voice. "She also pitched Netflix a structure in which her uncle is played by a different *actor* in each episode, which like . . . blew their minds. So then they offered her an overall deal."

"A what?"

"For whatever she wants to do." Jocelyn flushes, and for a moment neither of us can say anything over the rush of water. Then she asks, anxiously, "Did you hear me poop?"

"No," I say, distracted. "You're saying Tara-Jean Slater has an overall deal and she hasn't even graduated from Yale?"

"Yeah," Jocelyn says. "Well, she graduates in May." And then she adds, "I was worried you'd know I was pooping."

"No, I didn't know. Until you told me, I didn't know."

"I was just gonna hide in the stall and call you," Jocelyn says, "but then I realized I'd been at my desk for like, eight hours straight, and I better use the time in here wisely. You know?"

"Yeah," I say bleakly. My life is rushing before my eyes. When I hang up this phone, I will be sitting on a sidewalk in Los Feliz behind a Honda Fit. I will not be a person who has an overall deal with Netflix, and nobody will want to play my uncle on TV.

"Anyway, so that's why she's in L.A.," Jocelyn says. "I should get back. . . ."

"Yeah. Okay. Um. Thank you. For calling me."

"It's okay," Jocelyn says. And then she adds brightly, "Hey, about the other week? When you saved me from dying in a fire?"

"Yeah?"

"The ConEd guys were really nice. And this one guy—the younger one—he gave me his number? So I think we're gonna have sex."

I blink rapidly, trying to switch gears from the universe in which I am a crushing failure to the universe in which Jocelyn is fucking the ConEd guy. "Oh, whoa."

"Yeah, he's gonna come over tonight. We've been texting."

"That's . . . that's great. I'm glad."

"You really did me a solid," Jocelyn says, "so thanks for that." I hear the hand dryer roar to life for a few seconds, and I hold the phone away from my ear. When the dryer shuts off, Jocelyn says, "Okay, I'm headed back in now."

"Okay."

"Bye, Cass."

When Jocelyn hangs up, I sit for another minute. I have no idea what to do with myself. It occurs to me that I can't keep sitting on the sidewalk, so I stand up, and once I've stood, I go into the Punchbowl. I order the halvah smoothie that Dylan always gets, even though I feel nauseous. But it gives me a reason to stand there and do nothing: I am waiting for someone else to complete a task, in a place where it is proper and necessary to wait. I find myself playing with a stack of postcard-sized announcements for upcoming events, knocking them over with little flicks of my fingers and then restacking them. When I get a glance from the cashier, I make myself stop. I'm filled with an electric storm. I feel insane.

I glance at the top postcard automatically to see what it's for . . . and I freeze. Staring back at me are Tara-Jean Slater's narrow green eyes. A new play commission. Upcoming reading series. The Geffen. January.

Tara-Jean Slater will be in town, succeeding, for a whole month. She will breathe in oxygen and she will breathe out carbon dioxide, and her carbon dioxide will fill this city—the city where I have come to escape her—and I will not be able to breathe.

I think: *At least I have the movie.*

I think: *You try giving a bad review to a movie about a queer filmmaker who mentors a young lesbian, and there are Black and Asian people in it—like* Crazy Rich Asians *meets* Moonlight, *but also it's about female rage.*

I think: *I don't care where the fuck this story came from, I'm not getting left behind again.*

"Miss. Hey, miss. Your smoothie." The cashier is staring at me. He looks like he's daring me to knock over the postcard stack again. I wanted to hit it with one great open-palmed swipe, send those miniature Tara-Jean Slater faces flying all over the café.

"Thank you," I say haughtily. "I was just going."

And so I leave, and I take the postcard with me.

11

As we enter the last three weeks before Daniel leaves, Dylan and Daniel begin a period of politeness. It permeates the house: the sense that all of us are on our best behavior. It feels like being brought to an unfamiliar relative's home as a kid for a reluctant holiday visit, and all you can think about is not scuffing or spilling.

We are all aware of the countdown to Daniel's departure, although Daniel only packs when Dylan isn't home. It seems to be one of the unspoken tenets in the rewritten contract of their time together. Dylan is there less and less, and Daniel is there more and more. As he tapes boxes and ties up loose ends, he is lighter, more cheerful. I can tell he's gathering his wings under him, preparing for flight. Dylan can see it as well. And so, he stays away, coming home only late at night. If he and Daniel talk, it's in whispers, because no sound travels down the pipes from above.

Midweek, I ask Daniel if he'd like me to get an Airbnb for Christmas and New Year's Eve. He's in a rush out the door, driving his boxes to the post office, but when I offer this, he stops.

"No need—we'll go to Dylan's parents for Christmas. But New Year's Eve—it would be nice to have all three of us."

"That's your last night. Are you sure you wouldn't rather have the house for yourselves?"

"No, no," he says hastily. "Please stay." The note of plea in his voice is so unguarded that it takes me aback.

"Okay," I say, "if you're sure."

He starts to leave again and then hesitates, as if a new thought has struck him. "Actually . . . this is maybe crazy, but—would you by any chance want to go to Monterey with me?"

"Monterey?"

"I promised my aunt and uncle I'd come visit them before I leave, and I was going to drive instead of fly, because I'm bringing them the extra desk upstairs—Dyl said he wants to get another one—and this painting that my aunt gave me—and it's a five-hour drive, and I thought . . . As I'm saying this out loud, it sounds insane. Sorry."

"No," I say, "it's not insane." It crosses my mind that Hélène was recently—might still be—another hour up the coast, in Berkeley. I can't help it if Hélène lives near Daniel's relatives. This has nothing to do with her anyway.

"I don't have any holiday plans," I say. "Let me know when you're going."

Daniel's face lights up. "Really? That's—lovely, actually. I promise it won't be too terrible—beautiful coastline, and they're both very nice."

"Worse things have happened than a trip up the coast," my mouth says, while inside me all of my blood cells sing: *Hélène!*

*

The politeness between Daniel and Dylan mirrors the guarded politeness that B.B. is manifesting toward me. She doesn't bring up what happened. She doesn't talk to me at all if she can help it. Wherever I am, she is in an opposite space: across the room or out on the porch. Her rigorous absence unsettles me.

There have been any number of moments in which to ask Caroline casually about the origin story—How did this *really* start?—but I don't do it. At first I kept thinking I'd bring it up so casually that she'd just tell me the truth and then we'd be in this together again. *Cath is my number two.* But after seeing Tara-Jean Slater, I know that I won't.

When Christmas break begins, most of the girls will leave for family trips. So we double-down, trying to get some big scenes in before then.

Caroline has taken Chip's advice seriously, and now Post-it-note char-
acter arcs have popped up on the walls of her study. B.B.'s reads:
CLOSETED—>CATH GAY CONVO—>B.B. OPENS UP. Evie's reads: UNDER-
PRIVILEGED—>CONFIDENCE—>COLLEGE. Mona's just reads: EATING
DISORDER.

We shoot a couple more fights—at the Venice Beach apartment of
one of the Nickeys, in the Echo Park backyard of Mona's cousin—but
most of what we're shooting now are conversations, moments between
the girls. We spend a whole Sunday shooting Ming, ending with a scene
where she talks to the Nickeys about the familial pressure to go to a good
college. It's a particularly moving sequence—Ming tears up as she talks
about her mother's childhood at an orphanage in China, and how that
has shaped her mother's determination to see Ming go to Harvard. She
describes the windowless four-by-four-foot cell in which her mother
slept on a straw mat, surrounded by the sleeping bodies of other
unwanted Chinese orphans. She says that nearly all of the orphans were
girls, and then the Nickeys start crying as well. The scene ends in a hug,
with Ming's face over Nickey's shoulder, still facing the camera.

I have learned enough from my conversation with B.B. to no longer
make assumptions about where the authorial hand of Caroline begins
and ends. Something in me doesn't quite dare to ask Ming directly, so,
after the shoot ends, I ask Evie. It's one of the few times we've been
alone together; I'm hovering awkwardly in the mudroom while she pulls
on her sneakers. She tells me that Ming's mother is Swedish (Stock-
holm; former model), and her father is Chinese-American (Sonoma;
cardiologist), and Ming is taking a year off after high school to try to
launch her own modeling career. She doesn't betray any feeling whatsoever about the divide between the tearful scene we just shot and the facts
of Ming's life as she knows them to be.

I want to ask the decidedly upper-middle-class Evie how she feels
about her own character arc (UNDERPRIVILEGED—>CONFIDENCE—
>COLLEGE), but as I hesitate, she stands, grabs her satchel, and says,
"I'll see you tomorrow." She feels my hesitation and looks at me ques-
tioningly: *Is there something else?* But I don't know how to begin framing

a question that I myself can't answer. So: "See you tomorrow," I say, and Evie gives me a quizzical nod and is gone.

*

The last scene Caroline wants us to shoot before break is the one she's marked as CATH GAY CONVO. We decide we'll shoot it on the morning of the eighteenth, the first day of break. She talks me through it the night before, on her porch. The air is dry and cold, and we're bundled up, me in my tattered winter parka and Caroline in a stylish wool-lined leather jacket. I can imagine myself wearing that exact jacket at Sundance, on a particularly crisp and scenic morning. During an interview, even.

As Caroline pours us a nightcap, I ask casually where she got it.

"Oh this? I dunno, it's my mother's."

"Your mother!" I imagine my own mother. She mostly lives in secondhand fleeces augmented by bulky vests. New Hampshire.

"Yeah," Caroline says. "She loves shopping. She's a shopaholic." I open my mouth to say that sounds nice, and Caroline forestalls this: "No, she actually has a problem." She shrugs. "She always looks really nice, though. That's her thing: Always look nice. I got arrested once— did I tell you this?"

"No," I say, wide-eyed. I don't know if it's the proximity of the holidays, the thought of all the girls going off to their families, that has created this space for Caroline to talk about hers.

"Yeah," Caroline says, "well, it wasn't serious—high school, my boyfriend at the time hot-wired this car so we could go joyriding. *Anyway*, the point is, we got pulled over and brought down to the station, and when my mom came to get me, she was like . . . mad, but also, she seemed weirdly relieved? And then in the car she was like, 'I really think the way you dressed made all the difference.' And I realized I was wearing one of her skirts and one of her blazers, and my hair was nice—like, she thought they let me go because I looked nice." Caroline shrugs. "Her motto is: No matter what happens, look your best. When I was growing up, she alternated it with her other favorite: Look your best, be the best." Caroline sips, then cracks a smile, letting the whiskey warmth settle. "Please note the grammatical shift from 'your' to 'the.' Anyway." She turns to me, studies me. "About B.B."

Something knots in my gut. "Yeah?"

"The scene wants to be pretty simple," Caroline says. "We're gonna get a series of shots of you guys together—smoking, in the car, whatever. Simple stuff. And then we're gonna do the scene right here on the porch. You'll talk to B.B. about being gay, like you can tell her your coming-out story or whatever feels right. And then she's gonna open up to you. Like, this whole time she hasn't told the girls she's gay, and she'll say it to you."

"That sounds pretty simple."

"So, whatever you want to say to her—I don't know if your parents are cool with you or not, but . . . maybe they weren't? You know. For the purposes of this. Maybe you felt a lot of anguish. You felt like something was wrong with you. Like, there was this entire human machine, and you were—totally shut out. You know? More than lonely—you couldn't imagine being a participant."

Caroline has X-rayed my soul by accident. Even though she's inventing angst for my teen self, everything she described is what I've recently felt, although unrelated to desire. *No*, I correct myself. *Unrelated to sex.* Ambition is all desire, all the time. So is success. I'd take success over sex.

Caroline is looking at me searchingly. She can tell that something in there landed.

"Yeah," I say, clearing my throat. "I can talk to B.B. about that."

Caroline's face lights up. "Good," she says. After a second she touches my arm, a very light touch. "And obviously, I'm sorry," she says. "About your childhood. If that was . . . you know."

I want to tell her that my childhood was essentially fine, it's being an adult that sucks. But there's something about the way that she's looking at me—with warmth, admiration—that shuts me up. It's the way she looked when Ming was crying about her mother's life in a Chinese orphanage. She is looking at me and she is seeing resilience, determination, self-knowledge, the residue of suffering. Who doesn't want to be looked at like that? Even if you don't deserve it for this exact set of facts, you still deserve it. You *have* suffered in your life, you *have* felt anguish, even if it was for reasons that were technically different ones. Who cares about a technicality?

"It's okay," I say, self-conscious. "I'm fine now."

Caroline grins suddenly, leaning back on her hands. "You know, I thought I had a crush on a girl once?"

"Oh yeah?"

"There was this girl who transferred into my high school senior year. She was from Florida and she played basketball."

I wait for more to the story, but there isn't more. After a moment, Caroline lies down on the porch. "I fucked Thomas," she says, staring up at the porch roof. It takes me a moment to catch up.

"Thomas, the DP?"

"Yeah," Caroline says. "On Wednesday. You know, I spent all this time since we broke up working on my self-respect, like, my *boundaries*— and then I went ahead and fucked him. I can't tell if all that work is down the drain or what."

"Work from the shoot?" I ask, still trying to catch up.

"No," Caroline says, narrowing her eyes at me, "the work on my *self-respect*."

"Oh," I say. We're quiet. "Why'd you fuck him?"

I expect Caroline to reject the question, but instead she looks thoughtful. "I wanted him to want me," she says at last. "Whenever we were talking about the shots, or whatever, I'd just be focused on whether or not he still wanted me. So then I lost track of whether or not *I* wanted *him*. He came over here to talk about the footage, and it was getting late, and when he stuck his hand down my pants, I just—you know. Climbed on his dick." She sighs from a place deep within. "Do you wanna hear the worst part?"

"Maybe?"

"After he went home, I texted him. In my head, I was like: *This was a terrible mistake, this can't happen again*—but then I fucking *texted* him. I was like, Do You Want to Hang Out Tomorrow. And he didn't text me back. And I stayed up waiting to see if he would! Like, for hours,

I stayed up in case he texted! Was all that money I spent on therapy just a waste? I coulda put that into cameras, I coulda hired a better DP with all that money!"

"Huh," I say.

"Do you know what I mean?" Caroline sighs. "You seem so . . . I don't know. Like you never do this kind of stuff."

I'm startled into laughing, and for a moment I worry that I won't be able to stop. Caroline looks at me, wide-eyed but not alarmed.

"What's so funny?"

"Look," I say. "I don't even know where to start. I make a lot of mistakes."

"Like what?"

Something in me says *Be careful*. But it feels good to be talking like this. Caroline so rarely asks me about myself, and every time she does, I feel the high-watt incandescence of her attention and I want to make it last.

I choose the simplest thing. "I slept with a married woman," I tell her. "For months and months."

Caroline's eyes light up. "Ooh," she says. "Did you get caught?"

"No, I stopped in part because I was in love with someone else." This isn't exactly the truth, but it feels like a safe version—or the version I want Caroline to have.

"Who were you in love with?"

"A straight woman who rejected me." I grin at her. "See? Mistakes!"

Caroline bursts out laughing. It's warm, approving laughter. "That's so good," she says, like a kid who's been told an appealing joke. "Who woulda known." Caroline pours more into her glass, then into mine. "You're very easy to talk to," she says softly. "No wonder B.B. likes you so much."

"She doesn't . . ."

"Shut up, you know she does. With the rest of us, it's like . . ." Caroline mimes something like a constipated robot, arms at her sides, face blank. "But with you she's . . . a totally different human."

I feel a warmth spread through my chest, and then it's joined by a queasiness. "I don't think that's true anymore," I say.

"What, did you tell her to give you some space?"

"No, she kissed me."

Caroline sits bolt upright. "She did?"

I'm already regretting it. "Please don't say anything."

"What happened? Did you guys make out?"

"No! Jesus, she's—what—eighteen? No, I stopped her and then she . . ." I scrub a hand over my face. I have a dim sensation that Caroline is not the person to discuss this with, but it's also a relief to finally be talking to someone. Dylan and Daniel are so entrenched in their own misery that there isn't room for much else at the house. "She was hurt, obviously, and she—we haven't really talked. Since then. And I feel terrible. And now she hates me, or she hates herself, or probably some of each."

When I look at Caroline, her eyes are radiant. "Did she say anything? Like how she feels about you? Like that she's had a crush on you forever, and she needs to know how you feel, and she's never before felt this way about—"

"No, she just kissed me." As Caroline mulls this over, the uneasy feeling crawls further up my spine from the pit of my stomach. "You're not gonna say anything, right?" Caroline doesn't say anything for a long moment. "Caroline?"

Caroline turns her eyes back to me. They're wistful and faraway. "I wish there'd been a camera there," she says.

*

When I next call Jocelyn, she launches into the update right away without making me ask for it. "The Netflix meetings went well, they've decided to move ahead with having a different actor play her uncle in each of the episodes. Samuel L. Jackson developed a conflict with his shooting schedule, but they're out to Morgan Freeman. Also Tilda Swinton."

"As the uncle?"

"No, Tilda Swinton will play an adult version of Tara-Jean Slater, who encounters young Tara-Jean Slater, who will be played by actual Tara-Jean Slater. And Tilda will perform a dream ballet. What else." Jocelyn considers. "Tara-Jean Slater is depressed, she told Marisa she feels like it's depressing to create art within the confines of institutions."

"I mean, I'm happy to take over for her if she wants to quit."

Jocelyn continues as if she didn't hear me. "She's been writing a series of poems about her depression, and *The New Yorker* is going to publish them. The titles are—" A moment of shuffling, and then Jocelyn reads: "'Depression One,' 'Depression Two,' 'Rothko,' and 'Depression Three.'"

She stops, as if she's come to the end of her reportage. Then she adds: "I've been watching spy movies all weekend."

"Oh yeah?"

"Álvaro really likes them, he made me watch *North by Northwest* and *The Manchurian Candidate*. He loves American classics."

"Is that one of Marisa's new clients?"

"Oh, that's the ConEd guy. We're sort of dating. Or we keep having sex. It feels like dating?"

I realize by the pause after her question that I'm being called upon to offer an opinion. I pull myself back from the brink of Tara-Jean Slater and try to focus. "Uh, spy movies and fucking, that sounds like dating, yeah. How long is Tara-Jean Slater here, exactly?"

"Well, she's staying through the holidays," Jocelyn says. "The Geffen is doing a public presentation of her commission, when everything starts up again."

I don't tell Jocelyn that I already found the postcard for it. Instead, I say, "When did she have time to write a commission?"

"She wrote it in her Notes app during all the times she was in the waiting room," Jocelyn tells me. "For the eye doctor." There isn't accusation in her voice, just blunt fact. "The play starts as a first-person narrative from the perspective of the cyclops, after Odysseus puts out his eye."

"On her Notes app?"

"On her Notes app."

"In the waiting room."

"I mean, doctors in New York are always running late," Jocelyn reminds me pragmatically. "Every time I go to my gynecologist it's like . . . I wait for ninety minutes so that she can jam her fist in my vagina for less than ten."

It never occurred to me to write a first-person narrative play on my Notes app while in a waiting room.

I shouldn't ask. I have to ask, but I shouldn't ask, but then I can't help myself and I do ask. "Who . . . uh . . . who's playing the cyclops? In the workshop?"

"Cate Blanchett," Jocelyn says. "She happens to be in town after the New Year, and she's a big fan."

*

The afternoon of our last shoot, it rains all day, a steady December drizzle. B.B. shows up in rain boots with a miserable cough, gives me a wary nod, then vanishes into the warmth of the house before I can start a conversation. The rest of the girls are buoyant with the first day of break, chattering about where they're going. Thomas shows up in a black hoodie and stubble, followed by three or four guys who look like younger versions of him. They bustle around the end of the driveway, stringing up a plastic tarp to shelter the cameras, while Thomas stands with his hands shoved in his kangaroo pouch, gazing off into the trees.

Caroline brings me a mug of hot coffee and stands under the porch overhang with me. Her eyes follow Thomas as he blows his nose into his sleeve and yanks his hood down farther over his face. I am thinking that Thomas looks like the kind of person who would shoot up a mall. I can tell, when my eyes skate sideways to Caroline's face, that she thinks he looks like a tortured poet.

"He texted me last night," Caroline says, apropos of nothing.

"About today?"

"No, just a picture of his cock."

"Oh."

After a second Caroline says, "It's thinner than I remembered."

"Oh?"

"Like—I knew it was *short*, but I didn't remember it was so *thin*."

I try to imagine them having sex. I can't picture Thomas divested of his oversized hoodie. Maybe he has sex with it on.

"You and B.B. haven't talked about things yet, right?" Caroline asks, turning fully to me and away from Thomas's pencil dick.

"No," I say.

"Like, about the kiss or any of that stuff?"

"No, I've barely seen her."

"Great."

The warmth of her focus is exhilarating enough that it takes me a second to add, "You can't tell her I told you. You promised, remember?"

Caroline puts a hand on my shoulder. "Cath, this is good information to have. As a director, as I shape these scenes, it's just good information to have. So I really appreciate you being honest with me. That's all."

It's only after B.B. has come out to the porch—arms wrapped around herself—and Thomas has summoned us down to the end of the driveway that I realize Caroline's answer contained nothing in the way of a promise.

*

The first set of scenes are simple, wordless. We walk down the driveway together. We share a cigarette on the back porch. I open a soft drink and B.B. steals it to take a sip. Before each scene, Caroline tells us exactly what to do, and then we do it.

It is eerie to perform these gestures. We are repeating moments plucked out of the fabric of our real lives—moments that reveal to me how closely Caroline was observing, exactly how much she sees. We have lived all these gestures before, simply; and yet, now that the cameras are collecting them, they are harder to execute with a casual realness.

This isn't helped by the fact that B.B. feels completely closed off from me. I can't read her face. She tries not to look at me if she doesn't have to, tries not to touch me when she offers me a cigarette (Caroline: "B.B., give her your cigarette") or steals my LaCroix (Caroline: "B.B., I want you to steal her LaCroix"). I can feel her discomfort and my own, and because we feel it, so do the cameras. Bodies tell the truth, even when everything around them is lying. I can tell the shots aren't working because Caroline starts giving us more and more detailed direction: "B.B., get four inches closer . . . One more . . . Okay now look at her, then look away . . . No, *look* at her." The more detailed Caroline gets, the stiffer B.B. gets, until she's fumbling with things, dropping the cigarettes in a puddle, burning herself on the lighter. We haven't even gotten to the CATH GAY CONVO, and this is a disaster.

"Cut and take five," Caroline calls to Thomas. "Check the gates, next scene on the porch. Thomas, let's start with a long lens for the master, and then we'll bring it in." As Caroline moves away, still talking, I dart a look at B.B. Her face is cast downward, staring at the wet driveway. She's shivering.

"Hey," I say softly.

B.B. grunts, examining the wet toe of her sneaker.

"You okay?"

B.B. gives me a tight, closed-off look. "Sure."

"Is there anything you wanna talk about?"

"Yeah," B.B. says, dry as bones, "I wanna tell you on camera that I might be gay. Is there anything *you* wanna talk about?"

Caroline comes back before I can answer. Thomas and the flurry of assistants are moving with the steady focus of carpenter ants, their dark hoodies billowing in the cold breeze.

"Okay!" Caroline says, chipper. "So, we're gonna shoot this the way we talked about. Just for you to know, Thomas is gonna start with a nice long shot of you two sitting on the porch. After that, we're gonna come in close, mics will be hooked up the whole time. I'd say let's save the actual conversation for the next two sizes, the master can be this moment of silence, you're smoking on the porch, B.B., you're working yourself up to ask Cath for advice. Any questions?"

I'm quiet. B.B. is fascinated by the frayed edge of her shoelace. She shakes her head, and then I do too.

"Okay," Caroline says again when we don't say anything. And then an eagerness creeps into her tone—she can't help herself—and she says, as casually as she can but not casually enough: "While we're setting up for the master, I want you both to think about . . . how unspoken things can *affect* this conversation. You know? Why This Why Now. For example, B.B., maybe your character has *feelings* for Cath. Maybe there's a reason you're talking to her now. You know? Tension. Unspoken— Thomas!" Out on the driveway, a gust of wind has blown a camera tripod over. Thomas lopes toward it, and Caroline shakes her head, frustrated. "I'll be right back," Caroline says, and darts off the porch toward where the interns are picking up the camera, checking it for damage.

B.B. says, not looking at me, "You told her."

In the silence, a car goes by and the rain hisses in its tires. A dog barks. My voice lifts between us, thready and unconvincing: "What do you mean?"

B.B. looks at me. Steady, direct. I notice the purple thumbprints under her eyes. She hasn't been sleeping.

I start: "I mean, I think Caroline's just offering—like, as an *idea* for what could be *underlying*—"

"Cath."

"—and I think things feel a little bit—*tense* between us, and maybe—I mean, I think it's possible to *guess*—"

"Cath," B.B. says again. Her voice is very quiet and firm. She sounds like an adult.

"Yeah?"

"Fuck you."

She vaults off the edge of the porch and is walking down the driveway before I realize what she's doing.

"B.B.! Wait!" I jump off the porch as well, but she doesn't even hesitate. It's like the piano-key stairs all over again, except this time I'm in the wrong. "B.B., *wait*!"

She turns the corner and is gone. I jog down the driveway, but Caroline catches up to me: "Where are you guys *going*?"

"B.B. got mad," I say, out of breath. "She knows I told you."

Caroline sighs. "She'll be back," she says. "It's her big scene. She just needs to cool off."

"You shouldn't have done that." I turn to her, half-angry, half-pleading. "I asked you not to tell her."

"I didn't tell her anything, Cath, I gave her some direction." Caroline rolls her eyes. "They're teenagers, they get emotional. She's gonna cool off and come back, and until then, maybe you need to do the same thing."

A moment. The frost in Caroline's voice penetrates the buzzing in my ears. This doesn't feel good, Caroline looking at me like I'm the problem. It was good on the porch, drinking coffee, watching Thomas. It was good being a united front.

"I guess," I say, turning back to the porch. "I'm sorry."

We wait for two hours, but B.B. doesn't return, and when the rain picks up hard, Caroline calls it a day.

*

That night, I have a dream about Tara-Jean Slater.

We are in a giant theatre together, and I'm standing in the wings. Tara-Jean Slater is onstage. I can't see the audience, but I can feel the gathered weight of them, beyond the blazing lights—their attentiveness, the solidity of their bodies. Tara-Jean Slater is delivering a monologue, and I know that it is objectively the best monologue that anyone has ever delivered on any stage—not only in America but globally; in the global history of international theatre, this is the best monologue—but I can't seem to make out what she's saying. Her tiny mouth moves, and I hear sounds. I can feel in my body how the audience sighs, how they sway toward her, I can feel the tiny ripples of laughter or the convulsive sobs that she coaxes from them. But my brain can't seem to parse words into meaning. At first I wonder if I'm having a stroke. But then, eventually, it occurs to me: Tara-Jean Slater has written and is currently delivering the world's greatest monologue in a language so brilliant, so elegant, so refined, that I don't even speak it.

Someone to my left coughs. I turn, and it's Tilda Swinton.

She's wearing a red velvet dinner jacket and studying Tara-Jean Slater with keen appraisal. Her eyes flicker over to me.

"You'll have to kill her," Tilda Swinton says to me. "That's the only way."

"I can't kill her," I say to Tilda Swinton. But Tilda is no longer interested in my excuses. She has already told me what is obvious to us both. "Tilda," I say, "come on. I can't *kill* her!"

Tilda Swinton turns her back on me, and I wake myself up with the sound of my own voice. It's morning and my phone is ringing. Groggy, I reach for it—Caroline.

"Yeah?"

"Cath, do you know where B.B. is?"

"B.B.?" I rub my eyes, clear my throat.

"Yeah, her mom called, she didn't come home last night."

I sit up, wide awake now. "Have you called her?"

"Yeah, obviously, I've been calling and texting. It goes to voicemail." Caroline sighs again. "I better go. This is such a mess."

"Wait," I say, "should we be looking for her?"

"Looking for her where?"

"I don't know, but like . . . *looking* for her. Or doing something."

"I mean, her family is looking for her," Caroline says. "But I feel like we should definitely gather the girls together. Be here by ten-thirty, there should be enough girls for a scene by then."

"Wait a sec," I say, getting out of bed. "Caroline?"

But she's hung up. And after a moment, phone heavy in my hand, I do as well. I text B.B.: *Are you OK?* Then I call her. It goes straight to voicemail. Then I text her again: *Call me.* And she doesn't reply, and she doesn't reply, and as the day goes on, I think: *Here it is again. The moment where Cass shows up and ruins everything.*

12

In the week before Christmas, I find myself retracing the path across Silver Lake that B.B. and I took. I fall into a morning routine that begins by walking to La Colombe for coffee and then takes me down Sunset to the piano-key stairs, where I sit at the top while I finish my coffee. Scanning across the mountain ranges and then down to the sidewalk below. Looking for her, as if she'll come into view like a rewound tape, back up the stairs toward me, back to the moment right after she leaned in and kissed me with her chapped lips.

Sometimes I find myself talking out loud, saying the things I might say if I got to redo the moment. "B.B., you are such a special person. So, this is a no, but not the kind of no that you need to take home and worry about. It is not a sign that women will say no to you in future, or that you are a kind of person destined to receive rejections. It's just the no from someone who can see your future, and it is a bright future, and I am not in it." And sometimes B.B. gets it. Those days, a small smile flickers at the corners of her mouth. She says, "Jesus, relax." She says, "You're not such a catch." She says, "I was playing, who cares." And we sit up there on those steps for a while longer.

Sometimes in the fantasy, I apologize to B.B. for telling Caroline. Sometimes, I change the future by not telling Caroline, and B.B. isn't upset, and the shoot is corny but fine, and we all go to Sundance and win Grand Jury. Other times, the fantasy ends abruptly, the way reality did, with her narrow back bounding down the steps. And then, even when I imagine going after her, nothing turns out well. She's gone before I can reach her, evaporated into the flat glare of sunlight on cement. On those days, I call her, and her phone goes straight to voice-mail, again and again to voicemail, and I hang up.

In the morning I walk, but in the afternoon I borrow Dylan's van and I drive. I take Sunset Junction, turn onto Hyperion, continue on Fountain, and then loop in the opposite direction, connecting to Hoover. I scan the sidewalks as if I might see B.B. strolling along with her hands in her pockets. But I never do, and nobody seems to know anything. Caroline keeps saying that B.B.'s family has it under control, that they know where we are if they need us, that we need to give them space. The girls are worried—they didn't like her, but their foreheads bunch uncertainly when I ask them about her. What were places she liked to go? If she ran away, who would she stay with? What did her life look like outside Caroline's house? Their foreheads gather into frowns and their eyes skate away. They don't know. They never asked her. Evie tells me that she thinks B.B.'s family lives in Highland Park—the section that isn't so nice—but she's never been there.

It's clear to me that her vanishing is my fault, so clear that I haven't wondered *why* she vanished so much as *where*. But late in the week, I walk into Caroline's kitchen and the girls are all talking at once. Caroline is saying, "One at a time, one at a time," with her steady hand on the camera, but nobody is yielding ground. The cacophony of voices builds until Caroline has to yell over it: "Evie! You go!"—and the buzz hushes.

Evie is the only one who wasn't talking. When Caroline says her name, she looks up and her eyes travel warily around the semicircle of our faces.

"Tell us about what you girls heard today about B.B."

I feel my body shift on a cellular level. "What about B.B.?" I demand, and Caroline turns the camera on me as Ming says, "She killed herself."

"*What?*" I yelp, at the same time as Mona yells, "Oh my god, I'll tell it!" and one of the Nickeys starts yelling that, no, she'll tell it.

"Everybody shut up," Caroline orders, cutting through the noise. "Evie is gonna tell this."

"What happened to B.B.!" I demand. Caroline gives me a cool, measuring look, and then turns off the camera. "Hang on," she says. She crosses the room and kneels down on the carpet by Evie. She talks very softly and intently, her face close to Evie's ear, her hair swinging in a shiny curtain over her mouth and Evie's cheek. The girls and I stare at the visible side of Evie's face. She nods. She nods. I'm trying to figure out by her expression whether or not B.B. is dead, but I can't be sure. Adrenaline is coursing through my body and my fingertips feel numb. After listening for another few seconds, Evie nods a final time, and Caroline stands up.

"Okay," she says, "let's shoot this. Mona and Nickey, on the couch, please. Ming, I want you sitting at the coffee table with Evie. But you guys aren't gonna say anything, okay? We're gonna let Evie tell the story."

I feel like I'm going to jump out of my skin, but I know Caroline well enough to know that the fastest way to get what I want is to do what she wants. So I stand, my heart slamming into the wall of my chest, as the girls take their places and Caroline examines the arrangement through the small digital screen of one of Thomas's cameras. I don't know when his cameras moved into her house. "Mona, an inch to the left. And Ming, can you . . . ? Yes. Yeah, there, don't move." When she's satisfied, Caroline nods. "Okay, Evie. Can you tell me what you heard today?"

"I heard about B.B.," Evie says.

"And what did you hear?"

Evie licks her lips nervously. "Ming and Mona and me were at the mall with these girls from school. And they said that everybody's saying that B.B.'s ex-girlfriend is saying B.B. wrote her all these letters, after they broke up? These dark letters. And in the last letter, B.B. was like, *Tell me you love me, or I'll kill myself.* And Molly was like: *I never loved you.* And then B.B. went missing."

"And what do the girls think happened?" Caroline prompts.

"They think she killed herself," Evie says.

"And what do you think?"

Evie wasn't expecting this one. Her eyes dart to Caroline, then to me, then back to Caroline.

"Uh, I don't know," she says. "I guess I hope not?"

"But do you think it's possible?" Caroline pushes. "Do you feel like maybe that's sort of who she is?"

"I don't know," Evie says, "but I'd be sad if anybody killed themself."

"It has to be acknowledged," Caroline says thoughtfully. "There's a high suicide rate for gay teens in this country. B.B. has been bullied at school, she has issues in her family, she's a tough kid but she's also . . . frankly, she's been depressed. And the holidays are a tough time."

Ming sees exactly where Caroline is going. "She's always had a darkness about her," she says. "Like even at school you could tell there was something off."

If anyone is going to deliver, it's Ming. Caroline gives her a nod, and Ming is off. The other girls are mesmerized by her gift of speech; even if they already knew this story, they lean in, hanging on her every word. She talks about B.B. as an outcast, she talks about her as a stalker ("And they said she even followed Molly into the *bathroom stall*"), and she talks about her as an addict ("I mean, it's *genetic*, everybody knows that, and you could see it in the way she smoked, that she was gonna end up doing heroin"). She paints a picture of someone who has been in free fall since childhood, and whose sojourn with us was only a brief suspension in that plummet. Ming is sharp and uncompromising, but she stops short of unkindness. Every once in a while, she'll add something surprising that changes the texture of the story—that B.B. bought tampons for her once; that when she was worried she had an STD, B.B. was the only person she told, because she knew B.B. wouldn't tell anybody else. "And she never did," Ming says wistfully. "As far as I know, she never did."

Ming takes this story in a sharp left turn, right around the bend and straight toward the goalpost, where Caroline is waiting for her. She talks about how she herself has been depressed before, and that the only thing that has kept her from going missing is this group of girls, this space curated by Caroline. Mona starts crying, and by the way her face splotches up and she keeps rubbing her nose with her sleeve, I can tell she's forgotten about the camera. Actual Nickey puts a fingertip under her eyes without actually touching her mascara, which indicates that she has *not* forgotten about the camera. Evie looks mildly perturbed, like she isn't sure what's expected of her. And Caroline, in a coup that none of us saw coming, finishes the scene by kneeling next to Ming on the carpet, her arms around her, that curtain of hair falling over Ming's face until only Caroline's is visible, both of them framed in the camera's eye as she says, "You're safe here, you're safe with me."

*

Evie comes out on the porch and catches me smoking.

"I thought you went home already," she says.

"I was about to." We're quiet, and then I have to ask: "Are people really saying she killed herself?"

"I don't know," Evie says, "I didn't hear that till today."

"From the girls at the mall."

"Nah, I wasn't at the mall. Ming said it, before you arrived—her and Mona were at the mall. And then Caroline wanted me to tell it."

"But maybe it's not true."

Evie sighs. "I don't know. Like I said, I wasn't there."

"Why did she want you to tell it?"

Evie sounds very resigned and very adult when she replies. "Caroline says she wants a whole storyline about me being—I forget how she said it. Like, me being depressed, and then drawing a parallel to how B.B. musta felt. Caroline says that, historically, gay people and black people have been oppressed in similar ways, and this is an opportunity to have scenes where we talk about it." She shrugs. "But I don't really like cameras." Then she adds: "I told Caroline I don't like cameras, but she was like: *Don't be a quitter, Evie!* Like, *if you keep quitting things you'll never get anywhere.* Because I quit track last year. Which I also didn't like. So."

After Evie leaves, I place the butt end of my cigarette on Caroline's porch, so small she might not even see it but naked in its tiny rebellion, and I walk back across the street. I call B.B. five times in a row that night, but of course she never picks up.

*

On Christmas Eve day, B.B.'s phone goes dead, and Caroline summons me to talk about "the Twist."

She says it with a certain holy weight, a reverence: "You know, the Twist."

I shake my head, it's eight A.M., I don't know.

"The moment after which the narrative is never the same. The audience doesn't see it coming because the *generative artists* didn't see it coming. So it's like—on a structural level, and a personal, visceral level, it is . . . penetrative. It cuts through everything we think we are making or watching, and redirects us, all of us together. It is a guarantor of humanity in that way, and a . . . a sort of narrative equalizer . . . we are *equally* shocked by what has occurred . . . and it is also a guarantor of commercial success."

She leans over the desk toward me, eyes wide, trying to plug me into her hot current of potential energy. "Like in *S-Town*," she says, "when John dies halfway through, and the narrator is like, *This is not what I thought the story was*."

I shake my head.

"You never listened to *S-Town*?"

I shake my head. Caroline does the face that is shock, and dismay, and confusion, and then says, "Sorry, spoiler alert. Anyway, the main character, John—he's gay and depressed, he's this outcast genius in a small town. The narrator becomes his friend, the narrator is like: This is the story of a gay depressed genius. And we think it's gonna be, you know, this *vignette*. Of someone's *life*. But *then* he *kills* himself, and now it's suddenly this whole other thing."

"That sounds really sad," I say, because she's waiting for me to say something.

"It was! It was really sad! Everybody was crying and posting about it!

Everybody was like: *I just listened to episode two, and I can't stop crying. Like, all these people.* Caroline takes a sip of her coffee—she's been too excited to drink it. She adds, "*I* cried," a little defensively. Then she leans forward again: "*But:* compelling. We were all *compelled*. And I've been thinking a lot about it, and it feels like—B.B. is our Twist."

I'd been afraid she was going to say that.

I say, "B.B.?" like I never saw it coming.

"We're making a movie about these girls, and the audience is like: *This is a badass feminist film about teenage girls!* And then . . . *bam.* B.B. is gone. Where did she go? What happened? Who even *was* she?" Caroline spreads her hands, like *Who can know?* "And all of a sudden, the camera . . . is turned around. On us. The filmmakers. Who are faced with this *absence*, and everything it means."

"On us?"

"On me," Caroline says, "and on us."

I study my coffee cup. It's the same one she gave me that first morning in her house—TRIBECA FILM FESTIVAL on the side, the groove in the handle where my thumb has learned to fit. The house is empty except for us; all the girls are gone now. The silence hangs over us, eerie.

"Soooo," Caroline says, very carefully, "what do you think?"

I say, also carefully, "Have we heard anything more from B.B.'s mom?"

"No."

"But you went to go see her?"

"Yeah," Caroline says. "And—you know. They're really worried. As am I. As are we all."

"And the police . . . ?"

"Are looking for her," Caroline says, "and obviously are in contact with her family, not me. So what I'm talking about is what *we* can do, on *this* end, to . . . you know, honor what B.B. would have wanted."

"What would B.B. have wanted?" I ask, and then realize it sounds like I'm agreeing that maybe she's dead, and nausea rises in my chest.

"I think B.B. cared a lot about this movie," Caroline tells me, very calmly, "and I think she would have been really sad if she inadvertently stopped its *momentum*. Clearly, she was struggling—mentally, I mean—but I think she would have really wanted us to continue—"

"She's not dead," I say sharply.

"Well, I hope she isn't," Caroline replies, in that infuriatingly calm voice, and we stare at each other. Then Caroline leans back, fingers steepled, and says, "Cath, am I sensing that you're losing interest in all of this?"

I can't help myself. "You know this is our fault, right?"

"No," Caroline says, "I don't know anything of the sort." Her jaw is set hard. I recognize that steeliness, and I'm afraid of it. And maybe she's right, anyway—I'm the one who rejected B.B., I'm the one who betrayed her trust.

"Okay," I say, "*my* fault."

"Cath." Caroline's face softens into gentleness. She leans over the desk toward me. "Of course it isn't your fault." There's a way in which people say this phrase, where you see through the porousness of it, straight to the rigid core of their relief—that it *is* your fault and not theirs.

Caroline says a lot of other things that morning—about B.B. and about the movie and about our responsibility to this story, to the other girls in it, and about how responsibility to a story supersedes responsibility to an individual. She says things about the Twist, and she says things about assigning blame, and she says things about how great art comes when people are interested in something larger than assigning blame. She speaks for a long time, she is impassioned and eloquent and convincing, and none of it seems to sink in. I keep thinking of the look on B.B.'s face when she said, "Fuck you, Cath," right before she left. I wait until Caroline is done talking, is looking at me expectantly, and I nod okay, I give her what she wants, and then I leave.

*

Walking up my driveway, I realize that it's only ten A.M. It feels as if I've been with Caroline for days, not hours. Dylan and Daniel are leaving later this afternoon for Dylan's parents', and then the house will be as ominously quiet as Caroline's was. As I fumble with the front door, I think maybe I should have gone home to New Hampshire for Christmas. It had felt like it would be such an act of failure, to go home like this—empty-handed, nothing to celebrate, so much to avoid saying. I'd thought that I couldn't bring myself to do it. But maybe I should have done it anyway.

I kick my sneakers off in the hall, walk into the kitchen, and come face-to-face with a naked man.

We stare at each other, both of us stricken. I get a flash of early twenties, brown hair, wide startled eyes, dick like a coke can, and then he gives a dismayed hiccup and springs out of the kitchen and up the stairs. I consider the idea that we're being mugged by a nudist, but then the rumble of voices starts above me—his high and insistent, Dylan's lower and calming—and I file this entire thing into the sizable category of Not My Business.

Dylan comes down ten minutes later. I'm out on the patio, drinking my coffee and watching the hummingbirds come and go by the lemon tree. I hear a muffled conversation, the front door closes, and then Dylan leans in the open rectangle of the sliding doors, mug in hand.

"Hey," he says. His hair is bed tousled, low-slung sweatpants ride his hips.

"Hey," I say.

A moment, and then Dylan leaves the safety of the doors, arranging himself on the other lounge chair opposite mine. "What're you looking at?" he asks, following my gaze.

"Hummingbirds."

Silence. There isn't much more to say about hummingbirds. Dylan sips his coffee, then without a discernible shift in tone: "I know you ran into Clyde downstairs. He told me."

"He really didn't look like a Clyde."

"He said you looked at his dick."

"I mean, it was front and center."

Dylan grins, then sobers. "You think I'm fucking everything up."

"Look," I say. "Your relationship isn't my business, I don't know what agreements you guys have right now."

"We don't. I cheated."

"Oh." We drink our coffee. I have to ask, "Where's Daniel?"

"His work friends took him to Joshua Tree last night. A goodbye party. I knew he wouldn't have fun if I went, so . . ." Dylan shrugs.

"Are you still technically together?"

"Until he leaves, yeah. We said that once his plane takes off—when it reaches altitude? That's the breakup."

"That's very symbolic."

"Or cowardly. That we won't even look each other in the eyes when we do it."

"Whose idea was it?"

"Who do you think?" Dylan asks, with real bitterness, and I'm quiet. Then he says, "I agreed to it, though. I can't—that's me, always *agreeing*. And then I want things to be different but it's like, I can't complain when I was so fucking *agreeable* to begin with." After a second he adds, "I don't know why I fucked him. Clyde, I mean."

"Is he a friend?"

"No, I got him off Grindr. I don't even know if his real name *is* Clyde. That might be a thing, so he gets to say his line."

"What's his line?"

Dylan grimaces and laughs at the same time, and then, making his voice breathy, says: "Are you gonna be my Bonnie?"

"Oh god, stop."

"I mean . . . I did stop. I was like: *Never say that again*." Dylan puts his face in his hands, and I think it's about Clyde, but then from inside his hands he says, "Why'd I have to go ahead and make it *dirty*? You know? It's always been a lot with us, sometimes too much, but nobody ever cheated, nobody lied. And then right before the end . . ."

"Don't you think that's why you did it?"

Dylan drops his hands. "Why?"

"To sort of ruin it, so it's easier to let go of."

"Oh," Dylan says softly. After a long silence, he looks at me. "I'm gonna tell him."

"Okay."

"Shouldn't I?"

"I don't know."

"Or is that going to hurt him for no reason?"

"Maybe," I say. "But didn't you do this to punish him?"

"If I'd done this to punish him," Dylan says immediately, "I would have fucked a girl." Then he winces. "I'm sorry."

"No, I know what you mean." I give him a half smile. "My first girlfriend? When we were breaking up, she was like, *Just don't date a man after me*."

"I forget," Dylan says, "how you know exactly what I mean."

"Guys are the same, though. They're fine going in, but then all of a sudden it's like: *So, did you think my sister was hot?* And the ones who tell you it's not a big deal? It's gonna be the biggest deal for them."

"Yeah," Dylan says. "Well. At least Daniel never said it wasn't a big deal."

"And your friends?"

Dylan sighs. "Honestly, most of them met me with Daniel, and they think I'm gay. The minute you say you're bi . . . gay guys are vicious about that. And Daniel's been like . . . my adult life, so I haven't had to open that can of worms. Oh god," Dylan says as a thought strikes him. "What if I date a girl next?"

"Total shitstorm."

"Fuck me. It would have to be a state secret."

The same thought strikes us both at the same time. I see it hit him, and his jaw tightens. I'm not going to say it, but he does anyway: "Sounds familiar, huh."

I know he doesn't want that answered, so I don't try to answer it. After a minute, he nudges my knee with his. "Remember when we . . . ?"

"Yeah."

"So young," Dylan says. "So dumb."

"We were, what, eighteen?"

"Total idiots. You brought a bottle of peach schnapps."

"*Gross*. I did not."

Dylan laughs out loud. "You absolutely did. You brought this bottle of peach schnapps to my room—and I was like *Who the fuck is this girl*—"

"We were already friends by then!"

"No, I know, but in a whole new way, I was like *Who the fuck*—but then I drank it. We both did." Dylan leans his head back, letting the sun fall on his face. His eyes stay on me as he says, "I couldn't have been much good."

"Are you asking me if I remember whether the sex was good or not?"

Dylan's mouth quirks. He makes a gesture, like: *Maybe, maybe not.*

"Come *on*," I say. "Seriously? We were eighteen and wasted." And then I have to ask: "Does Daniel . . . ?"

"No," Dylan says fast.

"Because he'd hate me?"

"Because I'd have to say I didn't enjoy it," Dylan says reluctantly. "And I did. Enjoy it."

In the silence, we look each other straight in the face. It isn't flirtation. It isn't even that electric charge I know so well, that I spent months chasing with Hélène. It is pure recognition: rare and sad. It makes me ache.

"Maybe when Daniel leaves I won't date at all," Dylan says at last, "and then I won't have to lie to anyone."

"Maybe you should only date people you don't have to lie to," I suggest, and then we both start laughing. As if it's that easy. As if I have any advice worth giving.

※

When I wake up on Christmas Day, the house is bright and silent. I drink coffee, I wander around the block, I walk to Sunset Junction. Most of the stores are closed, and the haphazard decorations feel strange without snow. The day passes slowly. I try to read, but I can't concentrate. I browse movies on my laptop, but I can't decide what to watch. I order takeout and don't eat it. I look over the fence toward Caroline's house, but I can't tell if she's home or not. Maybe she's at a family gathering. Maybe she's sitting at a long table laden with food, and she's telling everyone about how B.B.'s disappearance is the cherry on the sundae, exactly like *S-Town*.

I call my parents and we chat briefly. The familiarity of their voices fills me with loneliness; I can almost smell the mustiness of their old house, the pine needles of the small tree my mother would have gotten outside Hannaford. Right now, being alone on Christmas feels like more of a failure than going home with nothing to show. After my parents say goodbye, I call Nico; he doesn't pick up, and I leave him a voicemail. And then, without intending to, I find myself calling Jocelyn.

Jocelyn picks up her cell on the fifth ring. "Cass!" she chirps. "How are you!" I can hear sounds in the background, people talking and laughing, maybe a TV, the low *tat-tat-tat* of TV gunfire.

"Hey!" I say.

"Hang on a sec . . ." Shuffling; the *tat-tat-tat* dies away. A door closes. "Hey! Okay. Hi."

"Merry Christmas," I say, too hearty.

"Oh, my family is Jewish," Jocelyn says, "but happy holidays. What's up?"

"I'm wondering if . . ." I hesitate, and then plow forward. Jocelyn has seen me in a cascading aria of low points, there is no more dignity to preserve. "I'm wondering if you could read me Tara-Jean Slater's poems."

"Her poems?" Jocelyn echoes.

"Yeah. If you wouldn't mind."

"You mean the depression ones?"

"Yeah."

"Right now?"

"Uh. I mean, I'll be up for a while. So if tomorrow—if tomorrow would be better . . ."

"No," Jocelyn said, "uh, I guess I can do it now. But I'm not good at reading poetry or anything. I don't really understand poetry."

"That's okay."

"Like, some people have a poetry-reading voice? And I don't."

"I think you could just read in your normal voice."

"I'm pulling it up on my phone," Jocelyn says. "Hang on." A long silence and then she says, "I just have the first two. I don't have the full set or whatever."

"That's okay, read the ones you have."

"'Depression One,'" Jocelyn announces. Then, sotto voce, "That's the title."

"I remember."

"Oh, right. Uh. Okay." Jocelyn clears her throat. She reads:

> I just keep circling
> the same bowl;
> Goldfish or
> toilet?
> I can't decide

A moment of silence as we both contemplate the poem. Then Jocelyn says, doubtfully: "I mean, it's about depression?" She sounds like she's no longer sure. "I don't get poetry, like I said."

"I mean, no, I think you're right."

"I'm not sure—like, with the line breaks, do you pause, or ram all the way through?"

"I don't really know."

"Huh." Jocelyn hesitates, clearly conflicted. Then: "I'm gonna try ramming."

"Okay."

She reads: "I just keep circling the same bowl goldfish or toilet I can't decide."

"I think pauses are better."

"Yeah, I think so too. Anyway, the other one I have is called 'Rothko.'" Jocelyn clears her throat again and reads:

> Rothko,
> you made so many attempts.

Everybody wants to hire me;
I am the village bike.
No wonder bicycles
are lonely.

I make her read it again, twice. Then I ask her to describe the punctuation. She gets hung up on the semicolon ("It's like . . . a period stacked on top of a comma, I forget what you call it?") and finally says, "Look, I'm gonna text you a screen shot, but you *cannot* tell anybody I shared it."

"Jocelyn," I say, "you are crazy if you think I am telling anybody anything about anything."

"Great," Jocelyn says. Then, "I'm gonna go back to my family now, but it should come through any sec."

"Thanks," I say, and she's right, because as soon as we hang up, it's waiting for me on my screen. A tiny little stack of a poem. I read it a few times. It makes a knot form in my stomach. I hope that means that it's bad. I hope that Tara-Jean Slater is massively untalented, that she is a fluke of the market. I want to dismiss Tara-Jean Slater as badly as I wanted to put a finger in her eye.

But something about that poem.

I lie in bed that night and I keep reading it. *No wonder bicycles / are lonely.* And then my eyes flick back up to the top and start again: *Rothko, / you made so many attempts.* The poem does something to me that may have nothing to do with the fact of its being a poem. Maybe it is a conduit. Maybe all poems are actually conduits. Some poems might be viaducts, others are tunnels, the ones I normally never understand would be complex systems of pipes and tubes. But each of them is a means of conveyance, a channel for some kind of nameless power that bubbles up from somewhere deep in a person and then needs to be directed out. When I think about it like that, I start to feel like I understand poetry. I think: *I should tell Jocelyn that.* But I fall asleep before I can text her.

13

Daniel and I drive to Monterey a few days after Christmas. I help him carry a giant framed painting from their bedroom to the back seat of the car, where we wedge it carefully to the side of the slightly deconstructed desk. It feels good to be useful in a way that is tangible.

"You're really the best," Daniel says as we take the 101 up the coast. "I wasn't expecting you to sign up for a five-hour drive."

"It's nice to get out for a bit," I say. Caroline has been away, presumably with her mother, and I haven't heard from her or any of the girls. Inside this holiday limbo, the thought of B.B. remains suspended over me like an anvil. Is she still missing? Or, even worse, did they find her body tucked into a crawlspace, a bottle of pills and a fifth of vodka?

"How's the movie going?" Daniel asks, as if he's read my mind.

"It's sort of . . . uh, hit a snag."

"Oh no." Daniel sounds genuinely concerned. "You mean financially?"

"No . . ." I briefly consider explaining the B.B. situation to Daniel. We would have to talk about the shoot, about Caroline. I would have to say the words "the Twist" out loud. I can't do it. "It's complicated," I say. "How are you feeling about going home next week?"

A moment while Daniel considers the road. Then he says, his voice soft and apologetic: "It's complicated."

We listen to music for the rest of the drive.

*

His aunt's house is beautiful and modern, surrounded by thick trees. As I get out of the car, I see the curve of headland, the steady blue of ocean beyond. The air smells fresh and sharp, reminding me of New Hampshire. Even from here, I can hear breakers churning on rock.

I don't know what I imagined, but Daniel's aunt and uncle are not it. Maybe I assumed some kind of strictness, a conservative coldness. His aunt comes out to greet us, offering up a big hug and a kiss, even before Daniel introduces me. She has long hair, blond that has grayed into a shimmering ash. Her Australian accent is lighter than his, but still there. "Your uncle is on the grill," she tells Daniel, "but Lucy and co aren't even here yet, I don't know who he thinks is going to be ready to eat."

His uncle is laconic, a big man with giant hands. He's hunched over the grill in back, cheeks flushed with heat. When he sees us, his face cracks into a large, shy smile. "Well now," he says, a few times, and gives me a hearty handshake. "Well now, Cass."

His aunt pours us each a glass of cabernet from an open bottle, and we awkwardly settle in the living room. She asks me about Los Angeles — how long have I been there, do I think it's safe. It can be rough, she wants me to know, she wouldn't advise walking around alone at night — and Daniel says, "She's not a kid," and his aunt tells him, "You're both kids to me."

Daniel's cousin Lucy arrives with three sticky boys between the ages of two and six. Her husband is parking the car, and he enters last. He resembles the largest of the sticky boys — same towhead, same blunt nose, same blue eyes. He shakes hands with the men, hugs Daniel's aunt, and turns a vaguely interested gaze on me. "Good to finally meet you," he says, and Daniel's cousin echoes it, folding me into a hug.

"I wondered when we'd get the chance," she says. Her accent is fully American, and her eyes are suspiciously bright. She darts a private look at her mom, so quick I almost miss it. Suddenly I wonder what Daniel told them about me. I shoot him a glance. His face is impassive. He refills his wineglass and then, in a gallant gesture, reaches over and tops off mine.

"See that, Petey?" Lucy turns toward her husband.

"Okay, okay," Petey grumbles, good-natured. He fetches a new bottle from the kitchen. When he returns, Lucy asks me, with studied casualness, "How long has it been, again?"

"Has what been?" I ask. Daniel dips a peeled shrimp into melted butter and bites it off at the tail. He offers me the small butter bowl for my shrimp.

"For the two of you," Lucy says. And then, laughing as Daniel's eyes dart up from the plate, "He's notoriously private about everything. His mum and dad are always asking us what he's up to, as if we'd know."

"Lucy," Daniel's aunt says, "don't tease your cousin, he just got here."

"When did you move to L.A.?" Lucy asks me, ignoring her mother.

"Oh, uh . . ." I look to Daniel, but he's staring back down at the melted butter. Without looking up he says, "Don't interrogate her."

"In October," I say. "I moved to L.A. in October."

"Not long, then," his cousin says in surprise, looking at her mother. "We thought it was much longer."

"Well, they *met* years ago," the aunt tells her. "But all the—back and forth, the travel, didn't you say, Daniel? That it was long distance?"

"More wine?" Daniel gets up, headed toward the kitchen without waiting for an answer.

"There's wine here," his uncle calls after him. "Dazza, there's wine here!" But he's vanished inside. After a second I say, clumsily, "I'll just . . . the restroom . . ."

"Past the kitchen on the left," his aunt says. "Shall I show you?"

"No, no," I lie, hastily, "I saw it on the way in." And I follow Daniel into the house without giving anyone a chance to accompany me.

He's standing in the kitchen looking miserable when I walk in. I wait for him to speak, and when he doesn't, I say: "You told them we're together." Not quite an accusation, just a statement—giving him the chance to tell me that I misunderstood. Instead, he grabs me by the wrist and pulls me after him down the hall. I yank my wrist back, pissed, but follow.

When we're sequestered in the small bathroom, Daniel's back pressed to the door, he says, "Look—" then stops, as if he isn't sure what comes next.

"Did you tell them we were dating?"

"Not at first . . ."

"But they *assumed*, and you didn't correct them."

Daniel nods.

"Is that why you asked me here? So you could parade a girl around and the news would get back home, and I'd be . . . what, living proof?"

When he mutters "no," so weakly that it sounds like a yes, I know I was right.

"That's fucked up."

"What's the big difference, anyway?"

I stare at him. "The *difference*, Daniel, is that we're *not* together. To start with. But also, more to the point, I'm queer and *you're*—" At the genuine alarm on his face, I stop.

"It's not like you don't fuck men too," Daniel whispers defensively. "It's not like you're a lesbian."

"*Excuse* me?"

"So the whole—I mean, we're not *together*, obviously, but it's not like you're *not* someone who would sleep with a man. So, what's the difference to you if they think I'm the man you're sleeping with?"

It takes a moment before I can find my voice, and when I do, it's harder and steadier than I thought it would be. "Because when I *do* fuck men, I'm sure as hell not *lying* about myself. That's the difference, and it's a pretty substantial one from where I'm standing."

In the silence I can hear an indistinct chatter of voices from outside. One of the little boys shouts something and everyone laughs. The sound of them refocuses Daniel back on me, a growing desperation straining his voice.

"Cass," he says, "I need you to—you don't have to *say* . . . You don't have to *tell* them any sort of . . . but let it be. Can you do that? I'm gonna leave, and it won't matter to you after this. But it will matter to me."

"You shouldn't have brought me into this. Not like this."

"Maybe not," Daniel admits, defeated. "But I knew you wouldn't . . . if I'd asked you, you wouldn't have."

"Been your cover? I don't know—but you didn't ask, you just *put* me—"

"I know," Daniel says. "And I know it's fucked up. But I really . . . I need this."

"Fuck you," I say, soft, and Daniel hears a kind of yielding in that, because I can see relief wash over him, and it's all in his voice when he says, "Thank you. Cass, thank you."

*

I call Hélène from the bathroom after Daniel goes back outside. Because it is instinct and not a plan—because I haven't even considered what to say—the truth comes tumbling out as soon as I hear her warm, quizzical "Cass?"

"I'm hiding in the bathroom of a house in Monterey and everyone thinks I'm straight and I've done everything wrong since I last saw you. Where are you?"

The amusement in Hélène's voice fills me with relief and longing. "Do you ever . . . I don't know, relax?"

"Yes, but those aren't the moments in which I call you."

She snorts. "Well, you're in luck. I'm in San Francisco—an hour north or so."

"Can I see you?"

"If I give you my address, do you have a car?"

"I can borrow one," I say with grim determination, and I write her address on a square of toilet paper.

I take Daniel aside under the thinnest of pretenses and when we're alone, I fold my arms. "Here's the deal. For the next two hours, I'm your devoted girlfriend. I'm so sad you're moving to Sydney, I can't stop holding your hand, there are so many memories of our life together that I'll get tipsy and spill. In return, I take the car for the night."

"For the *night*!" Daniel's accent is thicker than usual—a combination of being around his relatives and surprise. "Where are *you* going?"

"Deal or no deal, Daniel. Either you can have the Girlfriend Experience or I can tell them all I'm a lesbian. Big coming-out in the middle of holiday lunch. Tears."

"You're *not* a lesbian!" Daniel yelps.

"No," I say, "but I've decided I'm okay with lies—it's up to you which one I tell."

Daniel eyes me, both resentful and impressed. "You're tough as nails, aren't you?"

"You started this bullshit," I remind him. "Lemme know which way you'd like it to go."

I know he'll say yes before he does. His need is palpable. If I have learned nothing else from Caroline, it is how to recognize desperation in others and make use of it before they learn to tuck it safely away. Or maybe I knew that all along.

*

Hélène is staying in a basement apartment in the Castro; the guesthouse of a theatre donor, she explains when she lets me in. It's early evening, and the drive into the city took an extra hour because of traffic. She looks exactly like herself—smile lines deep at the corners of her eyes, a red wool sweater with holes in the elbows. I realize that only a few months have passed since I was in her East Village apartment. I feel like an entirely different person now—but here I am, showing up at her door, so then again, maybe I'm entirely the same person.

"Well," Hélène says, as if she's having the same thoughts: "You seem much less . . . moth-eaten than I expected."

"*Moth*-eaten?"

"You look fine, actually." She crosses to the countertop, gesturing to an arrangement of bottles. "Wine, scotch?"

"I'd take a coffee?"

"Lucky for you there's a Keurig right here, waiting to choke a landfill." Hélène flicks the top open and jams a pod in upside down, then extracts it and puts it in correctly. "So," she says thoughtfully, studying the machine while it hums and shakes. "You were in Monterey pretending to be a heterosexual."

I have imagined this moment many times over the past few months—being near Hélène somewhere, anywhere. I'd imagined correctly her wryness, her presence. My desire for her, akin to the sensation of everything inside me being pulled out to my edges by a large magnet. What I didn't imagine was that it wouldn't hurt. Instead, I feel a kind of vivid joy, like every cell inside me is awake but unharmed. With enough time, B.B. could have felt this too—about me, or about her high school girlfriend, or about someone else. This feeling, whatever you call it—*Is this love?*—could have become beautiful if I'd given her the privacy to feel it through to the end.

Hélène hands me a mug of black coffee. "I don't have any milk, but there's some unspeakable oat thing in the fridge."

"Black is fine."

Hélène leads me into the small living room and we sit across from each other, in strangely shaped armchairs. "Would you like to tell me all of the terrible things you've been doing?" she inquires.

I do and then suddenly I don't. "How's San Francisco?" I ask instead. A moment as she studies me, and I follow it up with: "I didn't think you'd still be here."

"Me neither, frankly. But I find holidays incredibly depressing. So here I am, hiding out in a basement far away from the family gathering." Hélène makes a wry, humorous gesture indicating the space, its subterranean isolation. "The show opened weeks ago, but luckily, none of my family understands what it means for a play to be open. The story is that I'm working around the clock, deadlines, press, etcetera."

I've never heard Hélène mention her family before. Or admit that she found anything depressing. This Hélène feels looser and less guarded than the one I remember. I wonder if she was drinking before I got here, or if this is how she is when she can be my friend and not my director.

"Where's the family gathering?"

"London, this year. My sister's house. She's a barrister—that's 'lawyer' to you. Three children, a husband. So many delicious accomplishments." She shakes her head. "And then me." She pitches her voice into a dubious key, speaking as her sister: "'So, Hélène, are you . . . making a play at the moment?'"

"You can't be trying to tell me that *you're* the black sheep."

"Theatre only feels like an accomplishment if you're part of the cult," she says crisply. "The rest of the world thinks we're all wasting our best years." Then, as if reminded: "Did you make the next thing yet?"

I think about the movie and I know better than to claim it. Not to Hélène.

"No," I admit, "not yet."

"That's all right. Urgency is the only messenger worth listening to. When it arrives." Then her wry smile deepens and she adds, "Then again, the thought of seeing my sister makes me *urgently* want to throw myself off a bridge. Or put a finger in her eye."

My heart plummets through the floor. "You heard—I mean, obviously you heard . . . ?" How had I managed to keep Hélène separate from all of that in my head? A trick of compartmentalization, I realize, or simple desperation.

"Obviously I heard," Hélène says. "It's all anyone cared to talk about for quite some time."

"I'm sorry."

"Don't apologize to me." She smirks. "Both my eyes are fine."

"Hélène!"

"Oh, lighten up, I'm not condoning your ridiculous behavior." After a moment, she sobers. "I thought of calling you, but I also thought about what I would need if I was you. And that was distance. When I heard you left New York, I felt I'd been right."

"You were, I think."

"And how is the distance serving you?"

"Not well enough."

This makes Hélène smile. "You know, that was why I moved to New York, at first. To get as far away as possible from a family of doctors and lawyers and . . ." She makes a gesture that signifies general, unforgivable success. "But, of course, the distance is never as far as you think it will be, since they're all still inside your head—commenting on your life even as you're living it."

I mean to ask Hélène any number of questions, but what comes out is: "Do you actually feel like you haven't succeeded?" When she looks at me, keen and probing, I stumble to shore up the question: "I mean . . . you *must*, in some part of yourself, feel like . . . you made it?"

"Like I made it," Hélène repeats, letting the words remain mine.

"Professionally, even."

"I'm proud of *what* I've made," Hélène says, slowly. "I think, most days, I'm proud of the way I live. The mistakes are many, but they are *mine*. But then . . . sometimes I ask myself, What do I have to show for it? All the plays, whether they went badly or well—they're over now. There's nothing you can hold in your hand when it's done. And my sister . . . Her life is so tangible, you see. It is a life of tangible measurements. A husband, children, a house. And mine . . ." She considers. "That doubt, when it gets into my bones, it feels like so much . . . failure. And I start to ask myself: How did I get here, and was there not a better place to be?"

We're quiet. In the silence, I love her even more for letting me see a side of her that, in all my worshipful lust, I'd never tried to imagine. After some time passes, she asks: "What were you fleeing from, anyway?"

"Me?"

"All the way to Monterey?" She lifts an eyebrow, challenging me. But I don't want to talk about myself. I thought I'd come here to—what? Tell her about B.B., and all the mistakes I've made since New York, and the weight of those mistakes on me? Ask for her forgiveness, both specific and general? What a bore for Hélène, I think, she didn't sign up to be my private god.

"Just a gentle jaunt," I say. "A friendly day trip."

Her eyebrows say, *Oh, really?* but she doesn't press. "You can sleep on the couch if you want," she says casually.

"Are you sure?"

"It's nearly midnight, Cass. I don't need you driving into the ocean and adding your death to my list of failures."

I brush my teeth in the small side bathroom with my finger and some toothpaste. Splash water on my face. When I emerge, Hélène is tucking spare sheets onto the couch. She folds a wool blanket down over the end.

"Thank you," I say. As I sink down onto the couch, I realize how exhausted I am.

Hélène bends and touches my cheek lightly with her fingertips. I can smell faded perfume, lemongrass, scotch. "My bedroom door will be locked," she says dryly, as if to make up for having been gentle.

There was a time when I would have been embarrassed by this reminder of my rejection. This time, the wry joke of it reaches me instead, her self-mockery as clear as her mockery of me.

"Let me know when you come to your senses," I say sleepily.

I hear the smile in her voice when she says, "I imagine you'll be the first to know."

*

I call Tara-Jean Slater the night before New Year's Eve.

The house is empty. Dylan and Daniel are both out, although not together. Since Christmas, they've orbited each other with care. Dylan tells me later that their visit to his parents ended up being tense; they didn't even get up the nerve to reveal that the relationship was ending. Maintaining the charade has burned out their last reserve of energy, and now they're giving each other space. Daniel and I are in a similar position. We haven't discussed Monterey; on the ride back, we listened to podcasts and barely spoke.

Home alone, I find myself reading Tara-Jean Slater's poem again and again, until I'm saying the words in a full voice: "Rothko, / you made so many attempts. / Everybody wants to hire me; / I am the village bike. / No wonder bicycles are lonely." I am saying it with the pauses ("Rothko . . . you made so many") and without them ("Rothkoyoumadesomany"), and then I'm moving with it, standing on my bed letting each sentence plummet into the silence like a declaration: "ROTHKO!! You MADE! So MANY! . . . ATTEMPTS!" And then I pick up my phone, find the Lansing Fellows email with its contact sheet, and before this recklessness can abandon me, I dial the number attached to Tara-Jean Slater.

On the other end, her phone rings and rings. And then, unexpectedly, she picks up.

That little voice, like a hot wire. "Hello?"

I don't say anything. I'm frozen.

"Hello?" Tara-Jean Slater says again, impatiently.

"Hi," I say, before I know I'm going to. "Hello."

"Who is this?"

"Uh. This is . . . Julie. From. *The New Yorker.*"

"Julie?"

"An intern, I mean. An intern at *The New Yorker.*"

"Okay." Tara-Jean Slater doesn't sound suspicious. "So, what's up?"

"I read your poems. Your poem 'Rothko.'"

"Yeah?"

"They were in the, uh, the stack of things we're publishing . . . ?"

"Yeah," Tara-Jean Slater says. "Is there a problem?"

"No," I hasten. "No, no. I—I liked them."

"Thank you," Tara-Jean Slater says in her small, dead voice. I try to imagine her eyes. I remember that she would be wearing an eye patch. I wonder if she has different colored eye patches, for different events or moods, or if it's always the lime-green one.

"And I wondered . . ." I'm not sure what I wonder. I wait to hear it from myself. "I wondered if you think . . . uh . . . if you think that the *narrator,* in these poems. Has any hope."

"The narrator?"

"Yeah, the narrator. If you imagine that the narrator has hope for joy."

"Well," Tara-Jean Slater says, "the narrator is me."

"Oh." I didn't know poets ever said that so directly, that anybody ever claimed the ambiguous *I* of poetry. I'd been taught, in a variety of writing classes, that you were only allowed to talk about characters as "the narrator"—even in one-woman shows that recounted painful breakups that you'd seen the writer-performer going through, you were still only supposed to give feedback about the experience of "the narrator." And here was Tara-Jean Slater, flouting convention once again.

"So," Tara-Jean Slater says, "I guess the answer is no, I don't have hope for joy."

"Oh."

Julie, intern from *The New Yorker*, fumbles for the next question. Maybe this question would be: "But Tilda Swinton wants to play your adult self, how is it that you have no joy?" But as Julie fumbles, Tara-Jean Slater hangs up with a *click*. The room becomes quiet once again, a quiet that spools outward and outward, that becomes the silence of the whole house, of the night, of the neighborhood—not even a dog barking—of the city, of the country, of the planet, of outer space. Somewhere in that silence, B.B. is tucked away like a chrysalis. But where? Becoming what?

Rothko, the silence says, *you made so many attempts.*

*

New Year's Eve comes, and we have Daniel's last supper in the backyard.

Dylan turns on strings of fairy lights wound around the lemon tree, and the yard glows. I buy a six-pack of Negra Modelo, a bottle of good tequila, and a bag of ice. Dylan unpacks a bag of tacos and an extra paper sack of fresh tortilla chips, and we dump a jar of jalapeño salsa into a bowl and squeeze lime over it. We play music off the outdoor speakers, filling the patio with Miles Davis. The air is cool and clear, surprisingly mild for the last night of December. We keep it light, talking lazily about movies, bands. Daniel volunteers that the weather in Sydney is very similar to California, and so we talk about that for a while. When the conversation turns fully to Sydney, it maintains its impersonal nature; Daniel tells us about flying foxes—bat-looking creatures that are actually marsupials. He tells us that they roost upside down in the shelter of the botanical gardens during the day, and emerge at dusk, chasing mosquitos and flies, turning cartwheels under streetlamps. He makes Australia sound like a cross between some kind of strange paradise and a Hieronymus Bosch painting.

After the paper plates are emptied and we've shared a few tequilas, we toast to the new year. We're still an hour from midnight, but the glimmer of the tiny string lights makes it feel as if we've entered into a space in which there is no time at all. We don't talk about our resolutions, or what we want the new year to hold. It's as if, by unspoken agreement, we're not acknowledging that this backyard dinner will end, and with it, their relationship. We have one more drink, and then I relinquish the yard to the two of them and head in. I pause in the doorway for a moment and glance back. Their heads are close together, gold and dark. Daniel is laughing, and Dylan is watching him with a look that is perceptive, loving, and entirely defeated. I close the sliding doors as silently as I can, and they don't look up.

I wake up with a start, because someone is in the room with me. I'm already bolting upright when my brain catches up to the moment and recognizes the unknown form as Daniel, saying softly, "It's okay, it's just me."

"Daniel," I say, groggy.

"I'm sorry, I didn't mean to wake you. I thought you might still be up."

"What time is it?"

"Late," Daniel says, and I hear in his voice that he's properly drunk but carrying it well.

"You and Dylan fight?"

"No, he's asleep." He hovers in the doorway, unsure, and I say, "Well, I'm awake now, come in."

He closes the door behind him with a click, and I see he has two glass tumblers tucked under his forearm, and the neck of a whiskey bottle between two fingers.

"Drink?" he asks.

"No thanks."

"You sure? Farewell nightcap. Last time." Daniel sits on the edge of my mattress without waiting for my answer, and it dips under his weight. He hands me one of the tumblers and pours a splash into each with steady hands. In the dark room, the whiskey is liquid black. We clink glasses and Daniel says, "Cheers." He drinks, I don't.

When he lowers his glass, he says, "What I asked you to do in Monterey was fucked up. You were right, and I'm sorry. I'm an arsehole."

"It's okay," I say, surprised.

"It isn't—I've thought quite a lot about it, actually. All the many reasons it was particularly loathsome."

"Well, I blackmailed you and made off with your car, so your apology is accepted."

Daniel laughs. "You know, if I were staying . . . I think we could've been great friends."

"As opposed to?"

"*Housemates,*" he says, with a nasal American accent, and for some reason it makes us both giggle. He takes another sip, and, lowering his glass, says: "Dylan cheated on me, didn't he?"

I choke. "What?"

"Didn't he?"

"Did he tell you that?"

"No. But." When I'm quiet, Daniel asks, casual, "A woman?"

"No."

"Oh." He drinks again.

"I ran into him by accident—the guy. It's not like . . . That's why I knew."

"I keep hurting him," Daniel says. "Even tonight. I knew he wanted . . . There's a way I could have been. That would have been . . . better."

"What way is that?"

"Sorry," Daniel answers me, after a moment of thought. "Very, very sorry."

"About leaving?"

Daniel rubs a hand over his face. "He would've come with me, you know."

"I didn't know."

"He said he'd move if that's what I wanted. And I said no."

When I'm quiet, he dismisses it: "Doesn't matter now, anyway. He'll find someone—a well-adjusted American, straight teeth, traumatic middle school experience, lots of therapy, ran the Gay-Straight Alliance at school." His teeth show when he adds, "They'll go surfing together."

"Daniel . . ."

"Kidding. Just kidding. Just being a tosser. But that *is* what I want for him. God bless his cowboy heart." Daniel takes a sip, discovers his tumbler is empty, pours more. Goes to top me off, but I put a few fingers over my glass, blocking it. He's quiet, and then he says, his voice rough, "You think I could do it?"

"Do what?"

"With a woman."

I look at him carefully, trying to take him in through the dark. "What do you think?"

"I don't know."

"Have you ever wanted to?"

He doesn't move, doesn't shake his head yes or no. The question seems to have unspooled a private rabbit warren of moments for him that he darts down and examines one after the other: *Did I then? What about then? And then?* After what feels like a long time he says, with a determination that tells me the answer at the end of each path was negative: "I never tried, though."

"Daniel, if you don't want to . . . probably you don't want to."

He examines this statement the way he did the other. Endless possibilities unfurl. After what feels like a long time, he says, "But Dylan can."

"Well . . . yeah."

"And you can."

"It isn't about whether you *can*, it's about *wanting* to."

After what feels like a long time, he lies back. Next to me, but not touching me. The heavy length of his body indents the mattress. Heat radiates off his shoulder, an inch from my bare arm. I can smell a mix of whiskey, sweat, and outdoor air emanating from him, not unpleasant. When I don't say anything, he shifts so that his shoulder rests against mine. I can feel Daniel listening, but I don't know whether he's alert for Dylan stirring upstairs, or for anything stirring within Daniel himself. Then he turns on his side, facing me.

"If you didn't know me at all, would you want to sleep with me?"

"Are you asking if you're able to suppress your subliminal gay emanations?"

To my surprise, I hear him smile in the dark. "Fuck you," he says, gravelly. "That's exactly what I'm asking."

"You don't have a neon arrow above your head, no," I say.

"This is an insane question, right?"

"A little bit."

"Like, politically unforgivable. Like, I'm setting us all back."

I hear the ghost of Dylan in those words. Whenever it was that Dylan said this, Daniel has held on to it.

"Sure," I say, "I guess so. But fuck politically. What about just for you? For your life?" I turn my head to him and his hair feathers against my chin, softer than I'd imagined. "It's one thing, I guess, what you said before—you don't need to shout your truth from the rooftops. Maybe that's too American. But if you have to worry all the time about . . . being a thing you're not . . . or *not* being a thing you are—then what are you standing on? How are you ever . . . home, I guess? It's like being in a . . . a third state, or a limbo . . . Being a stateless citizen, sort of. Do you know what I mean?" Daniel is silent, and I say, softer, "Daniel?"

He doesn't answer. His breathing drops and evens, slow and rhythmic, an undertow. He's fallen asleep. Or else he just doesn't want to talk anymore. I wonder if I should wake him up, send him upstairs. But there's something comforting about the heaviness of his body next to mine. Listening to his breathing, I slip under as well.

When I wake up, it's early afternoon on the first day of the new year and Daniel is several hours gone, beginning the first stage of his suspension over the Pacific, pointed like an arrow toward a Daniel far from the one I knew.

14

New Year's Day is a wasteland; the house is empty all day. The next day is much the same. Dylan's van remains gone; wherever he went, he's still there. I doze all morning, and dream that Dylan and B.B. are in the same place, and that I'm supposed to meet them there, but they forgot to give me directions. I wake up with a feeling like panic curling in my gut and make myself get out of bed and walk up and down in the backyard until I feel normal again.

Caroline calls me, then texts me. She's back from wherever she went. I know she wants to start getting ready for everything to start up again. For the Twist. The girls will be back soon, if they aren't already. But I don't pick up. Something in me can't seem to find whatever it would take to be Cath. I go for a run in the evening, taking Fountain Ave around to Hyperion so that I don't pass Caroline's house. I almost never jog, and it makes me damp and miserable. Halfway home, a twinge starts in my knee; when I slow down to walk, the wind blows through my sweat-soaked shirt, making me shiver uncontrollably. By the time I reach the house again, every part of me has succumbed to a pervasive chill.

I strip and climb into bed, pull my comforter around me, and open Gmail. It takes less than three minutes to open a new tab and create the account Julie_NewYorker@gmail.com.

Julie from *The New Yorker* emails Tara-Jean Slater.

Hey Tara-Jean, it's Julie—we spoke the other day on the phone.
Thanks again for chatting. I was wondering if you would send me
more poems?

I hit Send and collapse on my back, staring at the ceiling. I'm still
lying in that exact position an hour later when Dylan pokes his head in
my door. He is red-eyed and disheveled, hair matted. He looks like a sick
Labrador.

"Hey," he says, "we're both home."

I sit up and study him. "You look terrible," I tell him.

"I'm both hungover and still drunk," Dylan says. "Which I didn't
think was possible."

"Oh, it's possible."

"I threw up."

"When?"

"On the way home, I made Matthew pull over so I could throw up.
Twice, I guess. And then I thought I was gonna throw up on the porch
when I was letting myself in? But I didn't, and now I think I won't."

"Should you drink some water?"

"Oh." Dylan receives that like a brand-new thought. ". . . Yeah." He
leaves the doorway and I hear the tap running in the kitchen. He returns
sipping from a jar of water.

"Who's Matthew?"

"Grindr Matthew." When I don't recognize the name he says, "From
before."

"The twink with the big dick? Bonnie and Clyde?"

"Bingo," Dylan says, and finishes the rest of the water. "His real
name was never Clyde."

"Have you been fucking him for the last forty-eight hours?"

"Thirty-six," he corrects. "And I did coke—for the first time, can you
believe it? And I *really* hate it."

"You should be a motivational speaker," I tell him. "Like, in ele-
mentary schools."

"And I tried yoga. Daniel thought yoga was too L.A., so I never . . ."

Dylan's voice trails away. Then he clears his throat and continues, defiantly, "But I tried it."

"How did you like it?"

Dylan makes a face. "I was still drunk and high and my heart kept racing and I hadn't slept, so I can't really tell." After a moment he asks, "Have you heard from him?"

"No . . . haven't you?"

"Just that he landed." Dylan shrugs. "We thought it would be better to . . . sort of . . . cold turkey, right now. You know?"

I look at Dylan's matted hair, the swollen places under his eyes. His button-down is off by two buttons. "Yeah, maybe?"

Dylan feels my doubt. "Well," he says, "the alternative is to talk to him, and then he hangs up and goes back to pretending that he had a *roommate* named *Dylan* back in *Los Angeles*, and I'd have to be fine with that. And I can't be fine with that."

After he goes upstairs and I hear the shower start, I check the email account I've created for Julie from *The New Yorker*. My heart stutter-stops when I see one unread email sitting in the inbox. No attachments, only a message. I open it.

Julie—I've stopped writing poems.
The monetization of content is the death of content.
Which is to say: there is no joy in poetry. —TS

*

I approach the Geffen like a spy approaching a heavily guarded fortress.

As I enter the lobby, I expect someone to shout, "She doesn't belong here!" I imagine a brace of Tara-Jean Slater's bodyguards, husky Romanian men who seize me by the arms and drag me outside into the glare of the sunlight. But the lobby is cool and quiet; doors open to the back patio, where a small fountain leaps and people are milling gently. The early afternoon light spills in, making everything glow. Nobody stops me. Nobody looks at me.

I slip into the back row of the theatre, minutes before the reading starts. The room is vibrating with that low, anticipatory buzz that is not quite language—something closer to an incantation. The sound is as familiar as my heartbeat. I haven't heard it since the night of Tara-Jean Slater's opening. It rekindles an absence that threatens to become me.

Two reading stands are carefully placed along the lip of the stage; a stand and a chair are off to the side, the universal signifier for where the stage-directions reader will sit. Two bottles of water sit on the stage to the right of each stand. I scan the audience for Tara-Jean Slater, starting with the rows near me. I don't see her anywhere, and I wonder if she is sitting in the front. I've never met a playwright who had it in them to do such a thing. But if a playwright like that did exist, wouldn't it be Tara-Jean Slater? I strain my neck and then a cold hand closes around my heart as I make out a familiar dark bob, one row from the stage. Marisa. It hadn't occurred to me that she would be here. I slide down deeper in my seat.

The audience buzz quiets, and I look up as a woman walks onstage. She's wearing chunky heels and a chunky necklace, and she's not Cate Blanchett. She greets the audience and tells us that she is the director working with Tara-Jean Slater this week, on her brilliant new play, her feminist take on an inherently patriarchal canon, her disability-inspired window into *The Odyssey*, shored up by Tara-Jean's own lived experience of . . . The director hesitates guiltily after the first time she says the word "disability," like she's wondering if she should have used a different word. Then she plows on, clumsy but game: ". . . physical otherness."

She tells us that Cate Blanchett, sadly, couldn't make it today because of an unexpected conflict with her film shoot, but they have a very special surprise for us. The role of the cyclops will be read today by none other than Tara-Jean Slater herself.

The audience applauds enthusiastically. The director applauds as well, turning toward the wings. The stage-directions reader enters and sits in the chair on the side, opening his script binder. He does this very efficiently and confidently, like he has read many stage directions in the past and he will read many more in the future.

Tara-Jean Slater walks out onstage next to a stocky guy with a beard. This must be whoever is playing Odysseus. The audience claps harder, and he gives them a nod and a smile and takes his seat. Tara-Jean Slater doesn't even look at the audience as she sits. The stage-directions reader clears his throat and says, "*Cyclops*, by Tara-Jean Slater. Act one, scene one. A dark cave."

I want this play to be bad. Every cell in my body longs for it to be terrible. My skin wants it to be bad, my teeth want it to be bad, the hairs on my arms are standing at attention and they want it to be bad as well. I want the audience to rise to its feet and scream, "Fraud!" I remember the undergrad class in which I learned how the groundlings would pelt Shakespearean stages with rotten fruit when they were displeased, and I want this practice to instantaneously reignite itself. I want Tara-Jean Slater to receive an avocado to the head, and for the Geffen to call Cate Blanchett and say, "Everybody hated the play so much we can't possibly produce it," and for Cate Blanchett to say, "You know, I too thought it was a very bad play, and that is actually why I didn't show up."

And then, at the same time—in a place that is buried deep in my core—I want this play to be good. I want to be transported by it. I want it to fulfill its contract with me, the audience member—I want it to wrap itself around me, bring me someplace I can't get by myself. I want it to tell me things about myself that I can't bear to know, but tell them to me in a way that makes it possible to know them. I want Tara-Jean Slater to be a failure, but I want this play to be a success, and to give me two hours of my life that are transcendent, that make being here (in this row, in this theatre, in this body) worthwhile.

If you're wondering what it feels like to want two completely opposite things to the same degree, at the same time, for entirely different reasons—it feels insane. But then again, maybe it's hard to be alive on this planet and not know how that feels.

*

It takes me a few moments after the play has ended to realize that I'm crying.

Everyone around me is applauding; there is an entire row of elderly ladies to my right, and a pack of designer gays to my left, and all of them are applauding. I don't applaud. It feels like a ridiculous thing to do when there's an iron band wrapped around my chest and water is leaking out of my eyes. As soon as people start to stand, fumbling for jackets and purses, I slip out of my row. I'm the first one out the theatre doors, but everything is blurry. I see the restroom sign across the lobby and make a beeline for it. Only after I've locked myself into a corner stall, and 50 percent of the crowd has started funneling itself into this exact restroom do I realize the idiocy of trying to hide in a women's bathroom after a play reading. I imagine the line forming outside my particular stall door, and I waver on the edge of opening the door and fleeing, red eyed, past the hundreds of waiting women. But imagining them looking at me—imagining *Marisa*—is enough to keep me from leaving. I sit on the toilet lid, feet tucked up so that nobody can see me, and when a few impatient denizens start rattling the stall door (all around us, other toilets in other stalls are diligently flushing), I deepen my voice and announce, "Occupied!" And eventually the rattlers give up, although I hear an older woman say to her friend, "Do you think someone *died* in there?" Ten minutes pass, maybe longer. The flushing grows less frequent. Eventually the sink stops running, and the air dryers are silent. The herd has moved on.

When I am quite certain that everyone is gone, I lower my feet from the toilet seat and stand. I've stopped crying, although I'm not sure when that happened. I run my hands through my hair, take a deep breath. Compose myself. I turn the lock of the stall door and step out into the silent bathroom . . . and come face-to-face with Tara-Jean Slater.

A moment—suspended, breathless, deep-space—while we stare at each other.

She is perched on the lip of the bank of sinks, little legs dangling. Neon-yellow Chucks, skinny jeans. Hair pulled into a bun, little copper wisps escaping like smoke, curling around her pinched face. She looks like a kid that got away from her mother and is hiding in here, where no one would think to look.

"Hi," Tara-Jean Slater says in her flat voice.

"Hi," I say. I walk to the other end of the bank of sinks. I don't know what else to do. I stick my hands under the sensor and hot water sprinkles out of the tap. I stand with my hands under the water for a long beat, feeling Tara-Jean Slater's eyes on me. I add a drop of liquid hand soap, get very serious about washing my hands, then focus on drying them, using exactly one sheet of paper towel.

When I look up, Tara-Jean Slater is still watching me—that direct, expressionless stare. I realize that she has taken off the lime-green eye patch. The top of it sticks out of her jeans pocket. My gaze immediately skates to her left eye, I can't help myself. It looks normal.

"I know you," Tara-Jean Slater says. Her tone sounds anticipatory, like she's reaching back into the hat of her memory, rifling around for a rabbit. I don't know how to respond, so I don't say anything, and she keeps rifling. Then her hand closes around it, and her eyes widen, but her voice doesn't change when she says: "You're the one who put her finger in my eye."

"Yeah," I say.

"I don't remember your name."

"Cass."

"Cass," she echoes, like she's trying it on.

"Sorry about that," I say lamely. She ignores this completely, not in a hostile way, but as if it simply isn't interesting to her.

"Cass," she repeats again. "And we won that prize. Together."

"The Lansing. Yeah."

"The Lansing." She nods to herself—all the pieces have slid into place. "What are you doing here?"

"I was watching your reading."

"Oh?"

"It was . . . good."

Tara-Jean Slater is bored. "You don't have to say that."

"It made me cry."

Now she looks interested. "It's not a sad play, it's just a play."

I don't know what to say, so I don't say anything. Tara-Jean Slater studies me. She's silent for so long that I get nervous. I can't tell if she's waiting for me to do something or if she's reliving the last moment we were this close together, unattended. And then she says, abruptly, "Do you want to come over?"

"Excuse me?"

"Do you want," Tara-Jean Slater repeats, very slowly and distinctly, "to come over. To my Airbnb."

"Right now?"

"Right now," Tara-Jean Slater says, staring me dead in the eyes. And there are a thousand reasons why this is crazy, and a bad idea, and ridiculous. Tara-Jean Slater, more than any human I've ever met, is capable of a revenge killing. But:

"Sure," I say. "Okay."

*

Tara-Jean Slater's Airbnb is a glass box high up in Laurel Canyon. Chad's house is also somewhere in the junglelike thickness of nature, but I couldn't begin to say where. I'm focused on following Tara-Jean Slater, who drives like a bat out of hell. I lose her almost immediately, lumbering along in Dylan's van. But when the van finishes its ascent and rounds the bend, I find her parked at the curb. Tara-Jean is sitting on the hood, chewing her nails. As soon as I park the van and get out, she walks a slow circle around it.

"Yours?"

"My friend's."

"Why's there a shark face?"

"I don't know," I say. "I guess he felt like painting one."

Tara-Jean Slater gives the van a nod, then turns her back and walks toward the glass box. She punches in a code and the door *beeps* and opens. We step, one after the other, into a flood of late-afternoon light.

The Airbnb is spare, but in an expensive, minimalist way, not a low-rent, scarcity way. The floor is a concrete expanse leading off in all directions. A few benches are placed against the white walls, as if we're in a gallery but art hasn't yet been hung. A white shag rug thrown over the concrete delineates a living room, along with a low hard couch. The chairs are all odd shapes that aren't quite chairlike and don't invite you to sit on them. There are a few decorative vases that are also shaped unintuitively. The wall facing us is all glass, leading out onto a balcony.

"I hate this place," Tara-Jean Slater says, going to the fridge. She retrieves a large bottle of Pellegrino and then starts hunting around, opening and closing the crisper drawers. The refrigerator is almost entirely empty. My eyes flick up, and I notice a large deer head attached to the far wall, surveying us with glassy eyes. It seems entirely out of place, like it appeared just now, when we weren't looking—stuck its head out of the wall and thought: *Maybe here?*

"It seems expensive," I say.

"It's devoid," Tara-Jean Slater says, and I wait for her to add "of" and then a noun. When she doesn't, my brain does a few calisthenics: Did she say *the void*? *De void*? Or was she using "devoid" as a noun unto itself? If anyone was going to use "devoid" as a noun, it would be Tara-Jean Slater. She is nearly a fetus and she is pioneering language. I am thirteen years older and I am crying in women's bathrooms. That old familiar feeling of utter failure drops down, like a fleece blanket from a top shelf. *Swaddle yourself*, says Failure.

"Fuck," Tara-Jean Slater says. "We don't have any lemons."

"That's okay."

"I wanted a lemon."

"I have a whole tree in the backyard where I'm staying. If I'd known this was going to happen, I could've brought you a handful." I don't know why I said that.

Tara-Jean Slater lifts her little chin and stares at me, framed in the oblong of the open fridge. Then she says, thoughtfully, "I guess so," and shuts the fridge door. She pours seltzer water into two tall glasses, brings them over to the window, and hands me one. We stand side by side and drink.

"I hate all of L.A.," Tara-Jean Slater says thoughtfully, as if she's been considering this question for a long time and has finally arrived at the answer. I open my mouth to say something idiotic, like: "L.A. has grown on me, but of course I can see why you'd hate it, it's so different from New York"—and then Tara-Jean Slater says, "I hate New York too, though."

"Where do you like?"

I expect her to name some place really weird and cool—a small town that no longer exists, located in a region of the country formerly known as Yugoslavia, now it is only rubble in the aftermath of war—but instead she says, as if she didn't hear my question: "New Haven is like living under a ball sack."

"Oh?"

"Connecticut is death," Tara-Jean Slater says. "In general."

We're quiet. I find myself studying her reflection in the glass. I can't help it, but I'm doing it again—looking for the mark of fate. I can tell she's special. But why? It takes one powerful person to anoint you. After you've been anointed, other people can get on board without having to determine your value for themselves. And then your value snowballs, because now you're a sure thing, now everyone can celebrate knowing about you without fearing that their taste will be questioned. But what if nobody had anointed Tara-Jean Slater back at the beginning, and she was just a depressed twenty-one-year-old? Would she still have some innate, inarguable specialness?

I can't answer this question. Maybe because I'm afraid the answer is yes.

"I wish I had a twin," Tara-Jean Slater says out of nowhere. "But a twin boy. If it was a girl, I'd smother her in her sleep."

"Why?"

"Girls can't be friends. There's only so much space available. If it's a boy, it doesn't matter, boys have their own extra space. But if it's a girl, then the space she's in? It's your space."

"Wait," I say clumsily. "I don't think that's true?"

"Do you have any female friends?" Tara-Jean Slater asks. Not like she's trying to prove a point, but like she's genuinely asking.

I think about Hélène. I think about B.B. I feel for them both in ways that are fierce and proprietary, ways that have nothing to do with space.

Or maybe they do—Hélène wanted me to stay in one space and I wanted to invade another; B.B. wanted to join me in a space where I couldn't let her enter. And in the end, I'm not sure we're friends. So maybe Tara-Jean Slater is right. She seems to be right about what people want to see and what they want to buy; what if she's right about this as well?

When I'm quiet, Tara-Jean Slater says, resigned, "I might get a cat."

*

As the afternoon gets later, Tara-Jean unearths a bottle of expensive-looking champagne and fills a vaselike object with ice, and we sit out on the balcony while it chills. She tells me in passing that it was a gift from Netflix, after her deal closed. I keep waiting for a moment when it becomes clear that Tara-Jean wants me to leave, but that moment doesn't seem to come. We sit in silence a lot of the time, but there's something lulling about it, a sleepy quiet that we sink into. When the champagne is chilled, Tara-Jean Slater pops the cork, and it foams over her fingers. She pours it into two glasses that we found in a high cabinet. I don't think she'll do something so prosaic as "cheers," but she surprises me by clinking her glass against mine.

"Cheers," I say. "Thanks for the champagne."

"I thought I was going to drink this alone," Tara-Jean Slater says tonelessly; and then she takes a sip with her eyes on me, so I take a sip as well.

We're each on our third glass (they're small glasses—or they are seeming smaller with each subsequent glass) when Tara-Jean Slater says, "There's a pool, but I haven't been in yet."

"Why not?"

She looks at me over the rim of her glass. "You can't go in a pool by *yourself*."

"I think that's categorically untrue."

"If you're not a *swimmer*," Tara-Jean Slater tells me, "if that's not part of your *identity*, then it is sad to be in a pool by yourself. Like drinking by yourself."

"I love drinking by myself," I start to say, but then I realize that I haven't really done it since Caroline pulled me into her movie and I started to be Cath. So maybe I didn't love doing it.

"Let's go in." Tara-Jean stands decisively.

"I don't have anything with me."

"You can wear your underwear. Or you can wear my extra underwear so you have a dry pair afterwards."

"I don't think we have the same size underwear," I protest, but I get to my feet, because she's standing there expectantly. The top of her head reaches my collarbone. She grabs the bottle of champagne in one hand and her glass in the other and takes me down the concrete-floored hallway to the bedroom: white walls, a white bed in the center, thin rectangular windows below the seam where wall meets ceiling. Her suitcase is spilled open on the floor, as if she's been living out of it. Above the bed is a wolf head. Bam. Just like that.

"Jesus Christ," I say, startled. The wolf head looks at me with disdain.

"It's a wolf," says Tara-Jean, going through her suitcase. "I think the owner shot it."

"That's terrible."

Tara-Jean Slater retrieves a pair of minuscule panties and a minuscule bra. Both are the same shade of lime green as her discarded eye patch.

"Why is it terrible?"

"Well, for the wolf, for one. And for you. To wake up and stare at a wolf's head? No wonder you're depressed here."

Tara-Jean Slater studies the wolf as if she's asking herself if this is an accurate assessment of things. She seems to come to a definite conclusion, because she turns back to me and says, brightly, "I'm depressed everywhere." She thrusts the tiny scraps of green cloth at me: "You can change in the en suite. I'll be in the pool."

Tara-Jean Slater's green underwear barely covers my pussy, and the bra is a gesture toward the concept of bra, without providing any of the services specific to "bra." After a moment in front of the mirror, I leave the underwear on but ditch the bra. The champagne buzz is kicking in.

I get lost a few times in the concrete-floored maze, and by the time I make it out into the pool area, the first bottle of champagne is perched on the edge of the pool next to a newly opened second one, and Tara-Jean Slater is naked and splashing inside a rubber doughnut.

"Come in, the water's warm," she calls up to me.

I suddenly feel ridiculous standing there topless, in her lime green panties. I pull them off, drape them over the empty bottle with a flourish, and jump into the pool. As the water closes over my head, the world gets muffled briefly, and then it explodes again in color and sound. I shake the water out of my ears as Tara-Jean takes a pull from the second bottle, then holds it out to me. I take a pull as well.

"That one was from Cate Blanchett," Tara-Jean Slater tells me. "An apology for missing the reading. Marisa told her I like champagne."

"Do you?" I just want to hear Tara-Jean Slater say out loud that she likes something.

"Sure," she says, noncommittal. "It's fine." She takes the bottle back, splashes to the edge to set it down. Then, without turning around, she says, "We could basically be in a porno."

"Huh?"

"You know, two girls naked in a pool. Los Angeles."

"Oh," I say, "yeah, I guess." I wonder if Tara-Jean thinks I'm checking her out. There's always a moment with straight girls in which I wonder if they think I'm checking them out. And then, especially if I wasn't, I start acting weird, because I'm trying to make it clear that I'm not, but the more you try to act as if you aren't doing something, the more you seem like you are.

"Don't worry," Tara-Jean says, as if she's reading my mind. "I'm asexual."

"Excuse me?"

"It's because I was abused as a kid," Tara-Jean Slater informs me. "All your sexual instincts get warped, so then either you can make the choice to be asexual or you end up acting out what you learned and abusing people."

"Tara-Jean," I say, choosing my words carefully, "I think maybe—"

"Don't go," she says, like she's disappointed in me.

"I wasn't gonna go. I was gonna say I think maybe there are more choices than just those two."

"No," Tara-Jean Slater says, "I've thought about it. There aren't. So I'd rather be asexual." She looks at me accusingly, like I'm about to disappoint her again, and adds, "I'm not interested in *therapy* and self-*care* and whatever-whatever. It's like—if you have a headache, you are either a person who takes Advil or you're a person who doesn't. I'm a person who doesn't. Because the point isn't convincing myself that I'm fine, the point is knowing which things are wrong, and to what degree."

"I mean, I hear that," I say, "but—"

"It's okay," Tara-Jean Slater says. "I'm rich. I'm so rich now. I was in Beverly Hills yesterday for this dumb meeting and I saw this five-thousand-dollar handbag. In a window? And I thought: *I could buy that*. Like . . . I could have walked in there and bought it. And I didn't want it—it was actually a really ugly handbag—but it took me a while to know that, because, when you know you can buy something? That is the largest piece of information in your mind about that thing." She takes a swig of the champagne and says, earnestly, through the mouthful, "That's something new that I'm learning."

We drift in the pool and don't talk for a while. Tara-Jean Slater has gotten quiet, like she's reliving the handbag incident. I feel like I should reply to everything she said, but I don't know where to begin. Then she says, like we're still having the same conversation, "Everybody thinks it was my uncle. It wasn't, but they think it was."

I want to pretend I don't know what she means, but we've entered the twilight zone, and we've entered it together. For me to act like I didn't follow her here is beneath us both.

"Because of your play," I say.

"Yeah," she says, "because of my play." After a moment she adds, "Sometimes I think I should say something. But I'm not going to. But the more I don't, and the more people want to talk about my uncle, the more it's like . . . Do you sometimes feel like you're a version of yourself?"

"Yeah."

"And it's not *not* you. But it's a version. And the more time passes, the more people only know the version. And the more time you spend *as* the version. And then it's like: Well, which one is the version and which one is real? Because, if you've spent ninety-five percent of your time as the version, doesn't that make it real?"

I think about Daniel, and I think about Dylan, and I think about Cath, and I say, "I don't know. Does it?"

Instead of answering, Tara-Jean Slater flips over onto her stomach, clutching the rubber doughnut to keep her head out of the water. I realize that it's gotten dark, the sun has gone down and lights around the pool have automatically come on. Tara-Jean Slater looks like a small animal trying to find its way to shore.

"Aren't you gonna ask me who it was?" Tara-Jean Slater demands.

I hesitate. I don't know if she wants me to ask, or if it's a test—that anybody else would ask, and therefore I shouldn't. Tara-Jean Slater waits politely for a few beats, to give me the chance, but when I say nothing, she goes on. "I don't actually have an uncle. I keep waiting for someone to fact-check that and be like, *She doesn't have an uncle.* But that hasn't happened yet." She shakes her head. "I've had so much time to think up what I would say if that happened, but I haven't thought of anything."

She lets go of the doughnut. I've found my way to the shallow stairs at the end of the pool. Tara-Jean Slater swims toward me, pulling herself onto the stairs as well. I wonder how often she's wandered from room to room in this Airbnb, or sat by the pool, without letting herself go in, and thought about all the actors being cast as her nonexistent uncle. I wonder for the first time how she spent Christmas, and then New Year's Eve. Here, probably. By the pool but not going in. B.B. comes to mind, sudden and unbidden. They're nearly the same age. If you asked me what it means, what it says about what we're all doing with our pain, me and the generation under me, and—on the scale of Caroline's artistic ambitions—what it all means for *women*, I wouldn't begin to know. I don't even know what it means for B.B. and Tara-Jean, let alone for *women*.

I stand up and walk to the edge where the second champagne bottle got left. I'm dripping water everywhere and the night air has become sharp on my bare skin. When I reach the second bottle, I'm surprised by how little is left.

"We still talk," Tara-Jean Slater continues, not raising her voice. It carries to me across the still air. "We don't talk about what *happened*, but we talk." And then, as if she's heard what I was thinking, she adds: "I didn't go home for the holidays this year. Every other year I have. But this time, I felt like . . . if I'm writing about it, I shouldn't. I know I'm supposed to be mad, or whatever, like empowered and mad, but . . . I don't know. When I think about what I want as opposed to like . . . what I'm supposed to want? I mean, I just want to go home and sit at the table with everyone and not talk about things. So maybe next Christmas I'll go home."

She accepts the bottle when I hand it to her. She's shivering, and we realize it at the same time. "It got cold," she says.

"I know."

"We should go in."

"Sure," I say.

"If we go in, are you leaving?"

I grab a towel off the back of the nearest lounge chair and hand it to her. She wraps it around her shoulders but keeps looking at me.

"Tara-Jean Slater," I say. "I put my finger in your eye. Why do you want me here?"

Tara-Jean considers this, and then she says, very honestly, "I get tired of being alone."

"There are any number of people in this city who—"

"No," she says. "Not really. They all want something. It's worse than being alone. Or it's exactly like it. And you don't want anything I can give you, which is the same as not wanting anything. And today was nice."

We settle back in the living room, on the uncomfortable low couch. Tara-Jean Slater changes into leggings and an oversized hoodie, and I put my clothes back on. She's sleepy, curled up in a fleece blanket, watching me as I go through the cabinets to find something for us to eat. There isn't much, but I locate a packet of graham crackers and some canned sardines, and when I tell her firmly that she needs to soak up the alcohol with something, she obediently places each wet fish on its graham cracker and ferries them one by one into her mouth. I drank as much as she did, but the last conversation chased all the alcohol from my bloodstream. I feel alert, tired but fully back to myself. I find two overripe bananas in a fruit bowl that I thought was pure ornamental sculpture, and when Tara-Jean Slater declines ("Bananas are gross"), I eat them both.

We're quiet, and Tara-Jean Slater is fading, with her wet hair spread everywhere on a bumpy pillow. I think she's out, and then she says, from halfway underneath the fleece blanket, her voice muffled and dreamy: "I keep waiting for my dad to come to one of my plays."

"What's that?"

"Or I guess, in a year or two," she says, "he'll be able to turn on his TV and see my show. And if he were like, *I'm so sorry that happened* — even if he didn't *claim* it, even if he didn't say *I'm sorry for what I did* but just generally acknowledged that something might have happened to me at some point — I think everything would be so worthwhile. But I think probably that won't ever happen."

I don't know what to say to that, so I don't say anything. And soon after, Tara-Jean Slater falls asleep. I wait until her breathing is even and steady before I get up. I stand for a moment, looking down at her. I want to protect her, and I want to escape her, and I want to kill her and wear her skin, all at the same time and to the same degree. In the end, I pull the blanket up more closely around her shoulders — and she stirs a little but doesn't wake up, the contented burrowing of a small animal — and then I show myself out.

15

The first week of January ends, and B.B. has been missing for eighteen days. The girls have returned from their vacations, tanned and glowing and solid. They seem surprised to find B.B. still gone, as if they thought the whole thing would resolve itself while they were away. Caroline tells us that she spoke to B.B.'s family and that the police are continuing to work with them. She doesn't repeat what they said, but she encourages the girls to look inward at their own lives, and to talk on camera about what B.B.'s absence means to them.

One of the Nickeys talks about the time her grandmother died. She had been sad, but then during the viewing she'd realized that her grandmother had had such a hard time getting around and doing fun things, and probably she hadn't had sex in . . . decades? (Ming: "*Ew.*") And so now Nickey thinks that she's gonna kill herself once she starts to get old: You might as well live fast and die young, and maybe B.B. felt that way too?

Mona offers a slightly less direct connection, telling a story about the time she went to Florida on a school trip ("Band") and had this premonition that she was going to get eaten by an alligator ("I dreamed about one every night, like . . . a *prophecy*") but then actually in the end it didn't happen. ("We didn't even see any?") The takeaway seems to be: Like B.B., the alligators were missing. Or maybe: The threat of death looms everywhere.

Caroline herself is in front of the camera more and more. She becomes a new character, marking the post-Twist change in direction from fighting to talking. She is often barefoot, in a pair of casually torn jeans, clutching a mug of coffee, with a knit shawl thrown over her shoulders. Her hair is flat-ironed so it falls in a straight, shiny curtain, and she wears a layer of coral lipstick. Sometimes she wears silk bomber jackets, sometimes distressed leather boots with a high heel. She looks youthful and cool and authoritative, and she says things like *I saw a lot of my young self in B.B.* and *These girls are like little sisters to me* and *I keep asking myself, did B.B. ask me for help and I couldn't hear her?* She is likable and grief-stricken, and she becomes the emotional heart of this new section of the movie.

I find it increasingly hard to look at her. When I do, I feel my eyes bouncing away to the walls, the floor. My hands. At first it feels like a muscular thing, this inability, and then I realize that to look at her is to lie with my eyes. Somehow, over the hiatus, the ability to do that has drained away from me. I don't know if the girls miss the fighting, but I do; it was clean, a forceful and unmediated expression that transcended Caroline's planning. She may have been the one to imagine and then set up the fights, but when the girls were in the midst of it, a thing that was purely themselves leapt to the surface and expressed itself. This, the Twist, feels slippery and more violent.

I can't stop thinking about B.B., even when I'm home alone. I've started to lose the expression on her face after I betrayed her; it's wearing away like a cheap Polaroid exposed too often to the light. Now she comes to me in other moments, less fraught ones—in Whole Foods with a watermelon under her arm; hauling her tank top up with a grin to show me her purpling ribs. It seems impossible to me that this person should be gone—not "gone" as a euphemism, but utterly vanished.

I feel that I've failed B.B., yes, but by now even I have realized that the size of my guilt is sheer arrogance. B.B. herself would say this. She would scoff at me: "You think my life revolves around you?" She would say: "You don't think I had *anything* else to worry about other than a dumb kiss that you blabbed about?" I know this, and I know that what really chews at my guts is the knowledge that I've failed myself. I want to have been the version of myself that I felt so close to achieving: wise, trustworthy, a dispenser of wisdom, a steady shoulder. Cath was going to be so much better than Cass—that monster of ambition and selfishness—but somehow the whole new self I was building cracked wide open, and Cass popped out anyway. No matter how capable of self-destruction B.B. is on her own, the truth is that I wanted success, I wanted accomplishment at any cost. And the price was her, and I was willing to pay.

*

I don't know B.B.'s home address, but Caroline has everyone's information stored somewhere. I spend a morning shoot sneaking into her studio and rifling around while she and Thomas are in the backyard with the girls, but there seems to be neither rhyme nor reason to her methods of organization, and every time I hear footsteps approaching, my heart leaps into my mouth. Finally, by early afternoon, I get Evie alone and ask her if she can find out B.B.'s address for me.

We've been shooting a scene in which Ming tells Caroline about a moment in her relationship with Chad in which she felt suicidal. Caroline has invited Chad to drop by the house later in the day without telling him why, and the plan is to record a scene where Ming tells Chad that he's emotionally abusive. My chance comes when Evie goes out to her car to retrieve her phone charger. I follow her out and, keeping my voice low, I make my request.

She cocks an eyebrow, but all she says is "Okay." She whips out her phone and texts with ferocious intent. Moments later, her phone *dings*. She reads it and a furrow carves her forehead. She texts back. *Ding.* I shift nervously from foot to foot. *Ding.* Evie sighs, but all she says is: "Got it."

I have to ask: "Who were you texting?"

"Molly," she says. "She's like—she has a lot of feelings about B.B. Put your number in and I'll text you her address."

As I do, Caroline's voice cuts down the driveway toward us: "Cath!

Hey, Cath!" And then, performing surprise in a way that says she saw us talking from the window: "Oh, Evie, I didn't know you were out here."

"Hey," Evie says, subdued. "I was just coming in."

"Okayyy," Caroline says. "Well, we're sort of *mid*scene, for *Ming*, so."

"Should I wait?"

Caroline holds the pause for a long second, punishing her, and then says, "No, go in." I hand Evie's phone back to her, and Evie walks up the driveway and into the house. From the porch, Caroline squints her eyes at me and inquires, politely, "Are you coming in too?"

I open my mouth and, before I know what I'm going to say, I hear my voice: "I can't."

Caroline is clearly surprised. "You *can't?*"

"I have an . . . appointment."

"An appointment," Caroline repeats. She tilts her head to one side, staring at me. "It's just, we have this whole scene with Ming and Chad today."

"Yeah, no, I know."

Caroline holds her silence to see if I'll overexplain myself, weaken my position. But if I have learned anything, it is this technique of hers, so I remain silent as well, and we look at each other across the expanse of driveway.

"Well," she says finally, when I don't apologize and I don't approach, "I guess it is what it is."

"Yeah," I say.

"But it's too bad," she adds casually. "I was gonna have you direct."

"Direct?"

"Yeah," she says. "It felt like you might be ready to direct and that scene felt like—*your* sort of thing."

"What do you mean my sort of thing?" And now my feet are carrying me up the driveway toward her, even as I'm telling them not to, even as I'm ordering myself to hold my ground. But these sneakers belong to Cath, and they bring her to the lip of the porch, where Caroline stands over her, toenails freshly painted a militant cherry. Today her braid is fat and straight down her back, the Tomb Raider look from our first encounter.

"Well," Caroline says, answering my question after making me sit in the pause, the way she'd done with Evie: "It feels like you're very concerned about these girls' *feelings*, their *inner* lives. And if you were to have a directing credit, an associate directing credit, these would be the scenes at which you'd excel."

"I mean . . ."

"It's okay," Caroline chirps. "I guess you have a conflict." She turns to go back into the house and her braid whips around like a tail. The door closes behind her. I stand there for a moment. Go in or leave? I can feel it, the magnetic pull. How easy it is to yield to Caroline, how yielding always seems to be framed as getting what you want.

I take a deep breath and then another one, and on the third one, I turn away.

*

B.B. lives in Highland Park, which is geographically close but, in traffic time, could be a neighboring country. The traffic is already thick by the time I pull onto the on-ramp, and as the van inches forward under the low gray sky, I think about what to say to B.B.'s mom. I want to tell B.B.'s mom that B.B. is a good kid, and that having friends isn't necessarily the litmus test of whether or not your kid is good. I want to tell her that B.B. is funny and sweet underneath her sarcasm, and I hope that her mom will stop me and say, "I *know* that." I want to ask if I can help, and then—if there is an answer, a set of tangible things that I can do—I want to do them. Then maybe I'll know what comes next.

The drive takes longer than the GPS predicted, and by the time I get to Highland Park, it's raining. B.B.'s house is on a side street lined with ramshackle old houses. I park along the curb, between a jacaranda tree and a particularly complicated three-part sign that seems to be saying either that it's okay to park on weekdays between certain hours or else that it's okay to park at all times other than weekdays between those specific hours. I spend a few minutes squinting at the sign through the windshield while rain spatters the glass, blurring the lettering. Eventually I give up and leave the van where it is, its big shark smile glistening. I cross the curb and start counting house numbers.

B.B.'s house has nothing particular to distinguish it. I walk by it once, and only find it when doubling back. The paint is light blue, peeling. A faded patch of yard sits in front of it with one of those signs that let you know there's a home burglar system installed. I can't help wondering if that came about because of B.B.'s sister. I hesitate at the end of the walkway for a few seconds, and then take a breath, march myself up it, and knock.

The sound of a TV makes itself heard through the door—a brittle burst of cartoon noise. For a moment the sound creates an odd nostalgia in me—not for my childhood but for the days in which B.B. was parked in front of Caroline's TV with all the others. I knock again and a woman's voice calls, "Coming!" Her heavy steps start somewhere very far away and keep coming, heavier and heavier. Finally, she's on the other side of the door, and she says wearily, undoing the lock and pulling the door open: "I keep telling you, if you're gonna forget your keys, someday you're gonna get home and I'm not gonna even be—"

She stops when she sees me, and we stare at each other. I can see the B.B. in her square face and pugnacious underbite. She's younger than I expected, maybe in her early fifties, but tired in a way that has aged her up. A lick of dark hair falls forward into her eyes and she blows at it impatiently from the side of her mouth.

"Who're you?"

"I'm Cass," I say. "I'm—uh—I was friends with B.B."

I open my mouth to say more, but she's already clocked what she needs to. "B.B., huh?" she says, and turns away from me. I think she's going to close the door, but instead she yells down that impossibly long hall toward the source of the cartoon sounds: "Bijou! There's someone here for you!" When I hesitate, she turns back to me: "You can come in, she's in the den."

"B.B. is here?" I stammer.

"When isn't she?" her mother says. "If you can get her off the damn couch, I'll pay you a million bucks."

I walk down the hallway toward the den. My mind is racing. The cartoon sounds get louder, and then the doorway to the den gapes on my right. The curtains are drawn, and only the flickering light from the TV illuminates the shape of a sagging couch, and the lump of B.B. curled up on it, surrounded by pillows. She doesn't look up at first, and I stand awkwardly in the doorway taking her in. An old-school cartoon rabbit jigs manically, casting jags of light over her—the faded blanket pulled up to her chin, the stubble of her scalp, the sunken thumbprints right under her eyes. After a few seconds, her mom thuds down the hallway toward us, headed back to whatever she was doing at the back of the house, and as she passes me, she says: "You have a guest, B.B."

B.B. turns her head and sees me standing in the doorway. Surprise jolts itself over her face, and she starts to sit up, then catches herself. Unwilling to seem too impressed, she says, "What are *you* doing here?"

"Same question for you," I say.

On the TV screen, the rabbit sets off a barrel of fireworks. "I live here." B.B. watches me warily.

"I thought you were missing."

"Missing?" B.B. wrinkles her forehead at me. "I'm right here."

"Everybody's been *looking* for you."

"Who's been looking?"

I want to say "the police" and "your family," but I realize abruptly that I don't know if any of that is true.

"I called you," I say. My voice sounds pathetic. "I called you a bunch of times."

"Yeah," B.B. says, "I turned my phone off."

"But your school—the girls—everybody thinks you killed yourself."

"How come?" B.B. asks. "Because I stopped coming to movie practice? Because I didn't want to be somebody's token gay?"

Suddenly the TV is too loud. "Can we . . . ?"

I search for the clicker, can't find it. B.B. lifts it from the morass of blankets and hits Mute. The rabbit, who has blown itself up, cavorts in frantic silence with splinters raining from its singed fur.

"Everybody thought something terrible had happened to you," I repeat.

B.B. props herself up on her elbow, watching me. After a moment, she says, "Why'd you come here?"

"I got your address from Evie. Your mom called Caroline and said you went missing, and Caroline called me—because you vanished! Three weeks ago. Didn't you vanish?"

"I stayed out all night," B.B. says. "And then I came home."

"You—? But hasn't Caroline been . . . calling here, and talking to your mom, and . . . Haven't the police . . . ?"

B.B. laughs out loud. It doesn't sound like a bitter laugh. Just rusty, like she's out of practice. "My mom left Caroline a message and told her I came home. She never called back. My stepdad called school when vacation ended and said I was sick. Everybody knows where I am, Cath, the police aren't looking for me."

I'm silent. I don't know what to say. I'm working it through in my head: the fact that B.B. didn't vanish or kill herself. That her family wasn't wracked by grief, or at least not that kind of grief, Dramatic Grief, Documentary Grief—just the quiet, slow, chronic grief of daily life. Had each of these capital-letter ideas originated with Caroline? Had we all, each of us, swallowed them fully because we trusted her or because we, too, secretly wanted the Twist to lift up our movie and make it worthy?

"You said they thought I offed myself?"

I focus on B.B. She looks quizzical. Interested, even. "Yeah, Caroline said—apparently you wrote your ex-girlfriend all these letters . . . ? And you implied . . . ?"

B.B. sighs. "Yeah, I wrote Molly a letter," she says. "I told her she behaved like an asshole, and that if you wanna experiment with pussy, you should tell the person whose pussy it is that they're an experiment. I was *mad*, I wasn't like . . . gonna kill myself."

"Oh." We sit in silence, and then I ask, "What happened to you after you left Caroline's house? Really, I mean."

B.B. considers telling me to fuck off, I can read it on her face, and then she decides not to. "Everything got too much," she says. "So I wandered around all night. And then I came home. And I lay down on the couch. And it was gonna be just one day. And then it was two. And then it was a week. And then it was two weeks. And I couldn't get off the couch. But also, I didn't know why I should. And now it's—however long. You said three weeks?"

"And your mom . . . ?"

B.B. shrugs. "This is better than freebasing heroin."

"Have you . . . talked to someone, or . . . ?"

"I have a therapist," B.B. says, tired. "Everybody in this family has a therapist. We've been doing FaceTime, since I won't get off the couch."

"Oh."

"Everybody thinks the whole point is to be *happy*, but happy is a show you put on for other people. I don't know why it's better to put on a show than sit on your couch and feel whatever you're feeling. So that's what I'm doing right now."

"Oh."

"Do you have anything else you wanna say about it?"

"No." I think of the weeks after I attacked Tara-Jean Slater, before I moved to L.A. How I'd roamed around my apartment like a desperate animal, how takeout containers spread over all the surfaces like fungus, how it had never occurred to me that I needed help, because it felt so clear that I was beyond help. How I didn't have the ability to do what B.B. is doing: to sit and feel what I was feeling. How I had fled and not returned, unlike B.B., who returned. And I hear myself adding: "Just that . . . you might be a few steps ahead of me. I don't know, but it's possible."

A moment, and then B.B.'s face lights up, that smile I see so rarely. It's like her entire face is emerging in all its details from an otherwise blank screen. "Okaaay, Cath," she says, and everything in me rises to the surface to smile back at her.

*

We sit on her back porch, under the dripping awning. The wet air smells of soil expanding, roots stretching, secret things growing underground. B.B. has traded the blanket for a hoodie, and she blinks repeatedly in the gray underwater light, as if stunned by the realness of everything. The backyard is a small square, its low fence more like a backdrop than an attempt to keep anything out or in. Its crowning feature is an orange tree that seems too scrawny to have as many oranges as it does. Polished by the rain, their color is improbably glossy.

I ask, "How's your sister?"

"She's good. Been doing so good they're letting her start outpatient next week." B.B.'s tone is wry when she adds, "Every time I start to do bad, she does good again. At least my mom only has to deal with one fuckup at a time, even though she got saddled with two."

"You aren't a fuckup," I say.

"Yeah okay," she says, but she sits up straighter. After a moment: "Hey."

"Yeah?"

"Thanks for coming over."

I glance at her. She very deliberately doesn't look at me, instead staring off at the rain gathering itself into a white mist. The profile of her cheek and the snubness of her nose have become so familiar to me. A sharpness works itself loose in my chest. I put a rough arm around B.B.'s shoulder, pulling her closer.

"Hey!" she protests, but doesn't pull away.

"Thank you," I tell her, "for not being dead."

"You're so weird," she says, but after a second she rests the top of her hood on my shoulder, just for a moment.

When the rain stops, she walks me out. Her mom is in the front room as we pass, kneeling in front of a plant, newspaper and potting soil everywhere. Her eyebrow lifts when she sees B.B. is leaving the house, but she is enough B.B.'s mother to know that nothing, under any circumstance, must be said—and so she turns back to the plants without even a goodbye to me.

At the van, I ask B.B. if I should tell Caroline she's alive. When B.B. shrugs, I ask, "Or do you want me to say I came from seeing your body? Motorcycle crash, maybe."

B.B.'s grin flickers, but she sounds tired when she says, "I don't care what you tell her."

"Maybe I'll tell her you were actually straight the whole time."

"Watch all her Sundance plans shatter. Evie is actually not even Black. And Ming?"

"Is actually a robot. AI."

"And you?"

"I'm not even in the damn thing," I say. "I guess we never got our It's Okay to Dyke It Up scene. Wish you'd stuck around for that one."

B.B. laughs out loud, then sobers. "You know," she tells me, "the thing is? She's gonna make it. In life, I mean. Success. You know? I don't know anything about movies, but you can tell she's the type of person who is gonna get exactly what she wants."

"I know," I say. The first thing I ever knew about Caroline—arguably the only solid thing, still—was that she reeks of success.

"I thought I'd get what I wanted too," B.B. says, "but now I guess I don't know what that is. Or it isn't what I thought it was. Or I thought I would start to get it, at some point soon, but actually I kept losing—the more I was around those girls and all of them not looking at me, or not talking to me . . . or *Caroline* not seeing me unless there was like, a *gay moment* she wanted to . . . Like, the more that happened? The more I kept losing. And I only suddenly noticed. Like, very suddenly, I noticed that I had never felt like a loser until now, now when I'm doing this super cool thing that is supposed to make me a winner, but instead . . ." She shakes her head. "I don't know if I'm making any sense, but that's what happened." She shifts from one sneaker to the other as the rain starts to pick up again, but this time she looks straight at me, almost a challenge. "You asked what happened to me, and that's what happened."

"I thought it was my fault," I confess.

"You?"

I hesitate, trying to find a way to talk about what happened between us. She lets me hang for a long beat, and I think she's gonna play dumb, or else punish me—*What makes you think you're so important?*—but then B.B. smiles. "*And* you," she says. "*And* it was you. But not just you."

"Look," I say, "come find me after your first divorce. If the first one doesn't work out, come find me and we can see how it goes."

B.B. laughs and laughs, standing on one leg as her sneaker gets soaked through by the water racing into the storm drain. "What if I don't get divorced?" she asks.

"Then I was right," I tell her, "and there was someone better for you."

I wait until she's run back across the street and up her driveway before I start the van up. The tang of dead manta ray is still buried in the van's atmosphere, along with stale cigarette smoke. I crank down the window to let in the rush of fresh air.

*

Caroline, Ming, and Chad are mid-shoot when I walk in. Thomas and a multiplying number of interns are crouched on the far side of the room behind two cameras, and Caroline is behind them, focused on a single monitor hoisted high on its tripod. Ming and Chad are facing off in the center of the room; Ming is screaming—". . . men like you, for *centuries!*"—and Chad is protesting, a steady mumble, "C'mon, this isn't—what the fuck—this is *so* unfair." Someone has placed a bizarrely large vase of flowers on the table behind them, a checked tablecloth spread under it like we're shooting a scene about a couple in a farmhouse. The thought flashes across my brain that Caroline must have let an intern do the set dressing, but I'm so angry the thought slides right off again.

Jaki and Whitford try to stop me at the kitchen door—"They're rolling"—but I don't break my stride, and their tentative hands drop away as I shove past. I don't stop until I've reached the middle of the room, and then I come to a halt as Ming and Chad fall into confused silence.

"Cath?" Caroline asks. Her tone is simultaneously confused and expectant. She expected me back, but not in the center of the room.

"B.B. isn't dead," I say—and I don't know, until I'm speaking, what I will say or how compressed with rage my voice will be. "She hasn't *killed* herself, she isn't even missing, for fuck's sake."

A moment, and then everyone starts talking at once. Ming is saying, "What's she talking about?" and Mona is asking, "Why'd she talk to B.B.?" and the Nickeys are whispering, and Evie is asking me, "Was she there?" and Caroline is saying, "Everybody take ten, everybody clear the room"—and my voice cuts through it all, because I just keep talking, straight at Caroline—"And you *knew* it, you knew it all along, you told us she was *missing*, you told us the *police*—the fucking *Twist*—but she's been home this whole time. She won't get off her couch, and not one of us went to see her!"

Into the sudden hush Caroline says: "Will you all give us a moment?" Her voice is high and strained—a new voice.

The girls file out of the room slowly, reluctantly. Ming tries to linger, but Mona pulls her by the arm. I wasn't prepared to be as angry as I am, but now that fury has been released, it is filling my entire body like helium. I feel like I'm floating; my heart is racing and my hands are shaking. It is frightening to be this angry—frightening and exhilarating, a kind of giddy liberation. I turn my back and take a breath, trying to calm down.

I know the room has cleared when Caroline's voice comes from close behind me—closer than I expected. She's still speaking in that new careful voice, but the strain has gone out of it, and that makes me even more furious, that she thinks she's back in control.

"Cath," she says, "I know that you think of B.B. as—"

I whip back around. "I think of her as a fucking person," I say. "I think of these girls as *people*. This can be a movie and they can still be *people*."

"I know they're people," Caroline says, refusing to lift her voice. "And I also know that I am responsible for the shape of this film, its structure, its narrative, and its politics. That's what I'm responsible for. So if B.B. wants to stay home for three weeks, if B.B. needs a break from the movie, that's okay. She can have what she needs. But there's no reason we can't have what we need too. And the girls understand that—"

"So, they knew she was fine? Everyone except me knew she was fine?"

"The girls weren't *worried* about what was happening with B.B.," Caroline says, "because they were focused on what was happening *here*, with *us*, in this *room*. They understood the value of a character arc that—"

"Then isn't that a problem?" I'm almost shouting. "Wouldn't you say it's a problem that their classmate being real-life dead had exactly the same *weight* as her being real-life alive, since their focus was on making her into a *character*?"

Caroline gives me a long level look. I think she's going to deliver more of her Andrea Arnold / "this is not a documentary" spiel, but she surprises me. "Listen," she says. "I get it. You want to hurt me. So, hurt me."

I stare at her. Her face is completely composed and entirely serious. She lifts her chin a fraction of an inch, as if she's anticipating being punched. As if she's inviting that.

"Caroline," I say, "what the fuck are you talking about?"

"It's okay." Caroline soothes me. "You can be honest."

"This is crazy! That's not what I'm—"

But Caroline is talking over me, started talking over me the instant I started protesting, and when I stop, her voice rolls forward, resilient and calm. "Every woman has the instinct to harm, Cath. We spend our whole lives denying it, but it's there. And denying it only damages us. It doesn't actually help anyone—least of all the people we think we're protecting from ourselves. Because that instinct to harm? It leaks out in other ways. Darker, stranger ways—more insidious ways—until suddenly we've actually ruined someone's life instead of just punching them in the face. Don't you think they would have preferred a fist in the face, given the choice to choose?"

"Caroline," I try again, but she cuts me off, still calm.

"You play at being such an Enneagram Two. So *helpful*. And I think you are. Part of you is. But I also think you want to fucking tear things apart, and you never let yourself do it. You're obsessed with B.B.'s *feelings*, so my question for you is: What are *you* feeling? Let's look at *your* feelings."

"I'm trying to—"

"Fuck trying," Caroline says. "Fuck *worry*, and fuck wanting to be *liked*. If you didn't want to be liked, who would you be?"

Her eyes are very green, and she is so close that whatever is radiating off her—intensity, anger, conviction—makes my skin tingle. The fury in me sublimates into a kind of sweet, vicious ache. I am in the presence of a god of carnage. I open my mouth to tell her that this is the wrong question, that I've already done a thing that made me hated, that I've been living with my unlikableness—that it has brought me here, as a matter of fact—and then I round the other corner of that thought and I wonder if, in fact, it is exactly the right question.

I realize that Caroline has gone quiet, scanning my face with her mesmeric eyes. Whatever she reads on me is encouraging. "Violence can be honesty," she says softly, almost soothingly. "Not always, not when it's being wielded by people who are entrenched in positions of privilege, who are used to *other* people carrying out their violence for them. But for women . . ." Caroline tips her chin to one side, studying me. "We are so often required to lie. Aren't you tired of lying?"

"Yes," I say, before I know I will say anything.

"Then stop doing it." Caroline's voice is soft, coaxing. "You're furious at me. You think I—what? Mistreated poor B.B.? You think I'm not *invested* in her *sadness*, you think I'm heartless. And you're angry at me for that, and you're angry at me for all the times I made you buy toilet paper at Trader Joe's. And you're angry for—what else, Cath? What else are you angry for?"

"You talk to me like I'm your intern," I say.

"Yeah, go on."

"I'm your age, I had a whole life before I met you, and a whole career, actually. I have ideas, I'm not your fucking intern. Unpaid, your *unpaid* intern."

"Go on," Caroline encourages, no shift whatsoever in her face.

"And you can be selfish."

"I 'can be'?" Caroline's tone challenges my unwillingness to offend.

"You are," I tell her. "You *are* selfish. You just want what's best for you—you, then the movie, in that order."

"And what else?"

"You're being dismissive about B.B., but that's bullshit, because you picked these girls, you put them together—which you lied to me about, by the way, so that's another fucking thing—but you picked these girls, and now you're uninterested in who they are when their pain is *inconvenient*? Isn't that supposed to be the whole fucking movie? Who they *are*? So she didn't kill herself—she still isn't *okay*. How can you only care about her pain if it's *useful*?"

I grind to a halt, out of breath. My chest is blown wide open, like something buried inside has punched right through me and out. It feels exhilarating. Caroline has reached into some deep core and unlocked me. She leans in, her eyes large with anticipation, and she says, like a blessing: "Then hit me."

And I would have. I would have. I can feel the tension coiling its way from my stomach up my spine, through my shoulders, into my hands, how they curl into fists, how each inch of my skin is prickling and alive.

But there's something.

Something in her eagerness. Something that feels too familiar, too recognizable. Too specific.

I know Thomas is there before I even see him. I cross the room like a bullet, headed straight for the table with those goddamn flowers, that goddamn all-American tablecloth, and even as Caroline tries to stop me—"Cath, where are you going?"—I fling the tablecloth up and there he is, crouched under the table like a kid playing house, and the camera in his hand is pointed directly at me. He gapes up at me, weak jaw lowered to reveal the slightly acorn-colored row of his lower teeth.

"Cath," Caroline says hastily, a note of alarm breaking the coaxing softness of her voice. "Cath, wait!"

I grab the camera out of his hands and throw it down on the floor with all my strength. Caroline gasps. Before anyone can stop me, I bring my sneaker down hard and feel it give underfoot. Pain lances up my leg from the bottom of my foot, and I hop, briefly dizzy with it.

Caroline grabs my arm, spinning me in a half circle as Thomas crawls backward, trying to get out from under the table without approaching me. "Cath, stop it!" I'm pulling this way and that, she's clinging to me like a dog with a bone. I manage to kick over one of the camera tripods. The second camera hits a small rug and bounces harmlessly. I can't tell if it's on or off and I don't care, I want to destroy them all. I lash out with my injured foot and connect with the camera; it flies across the room like a soccer ball and hits the wall. A piece of it falls off. Caroline howls like a wounded animal. As she loses her grip on me, I grab the first camera, beating it against the hard wooden edge of the table. Plastic pieces and knobs fly off and the screen spiders a crack, bleeding liquid crystal.

"Fuck you," Caroline is screaming, a high background hum. "Fuck you, what are you doing!" She seizes me from behind, but I throw her off. We are suddenly WWE, we are Olympic champions, we are cage fighters. I crouch, arms up, ready to throw her off again, but she doesn't come at me. There's blood on her face, a red splatter. At first I think I must have hit her without realizing it, and then I realize that it's my blood. She has the same epiphany at the same moment. We both look down at the floor. My Chuck feels soggy, and when I glance down, I see it has filled with blood. Blood is pooling on the hardwood floor, there's blood on the nearest rug. Caroline's arms drop to her sides.

"Whoa," Thomas says. He's still on his ass, halfway under the table, staring at me in dismay.

"Fuck," Ming says, and I realize that she and the girls are crowded in the doorway. Ming looks exhilarated, Mona looks horrified, Evie looks like she's going to cry. The Nickeys, jostling behind them, all start talking at the same time—*Move, I can't see, oh my god, is she bleeding? Is this a scene? What's happening?*

Caroline takes a step away from me, and then another. And I realize that my rage is gone. It's drained out of me, maybe via my gashed foot. I feel very tired, and very old.

"Cath?" Evie is in front of me. "Do you want a . . . um . . . Band-Aid? Cath?"

"No, thank you," I say with great dignity, and I turn and walk out. All the way across the living room, through the kitchen, into the mudroom, out onto the front porch, and down the sidewalk. Nobody makes a move to stop me. I look over my shoulder once, and I see a trail of bloody footprints—one foot, distinct in its shape—marching itself forward. As I make my way down the street, I think of a parable that my high school math teacher used to tell us whenever we complained about her tests. A man is strolling on the beach of life, a set of footsteps next to him: Jesus, walking at his side. Then: a hard patch, tough going, just his footsteps alone. The parable ends with the man asking why Jesus has forsaken him, and someone—God? His mother? A passerby?—rebukes him: "That's when Jesus was carrying you."

That's when you gashed your foot on a camera, I tell myself.

That's when you fucked up Caroline's movie.

That's when you ruined your chances of being successful . . . again.

Success, I realize, makes you do bad things. It opens up a door inside you, and all kinds of evil swarms through that door. The evil fills you, it becomes you, and suddenly you are putting out people's eyes, without warning you are smashing their cameras and bleeding on their carpets. Worse than being evil, you have been made embarrassing. A punch line, again and again, for a joke that just keeps telling itself. The joke is success. And the punch line—every single time—is you.

As I walk up the long driveway toward Dylan's house, I think: *From now on, I will give it up. I will give up. I will be someone who does not succeed.* My gashed foot leaves a snail trail of blood up the tarmac, and I think: *I will become someone who exorcizes herself of longing. I will embrace mediocrity—nothing but simple satisfaction will be my god. A good sandwich. A quiet day. A paycheck. A cat—and feeding the cat. Dishes—and washing them. Getting by.*

And there is one set of people in the world I know who live like this, who seem genuinely satisfied by it, who seem to be *happy*, even, if that is a thing that one can put any stock in.

And they are my parents.

And so, I go home.

3

16

I exit the Greyhound station and the cold air slaps me awake. New Hampshire thaw, but barely: winter sun, a raw white light that illuminates but doesn't warm.

My mom's battered blue Toyota is parked at the curb, tires bleached with salt. I see my mother, leaning against the driver's side, before she sees me. Her face is tilted down, looking at the dark screen of her flip phone, her hair gathered up under a faded baseball cap—one of mine, from high school. She's wearing a gray fleece that used to be cream colored. Even before I see her feet, I know she's wearing the brown Uggs that I outgrew, then tried to explain to my mother were out of fashion and shouldn't be worn. "But I'm not fashionable," my mother always replied, reasonably, and so the Uggs remain, season after season. The unchangingness of this bus station parking lot, of my mother, of her boots, hits me like a wave and my throat tightens.

My mother lifts her head as if she feels my eyes on her, and her face breaks into a smile. But her forehead is creased; under the smile, she looks worried. And that is a constant as well—I have never known my mother to be without a steady background hum of worry. I wave, hike the duffel bag higher on my shoulder, and cross the gravel toward her, stepping gingerly on the ice.

"Cassie," she says, and hugs me hard, holds on for a second. My parents aren't big huggers. She must have been concerned, I realize—

not the background hum but something pressing, specific to me. She lets me go, studies my face, but all she says is: "That's it?"

I realize she means the duffel, and I nod. "I'll throw it in the back." I move around the car to open the slightly dented door on the shotgun side, and it creaks a familiar protest. This from the fall that I turned seventeen and was taking driver's ed; I'd miscalculated the amount of space between the side of the car and the dumpster I was inching past. Every so often, starting a week after that incident, my mother would say: "Maybe we should get the door looked at." But it has joined the same rhythmic, comforting, baffling continuum in which the Greyhound station and my repurposed high school clothes all exist, unchanging.

"That's all?" my mother asks again. "Did you mail any boxes, or . . . ?"

"No boxes," I say.

There wasn't much to take with me once I decided to leave. Some clothes, a few books, my laptop. *Another traceless exit*, I'd thought to myself, moving through TSA with only the one bag while all around me people juggled suitcases, backpacks, carry-ons. I'd offered to pay Dylan a month of rent to give him a chance to find a new roommate, but he said not to worry about it. I could tell that he was glad to lose his last daily reminder of Daniel; now he could come home to a house empty of us both and start over, in a way that you can't when you are sharing space with a person who knows what you are trying to start over from. But as the plane took off, I'd realized that I left my toothbrush back in Dylan's downstairs bathroom. And although at first it bothered me, by the time we landed at Boston Logan, it started to comfort me—the feeling that Los Angeles hadn't sealed shut behind me. Some small object remained, insisting that I had been there too.

My mother pulls out of the lot, gravel crunching under the wheels. Not many cars are on the road. Early evening now, already dark—an encroaching inky darkness. We talk in desultory fragments. About the winter—it's been a mild one, so far, a lot of snow but only a few power outages: "And the one time it got bad, we hired Ned's kid to dig us out—do you remember Ned?" My mother tells me about my father's classes at UNH—"He's talking about retiring," my mother says, as if he doesn't talk about it every year. She mentions the house—a leak in their bedroom, up in the corner of the ceiling where the runoff accumulates as soon as the gutters get blocked: "Another thing to take care of come spring." I remember the spreading stain from this leak, always the same leak and the same conclusion. The sameness is both comforting and soporific.

Strip malls give way to fields, farms, then woods. Pine forest, snow humped at the side of the road, a dirty mass turned blue with shadow. The car headlights are steady, tracking our progress: the next tree, the next fence, the next mass of shadow. My eyelids are getting heavy. I lean the side of my face against the window glass. The forward motion of the car brings me backward in time: I am seventeen, watching my dealer play Puck in his college auditorium; I am sixteen, I have one safety pin in my ear; I am fifteen, I am fourteen, I am ten, I am . . . home.

I wake up disoriented, no longer moving. My parents' driveway: loose gravel and dirt enslabbed by ice. The house: old, weathered blue paint peeling in strips. "Cassie," my mom says. Standing over me, my door ajar, the back of her hand on my forehead, so briefly. The anxious look hasn't gone away. "Cassie," she says again, but she doesn't follow it up with anything.

*

And the days blink past. A quick shutter, rising and falling, a staccato rhythm. When I fall into my childhood bed, my eyes shut and darkness drops. When my eyes open, it's light. I sleep deeply, and don't dream. Mornings, I wake late, make coffee in the kitchen. Linoleum, worn yellow. Exposed wood beams, knotted and rough with age. Dishtowels hung to dry; the same threadbare blue linen of my childhood. The house is always cold, and I find myself raiding my closet for clothes I haven't worn since high school: oversized hoodies, down vests, things that are ugly and shapeless and useful.

My father teaches early and is usually gone before I awake. Sometimes my mother is at the breakfast table when I get up, sipping black tea and flipping through a town circular; when she isn't, I look for the small Post-it notes on which she writes full sentences in her tiny, cramped writing: where she is, when she'll be back, what's in the fridge that I should finish.

Dinnertime is a convergence of all three of us, my mother and father and me, gathered around the old kitchen table stacked with magazines, articles marked with more Post-it notes, cups with broken handles waiting to be glued, mail that has been sorted into piles but not yet opened. Over dinner, my parents talk quietly about the weather, traffic, potholes that won't get fixed until spring. I remember these exact conversations from childhood too, except that my father looks older. Both of my parents do, I realize, and I'm not sure when that happened. Dad's hair is thinner; there's a bald patch at the top of his skull when he bends his head over the essays he's grading—a freshman seminar on ethics.

My father doesn't ask me questions, and I don't know whether it's because my mother has cautioned him not to or because he can't imagine whatever I've been doing clearly enough to ask about it. Either way, it's a relief. He is gentle with me, as he has always been—gentle and a little removed, staring into space. Occasionally he turns to me abruptly with a new thought—"The ethics of the *iCloud*!"—and jots down a note in the margins of whatever is nearby: a newspaper, a shopping list.

On the fourth or fifth day of being home, I check my bank account and realize that it's closer to empty than I remembered. The Lansing reserve has emptied out. Cold reality closes in. There's nothing to hold up for myself: no play, no movie that will send us all rocketing toward stardom, nothing on the horizon. This isn't that world anymore. This is the thing that happens after. Whatever that is. The compulsion rises in me, tidal-like panic, to figure it out.

I start reading job listings online. I go to a small coffee shop that didn't exist when I was a kid. It's almost always empty, staffed by gangly, stubbly boys who seem to be in high school or maybe community college. I park myself at a small table by the window and begin with New York. "A strong typist" is needed in Dumbo. Greenpeace is seeking "rainbow warriors" (whatever they are). Nonprofit canvassers are in demand in Brooklyn, although on further perusal this seems to be an unpaid volunteer position. ("You'll gain lots of experience!") I imagine being an executive assistant in Flushing; a caregiver near Woodmere ("Must be bilingual for Spanish"); a participant in a series of medical tests at various participating centers. ("Feeling alone with adult autism? Had a recent flare-up of Crohn's? Is heroin a problem for you?")

The problem is not that I can't imagine it; it is that I can imagine all of it, and each imagining fills me with bottomless despair. Not the despair of paralysis, which filled me in the wake of the Eyeball Incident. This is active and visceral. This despair propels me away from making each of those choices. This despair is the feeling of a hand approaching a hot stove—a whole-bodied imperative of rejection. And yet (and so?) I keep looking.

*

My mom goes to church now. This is new. The realization that my parents have changed in my absence—that they are capable of change—cuts into the familiar rhythms like a sharp new note. My father, in an act of mathematical synchronicity, has moved from agnosticism to atheism, so my mother goes by herself and only on Sundays. She tells me that the church is progressive and that they organize a lot of town events. She mentions a book sale every October and a bake sale in December, and she says that the Sunday school teacher has started organizing a puppet show for the kids on Easter. All the money they raise goes to local charities. "It's nice to do something to help," she tells me, wistfully.

I find myself wondering for the first time if she wishes she hadn't retired. If she misses high school English, the musky masses of interchangeable teenagers pouring in and out of her classroom. She doesn't seem regretful, though; she seems calm. Newly focused, maybe. Over the next few days I find myself watching my mother, trying to see past what I expect from her to what she actually is. Sometimes I catch her looking at me—across the dinner table, or over the kitchen sink—in the exact same manner. We don't ask our questions directly. Ours is not a family of emotion expressed outwardly. It is a family of sharp observations that you keep to yourself.

*

The job listings are interchangeable and unending. Queens, Brooklyn, and Manhattan ("Personal assistant needed, must be comfortable with ferrets") have given way first to Jersey City ("Cleaning jobs, flex hours"), then Albany ("GOT ECZEMA? GET PAID!"), then Middlebury ("Female dog walker wanted"), then Bennington ("Nude models, all body-shapes, $15/hr, THIS IS NOT A SCAM"). And then finally one day I'm reading them for this very place. A place in which, upon leaving for college, I had never again imagined myself doing something so committed as obtaining a job. "Insurance Inspector, Keene and surrounding areas." "Full-time licensed tattoo artist wanted, Salem, NH." "Wood floor refinishing apprentice, Hudson, NH." "Armed And Unarmed Security Guards Needed, Milford, NH."

"Hey." It's a short blond barista. He has a pot of coffee and he refills my mug without asking. "Whatcha looking at?"

"Job listings."

He makes a face. Then says: "Cassie, right? My mom is friends with your mom, they're doing the Easter show together."

"Oh yeah? Cool."

"My mom asked me to help out with the puppets — I was like: *Mom. No.*"

"Puppets?"

"Uh, yeah. My mom told me your mom said you're helping," he informs me accusatorially.

"I don't know anything about puppets," I say blankly. "Or the baby Jesus."

"My mom was like: *Cassie came all the way back here to help out. You go to college five minutes down the street and you can't give me a Saturday morning?*"

"I didn't — that's not why I moved back here," I say, increasingly thrown. "I mean — I don't even know what the Easter show is."

He shrugs. "Well, that's not how it got spun in *my* household," he says. "My mom thinks you're a fucking saint." And he moves on.

*

I've never thought of my mother as either ambitious or successful. She married my father at twenty-three, straight out of college; and although it was a good college (Williams), she taught high school English for the next forty years. She's written nothing, won nothing. She's never left New England. And yet, a fact about my mother is that generally she gets what she wants in the end. She is patient—ruthlessly so. It's how she managed being a teacher for so long. Perhaps also a parent. Slow, careful strategy: the Art of War. Under my mother's quiet, watchful gaze, all meals at our house stopped including red meat, despite my father's love for steak. I grudgingly passed classes that, through sheer apathy and disinterest, I had set myself on the path to failing. Even my recent and only trip to her church—"Just drop me off, Cassie, then you can have the car" and, on arriving, "Just come in, say hello to my friends"—is attributable solely to her force of will. My mother never says anything to mark the advent of her victories. She doesn't need to. You know and she knows that, eventually, she will bend you into compliance. It's something in the eyes.

My mother doesn't mention the Easter show to me at first. But now that I've been inadvertently warned, I am watchful. Perhaps she'd begun even during that first church visit, when I shook her friends' hands and stood by helplessly as they asked me questions like *Isn't it good to be home?* Perhaps even then, my mother had been observing as I shifted from foot to foot, and had imagined . . . what? . . . for me. So, in turn, I observe her and wait for her to show her hand. But she's too skilled to slip.

As I set the table for dinner, she asks how my day has been. "*Fine*," I say.

"Have you seen Emma yet, or Johanna? Or that girl—Tim's sister, you were close with her junior year."

Most of my high school friends still live here; I've learned from my mother that a number of them have babies. I keep waiting to run into one of them by accident—at the grocery store, at the coffee shop—but it hasn't happened yet, and I'm grateful to be spared. Now all I say is "No, not yet," and I wait. How will she do it? *You know, I've been helping out with the Easter show, and I thought* . . . But she just hands me the heavy ceramic salad bowl.

"I'm glad you're keeping busy," she says.

As the days pass, I can feel the weight in the air of a suspended plan—something larger than me, and inexorable. Watching my mother shape the world around her takes on a different meaning. Remaking the world is ambition. Succeeding at it is success. When I see her shuffling up the stairs to bed in her slippers, I think: *Who am I to quibble over a matter of scale?*

*

By the third week of my stay, even though my parents haven't asked how long I'll be here, I have stopped pretending that this is a brief visit, the precursor to an exciting next step. I have used it up, my allotment of next steps. Both Cass and Cath are dreams that have receded. Cassie was always going to live here, in the town where she was born, where all her old friends have married and procreated. Cassie is not someone who overreaches; she is pragmatic. And so, it's Cassie who keeps reading the job listings every day, and Cassie who finds a posting at the nearby community college—a lecturer, needed immediately, to cover the second half of a class on freshman composition. Its current teacher will be departing in several weeks, for reasons that the posting doesn't specify. I close my eyes and, briefly, imagine someone who has gotten a prestigious grant, a glamorous job. Someone who won the lottery and can't wait till the end of the term to leave New Hampshire. Something in me lifts a little—a banked glow, proximity to the idea of success, even if it's someone else's.

When I open my eyes again, it is gone, and I apply for the position.

17

Three days after I apply for the college job, William Chiang calls to tell me I have an interview. His voice is brisk and friendly on the phone, and I hear my voice take on a particular confidence and authority when I say that I'd love to, can't wait, looking forward.

I tell my mom about the interview that night. If I'm being honest, I'm trying to head off the Easter show conversation that has not yet occurred. She's folding laundry fresh out of the dryer, and I start helping her, to have something to do with my hands.

"Teaching," my mom says. "Well, that's nice."

"It's just finishing out the semester. Two months, maybe two and a half."

"Where's the current professor going?"

"They didn't say. I guess I can ask."

"Well, that would be nice if that works out," my mom says again. I can't tell what she really thinks.

"Just wait," I say, a dry joke. "Maybe I'll end up a teacher like you and Dad after all."

My mother flashes me a glance that seems pained. "We only ever want you to be happy, Cassie," she says, and I'm caught off guard—not by the words so much as by the way she says them. As if she's responding to an accusation.

"I know," I say. My hands are raised between us, half folding one of

Dad's old T-shirts, half fending off whatever my mother is responding to. "I know that, Mom."

But she says it again, "We only want you to be happy," and I know what I should say, so I do.

"I am, Mom. I'm happy."

*

William Chiang is in his early forties, and this turns out to be a problem, because it means he knows how to google.

At first, all seems well. I step into the small office—book lined, a large wooden desk beneath a desktop monitor and more stacks of books, windows facing out onto a green—a surprisingly nice office that turns out to be borrowed for these interviews from the dean, who is on sabbatical. "Italy," William Chiang says. Friendly small talk. "Writing a memoir, actually—her first." The small talk is so friendly, and so small, that I only realize something is wrong when I glance at his colleague and fellow interviewer, a thin woman with large glasses and long hair piled up on her head. She's somewhere between her late thirties and her early sixties, and she radiates a spidery anxiety that sounds a warning bell in the back of my head, soft and insistent, even as William Chiang is saying that he went to Venice once, it was *molto bellissima*, he never wrote a *memoir* there but one is always surprised by what life brings.

"Indeed," says the spidery woman, and clasps her hands closely together in her lap.

"Well," says William Chiang, "shall we get down to it?" and I am lulled away from the warning bell and into the easy particulars: where I did undergrad, what I studied, what I've been doing since ("We do love to hire working writers," William Chiang says. "It gives our students a *window* on the world"), and how lovely it is that I'm a local, William Chiang's wife is from here too, actually, we went to the same high school, albeit a few years apart. Things might have gone on in this vein for some time, except that William Chiang's nameless colleague gives a sudden dry cough and squeezes her hands together, and that seems to be a signal, because William's face draws into lines of regret and concern as he says, "We have one other question for you, Cass."

"Go on," I say, using my Cath voice—warm, inviting, in control. "Please."

"Well, you see . . . of course, we do a bit of homework, one must in this climate, you'd be surprised what people put online—we had a man last year, actually, who—" Another dry cough to his left, and William redirects himself. "Which is all to say—and this *is* a bit awkward, you'll forgive us—but we're hoping you can speak to us about the incident this past fall with, ahh . . ." He discreetly checks a note on his pad, but I know what he's going to say before he finishes the sentence: "Tara-Jean Slater?"

In the silence that follows I can hear a clock ticking outside the office, in the hall.

In the silence that follows I ask myself: *Is there any way to tell this that would make you want me to teach a class full of litigious children?* and I answer myself: *No, there is not a way.*

In the silence that follows—and it is a particularly deep and leaden silence—everything that I could possibly say swirls through my head, accumulates, builds pressure, and then comes to nothing. I open my mouth. I close it. Then I stand up.

The anxious woman looks genuinely pained as she says, bringing us all away from the depths of that awful silence: "Thank you for coming in." And William Chiang, grasping at straws, gasps out, "We'll call you later," even as we collectively realize this to be untrue.

As I walk to the car, I think: *So much for teaching.*

When my mother asks me about it later, I say: "They'd actually already decided on someone."

"Just this morning," I say. "If only I'd gotten there sooner."

By the end of the week, it is mid-February, and I get a job at CVS. The same job I worked at fifteen, sixteen, seventeen. There is no job posting; the blond kid who always refills my coffee simply mentions in passing that his cousin works at CVS and says they're hiring. It is as easy as falling down. It requires only submission to the laws of gravity.

*

The point, of course, is to be—not happy, but content. With the small things, the brief victories. The details, banal as they are. A paycheck. Unburnt coffee. A warm croissant from the bakery. A clean dishtowel, a freshly washed sweater. A satisfied customer. The light falling on your face in the morning; all your cells respond to that warm slant. My CVS vest smells like mildew; I take it home and wash it. Pulling it out of the dryer, I lift it to my face and inhale deeply: the crisp laundry scent. Is this contentment? I keep waiting to recognize myself in the normalcy of this. A sign that I have given up. A sign that I am growing. Time chops past like an old-timey movie: Cut To, Cut To, Cut To. Frame after frame. There is nothing to elongate the space between things; there is just doing. And soon it is March.

*

Most nights after work, I watch TV with my mother while my dad reads in his study. My mother likes National Geographic documentaries about animals, and I find myself increasingly drawn to them as well: the implacable rhythms of killing and eating and being eaten. It feels intimate and familiar, as if I'm watching a recap of everything that brought me here, but from a safe distance.

One night, a Humane Society commercial comes on in which a young, beautiful woman is asking us all to "adopt, don't shop." She looks like someone I know, and it takes a moment before I realize that, in fact, the woman is Liz. She has a new haircut and she's wearing Serious Casual Professional (blazer, slacks), but the way her smile wrinkles the lines under her eyes, the way she moves her hands as she talks—it's inarguably Liz.

We sit and watch her in silence, and a million thoughts flash through my mind. My mother is watching the dogs—a cheerful terrier, a sad-looking retriever. I want to say, "I dated that woman." I don't, because I don't know what the next sentence would be. *And she was married? And I was using her? And we were using each other?*

As I watch Liz with her new hair and her old mannerisms, I think that the rest of the sentence is that Liz actually liked me. She liked me and she liked my play, and she didn't know enough about either of those things to like them for what they were, as opposed to what she thought they were. But she was genuine in a way that I had not been. And I find myself wanting to apologize to her, here in the half dark, on the couch beside my mother. I know that the time for an apology has passed. To apologize would be to bring us back to a moment that we have both worked to escape. But as the last few seconds of the commercial flicker across the screen, I can't let it pass without saying anything—that feels too cold—so I say to my mother, "I know that actor."

"She looks so familiar," my mother agrees. I think she's going to put it together, then—*Wasn't she in your play?*—but instead she says, with an odd wistfulness in her voice: "That must happen a lot—that you turn on the TV and there's an actor you know."

"No," I say, taken aback. "Not so often, actually."

Another commercial takes the place of Liz and her shelter dogs. After a moment, my mom says, "You know, I acted in college."

Surprised, I glance at her. She's looking at me while blues and whites from the TV screen flash across her face. "I didn't know that," I say. The stories that I know about my mom from college are that she studied all the time; they'd only recently let in women, so there was something to prove; other people wasted their college days doing frivolous things like going to parties, and my mother did not. This was a lesson of sorts, held up for me when I left for college: *Other people will be careless with their educations, you must not be.* And so: my mother as an actor? This is new.

She's quiet, so I press: "What did you act in?"

"Oh, lots of things. *Long Day's Journey*—that one, the . . . well, long one."

"You were the mother?" I can't help laughing.

My mom laughs too. She seems to be relaxing into this, enjoying it. "Oh yes, it was so delicious. I forget her name. I was twenty, playing this old woman—drifting around in a nightgown, addicted to morphine—and the monologue at the end!"

"I can't believe you've never told me this."

"I was Ophelia too," my mom says. "After they saw my morphine-nightgown acting, they made me Ophelia. And I did a musical."

"You did not."

"I did! I forget what it was called. Lots of singing. And the director—he seemed very adult, but he must have been a recent grad, in retrospect—well, he had a Concept. Something that involved a lot of sequins. It was controversial."

"But you don't remember what the musical was called?"

"No," my mom says wistfully. "But, you know, everybody said I was very good." I've stopped laughing now; there's a look on her face that is so unguarded that, for a moment, she looks like a stranger. "*Everybody* said I was good," my mom repeats, and I understand that this isn't a brag—it's something that still seems remarkable to her, inexplicable and marvelous.

"I bet you were," I say. And even as I say it, I know I shouldn't, but I can't help myself: "But you didn't want to be an actor?"

My mother blinks at me as if returning from the far side of something. Our show is back on now, but she's muted it; leopards are stalking across the screen.

"An actor," she echoes.

"Yeah . . . after you graduated. Did you think about that?"

The faraway look is gone from her face, and she sounds exactly like herself when she says, with a laugh, "Oh, Cassie, I was never going to be an *actor*. It was *college*."

"Maybe," I say, "but—did you *want* to . . . ? Did it ever seem like you might . . . ?" I realize what I'm asking and stop myself. *Did you want more than this?*

My mother seems to hear the question anyway, though. She doesn't take offense. She tilts her head, looking at me, and then she smiles wryly. "I would have been unhappy," she says. "All that instability, that *want-ing*. It's harder for women." I open my mouth, reflexively indignant, but she cuts me off: "Or it was then. Having to compete for everything, but—no way to ever actually be in the running. You know, and women have children, so . . . you were just going to have to choose anyway. You were only ever going to have to choose, no matter how far you got, and I knew what I'd choose. And I did. So."

In the silence, she sees the look on my face. I don't know what it is—the immediate, unmediated emotion that is moving through me. "People stay younger for longer these days," she says. But my mom hastens to comfort me. "I see your life, and . . . there's more *space*, it seems. For you to—try things and—make mistakes and—I didn't have any space to make mistakes, it was always so . . ." She shakes her head, smiles again. "Well. It's a new world."

I realize, in that moment, that I have been living with the quiet, unexamined certainty that, in her eyes as well as my own, I've failed. I have been assuming her silence about my return home, my CVS job, is because there is nothing to say about a failure you watched come true over a decade of bad choices.

And yet.

It's a new world, my mother said. *I see your life, and* . . . Was there a note of envy in her voice as she said it? Or not envy but something just beneath the surface of it; wonder, perhaps? That the world has changed. That I, her daughter, am navigating it—no matter how different those navigations look from her own.

My eyes fill with tears, shocking me completely.

It's into this silence that my mother asks, as if the idea is occurring to her only then, for the first time: "Cassie, I wonder . . . This is only a thought, but—speaking of theatre—I wonder if you could help us out with the Easter show?"

*

The Sunday school teacher is named Ilse. She is not what I expected— nor am I, judging by the slight widening of her eyes as she takes me in, what she expected. She's in her late thirties, only a few years older than me—from Sweden, she says cheerfully. A smattering of freckles across her face. High cheekbones, wide gray eyes. Her husband is from here. We discover that he was a high school senior when I was a freshman; I remember his name but not his face. They have three children, Ilse says, although I only meet the baby, who is crawling around the floor at her feet as we talk. Ilse tells me his name, and it sounds like Farmer. "What did you say?" I ask, and she repeats the name with her gentle, lulling accent, and it still sounds like Farmer.

The Sunday school is in the basement of my mother's new church. The walls are painted an irradiant, optimistic daffodil, and small wooden shelves spill over with children's picture books and puzzles. I expect them to be Jesus themed, but when I give them a once-over, they seem to be regular books and puzzles. "Donations," Ilse tells me, "left over from the book sale."

"My mom mentioned there was a book sale."

"Yes, your mother organized the whole thing last year. She's a wonder." Ilse shakes her head, marveling. "So organized!"

"Yeah, well, she used to be a teacher." I don't say: *She didn't used to be religious*. I don't even know if my mother is religious now. Perhaps her religion is usefulness. Or perhaps religion is the ultimate organizational system: good and bad, order and chaos. My mind runs through each of these thoughts at lightning speed and then lands back at Ilse, who is looking at me with her wide, light eyes. I realize she's asked me something. "Sorry, what did you . . . ?"

"About the puppets? If your mother explained . . . ?"

"She said that you needed puppets. Of, uh, Jesus. *And* an Easter Bunny." I try not to sigh as I add: "*And* I don't actually know anything about puppets, to be completely honest with you, but I did . . . I worked in, uh, theatre . . . for a time. So my mom felt . . . I guess, she felt that I would know something about building puppets. Which I do not." I run into the end of my sentence and stop. Ilse is watching me with anticipation. I gather myself: "*But*, of course, I would be delighted to help."

This seems to be what Ilse is waiting for. "Well," she says buoyantly, "we have many art supplies—perhaps I can show you." She goes over to a large Rubbermaid tub in the corner and takes the lid off ceremoniously.

She waits. I walk over and peer in. Pipe cleaners, glue, felt, scissors, googly eyes of varying shapes and sizes, popsicle sticks, old socks. Even the art supplies are organized. "Your mother," she tells me with respect, "went to Michael's—she knew that there was a big sale. Two days only. She marked it on the calendar."

"Wow," I say.

Ilse patiently stands beside me until I have looked at every art supply in the box. If it seems like I'll miss something, she points it out helpfully: "You will see, right there, we have Play-Doh. I believe there is also a variety of, how do you call it, sculpting plastics?" When it's clear to her that we've finished, she picks Farmer up from the floor, efficiently removes a blue Matchbox truck from his mouth, and says, "Do you have any questions?"

"Uh . . ." I blink against the flickering fluorescent lights. The church basement feels oppressive; the heat has come on, and everything smells of wet wool. "No. I mean. I assume the deadline is, uh, Easter?"

"Yes," Ilse says. "Well—the morning before is when we would like to perform for the children. There's a mass on Easter itself, you know."

"Oh, of course," I say, as if I knew. "So—a month, give or take."

"From today, yes."

A question occurs to me. "Who will be doing the performing? With the puppets?"

"Ah," Ilse says, cheerfully, "I will do it with Cynthia. She teaches the younger children, twelve months to four years, and I teach four and up. Cynthia said that she can help operate the puppets, but she can't help with their, how do you say, construction."

Ilse's English is very precise. Her accent gives it a gentle, friendly roll, up and down, like a small boat at sea.

"And the story . . ."

"Yes, the story!" Ilse goes over to the bookshelf, laughing at herself. "Of course, you must forgive me. I am back from maternity leave very recently, my brain is still . . ." She waves a hand: scattered, maybe. She rifles around the shelves, and when she turns around, I think: *Oh, there it is*. The image I was expecting: a children's book, large primary colors,

Jesus on the cover. Long white beard, but his face oddly young. Blue-eyed, one hand raised in a benevolent gesture. Ilse hands me the book. "Your mother said you can make this into a play," she says hopefully.

I stare at it in dismay. The book is sticky in my hands—entire Sunday school classes have spilled their apple juice on it. I open it gingerly and a shower of crumbs rains down.

"A play," I echo weakly.

"Very short," Ilse assures me. "Five minutes at the most. The children will be so happy. I have circled—right here, you see?—all the puppets."

A very light pencil circle around: Jesus. A series of sheep. A shepherd. Some Romans.

"Very short," Ilse repeats. And then she smiles, reassuring: "It's not hard," she says, "when you have a Gift." The way she says the word lets me know that it has a capital g and is no doubt God related. "Your gift leads," Ilse finishes firmly, "and all you must do is follow." I want to dismiss this entire thing, but in that moment she reminds me of Hélène—*Urgency is the only messenger worth listening to when it arrives*—and so I can't say no, and so I say yes.

*

It is, after all, something to do. Like going to CVS is something to do; like taking lunch in the breakroom with a handful of other regular employees: a middle-aged woman who wears a daily uniform comprised of cheerful smocks (Sheila), a man in his sixties who has a mild form of cerebral palsy (Richard), the usual assortment of high school students for whom this is strictly an after-school job. All of this—manning the cash register, rolling out new stock, facing the shelves so that each item is displayed with delicate precision, taking expired items off the shelves, slicing and flattening cardboard boxes, shoving them into the trash compactor—is a series of things to do, and I do them. And then there are the puppets.

I agree to make Jesus and fifteen sheep and several shepherds (Ilse, shyly and progressively: "Perhaps one of them could be a woman"), and several Roman centurions ("Perhaps one of them, as well"), and Mary, and Joseph, and an Easter Bunny.

I ask Ilse if the Easter Bunny feels like, perhaps, it belongs to a different tale than the Jesus-centric story of How Easter Came to Be—even the progressive version, which involves female Romans. Ilse is undeterred by this: "Children get very excited about the bunny," she says pragmatically. "It is good to have built-in points of excitement for an audience."

"Like a gag," I say, despite myself.

"A . . . ?" Ilse looks confused. She mimes tying something around her mouth.

"Oh! No . . . like a trick. Like . . ."

"Maybe a trick," Ilse says doubtfully. And then her face lights up: "Sugar," she says. "You give the children vegetables but then you give them sugar."

I don't ask whether the fifteen sheep are the vegetables or the sugar. I do ask why fifteen of them, and Ilse says that she plans to hand each child in the audience a sheep puppet so that they can participate in being part of Jesus's flock.

After that, I stop asking questions entirely and start building Easter puppets.

It isn't hard once I realize that there's no real way to do it. Nobody is standing over my shoulder making suggestions. Nobody is giving me feedback. Nobody else wants to do it or thinks they can do it better. Nobody is vying for this opportunity, nobody is threatening to succeed before I do. Most of the time, nobody else is even there. Ilse is sometimes in her office at the end of the hall when I arrive, and I wave at her on my way into the Sunday school classroom, but once I shut the door it's just me and the beige carpets and the dry smell of indoor heating and the Rubbermaid containers full of supplies.

So, first, I make a sheep.

Felt. Cotton balls. I cut a straw into four bits for legs, paint the bits of straw brown. Tiny felt hooves. The sheep's face is a puff of cotton with ears. Googly eyes. A popsicle stick, so that it can be puppeted over the top of a table or curtain.

Once I've made a single sheep, a certain confidence creeps into me. I make another. I cut a long felt shape for its muzzle this time. Give its ears some definition. Maybe all the sheep can look different—there's a certain progressive angle to that as well, I decide.

The third sheep gets a tiny pink bow tie. This sheep is gay, and I find that immensely satisfying. Even if nobody knows it but me and the sheep.

The fourth sheep looks like Dylan: shaggy, overlarge hooves.

The fifth sheep looks like Tara-Jean Slater: streamlined and feral. I give it a miniature lime-green eye patch.

The pleasure I take in this is simple. It is a surrender to the inevitable (my mother) and also a break from the inevitable (CVS). It is a place to be where things are beautifully quiet—the creak and tick of an old building all around me—a place where even my mind slips into a hush, because it has been hijacked by a strange ballet: *Cut, paste, eyeballs? Pipe cleaner! Felt, felt, felt, cotton balls!*

It is—in a strange way—the first time I've felt at home. Although I couldn't say with what, or how. Maybe—as I place each completed sheep puppet in a row with its fellows—what I am feeling is a burst of accomplishment.

*

The Easter play is trickier. I try to write it at CVS, on the back of the spool of receipt paper that's lying on the counter. I get this far:

SHEEP: Baaaah.
JESUS:
SHEEP: Baaaah.
JESUS:
THE ROMANS: Kill him!

*

I text B.B. one night: *Still alive?*

The answer comes back almost immediately: *No, I offed myself. SOOO SADDDDD.*

I can imagine her, hunched over her screen in the dark of her bedroom, grinning.

B.B. was the only person I talked to before I left. We sat on her back porch, and she told me she hadn't started going to school yet, but that she *had* started going to the movies. We agreed this was a step in the right direction. She said her stepdad was talking to her about homeschooling, and that also felt like a good idea. She asked if I was coming back to L.A. and I said I didn't know, because that seemed kinder than saying no. When we said goodbye outside the van, she said, "Have fun in *New Hampshire*," the same way she'd said "*gay*" and "stupid" the first time I met her at Whole Foods, when she'd followed my shopping cart around with a watermelon under her arm. The familiarity of this rose up so strongly that I pulled her into a hug, expecting her to pull away, but instead she'd held onto my ribs, shoved her face deep into the shoulder of my T-shirt. After a long minute she straightened up and said, "Well, bye," and walked away without looking back.

Now, she texts: *Evie quit the movie.*

No way!

Yeah, she got tired of Caroline telling everybody it was like Moonlight when Evie didn't even get to do anything cool.

Are you and Evie friends now?

A pause, and then: *We hang out sometimes.* I can read the delicate hope between the lines and I don't push. After a pause, B.B. asks: *How's NH??*

It's OK.

A long pause, in which I wonder what else to say about my hometown, and then, from B.B.: *Wanna see the teaser? Evie showed me after she quit.*

I hesitate. But, of course, I say: *OK.*

B.B. sends me a link, and immediately there they all are: a long shot of a pack of girls walking down the street. As they get closer, I make out Ming in the lead, the Nickeys flanking her. I catch B.B.'s set jaw, Evie and Mona side by side. It looks sunny and warm; this must have been filmed in October, right before I arrived. The girls are laughing, rowdy.

The camera is close to them, as they approach. And then all of a sudden, it pans down to their hands at their sides, and we see that all their fists are bloody. The title smashes across the screen: THOSE GIRLS and then: A NEW MOVIE BY CAROLINE BIEL.

The teaser is about thirty seconds, and I watch it twice more before I realize that my name is absolutely nowhere on this thing. I don't exactly make the decision to google "Those Girls" and "Caroline Biel," but I don't stop my fingers from doing it either. I'm telling myself that a teaser is very short, you can't possibly fit all the necessary information inside a teaser. I'm telling myself that as soon as I see the name "Cath" even mentioned in passing, I'll stop googling. As I find myself slipping down the rabbit hole, I realize that this is the first time I've ever googled "Caroline Biel." My fear of what I would find on the Internet about myself has, for nearly a year now, effectively prevented me from stalking anybody else. Is this actually enlightenment, and now I'm throwing it away?

I learn that, in the two months since I left, Caroline has gotten a few high-powered producers on board who (*Deadline* says) are known for "strong female stories" and are particularly excited to embrace a "coming-of-age tale for the #MeToo era." There is also a *Vogue* spread of Caroline and the girls, in which Caroline is wearing an asymmetrical striped dress and high-heeled booties. This must have been right before Evie quit, because she and Ming are in the front row. B.B. is not there, but I see that Actual Nickey has gotten all of her hair chopped off and she's in the front row with Ming and Evie. Her short hair and sleeveless flannel styling look like a straight girl's idea of "classic lesbian." I can just hear Caroline pitching the Next Twist once it became clear that B.B. wasn't returning: *In the wake of B.B.'s absence, Nickey realizes that she's gay! She's been closeted all this time, but she can't stay silent any longer.*

And still, no mention of Cath.

I watch a brief interview clip in which Caroline talks about how difficult but rewarding it's been to make this movie, and how it's less *her* movie and more a collective ownership process, and she name-checks Thomas, the DP ("my longtime creative partner"), and even Jaki and

Whitford, but not a word about Cath. Not even *I had this collaborator named Cath who quit.*

It's as if Cath never existed.

I sit in the dark of my childhood bedroom, mulling this over. B.B. has stopped texting, maybe she's fallen asleep. It occurs to me that nobody outside of this movie ever met Cath or spoke to her or knew that she existed. And no one who watches the movie will feel her absence or wonder whatever happened to her—why she wasn't mentioned, what she did with her time.

Goodbye, Cath, I think. And like that, she feels truly gone.

*

Jocelyn calls me a few times. Reception isn't great here—there's a patch on the road between my parents' house and CVS where cell service picks up, and the parking lot of the church is also good for extended phone calls. Other than that, my phone becomes a paperweight. So I stop checking it, and occasionally at night I see that I've missed a few calls from Jocelyn, and I always intend to call her back, but then somehow I don't.

One afternoon I'm driving from CVS to the church when Jocelyn calls. And this time, because the phone is rattling in the cup holder right beside me—because to ignore it would be too intentional—I pick up.

"Jocelyn! What's up?"

"Cass," Jocelyn says, surprised. "I thought you were dead."

"Nope. In New Hampshire."

"What are you doing *there*?"

I open my mouth, close it again, consider, and then say, "It's a long story. How're you doing?"

Jocelyn clears her throat and her voice is very formal when she says, "I'm just calling to let you know that as of next Monday, I'll no longer be working at Creative Content Associates. My successor is named Debbie Turteltaub, and the email address you have for me will reach her, starting next week."

"Oh," I say, taken aback. "Okay. Did you get a cool new job?"

Silence, and then as I open my mouth to repeat the question, Jocelyn bursts into tears.

"Jocelyn?" I turn off the road into the church parking lot. Ilse's car is parked in the lot; otherwise it's empty. "Jocelyn? Are you okay?"

"Marisa fired me," Jocelyn sobs.

"Why?"

After a moment she gets her sobs in check and says, "Marisa says I'm not serious about my future here at this agency."

I pull into a parking spot next to Ilse's Land Rover. "Did you WikiLeaks or something?"

"I don't even know what that *means*."

"Well, what happened?"

"I ate all the snacks," Jocelyn says. "I'm always *here*, always working *late*, and she doesn't let you leave your desk for like, longer than it takes to *pee*, so—at night or like during lunch breaks, which are never lunch breaks, I would eat the snacks? And then a couple of the other agents' assistants started saying stuff? But like, *they* get to go buy lunch? And then on Tuesday, one of the agents was like, 'Marisa, I tried to offer a client a snack today, and there *were no snacks*, because your assistant has eaten them all!' And then Marisa called me into her office and told me that I am not serious about my future in this agency and then she fired me." Jocelyn takes a jagged breath and tries the phrase Marisa gave her: "Let me go." But it isn't strong enough, so then she says, "Fired me," and bursts into tears again.

"Okay," I say, at a loss. "Okay . . . Jocelyn? Jocelyn, can you hear me? You're gonna be okay. You're gonna be better off at a job where you can pee and eat lunch. I think most humans generally are better off in those circumstances, and this is probably for the best, even if it doesn't seem like it right now. Are you listening?"

Jocelyn sobs in a steady rhythm. I open the car door, and a cold March breeze sweeps in.

"Jocelyn," I say. "Did you even *like* your job?"

"That's not the point!"

"Then what is?"

"I got *fired*," Jocelyn wails. "I have a black *mark* on my name. I hate this fucking job, but I didn't want to be a failure!"

The sky has been steadily amassing clouds all day. Now the first heavy drop hits the blacktop, then another. I know I should run for the church before it really starts coming down, but I also know I'll lose reception once I'm in the church.

"Look, you're gonna fuck something up sooner or later. Might as well get it out of the way."

Jocelyn blows her nose. "Boys get comebacks," she says fiercely. "Have you noticed? All they have to do is be *sorry*. But where are the girls? Where's Hillary Clinton?"

"Rich," I say, "with a book deal."

"Be serious."

"Jocelyn, do you want a *comeback* to that terrible job? Do you even want to work in an agency at all?"

"I want to be a fucking star," Jocelyn says, still blowing. "I want a TV deal or like, a modeling contract or like. A brand. Some kind of brand. And I want to walk into this agency to meet with the fucking head of talent, and Marisa has to be like, 'Oh, Jocelyn, please come in, have a seat,' she has to be like, 'Can I get you a *snack*?' And then I'll be like: 'No, bitch, I don't need a fucking snack.'"

Rain speckles the parking lot, a steady pixilation.

"Jocelyn, I need to go in a minute, but I recommend you take an Advil and go home."

"It's five P.M.," Jocelyn says.

"My advice stands. You're fired anyway, right? So, go."

"Hey," Jocelyn says. "Before you go. Do you want me to tell the next girl about you? Like, to let you know if Marisa ever takes you off her DNC?"

"You know what?" I say, "it's okay."

"Is that a no?"

"That's a no." I close the car door behind me, lock it, and jog through the sprinkle toward the church awning. Just as I reach it, the sky opens up completely. I duck under the overhang; the achingly familiar smell of wet asphalt infuses the air. Jocelyn is quiet.

"Jos, the thing is, you're right—we don't really get comebacks. And that means we have to keep going until we get to the next thing. And sometimes the next thing is better. And sometimes it's not, and then we just keep going. I'd rather have a go-forward than a comeback, but I wasn't sure about that for a while. Are you still there?"

"Yeah," Jocelyn says, soft.

"I gotta go now, but—you're gonna be okay. And, someday, you will either be a star or you won't care anymore. Okay?" And I wait until she says okay before I hang up, and pull the heavy church door open, and slip inside.

*

It's after this that I start stealing from the church.

Nothing crazy. Just art supplies.

I know if I ask Ilse's permission she'll say yes. She'll assume I am taking things home to keep working on the puppets. I know she'll tell me: "Take what you need." And yet I don't ask her, because then I would have to put words to something that is wordless impulse—only a feeling. Something deep and secret, just for me.

At first, it's a few fistfuls here and there. Cotton balls. Pipe cleaners slipped into my bag. A single packet of googly eyes from among the plethora of sizes and shapes. Sheets of felt in different colors—eggplant, crimson, indigo—more intense than the palette for the Easter show.

Then I steal a hot-glue gun. And a pair of scissors.

And there's nowhere exactly to put all of this, so it starts spilling across my bedroom floor. I'm stepping on popsicle-stick splinters when I get up in the morning; I'm pulling flat googly eyes off the bottoms of my bare feet before I get in the shower. But there's something about it that feels—electric, somehow. Addictive. The mess, the spill. The chaos. In the church basement, I'm on sheep number eleven, I've hit a stride. But at home, I wake up with uncapped markers in my bed, streaking my sheets and ribs blue.

I don't consciously decide to make the first creation. It begins as an attempt at cleanup: picking things off surfaces, but then—instead of putting them on other surfaces—I attach them to each other. I don't know what I'm doing, exactly. I keep my mind very blank and very clean. But there is a buzz starting, a vibration at the base of my spine. And it is—oh, it is—so familiar.

I stop when it's time to leave for work. And I don't think about it at work. I ignore it deliberately. I ring up customers. I eat a PB&J in the break room with Richard, who is eating a salad. But when I'm in the stockroom, I see a few loose screws on the cement and I bend to pick them up. Before I know what I'm doing, I slide them into my pocket. And in the days that follow, I find part of a gear in the parking lot, a flap of torn canvas in the dumpster, the plastic lid of some oddly shaped container in the recycling, and I collect them all. And when I get home—from work, from the church, after dinner with my parents—I go up into my bedroom and I close the door and I return to the strange labor of a thing I can't yet name.

*

At first glance, they are strange and disturbing creations.

Eyes where eyes shouldn't be. Deformed, scraggly whiskers. Little jags of teeth—the broken tines of a plastic fork, a half-moon of metal spikes from part of that scavenged gear. Noses are crumpled, swollen, fat blobs of putty, narrow metal tubes, kitchen implements. Arms and legs are floppy, unwieldy, stiffly jutted out—distributed in triplicate, singularly, or not at all.

I don't decide when each one is done. I just lift it, look at it, and know that there is no more to do. It is as grotesque as it can bear to be.

And then I make the next one. And the next. And the next.

"You seem well," my mother says. Dinner. My father has brought a sheaf of student essays to the table. Ours has always been a family that reads at the table. My mother has a *National Geographic* open, but I realize that she's been watching me instead of the magazine.

"I'm good."

"Ilse says you've been by the church every day."

"I guess I have been."

A small line dents my mother's forehead. She says, gently, "Have you seen any of your friends yet?"

"I don't really know anyone here that well anymore," I say.

"Cassie, what about the girls you went to *school* with? You were so close."

"I'm sure I'll run into them." In my left pocket: a handful of orange plastic buttons. They were on the hall table in a jar that held quarters, safety pins, and keys to things that no longer need keys. In my right pocket, a sharp piece of metal is digging into my thigh—a piece of a bike, I think, although I'm not sure. I found it by the side of the road.

"It's so lovely of you to help with the Easter show," my mother says carefully, "but I don't want you to get *isolated*. It's okay to take a break from it."

"It's okay," I say. "We only have a couple of weeks left anyway. I don't mind."

"Ilse said she's turned it over to you," my mom says, "but I'm sure she could help. If you needed an extra pair of hands, she and Cynthia could—"

"It's okay," I say again, hastily. I like being alone. As I make the sheep, I think about creatures with three eyes and stunted jaws; I think about antennae where antennae shouldn't be, and tiny scrawny legs that could never support the weight of a body. I take flight to a place where everything is damaged and familiar. If I had to make polite conversation, I would be grounded.

My mother is looking at me, a sustained searching, and then my father breaks in enthusiastically, submerged in his student's essay— "Listen to this, this kid is writing about Leonard Cohen as essentially an arbiter of a new kind of *ethics*"—and the dinner moves on.

Later that night, the jagged bike part becomes somebody's semiexposed spine, and the buttons turn into a row of nipples, and I find a deep satisfaction that stays with me as I lie in bed staring up at the dark ceiling. Downstairs, my father is reading late into the night; outside the open windows, wood frogs twang and cluck, thawed by a week of rains.

Littered across my floor and desk and chair are all the strange creatures who are not fit for the Easter show.

This is the next thing, I say to Hélène in the dark. *I can't explain it, but here it is, arrived at my door.*

And—*Yes,* Hélène says, amused. *That's generally how it goes, isn't it?*

I choose to take this as a benediction, and I fall asleep.

18

Three days before Easter, I present the puppets to Ilse and Cynthia. The fifteen sheep are in a row; above them, a friendly Jesus with a long cotton beard, a cheerful Mary with a bonnet hot-glued to her sock-puppet head, an assortment of Romans, who are all smiling (two of whom have single hands lifted in friendly waves), and an Easter Bunny whose ears are glued to loops of metal wire and therefore can be bent at inquisitive angles.

"These are wonderful," Cynthia says appreciatively. She's in her late forties, so shy she rarely makes direct eye contact. Just little flicks of her eyes between your face and her hands or the wall. Her voice is apologetic no matter what she's saying. I can't imagine her in front of a room of children.

"Cassie is writing the text for us as well," Ilse reminds her.

"We're so grateful," Cynthia tells me.

I wait as they talk to each other about logistics: the number of children in the audience (thirteen, last count—ages two to ten); the puppet stage that will need to be set up (a long table with a black tablecloth over it); the backdrop (a painted drop of a winding path leading up to the cave from which Mary discovers that Jesus has vanished—this has been ordered from Amazon); the apple juice and cookies that must be obtained from Hannaford so the moms and kids can have snack time afterward. ("And some dads," Ilse says, and I can tell she's trying to be progressive again, because Cynthia gives her a pained smile, from which I understand that none of the dads will be coming to a puppet show about Easter.)

I wait for an opening, but one doesn't come, and so I don't mention the truth: that I have not been able to write a single line of dialogue for the Easter play. I've tried. I even took the children's book home with me and read lines like *Easter is a time for us to be close to Jesus*, and: *Surprise! Mary looked in the cave and Jesus was gone!* and *Where is Jesus? He has Ascended*, and I stared at Jesus's impassive beaming face both pre- and post-ascension and tried to imagine what his puppet would say. But nothing came to me, then or later.

What has been coming to me, unbidden, are other scraps of dialogue. The voices of the strange, horrible creatures I've been building late at night. They are urgent, importunate, self-hating, acerbic. It feels like being tuned into a radio signal from another planet. Scraps and sentences, brief utterances. At CVS, when there are no customers waiting, I unroll the long coil of the receipt paper, and Jesus and Mary are replaced by small, fierce voices that I start to associate with individual puppets: Three-Head, No-Eyes, Nose-Face, The Belly. At first, I don't write down what they're saying. There isn't a point, after all, I'm not actually *making* something. But then I think: *Maybe, if I write it down, I'll get it out of the way. Use it up. Be able to focus on this stupid Easter play.*

So then I do write it down.

And it keeps coming. So I keep writing. And the receipt spool gets longer and longer. And I start carrying it around in the pocket of my CVS apron in case the radio signal sweeps through and I hear something on the wind.

My father sees the spool of receipt paper once when I'm pulling it out of my pocket to jot something down. He's sitting in his armchair, reading, and I don't even know that he's paying attention until he says "Oh," with sudden laser-like interest: "Be careful with that. They're realizing that receipts—that kind of paper?—are coated with Teflon."

"Teflon?"

"A very thin layer, yes, but it comes off easily. It's an endocrine disruptor, there are studies about it. Cancer, etcetera. It's terrible, actually, you should wash your hands after you handle that—or use gloves. Probably when you're at work you should use gloves."

He goes back to his reading, and I do not begin using gloves, but the feeling sticks with me: *I am taking my life in my hands to record these voices.* And so, after that, it is even harder to hear whatever Jesus might say about Easter, because all I can think is: *What are the things I'd risk my life to write down?* And somehow it is the small, fierce voices that keep being the answer to that question.

"I'm so excited to hear what you're writing," Cynthia says now, turning back to me shyly. Ilse, standing next to her, bobs her head in agreement. And the spool of cancer-soaked death paper is heavy in my pocket when I say: "Me too."

*

My father sees them by accident.

He's knocked on my bedroom door and opened it without waiting for an answer. And then he stops before he's delivered whatever message he came to convey. He glances around the floor, the desk, the top of my bureau. I follow his eyes as he takes them all in.

"What *are* these?" my father asks.

I hear myself say, as if it's a name I've known all along: "The Grotesques."

My father picks up the one that I've been calling The Neck. It has a single bobbling eye on a stalk (repurposed mini-slinky), a swollen but obscenely creased belly (half-deflated balloon, covered in acrylic paint), and three tiny legs that stick out at odd angles, on which are hot-glued three different types of baby booties (from the lost and found basket at the church).

"Huh," he says, cautious but interested. "Are you making a . . . show, of some kind?"

"No," I say, "not really."

"You're just making them."

"Yeah."

My father looks at me curiously. Head tilted to one side. But all he says is: "Your mother wanted me to tell you that dinner is ready."

*

That evening, I get a notification: Julie at *The New Yorker* has a new email. My heart spikes in my chest. And when I log into Julie's account, there it is, like a missive from a faraway planet: an email from Tara-Jean Slater. Subject line: Seasons of Despair. I open it and find no message, just one of those tiny, stacked poems of hers that I've come to know so well.

Winter and
Spring and
Summer
and fall
and fall and
Fall

I read it silently, several times in quick succession. I still can't tell whether a poem is good or bad, and I still can't help secretly hoping that Tara-Jean Slater is capable of error. But my predominant feeling is one of unexpected relief. I had worried at her statement that there was no joy in poetry, especially once it became clear that she didn't say things she didn't mean. This poem, despite its title, is a tiny flicker of hope. I read it out loud, to the room of Grotesques. They listen, heads tilted back or falling forward, faces strange and slack. If Tara-Jean can still write poems, I think, I can write an Easter play. Jesus and the Sheep. Lady Romans. But when I glance around my room, all I can see are the Grotesques.

*

When I go downstairs at midnight that night, my father is still awake, sitting in the warm circle of lamplight. His armchair is surrounded by stacks of books and student papers, and Leonard Cohen is playing low on the record player.

"I didn't even know that still worked."

My father looks up from the essay in his lap and smiles. "It works, we just piled a lot of things on top of it." He gestures with his glasses, an invitation to sit. I lean on the arm of his chair. Leonard Cohen's voice rolls over us like gentle gravel at the bottom of a river: "Famous Blue Raincoat."

"I listened to this in college," I say.

"I always thought he was too depressing," my father says. Then he lifts an eyebrow. "Your generation listened to him in college?"

"Your generation didn't invent *everything*, Dad."

"We certainly invented Leonard Cohen," my father says, defensively. We both sit quietly, listening. "Chelsea Hotel #2" starts playing. "He wrote that for Janis Joplin," my father tells me, proprietarily.

"Oh my god, I know that."

We sit in silence. My father asks, "Is your mom asleep?"

"I think so."

I expect him to ask what has happened in my life outside of here. Or what the fuck is going on in my bedroom. But instead he says, "You know, Leonard Cohen went up a mountain for three years."

"He did?"

"Aha! See, there *is* something you don't know. He was living in a monastery, actually. He was a novelist until he was thirty-three, and then he started writing songs. And then, when he was sixty, he became a monk. For five years." He smiles at a joke I'm not in on. I notice again the thinness of his hair, the delicate pink of his scalp underneath. The net of wrinkles around his eyes, deeper than I remembered them. "And then he came down the mountain and there was a whole fourth life ahead of him still. Sixty-five, and he hadn't even finished leading all the lives he was going to lead." My father looks at me then, and I can see something in his eyes that is both a kindness and a sadness. "There are so many lives ahead of us all."

When I go to bed, my father is still listening to that rich baritone, head tilted back, eyes half-closed. The Grotesques are scattered on my bed. I crawl in next to them and fall asleep.

*

The morning of the Easter show is blustery and cold.

I'd stayed up late the night before, clutching the sticky children's book, trying to finish turning it into a play. Ilse had emailed around ten P.M. — in the chaos of tables and backdrops and cookies, she and Cynthia were looking for my printout and couldn't seem to find it. Where had I left it? I balanced questions of ethics and truth and reducing panic and covering my ass, and I wrote back and said that I would bring them hard copies in the morning, since I was making a few tweaks anyway. *Burst of inspiration*, I said. *Epiphany!* And then I spent the next five hours jotting down lines like *Be happy, my children, it is Easter!* and crossing those lines out, and descending into a spiral of self-loathing wherein I asked myself how I could have agreed to do this and how I can face my mother and her friends after letting them all down. I fall asleep by accident and wake up to my alarm.

The parking lot is full of cars when I arrive. I've never seen it so full. I end up parking behind the church, in a sliver of space between the edge of the gravel lot and a large oak tree. I sit in the car for a moment, taking deep breaths, watching families get out of their cars — moms in nice sweaters and skirts, helping their small kids out of the back seat. No dads in sight, as Cynthia predicted.

The Grotesques are in a laundry hamper in the back of the car. I ran around my bedroom that morning looking for the copy of *The Easter Story* that had magically vanished. I think I had the idea that I would find the book and somehow — in the minutes before I left for the church — know what the short play would be. I kept chanting, "A short play, a *short* play, a short, short, short . . ." And then I realized I couldn't find anything, because my entire room was covered in demented creatures, so I started throwing them all into an empty laundry hamper. I found the book where it had slipped between the edge of the bed frame and the mattress, and then, without interrogating the impulse, I carried the hamper full of Grotesques out to the car, with Tara-Jean Slater's Frankenstein sheep on the top.

On the drive to the church, I considered throwing them all out in the giant dumpster at the edge of the parking lot. There were so many of them—finished, half-finished, just begun. They aren't the sort of thing I could dispose of quietly, slipping them into the garbage container by the house. Bears knock the garbage over all the time in spring, and my parents are constantly opening it up to add trash bags, before they wheel it to the end of the driveway. No, getting rid of the Grotesques at home would involve some kind of conversation. This way, I can dump them all into the black steel church dumpster and be done with it. The Easter show will occur, the art supplies will be locked back away, I will be released from this strange mania, this odd fever. Toss in the increasingly torn and smudged Teflon receipt roll, and I'll live a long and healthy life. By the time I've parked under the oak tree, this seems like a solid plan. The only part of the plan that I haven't solved is the part where I need a play about Easter, and I still don't have one.

Okay, I think, getting out of the car. *I'll come clean. Forgiveness and sin are the currency of this whole thing anyway, right?* I imagine telling Ilse that I didn't write the play. I imagine her Swedish eyes narrowing in disgust: these lazy Americans. I revise my imagining. I'll tell Ilse that my computer erased the play right before I was going to send it to her. That my computer crashed. That I didn't make a backup copy. That she and Cynthia can improvise—they know the story after all, they have the puppets. They're in a better position than I am to know what Jesus would say, and why Easter is a miracle, and what it all means. They'll figure it out.

Ilse is nowhere to be seen when I enter the church. I go down the carpeted stairs and peek into the Sunday school classroom as I pass. It's already half-full. My mother is in the back, chatting and laughing with a younger woman, who keeps checking in with the small, dark-headed child hiding behind her legs. Other mothers are trying to get their kids to sit down, not to pull the black tablecloth off the long table/stage that's been erected. A few kids are crying preemptively, but most of them are wide-eyed, interested in the anticipatory commotion.

It surprises me that neither Ilse nor Cynthia are in the classroom, welcoming their students, talking to the parents. The wall clock says it's five minutes to eleven. I continue down the hall toward Ilse's office, tucked into its corner with windows facing the meadow and the back parking lot. The door is closed; I knock, wait, and then turn the knob and find it locked. This is an unexpected turn of events. I'm standing there stupidly, trying to figure out what to do, when Cynthia comes rushing down the hall toward me. She looks distraught. Her face is paper white except for two bright spots of red that stand out on her cheeks.

"Cynthia," I begin, but she's already talking. Ilse can't stop projectile vomiting. She got halfway down her driveway before she had to get out of the car and puke. She's not going to make it to the show. Cynthia is almost wringing her hands as she talks.

"Oh no," I say, at appropriate intervals. When she's finished, I decide to hit her with the bad news all at once. "My computer died? And I couldn't email the play? And there's no backup? So we don't have a play?"

Cynthia looks perplexed at first, and then, as my words sink in, a tide of terrified misery rises up and swamps her utterly. I feel, for the first time, a Christian stirring: I am looking into the face of Job, if he were a middle-aged woman who co-teaches Sunday school.

"Cassie," she says, urgently. "I can't."

"You can't what?"

"Do this. Do . . . *this.*" She gestures down the hall toward the classroom. A few mothers are hustling their children down the stairs toward the room—they must be late, by the looks of it, but when they see us talking at the end of the hallway they slow with relief.

"The . . . Wait, the puppet show?"

She nods and shakes her head at the same time, a frantic wagging of her whole body. "I have—anxiety," she says. "I get panic attacks."

I stare at her. "I mean . . . should we cancel it?"

"We can't cancel it," Cynthia whispers. "They—it's been—it's a whole—and they're already *here,* and . . ." She is looking at me with giant, pleading eyes. "Can you . . . I mean, you must remember whatever you wrote, could you . . . ?"

There are a number of things I could say. I only have two hands, and there is an entire series of sheep and Romans. I didn't actually write a play. I'm a liar and a bad person. And a bad playwright, probably, or not even a playwright anymore at all. I failed at being a playwright, and then I failed at being a ruthless filmmaking mogul, and then I failed at doing my mother a favor, and now I am failing at being—not just Christian, which was an expected failure, but *kind*.

"Okay," I say, shocking both of us.

"Oh, praise the Lord," Cynthia says, and throws her arms around me.

The last delinquent mothers slip into the classroom. From inside the awkward circle of Cynthia's arms, I hear a tide of chaos—bored kids crying, fussing, fighting. It's five minutes past eleven. We're late.

"Okay," I say again, detaching myself gently. "Uh, let's . . . uh. Let's do this." And together, shoulders squared, we open the door.

*

The kids hush when I crouch awkwardly behind the table.

Cynthia stands at the front of the room and, in a voice that can hardly be heard, explains that this is the Easter show, and it is about the miracle of Jesus and the ascension and rebirth, and it is for all ages. She adds that it will be followed by cookies and apple juice, and that, unfortunately, Ilse is ill, and we all pray for her swift healing. Then she nearly runs to the back of the room.

The kids wait to see what I will do. I wait to see what I will do. Someone—probably Cynthia, prior to Ilse's revelation—has laid out the puppets within reach, on a series of low stools. A whole basket of sheep— these were supposed to go to the kids, I realize—and then Jesus and Mary, and then the three friendly Romans, and the Easter Bunny. I'm not sure where to start. The kids are starting to rustle again, a many-legged, sticky-fingered sound that is not unlike an approaching army of cockroaches. A mother says to her child, in a stage whisper, "This is *very* exciting!" I hear, in that whisper, an entire universe of anxiety. The mothers can tell something is wrong. Their antennae are tuned to the threatening background hum of disaster.

I grab Jesus—after all, it's what we promised—and lift him up above the table.

"Hi," I say. "I'm Jesus."

A moment as the kids examine him. Then a baby starts to wail. Other kids turn to look at the baby. One of the little boys in the front row keeps trying to slide off his chair. The moms are trying to quell the mutiny, but it isn't working.

"I'm Jesus, and welcome to Easter!" I try to remember what the god-damn book said about Easter. "Easter is the day that I went up to Heaven! I was in a cave. The Romans put me there."

Another kid is howling now. Full-throated howls. His mom jiggles him on her lap.

"Time to meet the Romans!"

I pull Jesus off my hand, grab two Romans. A man and a woman.

"Hi! We're the Romans! We . . ." I open my mouth to say the word "crucify" and hesitate. Cynthia promised it was an all-ages show—how do you explain crucifixion to a roomful of children? Is it a word they already know? I glance at their bright, drool-crusted faces. A small, fat one is eating his own hand. He has never imagined the sensation of a nail going through that hand.

"We put Jesus on time out," I say in my genial, upbeat Romans voice.

The room is devolving into chaos. I'm losing them. Mothers are bent over their children, trying to shush them, but I can tell I've lost the mothers as well.

"We put him on time out because he kept saying he was the son of God!"

They're glancing at their phones surreptitiously, glancing at each other to see if anyone else knows how long this will limp on. I catch the helpless half-moon of Cynthia's face in the back—she's beaming at me as if she's trying to fast-forward this entire day with the power of her mind.

"And, uh, he was sent here to die for our sins, and we were like, 'What sins?!'"

My eyes dart to the back. My mother is sitting with her hands clasped in her lap, caught in a moment of compressed anguish. Okay, fuck the Romans. I toss them to the side and grab the Easter Bunny, thrusting him up above the table in a moment of desperation: "Hi! I'm the Easter Bunny!"—but it's too late. The kids don't care about a goddamn bunny puppet with pipe cleaner ears. They've seen more-elaborate rabbits on display in every CVS and Hannaford in the past month. The chubby fist chewer in the front row is now wriggling wildly, trying to break free of his mother so that he can fling himself onto the floor and make his escape. She looks like she wants to follow him. I don't blame either of them. I put down the Easter Bunny. I look at Mary, and the fifteen sheep, and I feel all of the will to do this exit my body. A new wind blows in.

I stand up fully, from behind the table. The kids hush, staring at me. The mothers tense.

"Please stand by," I say. I leave the room. I hear the mutter of voices begin behind me—*Where is she going? What's going on? Is the show over? Maybe she's getting the snacks*—and then the door swings shut and the hallway is bathed in blessed silence.

I take the carpeted stairs two at a time up to the front doors. Out into the breezy bite of early afternoon. I jog around the side of the church to where the car is parked, lift the old hatchback. Inside, the hamper waits. Expectant.

When I reenter the room clutching the laundry hamper, the wall of voices hushes again. I station myself in front of the table this time. I don't bother crouching down. I have already been exposed. I look around the room. The room looks back—large eyes, small ones. Wary, curious.

"Let's start over," I say.

And when I lift No-Eyes up into the air, the room erupts in glee.

19

THE GROTESQUES: A PUPPET SHOW

Lights up on NO-EYES.
It addresses us directly.

NO-EYES

> The story of Easter is that, no matter how badly you may fail,
> you can always just leave.
> This is also the story of Leonard Cohen.
> And me.
> There is a corollary to this story. The unspoken second half.
> It is: No matter how often and how successfully you leave,
> you always end up still being yourself when you arrive.
> This is the part we find much harder to reconcile.

Enter: WEIRD-SPINE.

WEIRD-SPINE

> I have a weird spine.

NO-EYES

I can't see your weird spine.
Because I don't have any eyes.

WEIRD-SPINE

Wherever I go, I will still have a weird spine when I get there.

NO-EYES

What about outer space?

WEIRD-SPINE

I think if I went to outer space, I would still have a weird spine.
But there wouldn't be any gravity, so maybe it wouldn't matter that
my spine was weird.

NO-EYES

If I went to a planet that was all dark, nobody would know if anybody
had eyes or not.
Because nobody would be able to see.

WEIRD-SPINE

Maybe there are environments in which we are not precisely
ourselves.
Or in which being ourselves is beside the point.

Enter: THREE-ARMS.

THREE-ARMS

Grab at joy.
That's my advice.
That's what I said to Jesus when they put him in the cave.

NO-EYES

Is that a Roman soldier?

THREE-ARMS

No, I'm just a three-arms. I was already in the cave when they put him there.

THE ROMANS appear.

THE ROMANS

We were like . . .
What is that?
It has three arms.
What did it say?

THREE-ARMS

Grab at joy.

THE ROMANS

Weird.
Bye!
Enjoy the cave!

They leave.

WEIRD-SPINE

What does joy look like?

THREE-ARMS

I've never seen it, but I've been led to believe that it looks like whatever you're grabbing.

Enter: TOO-MANY-FEET.

TOO-MANY-FEET

I used to think that joy was a place I wasn't in but needed to move to.
Then I thought it was a practice that I just needed to work harder at.
But now I think that joy is not tripping over all my feet all the time.
Every time I get up in the morning and I don't trip? I think that's joy.

Everybody thinks about this.

WEIRD-SPINE

What about the part right after you trip, where you get back up?

THREE-ARMS

What about the part right after you trip, where you decide to stay
where you are?

NO-EYES

Joy is a tricky proposition. I would rather invest in granite countertops.

Enter: SOMETHING-WICKED-THIS-WAY-COMES.

SOMETHING-WICKED-THIS-WAY-COMES

The story of Easter is that you can do your best and still get nailed to
the goddamn wall.
Because doing your best isn't necessarily an excuse for doing damage.
Sometimes you do an awful lot of damage.
And that doesn't mean you're a bad person.
But it does mean you aren't always a good one.

Enter: LEONARD COHEN.

LEONARD COHEN

I went up a mountain in San Bernardino county.

I was sixty years old, and I was ready to leave myself behind.

Some would say that becoming a monk is the ultimate expression of leaving yourself behind.

The people who would say that have never been monks.

Enter: TARA-JEAN SLATER, SORT OF.

TARA-JEAN SLATER, SORT OF

It is true that I have not left myself behind.

But it is *also* true that I am a person with a brand-new handbag.

So, in a way, I have transformed.

I can invest in a future of such transformations if there is nothing else to invest in.

There are many different philosophies that make this promise, but— for better or worse—capitalism is the only one that delivers.

Enter: FIFTEEN SHEEP.

THE SHEEP

Baaaaaaahhhhhhhh.

Enter: JESUS.
He takes us all in.

JESUS

Oh dear.

JESUS exits.

Enter: a METEOR.
It hits the earth at an impossible velocity.
It destroys everything.

METEOR

Sorry.

*Time passes, and from the char and rubble and mold and swamp, things
regrow. Slimy things. Sticky things. Things with hands where hands
shouldn't be, and eyes where eyes shouldn't be, and tails that are spiny or
spiky or flat or truncated, and faces that are in places you wouldn't think
would have faces. Things slip and shape-shift and become murk and goo
and regrow in larger and sturdier and more sustainable ways.*

*Eventually, out of the bubbling slick and wet ooze, one of these creatures
emerges, sans eyes.*

It looks like the NO-EYES *we met before the world was destroyed. It
speaks to us.*

NO-EYES II

I have started giving myself permission to be really, really ugly.
I don't know if anyone here has ever done that?
But it's incredibly freeing, actually.
I wake up in the morning and I drink an espresso and I think: *Be
hideous.* I take a shower and I feel the puffy, unboundaried bits of
myself and I think: *Be more hideous.* I think: *Is that the most hideous
you can be? I know you can do better.*
And then when someone rejects me, or when someone cuts me off
in line, or when someone succeeds where I'm failing, or when I find
someone I love to be so utterly incomprehensible that it's clear there
is something wrong with *me* and not with *them* . . . then, I think:
Good, you're being hideous enough.
And then I feel like I'm succeeding.

I think it's very important to succeed at something.

I used to think it mattered what that was, but I don't anymore.

Now I just think: *Dear God, please let me succeed in some small way, regardless of what it is.*

And if my own ugliness becomes the extent of my ambition, then . . .

at least I achieved something.

I think I achieved something.

Dear God, please let me have achieved something.

Amen.

Black-out.
End of play.

20

I'm having a cigarette in the parking lot when Cynthia comes out. It's the last one I stole from Dylan, and I'm relieved to see Cynthia instead of my mother, because I'm savoring it too much to put it out. Cynthia has thrown on a heavy parka but left it unzipped, and her whole body is fluid with relief. Her hair is frizzing into a halo around her face. I've never seen her this relaxed.

"They all stayed," she says wonderingly. "They're down there, eating cookies and juice."

"That's great."

"They filled the donation jar." Cynthia shakes her head. "I wasn't even gonna hand it out, but they went and filled it."

"That's great."

"The kids are all over your puppets. They might have already broken some—I can't really tell what's broken and what's . . ." Cynthia realizes this might sound rude, and her voice trails off.

"That's okay," I assure her. "I'm probably throwing them out anyway."

We stand together for a moment and then Cynthia can't help herself. "What did it mean?"

"What did what mean?"

"The . . . play? I guess? The things you said?"

"I have no idea."

"But you said it."

"I know, but I didn't really . . . *plan* it. It just happened."

I think Cynthia will accuse me of being deliberately obtuse, but a small smile lights up her face. "What a strange miracle," she says thoughtfully, and turns back toward the church.

As soon as I'd finished the show, the kids had rushed the front of the room like a pack of ravenous hyenas. They pulled the Grotesques out of the hamper, gnawed on their knobby ears or multiple arms, shoved their joyful faces against the distorted puppet faces. Their mothers seemed torn between bafflement at what they'd witnessed and relief that at least their children had been fully occupied for a period of time. My mom was talking to a cluster of women, and as I passed them, I heard her say grandly, "Well, Cassie was always *very* good with children." The nearby mothers seemed to relax into this reframing (nothing more sinister than children's entertainment!), and as I slipped out, one of them was saying bravely, "Yes, I've *never* seen Harry so engaged!"

After the mustiness of the church basement, the afternoon is sun drenched and clear. I tilt my head back. I can smell the thawing moss, the richness of the soil, the damp pine needles revealed by snowmelt. I close my eyes and imagine Lincoln Center. In my mind, I transplant my euphoric audience of toddlers, I grow them by several decades, I dress them in blazers and Italian-leather shoes. I imagine myself sitting outside Lincoln Center while, within, influential and Very Serious audiences mob the stage. To be loved like that by adults, by tastemakers . . . I try to summon the fierce longing that comes with these fantasies, the painful discrepancy between fantasy and reality, but somehow it isn't there. I feel loose limbed, light-headed. Peaceful. I knew the toddlers weren't listening to a word I was saying—but it hadn't mattered to me. I'd just needed to say it all out loud. I draw cool pine-tinged air into my lungs.

"Cassie? Are you Cassie?"

I open my eyes. A mom is standing in front of me, carrying the small, fat fist chewer from the front row. It's shoved into a quilted jacket, and pilled purple mittens are attached to the sleeves with alligator clips.

"That's me."

"I—gosh. I saw your—well, I don't know what I'd call that." Her hair is heavy and ash-blond, pulled back into a messy ponytail. She looks vaguely familiar; I'm not sure if we were in high school together. "I really did not know what to make of it, but . . ."

I open my mouth to tell her it's okay, but she keeps talking.

"—I found it, uh, I don't know. Immensely relatable." She's nervous. She shifts the fist chewer from arm to arm, and it stares at me through surprisingly long eyelashes. "The—the creature at the end? I don't know what it was, um, but—I–I felt . . ." She bursts into tears.

I'm frozen in place. "It's okay," I say awkwardly.

"I had Charles six months ago," she says, swiping at her face with one of the fist chewer's purple mittens. "And my body is—I mean, it's disgusting to me. Everything hurts and it's—stretched and distended and—*raw* and—you just could not imagine. You just couldn't. And of course you don't *talk* about these things to other people, I mean, my god, you are trying so hard to look like a human, even though you've basically become a *monster*, and . . ." She blows her nose into the mitten, tucks it into her pocket. "I'm changing his diapers and wiping vomit out of my hair and I went to *law school*."

"Oh," I say, impressed.

"Yeah. In Boston. I was a lawyer. I *am* a lawyer. Don't look like it now, though, huh?"

"I don't know," I say. "I don't know any lawyers."

She smiles. "Anyway. I just. That is the first thing I've seen that feels like . . . it was for me, somehow. This must seem really stupid to you."

"No, it really doesn't."

"I mean, your mother said you were living in New York—and Los *Angeles*—and you probably feel like all of this is so . . ." She makes a gesture: *small*, maybe.

"I'm living in my childhood bedroom," I tell her, but somehow for once I don't feel the need to apologize for it.

The fist chewer makes an odd noise, its face briefly contorted in ferocious concentration. I realize that it's pooping.

"*Charles*," its mother says. And to me: "We better get back."

"It was nice to meet you." I turn to Charles. "And you."

Charles blows a spit bubble, and then the frown comes back over his face. He's definitely pooping, again or still.

After their car pulls out of the lot, I lean back on my elbows and look up at the oak tree. Its branches cut against the blue of the sky. I think about the mothers and kids still in the basement. I think about Hélène: the night before we opened, when she smudged the theatre with Palo Santo and prayed for our success. How maybe her prayer had been only that we carry out our work, not that we were elevated for how we did it. Although that's nice, if it comes. It's just beyond the realm of prayer. Something even more tenuous than a wish. Nothing to stake a life on if you then intend to live the rest of that life.

I think of B.B., who knows when to quit.

I think of Tara-Jean Slater, who has not yet needed to know.

I think of Jocelyn, newly fired; and Daniel, masquerading as someone he hasn't had to be in a decade; and Dylan, exploring who he might be next; and my father, who understands that sometimes you have to go up a mountain in order to come back down; and my mother, who is proud of me for a reason that neither of us could have predicted; and I don't know how it sounds, a prayer for success, I've never learned how to pray at all. But I take a breath and then another and then another, until I can feel my heart slow, slow down, and it's just me, alone in this parking lot, and the sun is so warm on my face, and in this moment I have never been more unfindable, further from anywhere I expected to be, precariously—but thrillingly—suspended.

Acknowledgments

My love and thanks to:

My parents, Mark and Sue; my brother, Chris; and the Laffrey family, most especially Laurel.

My agent, Allison Hunter, for your enthusiastic championing of my story collection, and your certainty that I had a novel in me.

My editor, Caitlin McKenna. I am so indebted to your wisdom, your insight, and your leaps of inspiration. And to the whole Random House team, especially Emma Caruso, Vincent La Scala, Mimi Lipson, Erin Richards, and Jess Bonet; Rachel Ake for the beautiful covers you made for both *We Play Ourselves* and *The Island Dwellers*; and Kimberly Burns, for your passionate advocacy on behalf of this book.

The *Tales of the City* writers' room: our showrunner Lauren Morelli, Andy Parker, Pat Resnick, Marcus Gardley, Thomas Page McBee, Hansol Jung, and Eoin Bullock. I began writing the very first pages of this novel only days after I'd started the room for *Tales*. L.A. was an alien landscape and so was television writing. I learned an astonishing amount from you—not only about how to make a season of queer TV, but also what it is to belong to a community rooted in grace, empathy, and radical acceptance.

Mike Donahue: The day I finished the first draft, you bought me a fancy drink on Bondi Beach. The day I finished the second draft, we

shared a bottle of ham-flavored wine in Echo Park. The day I finished
the final draft, we were all in quarantine, but nonetheless: your abiding
belief in the reward system has sustained me across many projects.

Erin Chen: for putting that M.D.-Ph.D. to work when I call you
with emergencies not only medical but also aesthetic and intellectual.

Basil Kreimendahl: for your readiness to engage with both the exis-
tential and the mundane at any hour of day or night.

Swan Huntley: for your exquisite irreverence and your steady
friendship.

Kevin Artigue: for always getting down in the trenches with me,
across seasons and cities.

Max Posner: for years of reading each other delicate fragments and
dreaming about what they could be.

Nick Westrate: for regularly asking me how this book was doing, as
if it were a member of the family.

The P-Patrol: Samantha Sherman, for your great heart matched
only by your great daring, and Renata Friedman, for the clarity of your
perspective and the sharpness of your wit.

Chase Brock, Rob Berman, and Eric Dietz: for generously letting us
shelter in Modern Accord Depot. Thanks to you, this book was completed in a decommissioned train car.

A very particular thanks to Dr. Joseph Petitti, O.D. There are moments in which no one can help a writer so much as an eye doctor. Just
like my favorite authors, you are witty, compassionate, and detail oriented.

Theatre is an art form with many contradictions folded into it: the
deep intimacy of lifelong collaborations juxtaposed against an economic
model that can be lonely and brutal. My eternal thanks to the artistic
leaders, dramaturges, directors, designers, playwrights, and actors who
are my artistic family, and who have had a hand in shaping both my love
for theatre and my body of work there.

And finally, Dane Laffrey, my partner and closest collaborator on
plays, Sad Panda time-lapse videos, tarot decks, elaborate dinners, and a
life de- and re-assembled in various cities and countries. Your curiosity,
generosity, and bone-dry sense of humor are my guiding principles.